SIEGFRIED SASSOON DIARIES
1915–1918

The Infantry Officer

SIEGFRIED SASSOON
DIARIES
1915–1918

Edited and introduced by
RUPERT HART-DAVIS

faber and faber

*First published in 1983
by Faber and Faber Limited
3 Queen Square London WC1N 3AU
Printed in Great Britain by
New Western Printing Ltd, Bristol*

Library of Congress Cataloging in Publication Data

*Sassoon, Siegfried, 1886–1967
Siegfried Sassoon diaries, 1915–1918*

Includes index
*1. Sassoon, Siegfried, 1886–1967—Diaries. 2. Poets,
English—20th century—Biography. 3. World War,
1914–1918—Personal narratives, English. I. Hart-Davis,
Rupert, Sir. II. Title*
PR6037.A86Z472 1983   828'.91203 [B]   82–21058
ISBN 0–571–11997–2

British Library Cataloguing in Publication Data

*Sassoon, Siegfried
Siegfried Sassoon diaries 1915–1918
1. Sassoon, Siegfried—Biography
2. Authors, English—20th century—Biography
I. Title   II. Hart-Davis, Rupert*
821'.912   PR6037.A867Z/

ISBN 0–571–11997–2

CONTENTS

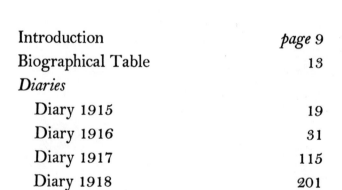

CONTENTS

INTRODUCTION

Siegfried Sassoon was almost twenty-eight when he enlisted on
3 August 1914. Till then, after education at Marlborough and
Clare College, Cambridge, he had lived at home, hunting and
playing cricket in Kent and Sussex, and writing agreeably
derivative poems which he had privately printed in very small
editions. It was the terrible impact of the Western Front that
turned him from a versifier into a poet.

His first three prose works—*Memoirs of a Fox-Hunting Man*
(1928), *Memoirs of an Infantry Officer* (1930) and *Sherston's
Progress* (1936)—were autobiography disguised as fiction, by
the changing of the names of everyone he met (except those of
Corporal Mick O'Brien in *Memoirs of an Infantry Officer* and
W. H. R. Rivers in *Sherston's Progress*) and by making no men-
tion of his being a poet. A close comparison of these books with
his diaries shows that they are faithful records of his experiences,
based on his contemporary descriptions, occasionally heightened
but never distorted. As time went on he came to rely more and
more on the diaries, and Part III of *Sherston's Progress* consists
entirely of quotations from them.

Introduction

Some may wonder why he took so much trouble to disguise fact as fiction, and I think the explanation lay in a lifelong dichotomy in his nature. He longed for praise and recognition, but he was so instinctively reclusive, so unsure of his gifts and afraid of making a fool of himself, that he preferred his poems to appear first in small and expensive limited editions, as a sort of safeguard to prove their worth and test readers' reactions. Even the first edition of *Memoirs of a Fox-Hunting Man* was published anonymously.

Of the three volumes of straight autobiography only the third, *Siegfried's Journey* (1945), deals with the war, complementing and filling out *Sherston's Progress*.

Siegfried's handwriting was always firm and legible, but these diaries were written in tiny notebooks, sometimes in pencil, often by the light of a solitary candle in dug-out or billet, and some of the names of French villages and hamlets are hard to decipher. I have checked as many as possible and left the rest as he appears to have spelt them. Obvious mis-spellings and slips of the pen I have silently corrected. He often used both ends of a notebook indiscriminately, but the date or position of an entry is usually clear.

I have included, where they occur in the diaries, many poems which their author thought worthy of publication only in a periodical or not at all. In their context they seem to me relevant to the prose entries, even though they may not warrant inclusion in the collected poems. Those that carry no note of publication are here printed for the first time. I have omitted repetitions, scribblings, half-obliterated beginnings of poems, and notes on drill and suchlike. Otherwise I have removed nothing of importance, though a few unimportant names are concealed by an initial. To all Siegfried's footnotes I have added his initials: the others are mine. I have extended all the abbreviations which he used to save space.

I have received much help and kindness in my work, and I am particularly grateful to Dr Robert Becker; Sir Ilay M. Campbell; Mrs R. E. Carter of Clare College, Cambridge; Major G. M. B. Colenso-Jones of the Royal Welch Fusiliers; Stuart Cooper; Mrs Enid Fry; A. G. Lee, Librarian of St John's College, Cambridge; Sir Anthony Lousada; Ernest and Joyce Mehew; David Newsome; Mrs Joanna Parker, Assistant

Introduction

Librarian of Somerville College, Oxford; George Sassoon; Martyn Skinner; Oliver Stonor; Roderick Suddaby of the Imperial War Museum; and Ann Thwaite.

For permission to reproduce copyright material I am grateful to Madame Virginia Eldin for the letter from Arnold Bennett; to J.-P. B. Ross for the letters from Robbie Ross; to Mrs Igor Vinogradoff for the letter and quotation by Lady Ottoline Morrell; and to Messrs Faber & Faber and the Viking Press for permission to reprint Siegfried's published poems.

Marske-in-Swaledale RUPERT HART-DAVIS
November 1982

BIOGRAPHICAL TABLE

1886	September 8	Siegfried Sassoon born at Weirleigh, near Paddock Wood in Kent, the second son of Alfred Sassoon and Theresa, née Thornycroft
1902–4		At Marlborough College
1905–6		At Clare College, Cambridge
1906–14		Lived mostly at home, hunting, playing cricket and writing poems, which he had privately printed in small editions
1914	May–August	Living in Raymond Buildings, Gray's Inn
	August 3	Enlisted as trooper in Sussex Yeomanry
1915	Spring	In hospital with broken arm
	May	Commissioned in Royal Welch Fusiliers
	November 24	Joined First Battalion R.W.F. in France

Biographical Table

1916	April 20	To Fourth Army School at Flixé-court for four-week course
	June	Awarded Military Cross for gallantry in action
	August 2	Invalided home with trench fever. In hospital at Somerville College, Oxford
		Convalescent at Weirleigh
	December 4	Reported to Regimental Depot at Litherland, near Liverpool
1917	February 16	Arrived at Infantry Base Depot, Rouen
	February 18–27	In 25 Stationary Hospital, Rouen, with German measles
	March 11	Joined Second Battalion R.W.F. on the Somme front
	April 16	Wounded in shoulder
	April 20	In hospital at Denmark Hill
	May 8	*The Old Huntsman* published
	May 12–June 4	In convalescent home at Chapelwood Manor, Nutley, Sussex
	June 20	Attended Medical Board at Liverpool. Sent to Craiglockhart War Hospital, near Edinburgh, where he was a patient of W. H. R. Rivers and met Wilfred Owen
	July 30	His statement against the continuation of the war read out in House of Commons and reported in *The Times* next day
	November 26	Passed fit for General Service
	December 11	Reported back to Litherland
1918	January 7	Posted to Limerick
	February 8	Posted to Palestine with Twenty-Fifth Battalion R.W.F.
	May 9	Battalion arrived in France
	June 27	*Counter-Attack* published
	July 13	Wounded in head; to American Red Cross Hospital, 98 Lancaster Gate, London

Biographical Table

	August 20	To convalescent home at Lennel House, near Coldstream in Berwickshire. Thereafter on indefinite sick-leave
1919	March 12	Officially retired from Army
	June	*Picture Show* issued
	October 30	*War Poems* published

1915

1915

November 17
1.15 Victoria. Got to Folkestone pier 6. Boat, *Victoria,* sailed
about 7 in bright moonlight; for Boulogne. Changed course
after an hour and reached Calais 9.30. Last hour rough. Went
ashore about 1 and slept on floor in hotel.

November 18
Left for Boulogne 11.15 in quiet grey weather. Very few
people to be seen in Calais. Got to Boulogne 12.30: did nothing:
left for base camp, Etaples, 9 p.m. Got there 11.30 and drew
blankets; slept all six of us in small tent. Weather cold and
frosty, but dry. 320 officers just got there, waiting to be posted.
Next morning went into Le Touquet on bike and saw Major
Thackeray at Duchess of Westminster's Hospital. Bike bust, so
drove back in cab.

November 20–22

Very cold and dry; nothing doing. Fed in Etaples at rotten café.

November 23

Went to Paris Plage after lunch: Hubert Jones posted to Ninth R.W.F. The rest of us think we go First or Second. Moving off to-morrow. Weather milder. Posted to First R.W.F.

November 24

Paraded with kit at 2.30 a.m. and went to station. Train started 5.30. Arrived Béthune 10.15 and found Battalion in billets there. After lunch went out to C. Company billets at Le Hamel, two and a half miles. The remainder at Le Touret, one mile further.

November 25

Went on working-party 3 to 10.30 p.m. Marched to Festubert village; a ruined place, shelled to shreds. About 4.30, in darkness and rain, started up three-quarters of a mile of light tram-lines through marsh, with sixty men. They carried hurdles up the communication-trenches about three-quarters of a mile, which took two hours. Flares go up frequently, a few shells go high overhead; the trenches are very wet; finally emerge in a place behind the first and second-line trenches, where we are digging new trenches with high command-breastworks.

November 27

Go out again, starting 9.45 p.m. in brilliant moonlight and iron frost. Dig from 12 to 2. Home 4.15. Men get soup in ruined house at Festubert. The moon shines through matchwood skeleton rafters of roofs. Up behind the trenches the frostbound morasses and ditches and old earthworks in the moonlight with dusky figures filing across the open, hobbling to avoid slipping, inhuman forms going to and from inhuman tasks.

1915

November 28

Walked into Béthune for tea with Robert Graves, a young poet, captain in Third Battalion and very much disliked.[1] An interesting creature, overstrung and self-conscious, a defier of convention. At night went up again to Festubert with working-party. Dug from 12 to 2 a.m. Very cold. Home 4.15.

November 29

Went with working-party 3 o'clock. Wet day. Awful mud up in trenches. Tried to dig till 7.30 and came home soaked. Home 9.45. A shocking night for the men, whose billets are wretched.

November 30

Started from Le Hamel 9 o'clock, in fine, bright weather and marched eight kilometres to Gonnehem where the Battalion are billeted fresh. Got there 12.15. C. Company in a nice farm. Good house joining a square of buildings. Men in large warm barn. Four big bedrooms for us, and a large mess-room—a sort of palace compared with Le Hamel.

December 1

Mild weather. Spent a quiet day. Battalion played Second Warwicks in the afternoon and won easily.

December 2

Quiet day. Rode with R. Ormrod after lunch. Tried to make black pony jump a ditch and failed utterly. Saw a heron, which sailed slowly away across the misty flats of ploughed land; grey, still evening, gleaming dykes, willows and poplars; a few lights here and there as we rode home, and flicker of star-shells in the sky beyond Béthune. Robert Graves lent me his manuscript poems to read: some very bad, violent and repulsive. A few full of promise and real beauty. He oughtn't to publish yet. Cotterill[2]

[1] Born 1895. His first slim volume of poems, *Over the Brazier*, was published on 1 May 1916. The David Cromlech of *Memoirs of an Infantry Officer*.
[2] Quartermaster of the First Battalion R.W.F. The Dottrell of *Memoirs of an Infantry Officer*.

[21]

and Ormrod to dinner, and the servants produced an awful
repast, worst ever known. Moving again to-morrow. Very wet
night. I dreamed of a sudden death.

December 3
Started 10.30 and had a dreary three hours' march to Bourecq
(two miles beyond Lillers) through the usual flat lands, along
liquid-mud-roads. It was raining and a mist hid the country.
We met an Infantry Brigade, Kitchener's army—Seventh
Sussex, Eighteenth Middlesex and Eighth Royal Fusiliers. Men
marching by, four after four, hideous, brutal faces, sullen,
wretched. Some wore their steel basin-helmets, giving them a
Chinese look. Strange to see, among those hundreds of faces I
scanned, suddenly a vivid red-haired youth with green eyes
looking far away, sidelong—one clean face, among all the others
brutalised. But their hearts are gold, I doubt not. The heavy
transport-horses plodding through the sludge, straining at their
weary loads; the stolid drivers munching, smoking, grinning,
yelling coarse gibes; worried-looking officers on horses; young-
looking subalterns in new rain-proofs. And the infantrymen, the
foot-sloggers, loaded with packs, sweating under their water-
proof capes, the men that do the dirty work and keep us
safe.

Got to Bourecq at 1.45. A squalid village street. The Com-
pany billeted in stables, dark and damp. Raining hard. We move
to Amiens on Sunday. Everything out here goes past me like a
waking dream. My inner life is far more real than the hideous
realism of this land of the war-zone. I never thought to find such
peace. If it were not for Mother and friends I would pray for a
speedy death. I want a genuine taste of the horrors, and then—
peace. I don't want to go back to the old inane life which
always seemed like a prison. I want freedom, not comfort. I have
seen beauty in life, in men and in things; but I can never be a
great poet, or a great lover. The last fifteen months have un-
sealed my eyes. I have lived well and truly since the war began,
and have made my sacrifices; now I ask that the price be required
of me. I must pay my debt. Hamo[1] went: I must follow him. I

[1] S.S.'s younger brother, who had been buried at sea on 1 November 1915 after
being mortally wounded in Gallipoli.

will. Bobbie[1] will come out soon. I shall be happy with him for a few months. And in the spring—who knows?

December 4
A quiet day. Weather mild and rainy.

December 5
Up at 6, as the kits have to be ready to go by 7.30. We start 10.30. So at 6.45 I escaped from the stuffy billet, where Tommy[2] was finishing his bacon and eggs by the light of a candle, and in the pallor of the morning went up the street of Bourecq, where the cocks are crowing, climbed the road to the high land southwest of the village, and so for an hour or two it is well with me.

For over the hill a mile or two of road brings me to a church and a few houses, clumps and lines of tall trees standing up against the faint colours of a watery daybreak; and the homely caw of a rookery, sailing out to their day's business. The curé gives me good morning as I trudge past his gate and round under the high garden-wall up the narrow lane with crazy buildings on the right side. And so out to the bare cornlands with a distant view of woods and ploughland, and steeples, and to the north and east the chimneys of some colliery-places. And I step out along a straight road, paved and poplar-guarded, until the light has broadened and it's full day—8 o'clock—and the church-bells come up from below, and from far and near. And a troop of mules clatters along to meet me, at their morning exercise, turbaned Indians and whistling Tommy Atkins leading them. So I must be turning back. But as I sit on a milestone the sun comes out and gives me his golden stare, and a thrush sings a little way off, the first I've heard in France.

At 10.50 we left Bourecq:[3] entrained at Lillers 12 noon. Crawled forty miles in ten hours, and detrained at Sadeux (three miles beyond Amiens). A dark, warm, still night, a little

---

[1] R. H. Hanmer, a pre-war friend of S.S., who in April 1917 was wounded when fighting with the Second Battalion R.W.F. There had been a shadowy engagement between his sister and S.S.
[2] David Thomas, the Dick Tiltwood of *Memoirs of an Infantry Officer*.
[3] I was here again in June 1918. S.S.

rain at times. After unloading and men getting tea, the battalion started at 12.15 to march to Montagne.

December 6

A straight, wide road with tall trees on either side; through a village—up a hill—then the road got bad. We passed a few villages, but very few isolated farms. Twice I saw our shadows thrown on to a white wall by a transport-lamp in rear of the column. Once it was a few colossal heads, with lurching shoulders and slung rifles, and again, on a dead white wall, a line of *legs only*, huge legs striding along, as if jeering at our efforts. And all the while we slogged on to the steady beat of the drums in front—up hill down dale; about 3.30 the sky cleared, and we marched under the triumphant stars, plough and bear and all the rest—immortal diadems for humble soldiers dead and living.

At 6 a.m. just before it began to get light, we halted (sixth halt) in a good village, with a fine church; and were told we had five kilometres to go (up a high hill). So at 7.15 we arrived at Montagne, a straggling village on the Picardy uplands, about eighteen miles north-west of Amiens. We had done sixteen miles since detraining, and everyone was about beat. We found the billets were rotten. After a wretched meal we got into bed at 10.45 and slept till 5. There have been no troops here before (except one troop of Bengal Lancers) and the rustic inhabitants don't seem overjoyed at seeing us. I sleep in an empty cottage with R. Ormrod. There is a nice brick-paved kitchen with a good open grate; we soon got a good blaze going, and the place looked quite cheery—a clock ticking slowly against the wall, and some good old furniture.

December 7

Took the Company out at 9 to some arable ground close to the village, which has plenty of woods near it, and small orchards adjoining the houses; one can see miles away over the country all round—rolling ploughlands and dark woods; only a few villages visible, with steeples, as in England. It is a little like parts of East Kent; and the Tickham hills. The fields are unfenced, and dotted with corn-stacks. And such a sky; it dominates the earth; but it is the sky of freedom, not a death-haunted appendage as in Flanders. And here there are flocks of starlings, and men ploughing with grey horses, and the roads wind away to a horizon that is not bounded by a line of armies entrenched. But there are no young men on the farms; only boys and grey old men. And long before the orchards break into blossom and the woods are charmed again into 'green pavilions', *we* shall have marched away, back to no-man's-land, with death in our hearts, mocked by the glory of the coloured earth—most of us blind to all but the dogged strife, the endless hardships, a few allured and heartened by the splendours of the spirit—the peace after sacrifice—the foreknowledge of beauty discarnate. I wonder when I shall see the wild hyacinths in the woods—'like a skylit water stood The bluebells in the azured wood'.[1]

December 8

Fine weather. South wind. Did outpost scheme on the hills north of the village. After lunch I rode the black pony for one and a half hours, out beyond Warlus, over the ploughlands and hills and made hunting noises and was quite happy with the corky little animal under me going so nicely. Saw no one but a few Bengal Lancers, very fine fellows, well mounted.

December 9

Rainy day. Rode black pony after lunch and got wet.

December 10

Fine and warm. Did attack on Le Quesnoy before lunch. Walked through woods beyond Le Fayel after lunch. Beautiful country—sat on edge of wood, under beech and cypress trees, looking across a valley of ploughland to grassy hills crowned with long dark lines of pine-covert—like a picture by Wilson Steer—a faint golden light over all, austere, and yet delicate in tone and outline. Wind blowing strong from south, and two windmills spinning round. Not a soul in sight but a big sandy

[1] A. E. Housman, *A Shropshire Lad*, xli.

hare and a brace of rabbits, and some pigeons wheeling above the pines. As I came out of the wood, the ploughmen were driving their last furrows and a man with his two dogs was driving a big flock of sheep to the farm, silver-grey on the dark stubbles, with Montagne away among its trees (and the R.W.F. fifes and drums playing down the street). This country is more like Arcady than anything I ever saw, but I expect all the woods are let to shooting syndicates.

And we can hear the big guns booming fifty kilometres away, and Armageddon is still going on. I have found peace here, anyhow, and the old inane life of 1913–14 seems lopped right off—never to return, thank heaven.

December 17

A week of routine, in rain and grey weather. A long letter today from E.J.D.[1]

Reading the new volume of Eddie Marsh's poets,[2] nothing new to me in it. Wish the Kaiser would let me go back to my work at writing poems. Slow and sure is my way, I'm sure, and the good work was bound to come along sooner or later. And now, if I get done in, I leave only a sheaf of minor verse, mostly derived from memory.

But I am happy, happy; I've escaped and found peace unbelievable in this extraordinary existence which I thought I should loathe. The actual life is mechanical; and my dreams are mine, more lonely than ever. We're safe for another year of war, too, so next summer ought to do something for me. Anything but a 'cushy' wound! That would be an awful disaster. I must endure, or else die. And it's nice to look back on my childhood which lasted so long (until I was twenty-three, anyhow). What a confused idea I had of everything, except beauty; was that time *all* wasted? Lovely now seem the summer dawns in Weirleigh garden; lovely the slow music of the dusk, and the chords of the piano-music. Loveliest of all, the delight of weaving words into verses; the building

[1] Edward Joseph Dent (1876–1957), musical scholar. Sometime Fellow of King's College, Cambridge. Professor of Music at Cambridge 1926–41. President of the International Society of Contemporary Music. Voluminous writer and translator of libretti.
[2] *Georgian Poetry* 1913–1915, published in November 1915. See n. 4, p. 130.

of dream on dream; oh the flowers and the songs, now so far away. The certainty of my power to touch the hearts of men with poetry—all faded now like a glorious sky. And then the July days, the afternoons of cricketing, and the silly joy I had when I managed to stay an hour or two at the wicket. And oh the quiet winter mornings when I rode to meet the hounds— and the dear nights when the tired horse walked beside me. Days at Ringmer—days at Witherley—good rides in Kent and Sussex—and the music of the hounds in the autumn woods— and talks by the fire with good old Gordon,[1] and my Nimrod. Good-bye to life, good-bye to Sussex.

BROTHERS

Give me your hand, my brother; search my face;
Look in these eyes lest I should think of shame;
For we have made an end of all things base;
We are returning by the road we came.

Your lot is with the ghosts of soldiers dead,
And I am with the fighters in the field;
But in the gloom I see your laurelled head,
And through your victory mine shall be revealed.

December 18[2]

Christmas

This country looks very attractive in the mild rainy weather. Rode after lunch out by Warlus and back through the woods behind Mericourt. The Somme valley looked fine in the twi-light; and the country westward with its wooded ridges against the yellow sunset low down under the dark clouds; the many little roads winding away over the slopes, wet roads gleaming in the last light, climbing and sinking, the roads that lead to the nowhere of romance. Dear are these fields and woods, dear the solitary trees against such evening skies. I am glad to be alive

[1] Gordon Harbord.
[2] Published in the *Saturday Review*, 26 February 1916, then in S.S.'s privately printed volume *Morning-Glory* (1916) and, slightly revised, in *The Old Huntsman* (1917). Later it was re-titled 'To my Brother'.

this Christmas, riding home in the dusk (as after a day with the hounds), the little horse stepping it out, and my heart musing in the old silly way—the heart that wants to find expression and always halts on the borderlands. No leaf here, no blossoming boughs—only the bare brown fields and the dark woods. And as I rode up Warlus wood in the gloom I met an old man with leather leggings and a great blue cloak with a pointed hood, and he stopped to peer at me, as if he were startled at my young face and the gallant little horse, so light-hearted—a dragon-slayer, perhaps. I slew the dragon in my heart when the war began, and it was only a little wheedling thing after all. The Angel is still there, Poetry, with bright wings prepared for flights into the dawn, across the cold hills, O joy—'wild and calm and lonely'.

Christmas night was jolly, by the log fire, the village full of maudlin sergeants and paralysed privates.

THE PRINCE OF WOUNDS

The Prince of wounds is with us here;
Wearing his crown he gazes down,
Sad and forgiving and austere.
We have renounced our lovely things,
Music and colour and delight:
The spirit of Destruction sings
And tramples on the flaring night.
But Christ is here upon the cross,
Bound to a road that's dark with blood,
Guarding immitigable loss.
Have we the strength to strive alone
Who can no longer worship Christ?
Is He a God of wood and stone,
While those who served him writhe and moan,
On warfare's altar sacrificed?

December 27

1916

1916

January 3
1916 comes along with a south-west wind and plenty of rain.
This morning we marched out at 8.30 along the Riencourt road
to Cavillon and Picquigny—delightful names—with the early
sun touching those hills across the Somme valley. Airaines
roofs clustering in the hollow and all the levels lit and shadowed
—a living masterpiece of landscape-painting. On the right are
the Riencourt woods, dark, with the sun behind them, and dark
the ploughland where rooks are settling and flapping their
wings. Ploughman whistles and halloos to his team of greys,
driving a cheery furrow—the world is jolly to-day, and the very
sludge of the lane is gilt with the sun's good humour.

This is only 'fine writing', but it was my happy heart this
morning, my heart singing its praise of life and landscape. The
men trudging behind chattered their war-jargon, but I was back
in an English day, walking alone on the hills with the mystery
of my joy strong in me. O the beauty, the glory of what I saw,
and see every day—so easily lost, so precious to the blind and

the weary; so heavenly to men doomed to die. The ghost of Apollo is on these cornlands—Apollo in Picardy; it was here that he ground the kern and plied the flail, and lived at the farm.

TO VICTORY

Return to greet me, colours that were my joy.
Not in the woeful crimson of men slain,
But shining as a garden: come with the streaming
Banners of dawn and sundown after rain.

I want to fill my gaze with blue and silver,
Radiance through living roses, spires of green
Rising in young-limbed copse and lovely wood
Where the hueless wind passes and cries unseen.

I am not sad: only I long for lustre;
I am tired of greys and browns and the leafless ash:
I would have hours that move like a glitter of dancers,
Far from the angry guns that boom and flash.

Return, musical, gay with blossom and fleetness,
Days when my sight shall be clean, my heart shall rejoice,
Where the blithe wind laughs on the hills with uplifted voice.

January 4[1]

January 9

I lay abed late and went out well rested about 11 to a sunny morning and a great cawing of rooks who had settled on the half-ploughed stubbles east of our remote Montagne. Not a cloud in the sky; and the cold air smelling wintry and good, a morning for the larks, but I could hear none aloft; only a few flocks of small finches; and once I saw some sort of hawk hovering near a clump of thorn-bushes round a solitary oak; there the small birds were congregated, chattering among the twigs, till Lord Merlin stoops and stands on the topmost branch

[1] Published anonymously in *The Times* 15 January 1916. Then in *Morning-Glory* (1916) and, slightly revised and dedicated to Edmund Gosse in *The Old Huntsman* (1917).

of their oak. For a while he surveys the world, till I scare him off his perch, and he wings away to the valley, where the bells of Airaines come up to me, very Sabbath-like in the stillness and clarity of the morning. On my right hand the sun and the dark ploughland, and further on the rich brown gloom of the woods, swept by faint winds and laced with flickering light.

And on my left, sunshine and yellow plains of stubble, straw-coloured, hued like pale honey, with two inky rooks and a few strips of covert, purple and grey and russet with chestnut, hazel and ash.

O this joy of to-day! My voice shall ring through the great wood, because I am glad for a while with beautiful earth, and we who live here are doomed to fall as best befits a man, a sacrifice to the spring; and this is true and we all know it—that many of us must die before Easter.[1] Some pigeons flew up from the homely stacks of a farm on my way back: the whistle of their wings brought a memory of Weirleigh lawns, but these were grey and puritan, and not flashing white as ours are.

I heard yesterday that Bobbie Hanmer is under orders for the Mediterranean Force. If only he were coming out here, as he hoped. But he may be safer there. Small chance for any of us in these attacks out here when they begin. Bless his heart; I never knew a nicer lad. Good-luck to his shining face. J.G.N. sends me a poem in irregular verse (not verse at all really) by F. Murray, addressed to *me!*

> Nature and you, walking hand in hand, speak to my soul
> like God's voice in a garden . . . Your words, like dewdrops
> on a spider's web, sparkle like jewels. The lark rises as he
> hears you come, and sings your name, then drops to earth,
> failing to find in heaven a soul so pure.

The funny part of it is that I quite agree with him in what he says.

January 13

Yesterday was a long Brigade field-day between Lincheux and Fricourt. We started at 7.10, with a lovely winter dawn coming up behind the woods; the sun appeared like a large

[1] Four officers dead by April 15. S.S.

orange, half-way to Camps, on our left. The charm of the day
soon wore off, and the operations lasted until 1.45. Then we
marched home and got there at 4.45, very tired. To-day I rode
out about 2.30 in half-a-gale of wind from the north, and the
huge gloom of a storm driving across the valley. As I went down
the hill to Warlus I saw a very noble picture. A rampart of
approaching rain, slate-coloured, blotting the plain; the fore-
ground striped with vivid green and rich umber, lit with a
gleam of sun, and a grand arc of iridescence spanning the storm.
A distant farm-cart with two horses, one dark, one white, was
the one thing needed to make the whole suitably impressive—
and it was there—the miniature of toil, so tiny—and the cloud
sky high, so grand.

Riding on toward Belloy the heavens were divided, the gold-
fringed darkness of the storm on either side, and between them
the glory of windswept blue; it was like the thought of two
nations divided by war. And then the road climbs and becomes
the street of Belloy—ramshackle houses, white-walled, their
roofs patched with green moss—here and there a touch of pale
peacock-blue from a door or shutter. And four solemn geese had
the village to themselves; four wise birds, footing slow, con-
tented in their survival of the Christmas feast, most seemly in
their gait, these matrons. As I turned in my saddle to look back
at them, two children in blue had run out at the sound of clatter-
ing hoofs and were staring after me. Still was the street,
sheltered from the gusty afternoon. At the hill-top the château,
grey-roofed and snowy-walled, showed me its many windows,
standing among trees—no face was there to see me pass. Only
a bronze lion guarding the well in the centre of the tangled lawn.
Huge clouds were flying in glory as I rode home through the
wooded ridges between. Magpies watched me from a wood.
The country looked wild and lonely and splendid. A silver
spinney of graceful birches welcomed me like a brother, as I
rode among them; my heart spoke to them as the wind speaks
to their answering boughs. How strange it is that I came to the
war prepared to suffer torments and to see horrible sights; and
I have found hours in heaven, and noble counties at my feet,
and love inhabiting the hearts of men. Somewhere Hell awaits
me, but it will be a brave place, where no devils are ramping.
As old Bridges says:

1916

If thou cans't Death defy,
If thy Faith is entire,
Press onward, for thine eye
Shall see thy heart's desire.

Beauty and love are nigh,
And with their deathless quire
Soon shall thine eager cry
Be numbered and expire.[1]

January 25
Riding out this morning in sunshine and stillness—the land-scape like a bowl of wine, golden; light spreading across the earth, and earth drinking its fill of light; down by Warlus the village shepherd stamps up and down the fallows on his numb feet, with his hood over his head; alone with his flock and his dogs and his two goats, and a hundred busy black rooks, and a few hares popping up and scuttling across the wheat, stopping to listen, and then away again—big sandy ones.

Since January 18, when R. Ormrod went on leave, I am Transport Officer; why does this safe job come my way when I wanted danger and hardship? But there is no way out of it, without looking a fool, so I must take it. And it is better fun than with the company. The old nags want a bit of looking after—and the whole show wants tidying up.[2]

Last Sunday (January 23) I left here to go to Amiens on a sunny morning, which had turned dull and cheerless by 1 o'clock. The train rambles in to Amiens in one and a half hours, about eighteen miles.

The Cathedral, as one stands in the nave, gives an impression of clear whiteness; the massive columns seem slender, so vast is the place; and the windows beyond the altar are high and delicate, with a little central colour, blue, violet and amber, and the rest white, with a touch of grass-green in the sombre-glowing glass lower down.

The architecture of the place, leading the eye upward, soars above the gaudy insignia of the service—shrines and candles and

[1] From *Shorter Poems*, Book III, no. 19.
[2] Gave up Transport on March 20. S.S.

[35]

pictures (like the great idea of religion—outshining all formulae of office and celebration). The rose-windows are full of dusky flames; with touches of scarlet, apple-green, sapphire, violet, and orange.

The noble arches and pillars are lifted up toward heaven to break into flowers, lilies of clear light, and the gorgeous hues of richer petals and clusters. And the voices of the great organ shout and mingle their raptures high overhead, shaking the roofs with glory.

Beyond the great wrought-iron gate, where the marvellously carven stalls are, the choir are a black bevy against the stars of the altar-lights. They fill the cathedral with their antiphons, while the French are at their meek orisons, old women and tired soldiers in blue-grey, children and white-haired men.

But the invader is here; a Japanese officer flits in with curious eyes; the Army Service Corps and Red Cross men are everywhere, walking up and down with the foolish looks of sightseers, who come neither to watch nor to pray. And the Jocks, the kilted ones, their arrogance is overweening, they move with an air of conquest; have we conquered France? For the old English knights and squires and varlets must have moved up and down just as these do, elbowing the fantastic Frenchmen against the wall; their eyes had the same veiled insolence five hundred years ago, I am certain. These wear long capes or cloaks which give them a mediaeval look.

January 26

> For I not for an hour did love
> Or for a day desire,
> But with my soul had from above
> This endless holy fire.

H.V.[1]

Old Vaughan the Silurist is the lad for me to-night; 'There is in God, some say, A deep, but dazzling darkness'; as he says,[2] and is often quoted by people who little know the truth and glory which shine from his words. And I am fortunate in having

[1] Henry Vaughan (1622–95), 'A Song to Amoret'.
[2] In his poem 'The Night'.

come to the blessed state of mind when earth and light are one;
I suppose it is what the mystics call finding Reality. I am part
of the earth which for me is soaked in the glory of sunlight and
past seasons—'sleep, and sunshine, and the autumnal earth' as
R.B. says.[1]

January 30
The Battalion left Montagne in raw and foggy weather and
marched thirteen miles by Picquigny to Vaux.

January 31
Marched to Pont Noyelles, by Bertangles and Allonville.
Weather cold and foggy. Bad billets. Heavy firing up the line.
Frise reported lost.

February 1
We marched ten miles to Morlancourt, a village about fifteen
miles north-east of Amiens and five miles south of Albert.
Battalion goes to the first-line trenches tomorrow, five or six
miles away—near Fricourt. To-day the sun shone and the air
felt keen. As we marched down to the village of Corbie, a flock
of pigeons circled above the roofs, the light shining through their
many sober-coloured wings. Very tiring day; on the run from
7 a.m. till 11.30 p.m. We relieve the Twelfth Middlesex: their
billeting officer is C. H. S. Runge. Hadn't seen him since I was
at private school with him. His two cousins, whom I used to
know, are fighting for the other side.

February 2
Went up with rations etc. about seven miles by road; started
2.45 and got back at 9.45. Very cold wind. Trenches only
sixty yards from the enemy in places and many mine-craters
between.

[1] Rupert Brooke, 'Safety'; 'sunshine' should be 'freedom'.

1916

February 3

Minshull Ford goes to take over the 91st Brigade. Major Stockwell[1] comes to command First R.W.F. Heavy firing by the French on our right (Frise about five miles away).

February 5

A memorable day. Brilliant sunlight and sailing white clouds all the morning. About 12.30 a German aeroplane came over and our anti-aircraft guns let off about two hundred shells—little puffs of white hanging aloft, dispersing slowly while the big hawk forged ahead and then turned and went back, superb and insolent. After lunch rode across to the Citadel under the same blue weather, startling the hares and partridges across the fallows and wheatlands, to find our batteries busily booming away at the Huns who had been playing hell with the trenches occupied by R.W.F. Got there at 4.30, and had some trouble getting up to C. Company and the front line, as the communication-trenches were very much knocked about. Found Greaves, Stansfield, Orme,[2] and Wadd all serene, and no one hurt, though they had been peppered with trench-mortars etc from 8.30 to 3.30. I left them at 7.45, when all the stars were out and the young moon on her back, and an owl flitting across the trenches. Through the dusk came the loud rattle of Hun machine-gun fire on the left; the sky soared unheeding of the war-lines, and the trenches ankle-deep in wet clay, and men grimly peering from under their round steel caps. The mare brought me home straight as a die across the four miles of plough and mud— gloom all around and stars, stars, overhead, and hanging low above the hills—the rockets going up behind, along the line— brief lights soon burnt out—the stars wheeling changeless and untroubled, life and deathless beauty, always the same contrast. So I still see the war as a looker-on; catching a glimpse of the grim places, and then ride back to village lights and evening talk with old Cotterill and the interpreter. But my time will come—never doubt it.

---

[1] The Kinjack of *Memoirs of an Infantry Officer*.
[2] E. L. Greaves, N. Stansfield, E. L. Orme = Barton, Mansfield and Ormond in *Memoirs of an Infantry Officer*.

IN THE PINK

So Davies wrote, 'This leaves me in the pink',
Then scrawled his name, 'your loving sweetheart Willie'.
With crosses for a hug: he'd had a drink
Of rum and tea; and though the barn was chilly,
His blood ran warm, for once; he'd pay to spend;
Winter was passing; soon the year would mend.

He couldn't sleep that night; stiff in the dark
He moaned and thought of Sundays at the farm,
When he'd go out as cheerful as a lark
In his best suit to wander arm in arm
With brown-eyed Gwen, and whisper in her ear
The simple, silly things she liked to hear.

And then he thought; to-morrow we must trudge
Up to the trenches, and my boots are rotten;
Six miles of stodgy clay and freezing sludge,
And everything but wretchedness forgotten.
To-night he's in the pink, but soon he'll die;
And still the war goes on; he don't know why.

February 10[1]

February 22

Battalion went to front line again on February 18. Weather
wet last week; very cold now but no snow. Major Stockwell
arrived yesterday to take command. He is aggressive efficiency,
very blatant, but knows the job. On going up with the rations
tonight I found a great noise of gunfire; coming over the hill
from Bray to Citadel the darkness toward Albert and Fricourt
was lit with flashes and glare of shells bursting and guns firing,
and over all Blake's evening star, 'Thou fair-haired angel of the
evening . . . washed the dusk with silver',[2] while men at war
painted it with flame and destruction. The Battalion were stand-
ing to, and rather expecting a German attack, but nothing came
of it and little damage done. And so home to bed, to be awakened
at midnight by Cotterill and told to go on leave to-morrow.

[1] Published in the *Nation*, 28 October 1916, and in *The Old Huntsman* (1917).
[2] Blake, 'To the Evening Star'.

February 23

Off to England; leave Mericourt 9.30 by a leisurely train to Amiens and Havre and get to town about 10 a.m. next day. Weather bitterly cold and hard frost. Very poor prospect for getting a hunt.

March 5 (On leaving Southampton)

Quiet evening, a smooth dusk of waters. The ships gliding, leaving a fan of eddies in their wake. Lights across the harbour—emerald, ruby and orange—sea-birds' creaking cries, like a sound of hauled windlasses and pulleys—sea-birds grey, floating, sailing, settling—and over all the sickle moon very slender, and one white star soon covered by wisps of films of thin cloud, and all the host of the lesser ones appearing in a sudden maze of remoteness, and a bugle sounding from the town, a lonely note like the last thought of home—lost in the greatness of the baffling seas.

March 6

Coming back to the war I find the country as I left it, under whiteness, snow; and this lovely vesture is like a sheet hung in a dark room; I see against it all the bright images which my ten days at home have brought me. The faces of my friends, smiling welcome, firelit rooms with books and noble paintings on the walls, the beauty of London streets by night with their mazes of red and orange lamps, passing and meeting, or burning steadily away into the vistas of streets like dark waterways between the mystery of lofty buildings. Woods and fields in Sussex, in clear sunlight of early March, and the scarlet-coated huntsman galloping his jaunty little grey nag, cheering his hounds to a find or casting them across the wet ploughs, and the violinist leading the orchestra from height to height of noble rapture, lost in the splendour of his task, an austere Apollo in a black coat.

March 13

Back from leave a week now. Weather last week very wintry; but yesterday was the first of spring, and again to-day the sun and the earth are lovers. All the farm-hens feel like laying eggs and make all their best noises outside our door. In bed in my canvas hut, after listening to the long roar of guns four miles away, and falling asleep to their cradle-song, I wake up to see bird-shadows against my roof, and to hear the busy clack and whistle of starlings on the fruit-trees and the red roofs of the farm where the transport is. And after breakfast I sit half-way between the fire and the sunshine to read the Laureate's anthology,[1] sipping small doses of Shelley who always makes such an effect when one reads him in small extracts. 'And the gloom divine is all round,' as he says in *Prometheus*. The 'gloom divine'—something like Vaughan's 'deep, but dazzling darkness'. And then the soldier-cook begins singing 'I want to go to Michigan' at the top of his voice about three yards away.

March 15

Looking across Morlancourt to the west from the hill where our billet stands, at 11.30 on a spring day. The last two days have soaked the earth in pure golden sunlight and warmth, leaving the air warm even when darkness had come and the stars were out. An air-plane drones overhead, and big prosperous clouds move slowly across the blue, trailing skeins and webs of white, flocks of them, far away to the edge of the sky, the furthest ones like pearls in their texture of light and vapour.

Birds wheel and clack round the vane on the grey church-tower with its slated peak. And a couple of miles away I can see the wood on the hill above Mericourt, tiny and delicate, beyond the angles of red and slate-hued roofs, rich and gleaming in the pale sunshine. The long line of the ridge goes all round, hiding the rest of the wood. Then I ride out toward Albert and Méaulte, with larks carolling very clear and two solemn black-and-white dogs staring at me from outside an R.E. hut on the ridge where the reserve-trench line is dug. From the slope, looking northwest, the country rises and falls, sparse green and drab and brown, to a skyline of trees in tiny delicate silhouette, with occasional dark line of woodland, the white seams of trenches dug in the limestone, and here and there a road winding away to nowhere (or the German territory, unexplored and sinister).

[1] *The Spirit of Man*, edited by Robert Bridges (1916).

Then there is Albert, with its two or three chimney-stacks and its ruined basilica tower showing above a line of tall trees that border the river, a medley of roofs, looking peaceful enough from here, but really a town deserted and semi-ruinous, in places destroyed. In the foreground two other villages by the river, with red roofs and church-tower, and patches of white walls and tall leafless willows growing by the river-sides. And Bécordel church-tower peeps over a shoulder of hill, the village hidden; and Fricourt only three miles away, but held by the enemy since I don't know when. And everywhere the rural spirit of the neighbourhood has been chased away by shells and soldiers, and supply-sheds and everything else; the very sky has lost its once bird-held supremacy and isolation; but to-day it is fair with clouds in the blue, and something of the spirit of the old countryside shines from the distant scene, as if it strove to assert itself in the early promise of spring, and the flowers would return to find their earth unchanged and the slaughter ended.

March 16

If anyone were to ask me how I remember Morlancourt, I should say that it is a village resting among the folds of long slopes and ridges of naked ploughland; where five roads meet, and the houses begin where each road descends a different part of the hills; at each end of the village is a church, and in the hollow centre of the place is a congregation of buildings with a sort of small square, or wide space, with a pond on one side of it. Looking down on Morlancourt, one sees a confusion of slate roofs and tiled ones, with touches of white and drab and ochre which are the walls of cottages and farm-buildings, a number of trees, slender and leafless, mingling with the houses. Then the eye roves beyond the village to meet the long line of the hills all round, with a few straggling trees, a team of greys ploughing or dredging, some horsemen trotting outlined along the white edge of the sky, or a hooded farm-cart, or a limber. There are strips of green wheat, and acres of drab fallow, mingled with the bright brown of the newly-ploughed land. And there are high banks where thorn-bushes grow, a cage for flitting birds that swing on the thorny twigs. The wind pipes across the open, soughing in the isolated trees, plane, willow or aspen. The open sky is full of lark-songs, as is proper for such places. And always the guns boom a few miles away, and the aeroplanes drone high up, looking down on the seams of unseen trench-lines with their tangle of wires and posts. It is a country of expansive skies and delicate miniatures of distant objects clear and neatly defined. The sunlight sweeps across it in a noble progress of wind and cloud; the rain comes down and blots it in scuds of grey; sunset brings it colour and mystery and sadness; and when night brings out the stars to watch over it, the hills fade, deep-hued and austere, and the whole region becomes an interminable dusk of looming slopes, with lights of village and bivouac picked out here and there, sparks in the loneliness and serenity of time.

Solving Social Problems
Quartermaster and Transport Officer
T.O. If the war goes on another twelve months the selfish hogs in England will begin to feel it; I mean the people who are clinging to their old easy ways of life, and trying to ignore the facts of the war; reading the war-news and sucking in all the fabrications that suit their hopes of a speedy end to it, and hell and extinction to the Huns.
Q.M. They're the b——rs I'm after! This war is being carried on by the highest and the lowest in the land—the blue-blooded upper ten, and the crowd that some silly b——r called the 'submerged tenth'. All the others are making what they can out of it and shirking the dirty work.

THE QUARTER-MASTER

Bad stations and good liquor and long service
Have aged his looks beyond their forty-five;
For eight and twenty years he's been a soldier;
And nineteen months of war have made him thrive.
He's got a face to match his breast of medals,
All stained and veined with purple and deep red.
His heart is somewhat bigger than his body,
And there's a holy anger in his head.

See where he sits before the evening embers,
Warming his knotted fingers at the blaze,
The man whose life is in the old battalion,
And all its battles in his gleaming gaze,
That looks you through and through: his smile is kindly,
And humbugs are the only thing he hates:
He's risen from a private to be captain,
And still he cracks a joke with his old mates.

But when the rum is hot, his eyes will kindle,
And all that's nearest to his heart he'll speak,
Lifting his banner over the tired and humble,
Who toil and die with nothing good to seek.
His words go questing in the swarming cities,
For men whose faces get no glimpse of green;
And he would march them out to win fresh fortune,
And freedom from injustice that has been.

He's chanced his arm with fate and found his glory;
He's swung the lead with many a roaring lad:
Good-luck to him; good-luck to all his kindred!
It's meeting men like him that makes me glad.

March 17

March 19

Riding out to the trenches last night the sky at 6.30 was angry
with a red smoky sunset; the village loomed against the glow;
it was a sultry, threatening dusk. But when I came home at 10
o'clock, everything was covered with exquisite moonlight and a
great star hung over Morlancourt, unbelievably light in the pale
azure heavens.

This morning came the evil news from the trenches—first
that 'Tracker' Richardson had died of wounds after being
knocked over by a shell last night in front of the trenches; this
was bad. But they came afterwards and told that my little
Tommy[1] had been hit by a stray bullet and died last night.
When last I saw him, two nights ago, he had his notebook in

[1] Lieutenant David Thomas. S.S.'s poems 'A Subaltern', 'The Last Meeting' and
'A Letter Home' refer to him.

his hand, reading my last poem. And I said good night to him, in the moonlit trenches. Had I but known!—the old, human-weak cry. Now he comes back to me in memories, like an angel, with the light in his yellow hair, and I think of him at Cambridge last August when we lived together four weeks in Pembroke College in rooms where the previous occupant's name, Paradise, was written above the door.

So, after lunch, I escaped to the woods above Sailly-Laurette, and grief had its way with me in the sultry thicket, while the mare champed her bit and stamped her feet, tethered to a tree: and the little shrill notes of birds came piping down the hazels, and magpies flew overhead, and all was peace, except for the distant mutter and boom of guns. And I lay there under the smooth bole of a beech-tree, wondering, and longing for the bodily presence that was so fair.

Grief can be beautiful, when we find something worthy to be mourned. To-day I knew what it means to find the soul washed pure with tears, and the load of death was lifted from my heart. So I wrote his name in chalk on the beech-tree stem, and left a rough garland of ivy there, and a yellow primrose for his yellow hair and kind grey eyes, my dear, my dear. And to-night I saw his shrouded form laid in the earth with his two companions (young Pritchard was killed this evening also). In the half-clouded moonlight the parson stood above the graves, and everything was dim but the striped flag laid across them. Robert Graves, beside me, with his white whimsical face twisted and grieving. Once we could not hear the solemn words for the noise of a machine-gun along the line; and when all was finished a canister fell a few hundred yards away to burst with a crash. So Tommy left us, a gentle soldier, perfect and without stain. And so he will always remain in my heart, fresh and happy and brave.

> For you were glad, and kind and brave;
> With hands that clasped me, young and warm;
> But I have seen a soldier's grave,
> And I have seen your shrouded form.

March 20

March 25

Snow yesterday, and the country all in white. To-day it has melted and the wind is south-west. I walked across to the hill looking over the Somme by Sailly-Laurette. A grassy juniper-dotted platform two hundred feet above the river, a steep bluff dropping down to it. A chain of steel-grey lakes by the river, and narrow pale-brown or buff levels of marshland. The hills rise gently beyond the river with its lines of trees and huddle of slated and tiled roofs, church-tower etc. Up here I find some purple flowers with yellow centres, scabious. About an inch long, shaped like gentians.

To-morrow I am off to do six days in the trenches with C. Company.

March 27

Last night it was cold starlight up in the front line from 8 to 12 while the men were piling sandbags on the parapet. This morning it was all blowing sun and showers and wind and lark-songs on the slope behind our dug-outs, and the skeleton village of Fricourt a mile away on the far hill beyond our trench-lines. Guns banging and puffs of smoke, and black columns of vapour and earth blown upward when they burst on the hill.

And this afternoon, sitting in the gloom of the steel dug-out, like being inside a boiler; reading a novel by candlelight with Greaves and Stockwell snoring on their beds, and the servants singing and joking next door, the patter of rain began on the roof, and I shivered and turned chilly, and thought of safety and home and years that might be. And Tommy's dead.

March 28

Wet and windy up in the line that night. This morning an R.E. officer called Sisson came in and talked about Hamo whom he knew so well up at Clare and spoke so nicely of H's intensely humorous way of looking at things.

The sky was pitch-black with pale blots: he could not see the man in front of him: when the flares went up beyond the hill the sky was inky at the edge and the dark line of the ground showed clear-edged and gloomy and forbidding.

On the bags above the deep trench a white sheen would settle and diminish upwards, a silver glimpse of mounded sandbags bleached and weather-worn.

In the morning of sun and cloudlands he would get glimpses of charming delicate landscapes, village, wood and hill, and trees along the crest; in no-man's-land nothing moves.

Prospects and aspects. A shell, whizzing over to the enemy lines, bursts with a hollow crash. Against the clear evening sky a cloudy column of dark smoke rises to drift away, driven by the faint breeze. Slowly it takes shape; curling in wisps, it is a gigantic form, hooded, with clumsy, expostulating arms, a figure draped in dingy whirling smoke. Then with a gradual gesture of acquiescence, it lolls sideways, falling over to the attitude of a swimmer on his side, and so dissolves into nothingness. Perhaps the shell had killed a soldier, for this was like the phantom of his departing and reluctant life; he was dead but he went in defeated anger, brandishing his ineffectual arms as he passed away to the inaccessible caverns of death.

March 30

7 o'clock on a frosty white morning with a lark shaking his little wings above the trenches, and an airplane droning high up in the soft early sunlight. At 5 it was quite light, with a sickle-moon low in the west and the dawn a delicate flush of faint pink and submerged radiance above a mist-swathed country, peeping out from tree or roof, all white, misty-white and frosty-white, men stamp their feet and rats are about on the crannied rime-frosted parapets. Folds of mist, drifting in a dense blur; above them the white shoals and chasms of the sky.

Here life is audacious and invincible—until it is whirled away in enigmatic helplessness and ruin; and then it is only the bodies that are smashed and riddled; for the profound and purposeful spirit of renascence moves in and rests on all things—imperceptible between the scarred and swarming earth and noble solitudes of sky—the spirit that triumphs over visible destruction, as leaping water laughs at winds and rocks and shipwrecked hulks.

Their temper is proven, the fibre of their worth is tested and revealed; these men from Welsh farms and Midland cities, from

factory and shop and mine, who can ever give them their meed
of praise for the patience and tender jollity which seldom forsake
them?

The cheerless monotony of their hourly insecurity, a mono-
tony broken only by the ever-present imminence of death and
wounds—the cruelty and malice of these things that fall from
the skies searching for men, that they may batter and pierce the
bodies and blot the slender human existence.

As I sit in the sun in a nook among the sandbags and chalky
debris, with shells flying overhead in the blue air, a lark sings
high up, and a little weasel comes and runs past me within a
foot of my outstretched feet, looking at me with tiny bright
eyes. Bullets sing and whistle and hum; so do bits of shell;
rifles crack; some small guns and trench-mortars pop and thud;
big shells burst with a massive explosion, and the voluminous
echoes roll along the valleys, to fade nobly and without haste or
consternation.

Bullets are deft and flick your life out with a quick smack.
Shells rend and bury, and vibrate and scatter, hurling fragments
and lumps and jagged splinters at you; they lift you off your
legs and leave you huddled and bleeding and torn and scorched
with a blast straight from the pit. Heaven is furious with the
smoke and flare and portent of shells, but bullets are a swarm of
whizzing hornets, mad, winged and relentless, undeviating in
their malicious onset.

The big guns roar their challenge and defiance; but the
machine-guns rattle with intermittent bursts of mirthless
laughter.

There are still pools in the craters; they reflect the stars like
any lovely water, but nothing grows near them; snags of iron
jut from their banks, tin cans and coils of wire, and other
trench-refuse. If you search carefully, you may find a skull,
eyeless, grotesquely matted with what was once hair; eyes once
looked from those detestable holes, they made the fabric of a
passionate life, they appealed for justice, they were lit with
triumph, and beautiful with pity.

How good it is to get the savour of time past; what living
skies, what crowds of faces, what unending murmur of voices,
mingle with the sounds of visions of to-day; for to-day is always
the event; and all the yesterdays are windows looking out on

unbounded serenity, and dreams written on the darkness; and suspended actions re-fashion themselves in silence, playing the parts they learned, at a single stroke of thought.

A WORKING-PARTY

Three hours ago he blundered up the trench,
Sliding and poising, groping with his boots;
Sometimes he tripped and lurched against the walls
With hands that pawed the sodden bags of chalk.
He could not see the man who went before him;
Only he heard the drum and rattle of feet
Stepping along the greasy planks, or sploshing
Wretchedly where the slush was ankle-deep.

Voices would grunt, 'Keep to the right; make way!'
When squeezing past men from the front line;
White faces peered, puffing an ember of red;
Candles and braziers glinted through the chinks
And curtain-flaps of dug-outs; then the gloom
Swallowed his sense of sight; the orange gleams
Faded; he felt his way; and someone swore
Because a sagging wire had caught his neck.

A flare went up; and shining whiteness spread,
And flickered upwards; showing nimble rats,
And mounds of sandbags, weatherworn and bleached,
Then the slow silver moment died in dark.
The wind came posting by with chilly gusts,
And buffeting at corners, piping thin
And dreary through the crannies; rifle-shots
Would split and crack and sing along the night
And shells came curving through the cloven air,
Bursting with hollow and voluminous bang.

Three hours ago he stumbled up the trench,
But he will never walk that road again;
He will be carried back; not carefully now,
Because he lies beyond the need of care,
And has no wound to hurt him, being dead.

1916

He was a young man, with a meagre wife
And two pale children in a Midland town;
His mates considered him a useful chap,
Who did his work and hadn't much to say,
And always laughed at other people's jokes,
Patient and dull, but kindly and reserved.

That night when he was busy at his job
Of piling sandbags on the parapet,
He thought how slow time went, stamping his feet,
And blowing on his fingers, pinched with cold.
He thought of getting back by half-past twelve,
And a tot of rum to send him warm to sleep
In draughty dug-out, stuffy with the fumes
Of coke, and full of snoring weary men.

He pushed another bag along the top,
Craning his body outward; then a flare
Gave one white glimpse of earth and what he knew;
And as he dropped his head, the instant split
His startled life with lead, and all went out.

That's how a lad goes west when at the front—
Snapped in a moment's merciful escape,
While the dun year goes lagging on its course
With widows grieving down the streets in black,
And faded mothers dreaming of bright sons
That grew to men, and listed for the war,
And left a photograph to keep their place.

March 30[1]

March 31

They put up three mines this evening between 4 and 5 but
did no damage at all. Last night, warmer and lovely with stars,
found me creeping about in front of our wire with Corporal
O'Brien. Got quite near the German wire but couldn't find the
sap which had been mentioned. Out about an hour and a half;
great fun. To-night I'm going to try and spot one of their

[1] Published, slightly revised, in *The Old Huntsman*.

working-parties and chuck some bombs at them. Better to get a sling at them in the open—even if on one's belly—than to sit here and have a great thing drop on one's head. I found it most exhilarating—just like starting for a race. Great thing is to get as many sensations as possible. No good being out here unless one takes the full amount of risks, and I want to get a good name in the Battalion, for the sake of poetry and poets, whom I represent.

No-man's-land fascinates me, with its jumble of wire-tangles and snaky seams in the earth winding along the landscape. The mine-craters are rather fearsome, with snipers hidden away on the lips, and pools of dead-looking water. One mine that went up to-day was in an old crater; I think it missed fire, as the earth seethed and spumed, but did not hurl debris skyward in smoke as they usually do. But the earth shook all right.

I am not going out for nothing to-night. I know I ought to be careful of myself, but something drives me on to look for trouble. Greaves tried to stop me going out last night; but that was child's play, only two or three sniper's shots at us, and the white rocket-lights going up while we lay flat and listened to our bumping hearts, and laughed with sheer delight when the danger was over: O'Brien is a topper.[1] I always knew it when he was in my platoon at Montagne.

April 1

Got back to Morlancourt by 1 o'clock on a bright day—east wind, glare and dust. Got through last night all right. About 9.30 I started creeping along the old sap which leads out to the crater where they put a fresh mine up in the afternoon; about forty yards from our parapet (it didn't explode properly). Our sentry had seen two men go down into the crater at dusk—covering-party, I expect—while the others worked on the lip. After crawling about forty yards I got to the edge of the crater and could hear them working about twenty-five yards away. Couldn't make out where the covering-party were, and was in mortal funk lest someone would shoot me. Crept back, and returned with Private Gwynne and four Mills bombs; we threw the bombs, I *think* with effect; a flare went up and I could see

[1] Killed May 25. S.S.

someone about five yards away, below me; fired six shots out of the revolver; and fled.

Gwynne was very steady, but I wish it had been O'Brien. Crawling out the first time was very jumpy work. Went out again at 8.30 this morning, and had a look, but could see no signs of work (or slaughtered Bosches).

I used to say I couldn't kill anyone in this war; but since they shot Tommy I would gladly stick a bayonet into a German by daylight. Someone told me a year ago that love, sorrow, and hate were things I had never known (things which every poet *should* know!). Now I've known love for Bobbie and Tommy, and grief for Hamo and Tommy, and hate has come also, and the lust to kill. Rupert Brooke was miraculously right when he said 'Safe shall be my going, Secretly armed against all death's endeavour; Safe though all safety's lost'.[1] He described the true soldier-spirit—saint and hero like Norman Donaldson and thousands of others who have been killed and died happier than they lived.

PEACE

Down glaring dusty roads, a sanctuary of trees,
Green for my gaze and cool, and hushed with pigeon's croon:
Chill pitcher'd water for my thirst; and sweet as these,
Anger grown tired of hate, and peace returning soon.

In my heart there's cruel war that must be waged
In darkness vile with moans and bleeding bodies maimed;
A gnawing hunger drives me, wild to be assuaged,
And bitter lust chuckles within me unashamed.

Come back to heal me when my feckless course is run,
Peace, that I sought in life; crown me among the dead;
Stoop to me like a lover when the fight is done;
Fold me in sleep; and let the stars be overhead.

April 2

April 4
What's all this rancour about? Is it my liver? Anyhow I am living in a sort of morose hunger for the next time I can get

[1] In his sonnet 'Safety'.

over the wire and look for the Germans with a bludgeon. Stockwell wants a prisoner, and I am going to try and get one for him, but it isn't for that I am going out. I want to smash someone's skull; I want to have a scrap and get out of the war for a bit or for ever. Sitting in a trench waiting for a rifle-grenade isn't fighting: war is clambering out of the top trench at 3 o'clock in the morning with a lot of rum-drugged soldiers who don't know where they're going—half of them to be blasted with machine-guns at point-blank range—trying to get over the wire which our artillery have failed to destroy. I can't get my own back for Hamo and Tommy that way. While I am really angry with the enemy, as I am lately, I must work it off, as these things don't last long with me as a rule. If I get shot it will be rotten for some people at home, but I am bound to get it in the neck sometime, so why not make a creditable show, and let people see that poets can fight as well as anybody else? And death is the best adventure of all—better than living idleness and sinking into the groove again and trying to be happy. Live is precious to us all now; too precious to keep long. 'And sweeter for the fading of those eyes The world seen once for all.'[1]

April 6

Tommy dead; and Bobbie Hanmer at Salonika; I can't keep them clear in memory; they fade, with their bright hair and happy eyes. I cannot recall the tones of their voices. And yet, when they were with me, I always tried to learn them by heart, like music, and said to myself, 'Only a little while; get all you can from them; make them happy if you can. And *don't* bore them.'

Back to the trenches to-morrow. 'Only a little more I have to write; Then I'll give o'er, and bid the world good-night.'[2]

Everything fades; the advancing spring only makes death more palpable—with attacks rumoured, and all the signs of preparation around us.

I am trying to put all the old life away from me. And it persistently returns, like the scent of lime-trees in June, 'gentle *far niente* existence', unbearably swift and alluring.

[1] Herbert Trench, 'Come let us make love deathless' ('sweeter' should be 'nobler').
[2] Herrick, 'His Poetry and his Pillar'.

And a telegram going to Weirleigh and Mother half-dead with agony. O God, why must these things happen?

April 11
After three days of sun and shrewd north-wind down at 71 North—the Company in reserve—we came up to the front line yesterday.

About 8.30 in the evening went out with two bombers, Grainger and Leigh, and O'Brien, to fetch in a supposed German body who was reputed shot the previous night when they came across cutting our wire. It was bright moonshine and very still. When we had got out about fifty yards and were up against our wire, we observed four Germans crawling over towards us. Withdrew fifteen yards to a big shell-hole and when they came to our wire we chucked twelve bombs at them and I pursued them, hoping to collar a wounded one. Most unlucky, they all cleared off. Then we got to the boots which had been seen from our trench and found a very old (French) body, at least six months old. Brought in the boots—one of them with half a leg attached (and sent it down to Battalion Headquarters).

To-day the weather has changed to wet. They sent over a canister at us last night when we were bombing, but it went over us and landed in our trenches, killing one good lad and wounding two others.

The sense of spring in England is very strong in me lately, and I dream of nice things and get rather weary of being out here. They say I am trying to get myself killed. Am I? I don't know.

April 12
Did a moonlight patrol with Leigh 12.45 to 1.45 last night. Got right up to the German wire, but everything was very quiet and nothing to be seen. To-day it is raining and very unpleasant.

April 13
We came away and reached Morlancourt about 1.30. Heavy firing on our right between 2 and 3 a.m. Then the dawn broke

quiet and chilly, the cloudy sky whitening, and the country below appearing sad and stricken; I could see the ruined villages of Fricourt and Mametz down below on our left, and the long seams of trenches on the other side of the valley, and the still-leafless trees, shivering sentries of the unhappy countryside.

And the larks were singing high up before the light began. And later on the voice of a thrush came to me from a long way off, muffled by the gusts of wind, a thrush singing behind the German lines.

Looking across the parapet at the tangle of wire and the confusion of mine-craters and old fortifications, the prospect is not cheerful. Nothing grows; everything is there for destruction. What eyes have stared across there while their brains and bodies were longing for sleep and home and desirable things! Eyes that see nothing now. But this moralising is in very bad taste indeed. We came back in a half-gale of wind from the north-west. Dandelions are flowering along the edges of the communication-trenches. And then I slept and slept, and woke dreaming of English landscapes.

April 14

The existence one leads here is so much a thing of naked outlines and bare expanses, so empty of colour and fragrance, that one loves these things more than ever, and more than ever one hungers for them—the music and graciousness of life. After six days up at the trenches in ugly weather, it was jolly to ride across to Heilly this afternoon, over the rolling plough-lands and through the strip of woodland on the hill above Mericourt and Treux. Sun shining and clouds flying with a boisterous north-west wind. And as I came back between 5 and 6 there were bluebells in the wood, 'like a skylit water,' between the stems of the trees—there is no undergrowth in that wood, so the cowslips and anemones and dog-violets are everywhere to be seen; and there are some tall wild-cherry trees in blossom; and thrushes were singing loud. And teams of horses harrowing on the uplands moved like a king's procession, their crests blown by the wind. And wheat's light green, and grass begins to grow, and leaves to sprout on sprays.

1916

THE GIANT-KILLER

When first I came to fight the swarming Huns,
I thought how England used me for her need;
And I was eager then to face the guns,
Share the long watch, and suffer, and succeed.
I was the Giant-Killer in a story,
Armed to the teeth and out for blood and glory.

What Paladin is this who bleakly peers
Across the parapets while dawn comes grey,
Hungry for music, and the living years,
And songs that sleep until their destined day?
This is the Giant-Killer who is learning
That heroes walk the road of no returning.

April 21 (Good Friday morning)

A lovely clear dawn, delicate and still, with the belated moon
hanging white in the west—the moon that rose so wonderfully,
like a large golden balloon with stripes of black cloud across its
middle.

April 22

I was on duty from 2 to 4; it rained and the trenches were
knee-deep, and falling in badly—at early dawn the sky was misty,
grey, clouded, ashen, but the larks were singing, singing, dis-
cordant sharps and quavers—dauntless as our spirit should be.
I stood in 75 Street listening to them; then sploshed through
the dismal water and down to the dug-out den to call the others
for stand-to. To-morrow I'm off for a month at the Army
School: heavenly to get a change and away from this—and these.
(*Vide* 'Stand-to: Good Friday Morning', versified from this at
the time.)

I'd been on duty from two till four.
I went and stared at the dug-out door.
Down in the frowst I heard them snore.
'Stand to!' Somebody grunted and swore.

Dawn was misty; the skies were still;
Larks were singing, discordant, shrill;
They seemed happy; but *I* felt ill.
Deep in water I splashed my way
Up the trench to our bogged front line.
Rain had fallen the whole damned night.
O Jesus, send me a wound to-day,
And I'll believe in Your bread and wine,
And get my bloody old sins washed white![1]

April 23 (Easter Sunday)

Out of trenches yesterday; the last two days have been wet and horrid. Yesterday evening the trees looked like ashen smoke rising from the rain-swept hills; to-day as I rolled along in a motor-bus from Mericourt to Flixécourt everything was golden and April's end—green trees, apple-blossom nearly out, steel-blue lakes and pools and rivers and canals—magpies in orchards —Corbie—Amiens—one or two men fishing—white tents at a Red Cross camp—a mill with water sluicing and broken wooden wheel—two women in black with veils flying—two girls in black-and-white—Easter and church. Started 8.45. Amiens 11.15—miller's waggon and four horses—Corbie church with two towers, and the chimney-stacks.

After this last period—since Tommy got shot—though spring was on the way, and trees putting on a vesture of faint green, though the sun shone on many days—yet most seem to have been dark and unhappy—since March 26. I have done eighteen days in the trenches, and those days and nights are a mechanical and strained effort. Coming away from it all—to find the world outside really acknowledging the arrival of spring—oh it was a blessed thing—the journey on a sunny morning, pleasantly blown by a north-west wind, about twenty-five miles in a sort of motor-bus—the landscape looking its best—all the clean colour of late April—the renewal of green grass and young leaves —and fruit-trees in blossom—and to see a civilian population well away from the danger-zone going to church on Easter morning—soldiers contented and at rest—it was like coming back to life, warm and secure—it was to feel how much there is

[1] Published in *The Old Huntsman*.

to regain. Children in the streets of towns and villages—I saw
a tiny one fall, to be gathered up and dusted, soothed, comforted
—one forgets 'little things' like those up in the places where
men are killing one another with the best weapons that skill can
handle.

And water—rivers flowing, taking the sky with them—and
lakes coloured like bright steel blades, their smooth surfaces
ruffled by ripples of wind—and a small round pool in a garden,
quite still and glassy, with vivid green blades of iris growing
along the edge. The great city of Amiens, Sunday-quiet, with
the cathedral lording it beyond the gleaming roofs, sombre and
unshining-grey, ancient, like a huge fretted rock or cliff, a train
moving out of a station when we halted at the crossing-gates
with rumble and clank of wheels on the rails. I had not thought
of a train or seen one since I came from England seven weeks
ago (it was at this very moment, on a Sunday, that I left
Waterloo, and saw the faces of my people left behind as the
carriage slid along the platform, all the world before me once
more, and the unfinished adventure waiting to be resumed).

And now fortune has given me another space to take breath
and look back on the grim days. Four blessed weeks in a clean
town with fresh companions and healthy routine of discipline
and instruction, and all this in the good time when spring's at
the full. At the end of May I shall return to the Battalion, eager
and refreshed, and glad to be with my fellow-officers again (but
one wants a rest from their constant presence to really appreci-
ate them). O yes, I am a lucky dog.

And at 7 o'clock I climbed the hill and gazed across the town
—the red wrinkled roofs of the great jute-factory below and the
huddle of grey roofs with their peaceful smoke going up in the
quiet air. I turned along a grassy, tree-guarded track that led to
where a half-finished house stood, red and white, overlooking
the town, with a lovely wood behind it. Sunset was fading, with
a long purple-grey cloud above the west: and oh the wood was
still, with slender stems of trees, all in their vesture of young
green—and bluebells were on the ground, and young fresh
grass, and blackbirds and thrushes scolding and singing in the
quiet, and the smell of wet mould, wet earth, wet leaves, and
voices of children coming up from a cottage below the hill. It
was a virgin sanctuary of trees, and blessed peace for my soul

and heaven for my eyes and music for my ears; it was Paradise, and God, and the promise of life.

April 24 (Flixécourt)

Waking up was heavenly. My clean little room with shuttered windows looks on to the angled street that climbs past the Mairie. I knew that the morning was fine: voices came from outside: sparrows chirped and starlings whistled. The bell in the church-tower tolled, and the clock struck the quarters. Waking up in a strange place, on a summer day or any fine morning, when you know you are in for a good time, and everything seems fresh and spotless. I had forgotten what it was to feel like that. Then after breakfast, walking up the hill with my pipe, I sat under a quickset hedge, all young leaves, and heard a nightingale singing in the garden-copse over the hedge. Really, this place seems to be laying itself out to flatter and soothe me for the half-wretched days I've had of late. Chestnut-trees are in their wonderful new liveries of bright green: an apple-tree looks over an old lichened garden-wall, with blossom showing and pink buds. Many of the houses have red tiled roofs, and clean whitewashed walls. And the inhabitants are friendly and delightful. The officers here (about a hundred) seem very pleasant.

There are several large châteaux on the hills looking over the basin where the town lies. A farm-yard over the way has a large pointed tiled dovecot, like a mediaeval tower.

April 25

There was a great brawny Highland Major here to-day, talking of the Bayonet. For close on an hour he talked, and all who listened caught fire from his enthusiasm: for he was prophesying; he had his message to deliver.

When he had finished, I went up the hill to my green wood where the half-built mansion stands. And there it was quite still except for a few birds; robins, and thrushes, and lesser notes. The church-bells were ringing in the town, deep and mellow. A pigeon cooed. Phrases from the bayonet lecture came back to me. Some midges hummed around my head. The air

1916

was still warm with the sun that had quite disappeared behind the hills. A rook cawed in the trees. A woodpecker laughed, harsh and derisive. 'The bullet and the bayonet are brother and sister.' 'If you don't kill him, he'll kill you!' 'Stick him between the eyes, in the throat, in the chest, or round the thighs.' 'If he's on the run, there's only one place; get your bayonet into his kidneys; it'll go in as easy as butter.' 'Kill them, kill them: there's only one good Bosche and that's a dead 'un!' 'Quickness, anger, strength, good fury, accuracy of aim. Don't waste good steel. Six inches are enough—what's the use of a foot of steel sticking out at the back of a man's neck? Three inches will do him, and when he coughs, go and find another.' And so on.

I told the trees what I had been hearing; but they hate steel, because axes and bayonets are the same to them. They are dressed in their fresh green, every branch showing through the mist of leaves, and the straight stems most lovely against the white and orange sky beyond. And a blackbird's song cries aloud that April cannot understand what war means.

THE KISS

To these I turn, in these I trust—
Brother Lead and Sister Steel.
To this blind power I make appeal,
I guard her beauty clean from rust.

He spins and burns and loves the air,
And splits a skull to win my praise;
But up the nobly marching days
She glitters naked, cold and fair.

Sweet Sister, grant your soldier this:
That in good fury he may feel
The body where he sets his heel
Quail from your downward darting kiss.[1]

[1] First published in the *Cambridge Magazine*, 27 May 1916, then in *The Old Huntsman*.

April 27
Another glorious day. Starlight on the mill-water and the
unrythmed music of the weir. And birds singing all day as if
they were trying to draw the heart out of me with dreams of
English woodlands and orchards.

May 20
My last day at the Fourth Army School. A cloudless hot
morning. Numerous generals rolled up for the bayonet work,
wiring, etc, and two mines were exploded; a brown spuming
hill of loose earth and chalk is hurled skyward; the ground
shakes and rocks; then there is a sound like a rain-storm gone
mad, and downward whizzing of clods and lumps, and stones,
and the hiss of smaller stuff: then a huge fountain of smoke goes
up over the debris, rising like a figure with draperies and
writhing arms to melt into nothing.
    After lunch I went into Abbeville with Marcus Goodall:[1] my
expedition with him to Amiens was a success, and this was
equally delightful. He is a very excellent companion, and
Marlborough talk always bridges the gaps.[2]
    We left Flixécourt at 3.45 in a bus, and did the twenty-two
kilometres to Abbeville along the straight dusty road in about
forty-five minutes: the green expanses of country on each side,
rolling away into the hot hazy distance, every tree proud of its
young leaves, splashes of white and pale blossom in orchards
and gardens, lovely glooms of sun-glinted woods, vivid patches
of clover-red, silver of daisies in lush grass, and yellow glory of
buttercups. Acres of green barley and rye and wheat and oats,
besomed by the breeze, and leagues of rust-coloured ploughland.
O those leagues of open country, glorious under the sky!
Goodall nudges me when he sees something he likes, and I do
the same; sometimes we both nudge at once: I want many more
eyes than two on such a rushing journey through a delightful
unfamiliar country; we met a shepherd boy at the head of his
large flock of ewes and three-parts-grown lambs; he looked about
fifteen, and very Arcadian with crook and slouchy hat, brim
turned down. The villages look so clean with their white

---

[1] The Allgood of *Memoirs of an Infantry Officer.*
[2] M.H.G. was killed on 22 July 1916. S.S.

cottage-walls and charming orchards and gardens; so different
from the same winter-villages of squalor and mud and chilliness.
How May changes everything!

And the roads that wind away over the ridges; what magic
is in their hidden miles; and to what happy places might they
lead? Dear lands of Nowhere. Any road that leads away from
the trenches is a good road. No one else in the bus but me and
my friend seems to take any notice of the country we pass. They
talk of war and folly, and sing snatches of 'Maconachie' and
'Charlie Chaplin Walk'. Soon we are rolling down a long hill,
and the town lies below between the wooded ridges; the usual
tall trees lining the river-side; the distant towers and roofs and
chimneys and surrounding tree-muffled country, seen through
the haze and dust of the hot glaring afternoon sunshine.

Of course the place is fringed with the usual Army Service
Corps camps—huts, tents, waggon-lines and so on: soon we
two are off exploring narrow streets near the big beetling
church—charming old streets; the town is quiet and easy-going
—like an English market-town—none of the clang and hurry of
Amiens. And we find the Somme slipping under a bridge and
making jolly ripples and eddies and whorls in the sunshine, and
we lean over and look down at the weedy water in great content.
Gardens run down to the waterside, green and sheltered. Beyond
tall trees the church and high buildings are seen, looking
quite noble, and a sound of six o'clock bells comes chiming on
the summer air: for a moment it seems like Oxford. Anyhow, it
was damned nice. I thought of Debussy's *'Cloches à travers les
feuilles'*. Back we wandered, heard the last bird-note in a garden-
tangle or flowering chestnut-tree over a high red-brick wall—
down an empty street—staring into a curio-shop full of R.C.
rubbish. In the square is a statue of some Early-Victorian-
looking Admiral, with naked females sprawling around his
heroic attitude. We dine at the Tête de Boeuf, an old-fashioned
sort of hotel: sitting outside afterwards I thought of the Red
Lion at Cambridge last August—and the two I used to be with
—both dead now. Of all the officers having dinner, I saw no
face with any touch of distinction in it. They were either
utterly commonplace and self-satisfied, or else tired-looking,
feeble, goggle-eyed, or otherwise deficient. Why does one see
so few proper-looking officers? Yet our army does all right.

Coming home, the bus dashed and lurched along in the warm, dark, starry night: along the white road—with trees slipping to meet us out of the gloom—like people surprised, standing still and hoping not to be noticed—some of them looked as if cut out of cardboard—stage-trees—in the white glare of our headlights. And at other times I could fancy their boughs were laden with glimmering blossom—but it was only the light shining on the young green leaves.

Back at Flixécourt, and goodnight to Marcus Goodall. I wonder if I shall ever see him again after to-morrow. His is the only face I shall remember with any interest—of all the two or three hundred I've seen since Easter. The others were all shadows—his is a real personality, which responds to mine. The others make military (and unmilitary) noises with their mouths; he talks, and answers with his eyes.

But let anyone who reads this know that I was four weeks at Flixécourt, and four weeks happy and peaceful—and free, with my books and my work and the heaven of spring surging all round me over the noble country, and lighting the skies with magnificence.

May 22

Got to Morlancourt about 7 yesterday. As we came down the hill off Corbie road there was the sun low in a hot blue sky, hurling his evening rays across the bare slopes and distant haze-hung valley. The glaring beams striking the ground made a fiery mist; I thought of a flock of sheep moving along a dusty road—'their fleeces charged with gold'.[1] I found the village quiet and dusky.

This morning there's warm green and light in the tangled garden behind our billet, chirping of birds among the fruit-trees, sunshine on the vine-covered plaster walls of the house; a few pink roses, and some red peonies: the horse-chestnut in flower in front of the house.

8.30 p.m. At Bécordel crossroads; a small bushy tree against a pale yellow sky, dark-leaved and still; a slate roof gleaming in the half-light, two hundred yards to the left down the road in the village. A noise of carts on the evening air; occasional bang

[1] From 'Nod' by Walter de la Mare.

of our guns, close to the village. The church-tower gloomy, only the front remains; more than half of the tower is shot away, and three-quarters of the church. A light sparks and glows somewhere among the roofs: in foreground two ruined sheds with skeleton roofs. A quiet cool evening after a shower. Stars coming out. The Royal Engineers stores are dumped around a French soldier-cemetery. At the crossroads here the communication-trench (South Avenue) begins. Voices of men in the dusk. Dull rattle of machine-guns on the left. A low grey blur of moving rain-cloud now (north above the village). I talk with a Northumberland Fusilier officer, who drops aitches. Too dark to write.

May 23   6.15 p.m.
On Crawley Ridge. A very still evening. Sun rather hazy but sky mostly clear. Looking across to Fricourt: trench-mortars bursting in the cemetery: clouds of dull white vapour slowly float away over grey-green grass with yellow buttercup-smears, and saffron of weeds. Fricourt, a huddle of reddish roofs, skeleton village—church-tower white—almost demolished, a patch of white against the sombre green of the Fricourt wood (full of German batteries). Away up the hill the white seams and heapings of trenches dug in the chalk. The sky full of lark-songs. Sometimes you can count thirty slowly and hear no sound of a shot: then the muffled pop of a rifle-shot a long way off, or a banging 5.9, or our eighteen-pounder—then a burst of machine-gun westward, the yellow sky with a web of whitish filmy cloud half across the sun; and the ridges rather blurred with outlines of trees; an airplane droning overhead. A thistle sprouting through the chalk on the parapet; a cockchafer sailing through the air a little way in front.

Down the hill, and on to the old Bray-Fricourt road, along by the railway; the road white and hard; a partridge flies away calling; lush grass everywhere, and crops of nettles; a large black slug out for his evening walk (doing nearly a mile a month, I should think).

Stansfield talking about Canada and times when he was hard up—this afternoon (twelve and a half cents a meal). Two Manchester officers this morning.

May 25

Twenty-seven men with faces blackened and shiny—Christy-minstrels—with hatchets in their belts, bombs in pockets, knobkerries—waiting in a dug-out in the reserve line. At 10.30 they trudge up to Battalion H.Q. splashing through mire and water in the chalk trench, while the rain comes steadily down. The party is twenty-two men, five N.C.O.s and one officer (Stansfield). From H.Q. we start off again, led by Compton-Smith: across the open to the end of 77 Street. A red flashlight winks a few times to guide us thither. Then up to the front line —the men's feet making a most unholy tramp and din; squeeze along to the starting-point, where Stansfield and his two con-federates (Sergeant Lyle and Corporal O'Brien) loom over the parapet from above, having successfully laid the line of lime across the craters to the Bosche wire. In a few minutes the five parties have gone over—and disappear into the rain and dark-ness—the last four men carry ten-foot light ladders. It is 12 midnight. I am sitting on the parapet listening for something to happen—five, ten, nearly fifteen minutes—not a sound— nor a shot fired—and only the usual flare-lights, none very near our party. Then through the hazy dripping skies the 5.9 shells begin to drone across in their leisurely way, a few at first, and then quite a flock of them. I am out with the rear party by now —about twenty yards in front of our trench (the wire has been cut of course), the men (evacuating party) are lying half-down a crater on the left, quite cheery. In the white glare of a flare-light I can see the rest of the column lying straight down across the ridge between the craters. Then a few whizz-bangs fizz over to our front trench and just behind the raiders. After twenty minutes there is still absolute silence in the Bosche trench; the raid is obviously held up by their wire, which we thought was so easy to get through. One of the bayonet-men comes crawling back; I follow him to our trench and he tells me that they can't get through: O'Brien says it's a failure; they're all going to throw a bomb and retire.

A minute or two later a rifle-shot rings out and almost simultaneously several bombs are thrown by both sides: a bomb explodes right in the water at the bottom of left crater close to our men, and showers a pale spume of water; there are blinding flashes and explosions, rifle-shots, the scurry of feet, curses and

groans, and stumbling figures loom up from below and scramble
awkwardly over the parapet—some wounded—black faces and
whites of eyes and lips show in the dusk; when I've counted
sixteen in, I go forward to see how things are going, and find
Stansfield wounded, and leave him there with two men who
soon get him in: other wounded men crawl in; I find one hit in
the leg; he says 'O'Brien is somewhere down the crater badly
wounded'. They are still throwing bombs and firing at us: the
sinister sound of clicking bolts seems to be very near; perhaps
they have crawled out of their trench and are firing from behind
their advanced wire. Bullets hit the water in the craters, and
little showers of earth patter down on the crater. Five or six of
them are firing into the crater at a few yards' range. The bloody
sods are firing down at me at point-blank range. (I really
wondered whether my number was up.) From our trenches and
in front of them I can hear the mumble of voices—most of them
must be in by now. After minutes like hours, with great difficulty
I get round the bottom of the crater and back toward our trench;
at last I find O'Brien down a very deep (about twenty-five feet)
and precipitous crater on my left (our right as they went out).
He is moaning and his right arm is either broken or almost
shot off: he's also hit in the right leg (body and head also, but
I couldn't see that then). Another man (72 Thomas) is with
him; he is hit in the right arm. I leave them there and get back
to our trench for help, shortly afterwards Lance-Corporal Stubbs
is brought in (he has had his foot blown off). Two or three
other wounded men are being helped down the trench; no one
seems to know what to do; those that are there are very excited
and uncertain: no sign of any officers—then Compton-Smith
comes along (a mine went up on the left as we were coming up
at about 11.30 and thirty (R.E.s) men were gassed or buried).
I get a rope and two more men and we go back to O'Brien, who
is unconscious now. With great difficulty we get him half-way
up the face of the crater; it is now after one o'clock and the sky
beginning to get lighter. I make one more journey to our trench
for another strong man and to see to a stretcher being ready.
We get him in, and it is found that he has died, as I had feared.
Corporal Mick O'Brien (who often went patrolling with me)
was a very fine man and had been with the Battalion since
November 1914. He was at Neuve Chapelle, Festubert and Loos.

I go back to a support-line dug-out and find the unwounded
men of the raiding-party refreshing themselves: everyone is
accounted for now; eleven wounded (one died of wounds) and
one killed, out of twenty-eight. I see Stansfield, who is going on
all right, but has several bomb-wounds. On the way down I see
the Colonel, sitting on his bed in a woollen cap with a tuft on
top, and very much upset at the non-success of the show, and
the mine disaster; but very pleased with the way our men tried
to get through the wire. I get down to 71 North about 2.15,
with larks beginning to sing in the drizzling pallor of the sky.
(Covered with mud and blood, and no tunic on!) I think it was
lucky the Colonel refused to allow me to go out with the raiding
party, as I meant to get through that wire somehow, and it seems
to have been almost impossible (we had bad wire-cutters) and
the Bosches were undoubtedly ready for us, and no one could
have got into their trench and got out alive, as there were
several of them. They certainly showed great ability and cunning,
but I suppose they generally do. This morning I woke up
feeling as if I'd been to a dance—awful mouth and head.

There was no terror there—only men with nerves taut and
courage braced—then confusion and anger and—failure. I think
there was more delight than dread in the prospect of the
dangers; certainly I saw no sign of either. But on the left where
the mine-explosion took place at 11.30 there were gassed men
lying about in the trench in dark rain and all sorts of horrors
being gallantly overcome.[1]

> *From GH.Q. communiqué—Friday May 26*) 'At Mametz
> we raided hostile trenches. Our party *entered without
> difficulty* [!!!] and maintained a spirited bombing fight,
> and finally withdrew at the end of twenty-five minutes.'
> The truth which is (less than) half a truth!!!

May 26   8.15 p.m.
Looking west from the support line; the brown, shell-pitted
ground gloomy in the twilight—beyond, the receding country,

[1] It was for this action that S.S. was awarded the Military Cross. The official
citation runs: 'For conspicuous gallantry during a raid on the enemy's trenches.
He remained for 1½ hours under rifle and bomb fire collecting and bringing in
our wounded. Owing to his courage and determination all the killed and wounded
were brought in.'

dim-blue and solemn, a distant group of thick-topped trees on a ridge dark against the low colour of fading sunset, deep-glowing-ruddy-amber, fading higher to pale orange and yellow; above that a long dove-coloured bar of cloud faintly fringed with crimson. And over all the proper star of dusk.

The guns rumble miles and miles away, carts can be heard on the roads behind Fricourt. Everything is very still, until a canister comes over and bursts, throwing up a cloud of purple-black smoke that drifts across the half-lit sky, and 'the blue vaporous end of day'. A rat comes out and nips across among the tin cans and burst sandbags and rubbish. And I turn away and go down the fifteen steps to a dark candle-yellow dug-out to fetch my bally revolver.

May 27

Sitting on the firestep in warm weather and sunshine about 10 a.m. with the lark above and the usual airmen. Can't remember Thursday night's show very clearly: it seems mostly rain and feeling chilled, and the flash of rifles in the gloom; and O'Brien's shattered limp body propped up down that infernal bank—face ghastly in the light of a flare, clothes torn, hair matted over the forehead—nothing left of the old cheeriness and courage and delight in any excitement of Hun-chasing. Trying to lift him up the side of the crater, the soft earth kept giving way under one's feet: he was a heavy man too, fully six feet high. But he was a dead man when at last we lowered him over the parapet on to a stretcher: and one of the stretcher-bearers examined his wounds and felt for the life that wasn't there, and then took off his round helmet with a sort of reverence —or it may have been only a chance gesture. I would have given a lot if he could have been alive, but it was a hopeless case—a bomb had given him its full explosion. But when I go out on patrols his ghost will surely be with me; he'll catch his breath and grip his bomb just as he used to do.

May 30   6.30 p.m.

Sitting on a milestone which says 'Amiens 29.7k. Péronne 22.9k'. A cloudless white evening—the tall green wheat shaking in a light southerly breeze. A steam-roller puffing and crunching a couple of hundred yards down the road toward Corbie (12.3k. Bray-sur-Somme 4.4k).

Some guns thudding a few miles away; and the long dark-green line of the Bois de Taille (full of Devons and Border Regiment) with telegraph-poles standing in the foreground. Rode over to Corbie this morning and saw Stansfield at the clearing hospital there. He is out of danger. A nice ride—with our cheery Medical Officer—in cool grey weather after a rainy night. Had a narrow squeak on Friday night when I went out to try and collect the debris of the raid: a bomb (from a catapult) fell about a yard from me, but I was lying flat, so everything passed over me, and I was only half-deafened by the noise. Got three axes and a knobkerrie, but I don't think it was worthwhile. Still, my luck seems to hold. Name been sent in for M.C. (so rumour says). Lord, how pleased everyone will be if I get it.

Walking home, there was an acre of thick wet clover, deep-red and tipped with paler pink, and in those lush tangles were a few small scarlet poppies. And the sun was low above delicate, watery-green landscapes tufted with trees; and Morlancourt in the basin with smoke going up looked very peaceful: and brown bees were in the clover-patch, and the sun went down like a poppy.

May 31   10.30 a.m.
Looking north from the hill behind Morlancourt. The cloudless morning sky meets the naked line of the ridge, green with grass and crops, and powdered with saffron and gold of weeds and buttercups, with three trees standing alone. On the opposite slope one sees the red and grey roofs of the village outskirts, with some bushy trees among the houses. Then, in the low ground, a bare pale-buff camp—horse-lines, some dirty white bell-tents, an iron-roofed shed, and a line of limbers and waggons. The picketed horses a brown mass with two or three grey horses among them. One can see their tails switching, and men grooming their legs. In foreground an upward slope and more yellow and gold.

Then walked out to the bluff above Sailly-Laurette and the Somme with its chain of lakes; and looked across the same view

as one afternoon at the end of March. The water shone dull
silver and breeze-ruffled to-day. The sun was not bright, and
the country looked hot and hazy and muffled with green. The
woods are full of bivouacked troops in low green-painted huts.
On my way home I went along a solitary part where the
thickets swung and rustled and birds were jocund—nightingale,
throstle and linnet—and there were a few wild-roses—the first
I've seen here. It was good to sniff them. And little blue
butterflies were fluttering across the short turf and settling on
clumps of low blue flowers.

June 1
Very successful R.W.F. concert, held behind Quartermaster's
Stores in the evening. Divisional Band, Basil Hallam[1] etc. The
horse-lines only a few yards away; they were standing there in
the dark—at the back of the pit, as it were: I wonder what they
thought of it. I can't read or enjoy poetry at all since I came
back here. Two new officers in C. Company since Stansfield
went—G. Williams, who was hit a year ago, and Morris—a
Sandhurst one. Neither of them at all interesting. Heard from
Robert Graves, now at Litherland; he says he 'wants to come
home—to France'. I only wish he would.

June 2
Up on the redoubt last night, between 10 and 11, the whole
horizon winked incessantly with gunfire and shells bursting.
Guns banged and boomed, red lights went up; quite a cheery
show. Marching up to Bécordel on a working-party at 7.30 this
evening there was a very red sunset: the light streamed across
the quiet green land and my party of men were moving in a
crimson glare and glow—the dust was crimson-gold; it was a
light most beautiful and blood-red and we were all in it. After-
wards a purple flush lay on the green slopes westward, and the
tall trees stood up against a flaming orange sunset. Purple dusk
came on, while the men lay on a bank by the roadside. Two
limbers with six horses in each rattled by and the spell was
broken.

[1] Popular actor and singer. Killed in action 20 August 1916, aged twenty-seven.

1916

June 3

Lorries a mile away, creeping along the green and yellow ridges of the June landscape like large insects. A partridge runs out of the rustling blades of corn, and hurries back again. The afternoon sky is full of large clouds, and broad beams of light lead the eyes up to a half-hidden sun. A fresh breeze comes from the north-west. Miles of green country as far as I can see, and trees dark green against the sky's white edge. A lark goes up, and takes my heart with him. Seven soldiers straggle across the view; one wears a cape. A team of horses drags a harrow; three greys and a brown, with a French boy riding, and calling to them.

I was thinking this evening (as I sat out in the garden with the sun low behind the roofs and a chilly wind shaking the big aspens) that if there really are such things as ghosts, and I'm not prepared to gainsay the fact—or illusion—if there are ghosts, then they will be all over this battle-front forever. I think the ghosts at Troy are all too tired to show themselves— they are too literary—and Odysseus has sailed into the sunset never to return. The grim old campaigns of bowmen and knights and pikemen may have their spectral anniversaries—one never hears of them. But the old Flanders wars have been wiped out by these new slaughterings; and the din of our big guns that shatter and obliterate towns and villages, and dig pits in every field, and lay waste pleasant green woods—this must have scared the old phantoms far away. Or do they still watch the struggle?

I can imagine that, in a hundred or two hundred or two thousand years, when wars are waged in the air and under the ground, these French roads will be haunted by a silent traffic of sliding lorries and jolting waggons and tilting limbers—all going silently about their business. Some staring peasant or stranger will see them silhouetted against the pale edge of a night sky—six mules and a double limber, with the drivers jigging in the saddle—a line of cumbrous lorries nosing along some bleak main-road—a battalion transport with the sergeant riding in front, and brake-men hanging on behind the limbers, taking rations to the trenches that were filled in hundreds of years ago. And there will be ghostly working-parties coming home to billets long after midnight, filing along deserted tracks among the cornlands, men with round basin-helmets, and rifles slung on their shoulders, puffing at ambrosial Woodbines—and sometimes the horizon will wink with the flash of a gun, and insubstantial shells will hurry across the upper air and melt innocuous in nothingness.

And the trenches—where the trenches used to be—there will be grim old bomb-fights in the craters and wounded men cursing; and patrols will catch their breath and crawl out from tangles of wire, and sentries will peer over the parapets, fingering the trigger—doubtful whether to shoot or send for the sergeant. And I shall be there—looking for Germans with my revolver and my knobkerrie and two Mills-bombs in each pocket, having hair-breadth escapes—crawling in the long grass —wallowing in the mud—crouching in shell-holes—hearing the Hun sentries cough and shift their feet, and click their bolts; I shall be there—slipping back into our trench, and laughing with my men at the fun I've had out in no-man's-land. And I'll be watching a frosty dawn come up beyond the misty hills and naked trees—with never a touch of cold in my feet or fingers, and perhaps taking a nip of rum from a never-emptying flask. And all the horrors will be there and agonies be endured again; but over all will be the same peaceful starlight—the same eternal cloudlands—and in those dusty hearts an undying sense of valour and sacrifice. And though our ghosts be as dreams, those good things will be as they are now, a light in the thick darkness and a crown.

June 4   11 p.m. (At 71 North)

A pitch-black night with a chilly wind and light rain blowing over at times. Two raids are fixed for to-night, by the Divisions on our left, north of Albert and Fricourt. There has been a bit of a bombardment since 9.30, quite severe since 10.30. Incessant bang, bang and whistle of shells overhead—and the sky winking and flickering—flares going up over the hill—din of explosions down in the valley by Fricourt—echoing and reverberating— a most hellish performance. The little wooden vanes on the roof of our dug-out keep spinning and rattling as if nothing were on. The sky looks like a thunderstorm gone crazy—in the swift glare of bursting shells can be seen the floating smoke and little clouds from shrapnel-bursts. Sometimes the glare is almost ruddy—suggesting burning cities and ruin and all horrors and confusion.

And somewhere a mile or two away the raiding-parties are waiting till it's time to go across—men with blackened faces and grim clubs and axes and bombs—men with knocking hearts, stifling the yawns of nervousness—wondering if our shells have cut the German wire—knowing that the enemy are ready for them—knowing they will probably be killed or wounded or caught like rats. O this bloody war! It will be my turn to go on a raid soon, I suppose.

June 5

A heavy bombardment along by La Boiselle, two miles to our left. I watched it from our support-line, where I was out with a wiring-party. It was a battle seen in miniature against a black screen of midnight. Men were invisible: it was a struggle of giants hurling thunderbolts. Star-lights and flares, red and white, kept curving up from both lines—the wind was against the Germans. The noise was a continuous rumble and grumble and thud, which lasted for over an hour. The glare of the high-explosive bursting was a fearful sight. One couldn't imagine anything living in that hell. Orme and Morris were hit on Sunday night when up with the working-party.

June 6

The clouds are like giants tumbling and striving and leaping round the edge of the clear blue sky. They are smoky-white and grey and golden-white. They strike huge attitudes and are blown shapeless again. I see colossal faces of Socrates and Diogenes—bearded sages—and slowly they lose their features. The evening sun strikes the glinting wings of an aeroplane forging away westward—and it is a tiny speck of gold glinting high up. Swallows skim above the long grass that almost hides the low wire in front of trenches; they are companions of light breezes, close to earth they sail, heedless of rifle-grenades.

1916

June 7   7.30 p.m.

Sitting in a dark dug-out twenty steps down after tramping about the sticky trenches all day. I suppose this cramped cellar is really rather 'picturesque', with its three candles and six thick wooden props down the middle and beams overhead, but the smell of earth and the frizzle of frying meat in the kennel of a kitchen are the things that strike me most forcibly. Here I sit reading the *Saturday Review, New Statesman* etc and feeling rather humpy. I suppose I've caught it off Greaves who came back from leave to-day in the usual condition of misery people suffer on these occasions. And I'm feeling a bit worried about being given the job of Sniping Observing Officer (knowing nothing about sniping or map-making) though it's a less strenuous job than being a company officer. On these rare occasions when I lose my courage to face the future, there is usually some explanation for it. Liver or over-smoking or wet weather. I shall have to go out and do a patrol in the long grass to-night to get rid of this hemmed-in feeling.

I don't often descend to the desire of a 'blighty one' which everyone talks about. If I get one I'm sure it won't be a 'cushy' one. And I rather want to see the summer out, and get the experience of the big battle which must surely come next month. And, as for dying, I know it's nothing, and there's not much for me to lose except a few years of ease and futility. What I'm doing and enduring now is the last thing anyone could ask for; I'm being pushed along the rocky path, and the world seems all the sweeter for it. The world seen from exile; I can't see things in proportion at all to-night. Death seems the only fact to be faced; the rest all twaddle and purposeless energy. Lord Kitchener is drowned—there's another shock to everyone's tender hearts.[1] And yet, why shouldn't he die? We're all dying. And the war will go on and on till we can't stick it any longer, and Victory will greet us with a very wry smile and a 'dud' shell in each hand. I suppose I'm feeling what Robert Graves felt when he wrote 'Is this Limbo?'. Shut in; no chance of escape. No music; the quest for beauty doomed. But I *must* go on

---

[1] Field-Marshal Earl Kitchener of Khartoum, the Secretary of State for War, was drowned on 5 June 1916, when H.M.S. *Hampshire*, which was conveying him to Archangel for consultations with the Russians, struck a mine west of Orkney and sank immediately.

finding beauty *here* and now; not the sort of beauty I used to look for.

And then I shall be going home on leave next week. There'll be the tedious train-journey down to Havre, and the boat waiting in the twilight, and chatter of officers going home like me. Then the beastly hours of trying not to feel ill; and Southampton, and the sentimental thrill as one sets foot on an English railway-platform (the eyes should fill with unbidden tears—England, my mother, and so on). Then London, and luxury, and being clean and tidy, and going down to Paddock Wood, and the Weirleigh garden in the June sunset; and poor old Mother trotting out to meet me. It's all so nice, but do I really long for it (to keep me safe) as much as I long to keep my freedom out here? For it *is* freedom, even when it rains and I get the blues. And I *have* been most awfully slack in every way till I had to be a soldier. Really, I'm in a desperate muddle to-night, and I haven't written down anything which will bring this hour back to me vivid and true. It's the little details that speak out clear.

June 8

It rained nearly all night. I was out from 9 till 3; with the wirers from 10 till 1.15. Everyone was getting soaked and the mud and water in the trenches were quite nasty, and the sentries had no protection except the inadequate waterproof sheet. No one was looking his best at stand-to (2 a.m.) but the rain had stopped and the east was shoaled and broken with a colourless dawn beginning, a solemn effect of black and white, or slate and silver (but as though washed over with faint grey-green) and afterwards a glow of amber and rose broke gradually upwards, and the sooty cloud-bars grew softer and more purple, and the arches of heaven soared above the shrill soaring larks. And down in the craters the water gleamed, and the tangle of wire and leaning posts showed clear against the dawn—the same old scene of desolation crowned with lovely promise of morning. So about 3.30 I splashed back to the dug-out, not so very ill-content with life and my wet feet, and snoozed till the Forward Liaison Officer came in to gossip with Anscombe.

1916

June 9

Another wet night—the trenches swilling with mud and water, and one's boots ditto, quite reminiscent of the winter. Everything very quiet after 9.30, both sides working. Out with the wirers from 10 to 1.15. I can't imagine anything much more unpleasant than lugging coils of 'concertina' wire along a narrow trench and stumbling with it over shell-holes and trip-wires in inky gloom and pouring rain. However we got a lot out.

This morning the sun shone warm and the liquid mud slowly becomes like glue or porridge. Sitting on a heap of bags behind the support trenches and scraping the caked mud off my tattered puttees, I thought things didn't seem so very bad after all. But I do hate that smelly dug-out, and the meals, when a mouse comes and stands on his head in the sugar-bowl, and one dare not think of the recent history of the things that one eats. And the sound of cautious-nibbling rats in the roof and behind the walls, and the dull boom of things bursting above-ground. But I think I get less fed-up than most of us.

In the evening my leave came in. So I rode down to Morlancourt with the Quartermaster in a perfect sunset, clover-red and glittering; the muddy road as we walked away from the Citadel was red before our feet—blood-red. And they were strafing the Maple Redoubt with their usual vehemence. Driving down to Mericourt station on a sunny morning, with strong fresh north-west breeze, the green hills looking fresh and fair. Passing slow Army Service Corps waggons, the ponies lazy and stumbling. Then the train goes out and we get out for an hour at Amiens. Crowds of men and officers in the echoing buffet—cardboard lunch-boxes—dingy-gilt chandeliers—clank and whistle and rumble of the bustling station. As we steam out of Amiens a long trainful of Australians—slouch hats, some adorned with a red or white flower—clean-shaved faces—young, keen, wild as hawks—shouting and craning out of crowded windows—the usual buck and banter—'Straight to Berlin', 'They say there's a war on' etc.

As we roll out of the station, on the gloomy-lit platform we pass the strange-looking throng of people—Frenchwomen, some in black, girls collecting for the Red Cross; blue-clad elderly officers, with glasses and medals and moustaches; English Lines of Communication staff-officers, trim, and carefully dressed, and

[76]

pleased with themselves; a few black priests, pursy or lantern-jawed; railway officials, mostly old and crooked and grey; and a litter of bales and deal boxes and crates and straw-swathed things. Everyone standing still—with eyes gazing straight or sidelong at the departing train. And we are all going home.

It is raining when we are clear of the city; three Manchester officers and one Suffolk in the carriage: all of them the last word in nonentitude and flatness and commonness. How rotten these people seem compared with the men who get orders from them, and go on leave once in twelve months if they are lucky. I can't see that the officer-class (second-rate) have any more intelligence than the private soldier. And their chief standard seems to be the *London Mail* and the illustrated papers with pictures by 'Kichener' and (for a treat) *La Vie Parisienne*, and eternal dull trench-shop, unlightened by any touch of originality or freshness of vision. And they are at their worst while they go on leave.

The train crawled; reached Montrouillet-Buchy at 4.30, for the well-known hour and omelette and red jelly and coffee at the Nord Inn. Hung around Rouen while the clocks tolled seven, and there was a noise of low, mellow bells afterwards in the quiet evening air, seeming to fill the populous hollows among the tree-muffled hills with musical vibrations—*cloches*, better than *bells* somehow. The first time I went this way it was night, lit with pallor of snow. And when I came back it was still snow and March winter. Now I'm going back to clustering roses and green trees and hayfields and bird-sung dawn. The officers in the carriage talking ('skiting') about their battalions, which are very small beer, I know. And one ass talked of 'a bull who produced sixty black-and-white calves'!

June 11

Arrived at Southampton beat to the world at 10.30 this morning in showery weather with bright clouds over it all. And the smooth water and the low green Isle of Wight.

Very strange to be in Melbury Road[1] again with someone playing on a piano over the way and the late June evening only

---

[1] The home of the Donaldson family (Mrs Donaldson was Mrs Sassoon's sister) with the studio of their brother Hamo Thornycroft attached to it.

just dusk at 9.30 (but of course it's the extra hour that deceived me).

June 19

  Got back from leave.

BEFORE THE BATTLE

Music of whispering trees
Hushed by a broad-winged breeze
Where shaken water gleams;
And evening radiance falling
With reedy bird-notes calling.
O bear me safe through dark, you low-voiced streams.

I have no need to pray
That fear may pass away;
I scorn the growl and rumble of the fight
That summons me from cool
Silence of marsh and pool
And yellow lilies islanded in light.
O river of stars and shadows, lead me through the night.

June 25[1]

June 26

  Up and away by 8.15 on a perfect morning with some clouds in the sky. The men were putting their kits together in the green orchard behind C. Company Mess, and I walked away to the riverside, where I sit now, with the twenty-foot stream sliding along at my feet, the long green weeds swaying with the current like nosing fishes slowly curving their way up-stream. The tall trees are full of bird-notes. A long way off seems the fighting line: one can just hear the distant bumping and dull thudding of the bombardment. The gun-flashes were lurid last night. Further up the river, along the marsh, there are yellow irises among the reeds, and little dark-green and gold frogs in thousands, and waterside birds crying and calling

[1] Published in *The Old Huntsman*.

and swinging on the bullrushes and tufted spires, by the smooth grey-green pools and creeks along the river-margin. Last evening the sun went down behind the low hills while I sat there on the *marais* reading *Tess* and watching the dimpling water. The last beams struck between the poplar-stems (they grow orchard-like in that green flat place) and the tree-shadows lay across the grass gigantic; but all was peace; there was nothing violent; the air was quite calm. Only the faint bump and thud on the horizon.

To-day we march eleven miles back to Morlancourt. Molyneux (my servant)[1] was very communicative last night; his tongue was slightly loosened by beer. His mind seemed in total confusion—a mixture of grievance against one of the other servants, and desire to be with me in the show, and something about the Company refusing to do anything unless I go with them. He told me he loved me like a brother—very nice of him; he *is* a dear.

Reached Morlancourt at 12.45. As we came along the Corbie road there was a lot of white smoke to be seen along the line, but not much noise to be heard. Morlancourt full of troops and supply-columns. We passed a big new Main Dressing Station about half-way between Corbie and Bois de Taille—mostly tents painted in camouflage.

Back in our old billets—self and Anscombe in the room with Eiffel Tower picture, and the pale-blue and pink oil-painting of jocular Jesus in his boat preaching.

It rained most of the night. I came in from a smoke with Rowley, Cotterill and Holmes about midnight. Soon after I got to bed, two five-nines came over and one went off just behind the Company office. The blackness of the night seen through my window was lit with continuous glare and flash of guns. Some limbers rattled down the street. I fell asleep to the sound of rainwater trickling and gurgling into the well—a noise of full gutters and rain pouring with a hollow echoing sound.

June 27
Rode up to the line after lunch. Things looked much the same as usual, except for the noise of our guns and the quantity of

[1] The Flook of *Memoirs of an Infantry Officer.*

stuff about the lines. The Germans have not retaliated much yet.
Fricourt was being shelled as I went along Kingston Road
Trench, where the Company goes to-morrow. Poppies growing
and leaning across the trenches. Little printed names in violet
indelible pencil on a tiny board hung in the trench. Men of
Royal Irish Rifles scuffling along 71 North, one with head under
another's arm. Sickly-sweet smell from a gas-shell at Gib. I
thought it was the yellow weeds.

4 p.m. We've just been told that all arrangements for the
show are 'temporarily in abeyance' and the Battalion is going
up to-night to take over C.1 and C.2 (the Brigade front only),
two companies in the front line. What does it mean? No doubt
a ruse to deceive the enemy! Rather a pity as everyone was
worked up to concert-pitch and the bombardment has been
great. C. Company are going to the trenches in front of the
cemetery by Fricourt station.

Marching up by Bois de Taille 5 – 8.30. Mud. Army Service
Corps officer with eyeglass. Dark-blue weed. Relieve Seventh
Borders. Quiet night. Mud-and-water bad.

June 28

Here I sit in this dog-kennel of a dug-out in 85 Street with
the shells hurrying and hurooshing over to Germany, or
thereabouts, and banging away on the slopes on each side of
Fricourt and away to Contalmaison. Wet feet—short of sleep
—trench-mouth—very beastly it all is—*on the surface*. But all's
well really. I wonder what's happening down in Sussex. A grey
day—the dark-green dense woodlands with pigeons circling
above the tree-tops. Dogs barking and cocks crowing—all the
peaceful hum of the countryside. Moffat-Smith at Ringmer
walking out in his white coat on the Broyle with the bitches—or
coming in to tea after a motor-drive to see some farmers or
keepers. Old man Harbord gardening at Colney. Everything
more or less stodgy but rather attractive to the jaded soldier.
Intense bombardment from 4.20 to 5.20 with smoke-bombs to
finish up. How long will it last?

Reading Hardy's *Tess* now. *Dawn at Talbothays.*

1916

June 29

Steady bombardment. Enemy quiet (up to 1.30 p.m.), weather cool and cloudy, no rain.

SPIRIT OF THE EARTH

What of the Immanent Will and Its designs?

SPIRIT OF THE YEARS

It works unconsciously, as heretofore,
Eternal artistries in Circumstance,
Whose patterns, wrought by rapt aesthetic rote,
Seen in themselves Its single listless aim,
And not their consequence.

SPIRIT OF THE YEARS

Yet but one flimsy riband of Its web
Have we here watched in weaving—web Enorme,
Whose furthest hem and selvage may extend
To where the roars and plashings of the flames
Of earth-invisible suns swell noisily,
And onwards into ghastly gulfs of sky,
Where hideous presences churn through the dark—
Monsters of magnitude without a shape,
Hanging amid deep wells of nothingness.

(from Hardy, The Dynasts)

June 30   6 p.m.

Yesterday: smoke-bomb show 5.15. Wounded R.E. 10.15–11.30 heavy shelling of front trench and supports. Collecting wirers. Weather cloudy and cool. Out cutting our wire from 12 to 3.30. Driven in once by shelling—Gurner wounded. In the afternoon dead body by trench-mortar, trussed in waterproof sheet. Blood. Young yellowhammer in trench. Phosphorus-bombs burning up the hill in the darkness.

[81]

1916

This morning warm and breezy. We go down to Kingston
Road. Jordan and self out cutting wire from 10.30 to 11.30.
No one noticed us. Pleasant trenches; mustard, charlock and
white weeds growing across the trenches. Another dead man
lying on the firing-step. News of M.C. before lunch. Letter from
Nick. Greaves typical. Battle begins to-morrow. C. Company
dispersed on carrying-parties etc. Gibson's face in the first grey
of dawn when he found me alone at wire-cutting. Brow and eyes
good: rest of face weak. Jaunty, fag-smoking demeanour under
fire.[1]

July 1[2] *7.30 a.m.*
Last night was cloudless and starry and still. The bombard-
ment went on steadily. We had breakfast at 6. The morning is
brilliantly fine, after a mist early. Since 6.30 there has been hell
let loose. The air vibrates with the incessant din—the whole
earth shakes and rocks and *throbs*—it is one continuous roar.
Machine-guns tap and rattle, bullets whistling overhead—
small fry quite outdone by the gangs of hooligan-shells that
dash over to rend the German lines with their demolition-
parties. The smoke-cloud is cancelled as the wind is wrong
since yesterday. Attack should be starting now, but one can't
look out, as the machine-gun bullets are skimming.
Inferno—inferno—bang—smash!
7.45 a.m. The artillery barrage is now working to the right
of Fricourt and beyond. I have seen the 21st Division advancing
on the left of Fricourt; and some Huns apparently surrendering
—about three-quarters of a mile away. Our men advancing
steadily to the first line. A haze of smoke drifting across the
landscape—brilliant sunshine. Some Yorkshires on our left (50th
Brigade) watching the show and cheering as if at a football
match. The noise as bad as ever.
9.30 a.m. Came back to dug-out and had a shave. Just been
out to have another look. The 21st Division are still going
across the open on the left, apparently with no casualties. The
sun flashes on bayonets, and the tiny figures advance steadily

[1] Lance-Corporal Gibson—the best of C Company wirers. A lad of nineteen from
Whitehaven in Cumberland. Quite fearless. Killed on July 16. S.S.
[2] Opening of the Battle of the Somme.

[82]

and disappear behind the mounds of trench-debris. A few runners
come back, and the ammunition-parties are going across.
Trench-mortars etc are knocking hell out of Sunken Road
Trench and the ground where 22nd Brigade will go across soon.
The noise is not as bad, and the Huns aren't firing much now.

9.50 a.m. Fricourt is half-hidden by clouds of drifting smoke—
brown, blue, pinkish, and grey; shrapnel bursting in small blue-
white puffs, with tiny flashes. The smoke drifts across our front
on a south-east wind, just a breeze.

The birds seem bewildered; I saw a lark start to go up, and
then flutter along as if he thought better of it. Others were
fluttering above the trench with querulous cries, weak on the
wing.

The uproar isn't as bad as it was an hour ago. I can see seven
of our balloons, half-right, and close together. Seven or eight
aeroplanes are above our lines and the German front-trenches,
also half-right. Our men still advancing in twenties and thirties
in file, about a mile to the left. Another huge explosion in
Fricourt, and cloud of brown-pink smoke. Some bursts are
yellowish.

10.5 a.m. I can see the Manchesters in our front trench getting
ready to go over. Figures filing down the trench. Two Hun
shells just burst close to our trench-mortar positions at 84
Street. Two of the Manchesters gone out to look at our wire-
gaps (which I made night before last).

Just eaten my last orange. I am looking at a sunlit picture of
Hell. And still the breeze shakes the yellow charlock, and the
poppies glow below Crawley ridge where a few Hun shells have
fallen lately. Manchesters are sending forward a few scouts. A
bayonet glitters. A runner comes back across the open to their
Battalion H.Q. in 84 Street. (I am about five hundred yards
behind the front trenches, where Sandown Avenue joins
Kingston Road.) The Huns aren't shelling or firing machine-
guns. 21st still trotting along the skyline toward La Boiselle.
Barrage going strong to right of Contalmaison ridge. Heavy
shelling by us of Hun trenches toward Mametz.

12.15 p.m. Things have been quieter the last hour: 20th
Manchesters not gone across yet. Germans putting over a few
shrapnel-shells. Weather hot and cloudless. A lark singing
overhead.

1.30 p.m. 20th Manchesters attack at 2.30. Mametz and Montauban reported taken; Mametz consolidated.

2.30 p.m. 20th Manchesters left New Trench and took Sunken Road Trench. We could see about four hundred. Many walked across with sloped arms. About twenty-five casualties on the left (from a machine-gun in Fricourt). I could see one man moving his left arm up and down as he lay on his side: his head was a crimson patch. The others lay still. Then the swarm of ants disappeared over the hill. Fricourt was a cloud of pinkish smoke. Hun machine-guns were firing on the other side of the hill. At 2.50 no one to be seen in no-man's-land except the casualties (about half-way across).

5.30 p.m. I saw about twenty or thirty men of A. Company, Second R.W.F., crawling across to Sunken Road, from same place as the 20th Manchesters, and lit a red signal. Huns put a few big shells on to the cemetery—and traversed Kingston Road with machine-gun bursts. Manchesters' wounded still out there. Remainder of A. went over after, about a hundred in all. I was in dug-out till 6, nothing to be seen meanwhile. At 7.15 p.m. people could be seen moving about the Hun lines beyond Sunken Road, and crossing the craters by 82 Street. Very little firing was going on. Yorkshires (50th Brigade) reported to have made a mess of clearing Fricourt: the Sixth Dorsets (two companies; C.O., Adjutant, and Major) came along Kingston Road, evidently got to finish the job. Weather clear and warm and still. Our dug-out heavily shelled with five-nines between 1.30 and 2.30.

8 p.m. Situation as reported by Staff Captain of 22nd Brigade to Greaves. Montauban and Mametz taken and consolidated. 20th Brigade (on our right) got their objective with some difficulty.

20th Manchesters are held up behind Sunken Road Trench. 50th Brigade have done badly in clearing Fricourt. 21st Division have done very well, and reached north-east corner of Fricourt Wood. A good number of prisoners have been brought in on our sector (reported several hundred).

9.30 p.m. Our A. Company holds Rectangle and Sunken Road: Manchesters Bois Français Support. C.O. 20th Manchesters killed. Greaves and I stay in Kingston Road: Garnons-Williams gone with carrying-party, so C. Company is reduced to six runners, two stretcher-bearers, Company Sergeant Major, Signallers, and Ryder! Things are quiet at present. Sky cloudy westward; five grey wisps: red sunset.

10.45 p.m. Heavy gunfire on the left round La Boiselle. Fairly quiet opposite us. Some of the Sixth Dorsets are in Kingston Road. That battalion attacks Fricourt in the morning.

July 2   11.15 a.m.

A quiet night. Fine sunny morning. Nothing happening at present. Fricourt and Rose Trench to be attacked again to-day. Everything all right on rest of XV Corps front. Greaves and I are to remain in Kingston Road.

2.30 p.m. Adjutant just been up here, excited, optimistic and unshaven. Fricourt and Rose Trench have been occupied without resistance (there was no bombardment). Over two thousand prisoners taken by Seventh Division alone. First R.W.F. took over two hundred. Germans have gone back to their second line.

I am lying out in front of our trench in the long grass, basking in sunshine where yesterday morning one couldn't show a finger. The Germans are shelling our new front line. Fricourt is full of British soldiers seeking souvenirs. The place was a ruin before; now it is a dust-heap. Everywhere the news seems good: I only hope it will last.

A gunner Forward Observation Officer just been along with a Hun helmet; says the Huns in Fricourt were cut off and their trenches demolished. Many dead lying about—he saw one dead officer lying across a smashed machine-gun with his head smashed in—'a fine-looking chap' he said (with some emotion).

Next thing is to hang on to the country we've taken. We move up to-night. Seventh Division has at any rate done all that was asked of it and reached the ground just short of Mametz Wood; the Second Queens are said to have legged it as usual when the Bosche made a poorish counter-attack.

July 3   11.15 a.m.

Greaves, self and party left Kingston Road at 6.45 a.m. The battalion assembled at 71 North and we marched across to a point north-west of Carnoy where the 22nd Brigade concentrated. The four battalions piled arms and lay down in an open grassy hollow south of the Carnoy–Mametz road, with a fine view of the British and (late) Bosche lines where the 91st Brigade attacked on Saturday, about six hundred yards away. Everyone very cheery—no officer-casualties yet. C. D. Morgan, Dobell and Peter with A.: H. B. Williams, Alexander, Smith B.: C. self and Greaves and Lomax. Hanmer-Jones and Baynes with D.: Stevens and Newton with Bombers. Anscombe (Lewis guns), C.O., Medical Officer and Reeves—Brunicardi (observing for Brigade) and E. Dadd. Weather still, warm, sky rather cloudy. Sorry to say most of C. Company are on special parties—carrying etc; poor old Molyneux will be in an awful state at not being near his master. I think we move up this evening and probably attack Mametz Wood to-morrow. (This is only a guess.) If so, we'll probably get cut up. Greaves and I are lucky to have had such an easy time lately. A. and B. Companies have had no sleep for two nights.

5.45 p.m. Everyone has been dozing in the sun all day. Minshull Ford rode round after lunch, and bucked from his horse about what his Brigade had been doing. K. Fry took his M.C. ribbon off and sewed it on me. R.W.F. about four hundred and twenty strong.

20th Manchesters reduced to about two hundred and fifty. Second Warwicks and Royal Irish haven't been in action yet. As I dozed I could hear the men all round talking about the things they'd looted from the Bosche trenches.

Evening falls calm and hazy; an orange sunset, blurred at the last. At 8.45 I'm looking down from the hill, a tangle of long grass and thistles and some small white weed like tiny cow-parsley. The four battalions are in four groups. A murmur of voices comes up—one or two mouth-organs playing—a salvo of our field-guns on the right—and a few droning airplanes overhead. A little smoke drifting from tiny bivouac-fires. At the end of the hollow the road to Mametz (where some captured German guns came along two hours since). Beyond that the bare ground rising to the Bazentin ridge, with seams of our trench-lines and those taken from the enemy—grey-green and chalk-white stripes.

AT CARNOY

Down in the hollow there's the whole Brigade
Camped in four groups: through twilight falling slow
I hear a sound of mouth-organs, ill-played,
And murmur of voices, gruff, confused, and low.
Crouched among thistle-tufts I've watched the glow
Of a blurred orange sunset flare and fade;
And I'm content. To-morrow we must go
To take some cursèd Wood . . . O world God made!

July 3[1]

July 4   4.30 a.m.

The Battalion started at 9.15 p.m. yesterday and, after messing about for over four hours, got going with tools, wire, etc and went through Mametz, up a long communication-trench with three very badly mangled corpses lying in it: a man, short, plump, with turned-up moustaches, lying face downward and half sideways with one arm flung up as if defending his head, and a bullet through his forehead. A doll-like figure. Another hunched and mangled, twisted and scorched with many days' dark growth on his face, teeth clenched and grinning lips. Came down across the open hillside looking across to Mametz Wood, and out at the end of Bright Alley. Found that the Royal Irish were being bombed and machine-gunned by Bosches in the wood, and had fifteen wounded. A still grey morning; red east; everyone very tired.

12.30 p.m. These dead are terrible and undignified carcases, stiff and contorted. There were thirty of our own laid in two ranks by the Mametz-Carnoy road, some side by side on their backs with bloody clotted fingers mingled as if they were hand-shaking in the companionship of death. And the stench undefinable. And rags and shreds of blood-stained cloth, bloody boots riddled and torn. This morning the facts were: R.W.F. and Royal Irish were sent up to consolidate trenches close to the south-east end of Mametz Wood and to clear the wood outskirts. The Irish got there and found enemy machine-guns and bombers and snipers in the wood, which is of big old trees. Our A. Company

[1] Published in *The Old Huntsman.*

went forward to join them, but were sniped on the road, and got into a quarry where they lost four wounded and one killed. The Irish meanwhile had tried to bomb the Bosches in the wood, failed entirely, and suffered sixty casualties (one officer killed and one wounded). Our guns then chucked a lot of heavy shrapnel over the wood and the Irish got away. The whole thing seems to have been caused by bad staff-work (of the Division). We were out eleven hours and got back to our field about 8.30 a.m. Mametz is as badly smashed as Fricourt. A few skeleton-sheds and one small white fragment of a church-tower, no more than fifteen feet high. Hun communication-trenches quite decent. Eight-inch guns firing three hundred yards from our bivouac. Rumour has it that the Seventh Division are to be taken out of the show soon. Not for long, if they are! Great fun these last two days.

9.15 p.m. The Battalion just moving off for the attack on Quadrangle Trench, by Mametz Wood. The XV Corps attack at 12.30 a.m. It rained in sheets from 1 to 4.30, but everyone has recovered, though all got soaked. The attack-scheme was sprung on us very much at the last moment.

C. Company can muster only twenty-six men, so we are carrying R.E. stuff. B. and D. attack. A. are in reserve. We attack from Bottom Wood on a six-hundred-yard front.

July 6

We are now back at Heilly-sur-l'Ancre. Got here at 7.45 this morning. We are under canvas along the marsh—not a very nice place. Heilly is a good village.

On Tuesday night (*July 4*) we struggled up to Mametz and on to Bottom Wood in awful mud. I sat with C. Company in a reserve trench till we were sent for (about 2.30 a.m.) to reinforce. This order was cancelled before we got there, but I went on to see what was happening (and got cursed considerably by the Colonel for doing so!). It was beginning to be daylight. I crossed from Bottom Wood, by the way they had attacked, and found our D. Company had got there all right, but things seemed in rather a muddle, especially on the right, where B. did no good —got lost or machine-gunned—and A. had gone up and saved the situation. The Companies advanced at 12.45 a.m. after a short bombardment by our guns. They had to cross five hundred yards of open ground and occupy Quadrangle Trench (a half-finished work the Germans were said to be holding lightly). There seems to have been a working-party there digging, but they cleared off without showing fight (except for a little bombing). Our attack was quite unexpected.

When I got there, morning was just getting grey; the trench taken had some wire in front, but was quite shallow and roughly dug. On the right loomed Mametz Wood—in front open country, a Bosche trench about five hundred yards away. Our men were firing a good deal at Bosches they couldn't see, and were rather excited, mostly.

The enemy were bombing up a communication-trench from the wood. The Royal Irish had attacked on our right and failed to get into the enemy trenches (Strip Trench and Wood Trench). We got a bombing-post established on our right where the Quadrangle Trench came to a sudden end. The Germans had fled, leaving their packs, rifles, bombs etc on the edge of the trench. Several of them were lying face downwards in the mud. We began digging the trench deeper, but the men were rather beat. After daylight the enemy sniped a lot from the wood, and we had five men killed and several wounded (C. D. Morgan got hit in the leg—not badly). I went across from our bombing-post to where Wood Trench ended, as there was a Bosche sniper: the others fired at the parapet, so they didn't see me coming. When I got there I chucked four Mills bombs into their trench and to my surprise fifty or sixty (I counted eighty-five packs left on the firestep) ran away like hell into Mametz Wood. Our Lewis-gun was on them all the way and I think they suffered. (Ask someone else about this show!) We had got the Quadrangle Trench well held by mid-day—no counter-attacks, only a little bombing (and the damned snipers playing hell).[1]

Quadrangle Trench was then the most advanced position held by the XV Corps. The Fourteenth R.W.F. relieved us at 9.30 p.m. and we started back for Heilly (about twelve miles). Coming through Mametz we were heavily shelled. The total casualties of First R.W.F. for the last seven days have been a

[1] For this exploit S.S. was recommended for a further decoration, but the award was disallowed because the whole attack had been a failure.

hundred and thirty, and two officers (only fourteen dead of this lot). We have been very lucky: gained our objective in two attacks (the night one a very chancy affair). The 20th Manchesters lost sixteen officers and did no good. The Second Warwicks were never in action and lost seven officers (four killed). The Royal Irish lost nearly two hundred and fifty, and several officers, and did no good. Our C. Company lost two killed and seventeen wounded.

We took a long time getting back, owing to congestion of artillery in Fricourt; we reached the hill above Bécordel at 1.45. Slept for an hour in the long wet grass, with guns booming and flashing all round in the valley below, and in the glimmer of a misty dawn—cold, with clear stars overhead—the Battalion fell in and marched on to Heilly, which we reached in hot weather about 7.45, all very tired and sleepy. We are in a camp on a sort of marsh by the river Ancre. Not very nice. I slept from 10 to 1 and was wakened to go to the Brigadier's conference of officers, where a lot of people bragged and made excuses for what they'd done and left undone. The next day it rained and the place was muddy and wretched. On Saturday (July 7) I went to Amiens with Greaves, Reeves, Cotterill and Julian Dadd,[1] and we lunched in style at Godbert and had a jolly day in fine weather. Rode to Querrieux, about four miles, and motored the other seven in Parker's car.[2] The country looked fine: grey-green and pale yellow and rain-washed, and the valley by Pont Noyelles patched with yellow and buff of ripening corn and deep-green clover, the ridges crowned with dark-green woods, a slow, rich, quiet sunlight brooding over all the calm landscape. On the way home we met a motor in a cloud of dust, with a German prisoner handcuffed, being whirled back to Army H.Q. to be questioned. All prisoners seem glad to be taken.

July 9

A fine day. Rode over to Corbie in the morning and saw Norman Loder[3] (Assistant Provost Marshal to XIII Corps

---

[1] The Julian Durley of *Memoirs of an Infantry Officer.*

[2] Captain E. A. Parker, formerly Quartermaster of the First Battalion R.W.F., now Quartermaster at Fourth Army Headquarters.

[3] A pre-war hunting friend of S.S. Master first of the Southdown, then of the Atherstone. The Denis Milden of *Memoirs of a Fox-Hunting Man.* S.S. dedicated his poem 'The Old Huntsman' to him.

H.Q.). He lives in a very fine billet. We sat on the grass in a
charming garden behind his office—a walled garden off the
place. It was splendid seeing him again.

In the evening we heard that the Seventh Division move up
to the line again to-morrow. Mametz Wood not taken yet.
Riding home from Corbie, stopped to let the mare graze by
still pools with lilies and tangled weeds. Green trees, and
swathes of new-cut hay, and Sunday afternoon peace and sun-
shine and midsummer richness of earth and air.

July 11   10 a.m.

The Battalion marched away from Heilly at 4 o'clock yester-
day afternoon in hot dusty weather. Five officers and fifty-seven
men from Twentieth Battalion came last night. Sir Douglas
Haig[1] passed us between Mericourt and Treux. Through
Morlancourt—doctor in white coat standing at church-door.
Along the red road and to the Citadel in rich yellow evening
light. Got to Citadel about 9, bivouacked on the hill behind.
Stood-to about 10.45, and the Battalion started for Mametz at
11.30—only to be brought back after going a quarter of a mile.
Slept well under a clear starry sky. There was a half-moon
shining last night—set about midnight. Heavy firing toward La
Boiselle. This morning we are still here—the sky full of rainy-
looking clouds and wind in the west. Fell asleep to the sound of
guns and rattling limbers on the Citadel road, and men shouting
and looking for their kits. Julian Dadd and self are left out this
time. Frenchmen working on railroad at the Citadel. Crowds of
guns up here.

July 12

I am with seven other officers, in reserve at Transport
Lines close to Méaulte. Windy and dusty, flapping tent and dry
mouth. Slept heavily last night owing to copious rum and tea
before turning in. Rode up to Citadel this morning: most of
Seventh Division seems to be there. French seventy-fives up at
Maple Redoubt. Sky grey but no rain. Everything looking
rather parched and hueless, except the poppies, and many of
them are withered. The guns slam away over the hills.

[1] Commander-in-Chief of the British Armies in France since December 1915.

1916

July 13

Still we remain in this curious camp, which leaves a jumbled impression of horse-lines and waggons and men carrying empty deal shell-boxes, and tents, and bivouacs, and red poppies and blue cornflowers, and straggling Méaulte village a little way off among the dark-green July trees, with pointed spire in the middle, and a general atmosphere of bustle while we remain idle at this caravanserai for supplies and men and munitions. There is a breeze blowing and grey weather.

Sitting at the tent-door last night about 9.30 I was watching a group of our officers and three from the Second R.W.F. who have arrived from Béthune. All were voluble—their faces indistinct but their heads looming against the last grey luminous gleam of evening.

I keep reading *Tess* and *The Return of the Native*—they fit in admirably with my thoughts.

Here with me are Dobell and Newton,[1] fresh from Sandhurst, cheery and attractive, and old Julian Dadd—the good soul, and Hawes, full of jokes, and Hanmer-Jones, blundering old thing, as stupid as an owl, but kind, and two others.

The Battalion are still waiting at the Citadel, three-quarters of a mile away, over the thistled slopes. Haven't seen Robert Graves yet: he is near, with the Second Battalion—unpopular, of course, poor dear.

Indian cavalry ride past along the Méaulte–Bray road. The landscape looks grey and withered to-day, and the poppies leap at one in harsh spots of flame, hectic and cruel.

This life begets a condition of mental stagnation unless one keeps trying to get outside it all. I try to see everything with different eyes to my companions, but their unreasoning mechanical outlook is difficult to avoid. Often their words go past me like dead leaves on the wind; one gets used to them, like banging guns that scourge the landscape and raise huge din; and then, after being merely irritated by them, they are suddenly dear and friendly, not to be lost.

> The quicksilvery glaze on the rivers and pools vanished; from broad mirrors of light they changed to lustreless sheets of lead. (*Return of the Native*)

[1] Dobell killed 1918. Newton killed on September 1 at Ginchy. S.S.

Sometimes when I see my companions lying asleep or resting, rolled in their blankets, their faces turned to earth or hidden by the folds, for a moment I wonder whether they are alive or dead. For at any hour I may come upon them, and find that long silence descended over them, their faces grey and disfigured, dark stains of blood soaking through their torn garments, all their hope and merriment snuffed out for ever, and their voices fading on the winds of thought, from memory to memory, from hour to hour, until they are no more to be recalled. So does the landscape grow dark at evening, embowered with dusk, and backed with a sky full of gun-flashes. And then the night falls and the darkness of death and sleep.

July 14

Awoke about 2.30 a.m. to hear an intense bombardment shaking the surrounding hills and ridges—the dark sky livid with flashes. Dull rainy weather to-day. Puff my pipe in the tent and read Hardy and wait for tidings of the battle. Many prisoners coming down and lots of our troops going up.

The Second Battalion are bivouacked three hundred yards away by the Bécordel road. I had a long talk with Robert Graves, whimsical and queer and human as ever. We sat in the darkness with guns booming along the valleys, and dim stars of camp-fires burning all around in the dark countryside; and a grey cloudy sky overhead, and the moon hid. And there I left him, with his men sleeping a little way off. To-morrow they'll be up in the battle, where things are going well for us, but no definite news has come back yet.

July 15

Awoke at 5.45 this morning when the Transport got back from the line. The Seventh Division have reached their objective: Greaves slightly wounded: also young Brunicardi and Smith. Baynes and G. P. Morgan killed. Hawes gone up to take C. Company. Only eight left of the Montagne lot who came hither on January 30—Brunicardi, Stevens, Davies, Hawes, Julian Dadd, E. Dadd, Reeves and self.[1]

[1] Davies and E. Dadd killed on September 3 at Ginchy. S.S.

July 16

We've just had dinner, in the tent, where you can see the camouflage paint-smears against the light, like birds flying stiffly, and all sorts of queer shapes. It's a drizzly cool evening and the Battalion are still up by Mametz Wood and there's no fresh news to speak of. And the others are sitting about the tent talking futile stuff, and the servants are singing together rather nicely by their light shell-box-wood fire outside in the gusty twilight.

And I'm thinking of England, and summer evenings after cricket-matches, and sunset above the tall trees, and village-streets in the dusk, and the clatter of a brake driving home. Perhaps I've made a blob, but we've won the match, and there's another match to-morrow—Blue Mantles against some cheery public-school side, and there's the usual Nevill Ground wicket, and I'll be in first—and old Kelsey and Osmund Scott and all the rest of them. So things went three years ago; and it's all dead and done with. I'll never be there again. If I'm lucky and get through alive, there's another sort of life waiting for me. Travels, and adventures, and poetry; and anything but the old groove of cricket and hunting, and dreaming in Weirleigh garden. When war ends I'll be at the crossroads; and I know the path to choose. I must go out into the night alone. No fat settling down; the Hanmer engagement idea was a ghastly blunder—it wouldn't work at all. That charming girl who writes to me so often would never be happy with me. It was my love for Bobbie that led me to that mistake.

To-night I am hungry for music. And still the guns boom, and the battle goes on three miles away. And Robert's somewhere in it, if he hasn't been shot already. He wants to travel with me after the war; anywhere—Russia for preference. And whenever I am with him, I want to do wild things, and get right away from the conventional silliness of my old life. Blighty! What a world of idle nothingness the name stands for; and what a world of familiar delightfulness! O God, when shall I get out of this limbo? For I'm never alone here—never my old self—always acting a part—that of the cheery, reckless sportsman—out for a dip at the Bosches. But the men love me, that's one great consolation. And some day perhaps I'll be alone in a room full of books again, with a piano glimmering in the corner, and glory in my head, and a new poem in my notebook.

Now the rain begins to patter on the tent and the dull thudding of guns comes from Albert way; and I've still got my terrible way to tread before I'm free to sleep with Rupert Brooke and Sorley[1] and all the nameless poets of the war.

July 18
In the brown twilight of the tent the paint-smears on the outside seem like ungainly shapes of birds with stretched wings, fishes nosing and floating, monkeys in scarecrow trees, and anything else one's idle brain likes to imagine. In one place, where the painter had spasms of activity, there's a fight going on (a sort of Marinetti[2] fight). One figure whirls upward a huge stave, striding forward with shapeless head tilted backward, while his adversary, taking a sideways leap, appears to be catching it hot from a bomb-explosion, for his right leg is flying away, and one of his arms has disappeared; nevertheless he's putting up a good show.

When the gusty breeze comes, white gaps and rents show the blank hazy sky. From the camp outside come certain noises, such as men whistling, carts rumbling and rattling, larks singing, guns thudding and echoing along the valleys, and a jumble of chatter and shouting of soldiers. Inside the tent a golden candle burns and officers puff pipes and talk second-rate rubbish and tired war-shop out of the *Daily Mail*. And I've been here a week.

July 19
An evening of massed stillness, and smoky silhouettes. Albert and its tall trees were flat grey-blue outlines and the shattered tower might have been a huge tree. There were figures of soldiers against the sky, and horses; and everything was quiet —the balloons swinging slowly aloft, their noses pointing toward the German lines, and a few aeroplanes droning like huge insects: only the distant thud of gunfire broke the peace,

[1] Charles Hamilton Sorley, killed in action in October 1915, aged twenty. He and S.S. were both educated at Marlborough.
[2] Emilio Marinetti (1876–1944), Italian poet and writer, founded the Futurist movement in 1909.

and that sounded more like someone kicking footballs— a soft bumping, miles away. Low in the west pale-orange beams were streaming down on to the far-stretching country; the sky mostly veiled with hueless cloud. I watched the Indian cavalry in the horse-lines by the river: their red head-caps made occasional spots of poppy-colour: the rest was browns and duns and greys—like the huddle of horses and waggons and blankets, and the worn grassless earth. Higher up was the pale-yellow barley, decked with vivid blue and scarlet flowers. I could almost catch the evening smell of autumn that always reminds me of early cub-hunting—a sort of chilly mingling of mist and fading woodlands and twilight stubbles; and gardens where robins pipe among apple-trees and dahlias. I like that smell and that feeling —half-sad for summer, half-glad for winter and sport. And to-night it caught my heart for a little and I turned back to the camp in an unheroic mood—and found the Manchesters' band tootling; then the sun came out for a last reddish stare at the war, and I was back again in the same tedious existence.

But I'd found comfort for a while in being something like my old solitary self—leaning over a rough wooden bridge to gaze down into the dark-green swaying glooms of the narrow river, full of weeds—watching the queer, swarming war-landscape and thinking my own thoughts, undisturbed by the mechanical chatter of my daily companions: and how seldom I get free from them, good people as they are. But they dull my impressions of the vivid scenes here; they make the strangeness commonplace. And the Battalion are still up beyond Mametz: they are gone further up again for an attack on High Wood.

This evening ended clear-skied after all; and I walked up and down by the green wheat and puffed a cigar, and dreamed about my old horses, I don't know why. And the silver-white tents glimmered across by the village, a cluster of mushrooms; and the fires glowed red and golden, and men talked and sang rather peacefully in the sober stillness. The place is strewn and piled with endless shell-boxes, which are burned and used to make little bivouacs. And the shells have all flown away to smash Germans.

I wonder what Thomas Hardy would think of the life out here. How the Pre-Raphaelites would have loathed it. Ten years ago I was busy writing my first lot of poems—Joan of Arc and things like that—under their weary influence. If I'm alive in July 1926 I'll be a decent poet at last.

July 21   8.30 a.m.

Transport (and us) moved to hill south-west of Dernancourt yesterday evening, Battalion expected to return from trenches about midnight. (They arrived at 5.45 a.m.) The Seventh Division were coming out after over a week in the show. The sun went down in glory beyond the Amiens–Albert road, horizon-trees dark grey-blue against the glare, a sort of mirage in front on the golden haze and aura of brightness. Continual lorries creeping along the highway. The country, vale and slope south-east with the large trees by the river and the villages, Ville-Treux etc, down to Corbie, swarming with camps. The low sun made it all look very peaceful and gracious—the cool green of unripe oats, and darker wheat, and the naked skyline starting from Corbie. The eye follows the Bray–Corbie ridge, and then sweeps round to the old English line ridge—beyond one can just see the top of Mametz Wood. Later on the country glowed and glinted with camp-fires. About 11 a red half-moon came up.

We waited at the crossroads for the Battalion from 11.30 to 5.30. I walked about most of the night, saw to moving tents up the hill, which had to be done at the last moment. The road where I sat was a moonlit picture (I sat among some oats and watched the procession of the Seventh Division). Guns and limbers, men sitting stiffly on tired horses—transport—cookers —they rolled and jolted past in the moonshine. Then, like flitting ghosts, last began to come the foot-weary infantry— stumbling—limping—straggling back after eight days in hell —more or less. They came silently—sometimes a petrol- (water-) tin would sound as it rattled chiming against the bayonet at the side. Then moonshine and dawn mingled their silver and rose and lilac, and a lark went up from the green corn. The kite-balloon, too, on the hill, began to sway huge and bulbous—upward—another was seen far off against the rosy east. All night the distant waves of gunfire had crashed and rumbled, soft and terrific with broad flashes, like waves of some immense tumult of waters, rolling along the horizon. As dawn

broke, and I came down the hill again, I heard the clear skirl
of the Second Gordons piping into their bivouac—a brave note,
shrill as the lark, but the Jocks were a weary crowd as they
hobbled in. Before dawn a horse neighed twice, high and shrill
and scared. And then I began to see the barley-tops swaying
lightly against the paling sky. And the hills began to gloom in
the dusk, stretching away and upward, and the huge trees along
the river stood out dark and distinct and solemn. The camp-
fires burned low. The east was beginning to be chinked with
red flames and feathers of scarlet. A train groaned along the
line, sending up vast columns of whitish fiery vapour—a red
light shone from behind.

And now I've heard that Robert died of wounds yesterday,
in an attack on High Wood. And I've got to go on as if there
were nothing wrong. So he and Tommy are together, and
perhaps I'll join them soon. 'Oh my songs never sung, And my
plays to darkness blown!'[1]—his own poor words written last
summer, and now so cruelly true. And only two days ago I was
copying his last poem into my notebook, a poem full of his best
qualities of sweetness and sincerity, full of heart-breaking gaiety
and hope. So all our travels to 'the great, greasy Caucasus'[2]
are quelled. And someone called Peter will be as sad as I am.
Robert might have been a great poet; he could never have
become a dull one. In him I thought I had found a lifelong
friend to work with. So I go my way alone again.

July 22

First R.W.F. took train at Mericourt this afternoon and came
to Hengest: marched seven kilometres to La Chausée (one
kilometre from Picquigny). A golden, dusty evening march
through green country and quiet white and grey and red
villages. We are back here for a fortnight.

---

[1] From Robert Graves's poem 'The Shadow of Death', published in his first book
Over the Brazier (1916).
[2] In the first draft of Robert Graves's poem 'Letter to S.S. from Mametz Wood',
which he sent to S.S. on 14 June 1916, he suggested that 'the great, greasy
Caucasus' should be visited by them both after the war. In the published version
in *Fairies and Fusiliers* (1917) this became 'the great hills of Caucasus'.

1916

July 23

Feeling very ill. Temperature 105 at 9 p.m. Went to New
Zealand Hospital at Amiens on Monday morning.

July 28

Still in hospital. Marcus Goodall dead of wounds.

ELEGY: FOR MARCUS GOODALL

Was it for English morning, spilled and flowing,
Across grey hummock'd fields, dim cattle showing,
Was it for this I longed? The glittering brass
Of rays low on brown roofs and steaming grass,
A garden spiked with blue and splashed with white,
Yellow and red and all the eye's delight.
Was it for these I longed, while you were dead,
Your mirth destroyed and from your lolling head
The racing thoughts gone out like smoke on air,
Thinning and whirling and subsiding—where?

Sad victim, could you see your body thrown
Into a shallow pit along that wood
Thronged by the dead? O, there you lie not lone,
Under the splinter'd trees; for the brotherhood
Of discontented slain, with eyes that scowl,
And bristly cheeks and chins all bloody-smears,
Will hug their rank red wounds and limp and prowl,
Squatting around your grave with moans and tears.

But soon, I hope a monster shell will burst,
And all such filth be blotted and dispersed:
You'll no more need to cling to the dead clay,
Dancing through fields of heaven to meet the day,
Slow-rising, saintless, confident and kind,
Dear, red-faced father God who lit your mind.[1]

---

[1] S.S. never published this poem, but he used its two last lines in 'To his Dead
Body', which was written at about the same time and refers to Robert Graves,
then believed killed in action.

July 30
Left N.Z. Hospital 1 o'clock. Ambulance to Corbie. Train started 5 o'clock. Reached Rouen No. 2 Hospital 2.30 a.m. Four hundred and fifty on board the train.

August 1
Left No 2 Hospital and got on board hospital ship *Aberdonian* at 10.15 a.m. A brilliant morning. Feeling better. Get to London this evening? Think I deserve a holiday, but feel rotten at forsaking the Battalion, when I could have been fit for work in three or four weeks. But fate is kind to me as usual.

August 2
Reached Southampton about noon. Got on train and came to Oxford about 4 p.m.—No 3 General Service Hospital at Somerville College. Paradise. Strange thing getting landed at Cambridge in August 1915 and Oxford in August 1916.
Lying in a hospital train on his way to London he looks out at the hot August landscape of Hampshire, the flat green and dun-coloured fields—the advertisements of Lung Tonic and Liver Pills—the cows—neat villas and sluggish waterways— all these came on him in an irresistible delight, at the pale gold of the wheat-fields and the faded green of the hazy muffled woods on the low hills.[1] People wave to the Red Cross train— grateful stay-at-homes—even a middle-aged man, cycling along a dusty road in straw hat and blue serge clothes, takes one hand off handlebars to wave feeble and jocular gratitude. And the soul of the officer glows with fiery passion as he thinks 'All this I've been fighting for; and now I'm safe home again I begin to think it was worth while'. And he wondered how he could avoid being sent out again.
Weather golden and sweet and gracious. The harvest landscape slipping past me as I lay in the train—all pale-golden wheat and silver-green barley and oats. Then Oxford bells chiming 5 o'clock and a piano sounding from across the lawn— someone strumming emotional trash—and the tall chestnuts

[1] Cf. S.S.'s poem 'Stretcher Case', published in the *Westminster Gazette*, 28 September 1916, then in *The Old Huntsman*.

swaying against the blue, as I lie in a little cream-white room. What an anodyne it all is after Fricourt etc. No need to think of another winter in the trenches, doomed though I am to endure it. Good enough to enjoy the late summer and autumn. And then, who cares?

August 12
From Oxford to Burford—nineteen miles along the Glouces-ter road. A grey village climbing a hill—with brown and golden and yellow and silver-green of harvest-fields all around. And the little Windrush running under a bridge at the lower end of the wide street. Uncle[1] at the Bull Inn. The Priory—a good old house with Mr Horniman owning it.[2]

Written on a grey evening at 8.15 at Shipton station, with a south-west breeze blowing and the country very quiet. A long line of willows and narrow stream by the station. Wireless-poles on the hill to the east. Uncle had been harvest-working: I passed the field, but many of his oat-stooks had collapsed. Brown kitten and brown fodder-trusses. Shipton spire half a mile off among dark-green trees. Old man driving bus up to Burford. Dust blowing. Grain-crops patching the landscape different hues of pale-brown-buff, primrose straw. Child running to his father (soldier on leave?) with little arms reaching up, very pathetic and humanly sweet. Very old small woman at the Bull, shrivelled and wrinkled, but erect. Horniman's water-clock—1635—a Chinese lacquer screen, delicate greens and reds. Wyatt the saddler. Boy-scouts falling in with bugle; sailor-boy at attention on right flank. *End of a good day.*

FOR ENGLAND

He ducked and cowered and almost yelped with fear,
Thought 'Christ! I wish they wouldn't burst so near!'
Then stumbled on—afraid of turning back—
Till something smashed his neck; he choked and swore;
A glorious end; killed in the big attack.
His relatives who thought him such a bore,
Grew pale with grief and dressed themselves in black.

[1] S.S.'s uncle Hamo Thornycroft.
[2] Emslie John Horniman (1863–1932), whose recreations were art and travel

THE STUNT

One night he crawled through wire and mud and found a score
Of Saxon peasants half-asleep, and wet and scared.
Three men he killed outright, and wounded several more.
But Gentle Jesus kept *him* safe; his life was spared.
At dawn we took the trench; and found it full of dead.
And for his deed the man received a D.S.O.
'How splendid. O how splendid!' his relations said,
But what the weeping Saxons said I do not know.

VIA CRUCIS

'Mud and rain and wretchedness and blood'.
Why should jolly soldier-boys complain?
God made these before the roofless Flood—
Mud and rain.

Mangling crumps and bullets through the brain,
Jesus never guessed them when He died.
Jesus had a purpose for His pain,
Ay, like abject beasts we shed our blood,
Often asking if we die in vain.
Gloom conceals us in a soaking sack—
Mud and rain.

[S.S. spent the next three months at Weirleigh, riding and
hunting. There is no surviving diary from here until the end of
S.S's sick-leave in December, so we lack his immediate impres-
sion of his first meeting with Lady Ottoline Morrell. This
remarkable lady (1872–1938) was half-sister to the sixth Duke
of Portland. In 1902 she had married Philip Morrell, a Liberal
politician (1870–1943), and in 1915 they had come to live in
the lovely Garsington Manor, near Oxford, where they har-
boured and befriended many leading pacifists and intellectuals.
S.S's friend Robbie Ross[1] came down to Oxford for the day
and drove S.S. over to Garsington. S.S. vividly described the

[1] Robert Baldwin Ross (1869–1918). Literary journalist and art critic. Faithful
friend of Oscar Wilde. S.S. had first met him at the Gosses' in 1915. See
Siegfried's Journey.

occasion years later in *Siegfried's Journey*, pp. 7–11, but Lady Ottoline's contemporary diary entry was printed in *Ottoline at Garsington* (1974):

> Daisy came to say, 'Mr Ross has come to see you.' Looking down I saw standing in the doorway a young man in khaki.
>
> Robbie Ross said, 'This is Siegfried Sassoon.'
>
> I could hardly believe it. Ever since I had read his poems I had thought of him, and had wondered if we should ever meet, and here he stood.
>
> We went to tea, which was already laid in the garden. While he and Philip and Robbie Ross were talking I watched him. He sat up very erect and turned his head in a peculiar stiff movement to one side. Although he talked a good deal he had a trick of hesitating over his sentences as if he were shy, but still he was full of humour and laughed and was gay, always keeping his head erect and looking down. Perhaps it was his way of turning his head, and the lean face with green hazel eyes, his ears large and rather protruding, and the nose with wide nostrils, that made me think of a stag's head or a faun. He was not exactly *farouche* but he seemed very shy and reserved, he was more *sauvage*; and, as I looked at his full face I said to myself, 'He could be cruel.'
>
> They did not remain very long, as Siegfried Sassoon had to return to the hospital in Oxford, having been ill with fever. They drove off in a taxi and as they disappeared I saw them laughing gaily together, each holding up in front of their face a peacock feather that I had given them.]

When thou must home to shades of underground,
And there arrived, a new admirèd guest,
The beauteous spirits do engirt thee round,
White Iope, blithe Helen, and the rest,
To hear the stories of thy finished love
From that smooth tongue whose music hell can move;

Then wilt thou speak of banqueting delights,
Of masques and revels which sweet youth did make,
Of tourneys and great challenges of knights,
And all those triumphs for thy beauty's sake:
When thou hast told these honours done to thee,
Then tell, O tell, how thou dids't murder me!

(Campion)[1]

I fall into the claws of Time:
But lasts within a leavèd rhyme
All that the world of me esteems—
My withered dreams, my withered dreams.

(Francis Thompson)[2]

December 22

Been at Litherland[3] since December 4. Robert Graves went on leave to-day, and will be going to France quite soon.[4] Haven't been able to get a hunt with the Cheshire since December 9 owing to hard weather. An occasional round by myself at Formby and several expensive gorges at the Adelphi have been my only pleasures (*sic*). Went to *Elijah* last Tuesday and was bored stiff. Mendelssohn is futile.

The only merit of this hut-life is that there are no women about. Plenty of fifth-rate officers—'Capel Sion Light Infantry'.[5] Orme, Morgan (C.D.), Bill Adams and R.G. the only First R.W.F. officers I know.[6] Julian Dadd came to Liverpool for one night. He has lost his voice, being hit in the throat; it was queer to see him so excited, telling us about the First Battalion show at Ginchy on September 3 in a strained whisper. Memory supplied his old voice.[7]

[1] *'Vobiscum est Iope'*.   [2] From 'The Poppy'.
[3] The R.W.F. Regimental Depot, near Liverpool.
[4] He went on January 20. S.S.
[5] Capel Sion was the setting of two volumes of savage stories about the peasants of West Wales—*My People* (1915) and *Capel Sion* (1916)—by the Welsh writer Caradoc Evans (1878–1945). They caused an outcry in Wales, were banned by the police, and copies of the books were ceremonially burnt in various villages.
[6] E. L. Orme killed 27 May 1917 with Second R.W.F. [S.S.'s poem 'To Any Dead Officer' was addressed to his ghost.] J. B. P. Adams killed in February 1917 with First Battalion. S.S.
[7] Cf. S.S.'s poem 'A Whispered Tale', published in *The Old Huntsman*.

I shall not go out till February unless I can't help it. The long
nights and cold weather are more than I can tackle.

Last Christmas was at Montagne. Richardson, Edmund Dadd,
Davies, Jackson, Pritchard, Thomas, Baynes, have been killed
since then.[1] The officers still with the Battalion who were there
then are Reeves, Brunicardi and Hawes, and of course old
Cotterill. I am more than twelve months older since then. 1916
has been a lucky year for me. This is a dreary drab flat place—
fog and bleary sunsets and smoky munition-works at night with
dotted lights and flares, and bugles blowing in the camp, and
sirens hooting out on the Mersey mouth, and the intolerable
boredom of Mess and not enough work to do, and people waiting
their turn to go out again. No one is at his best here. And the
men are mostly a poor lot—ill-trained truss-wearers, and
wounded ones. The year is dying of atrophy as far as I am con-
cerned, bed-fast in its December fogs. And the War is settling
down on everyone—a hopeless, never-shifting burden. While
newspapers and politicians yell and brandish their arms, and the
dead rot in their French graves, and the maimed hobble about
the streets. And the Kaiser talks about Peace because he thinks
he's won.

I seem to be acquiring the reputation of a *bon viveur*—the
result of melting fivers at the Adelphi. Some man said in Mess
to-night: 'These new regulations for food will tax your in-
genuity in ordering a dinner!' And the result is a disordered
liver, and cynical poetry. I wrote a beastly thing about a
butcher's shop to-day. I don't suppose it's any good either. I
wonder whether my boat will ever touch the shores of beauty
again. Those garden-dawns seem a very long way off now. And
nothing before me but red dawns flaring over Ypres and
Bapaume. And people still say the War is 'splendid', damn their
eyes. And the Army in France can contemplate a 'patched-up
peace' because it is so weary of the ways of death.

Christmas Eve

I have been wondering whether I shall be any better off
through going to the War again next year. Of course I've *got* to
go—I never doubted that; but if I'm there *another* eight months,

[1] And ten others wounded. Only four left of the old lot. S.S.

and come back *safely wounded* (!) shall I have anything more to say about it all, or shall I be more bitter, and unbalanced and callous? Not much use enquiring. It will be good fun in its way; and reading Sorley's letters has given me a cheer-up.[1] He was so ready for all emergencies, so ready to accept the 'damnable circumstance of death'—or life. Out at Formby to-day there was sunlight on the sandhills and low fir-trees, and the glory of clean air. And even Seaforth looked a better place than it is in the morning brightness—'a thicket of sunshine with blue smoke wreaths'—all roofs and chimneys and industry.

A sensible sort of man came into the hut after dinner, Owen of the one-leg, a Ceylon planter who got hit before he'd seen the Dardanelles two days. He asked me why there are no women in my verse. I told him they are outside my philosophy. He approved of 'Died of Wounds'—said he'd felt like that in hospital.

Christmas Day

Thirty-six holes at Formby: played alone before lunch. Afterwards played the best ball of two cheery Navy men, Fawcett and Dolphin, and beat them at the last hole. Fawcett had played cricket and hockey for the Navy *v.* Army. He told an amusing yarn of a Naval Rescue man in command of a mine-sweeper which struck a mine and sank in forty-five seconds. He was blown into the air and came down heavily through the chartroom skylight or somewhere, with a ton of water on his back, and laughed; the only impression he got was of men all round with hugely distended Boreas cheeks and bulging eyes, blowing up their lifebelts.

They say the U-boat blockade will get worse and there will be a bad food-shortage in England in 1917. The sideboard in this Formby golf-club doesn't look like it yet; enormous cold joints and geese and turkeys and a sucking pig and God knows what, and old men with their noses in their plates guzzling for all they're worth.

'On pain of death, let no man name death to me'

says John Webster.[2]

---

[1] *Letters from Germany and from the Army* by Charles Sorley, privately printed in 1916. A full edition of his letters was published in 1919.
[2] In *The White Devil*, V, sc. 1.

1916

'Death be not proud, though some have called thee
Mighty and dreadful, for thou art not so;
For those, whom thou think'st thou dost overthrow,
Die not, poor Death, nor yet canst thou kill me.'

says John Donne.[1]

And

'When you see millions of the mouthless dead
Across your dreams in pale battalions go,
Say not soft things as other men have said,
That you'll remember. For you need not so.'

says young Sorley.[2]

And when these professors have said their say, what shall I utter concerning the old ruffian? Nothing. I have jabbered at him too often. He'll glance his eye at me and tell me to wait my turn like a good lad.

Since Robert went away and I have been alone, I've been able to work. Some of the stuff may be all right. This Christmas night I did a grim, jeering, heart-rending sort of thing about a General taking the salute as we marched past him.

THE MARCH-PAST

In red and gold the Corps-Commander stood,
With ribboned breast puffed out for all to see:
He'd sworn to beat the Germans, if he could;
For God had taught him strength and strategy.
He was our leader, and a judge of port—
Rode well to hounds, and was a damned good sort.

'Eyes right!' We passed him with a jaunty stare.
'Eyes front!' He'd watched his trusted legions go.
I wonder if he guessed how many there
Would get knocked out of time in next week's show.
'Eyes right!' The corpse-commander was a Mute;
And Death leered round him, taking our salute.

And I remembered old wine-faced Rawlinson[3] at Flixécourt last

[1] In his sonnet 'Death'.
[2] From No. xxvii in Sorley's *Marlborough and Other Poems* (1916).
[3] Lieutenant-General Sir Henry Rawlinson (1864–1925), Commander of the Fourth Army.

May, as we swung down the hill with the band playing, two hundred officers and N.C.O's of his Fourth Army; and how many of them are alive and hale on Christmas Day? About half, I expect; perhaps less. But I'll warrant old Sir Henry made a good dinner in his château at Querrieux, good luck to him and his retinue! And now I'm going to sip some seventeenth-century poetry to send me happy to bed with the wind moaning round the huts, and the stove-light dying redly in the corner.

> For 'tis a duteous thing
> To show all honour to an earthly king,
> And after all our travail and our cost,
> So he be pleased, to think no labour lost.
> But at the coming of the King of Heaven
> All's set at six and seven:
> We wallow in our sin.
> Christ cannot find a chamber in the inn.
>
> (Fragment from Christ Church MS)

> Let not the dark thee cumber;
> What though the moon does slumber?
>   The stars of the night
>   Will lend thee their light,
> Like tapers clear, without number.
>
> Herrick[1]

Boxing Day

Quite an interesting evening. I went in to Mess feeling low and rotten; drank three glasses of champagne, port, liqueur brandy, and sat by the stove in the Mess-room while someone played the tin-kettle piano: felt happily semi-tight; cigar in one corner of mouth. Then a man called Syrett[2] began to play, flashy Bohemian-style of rattling off ragtime, sentimental songs, anything suitable to the occasion, ending with a Bowdlerised version of Debussy's *Clair de Lune*. So I asked him to come and smoke a cigarette in my hut. And he transpired to be a quite interesting, semi-theatrical cosmopolitan. Seemed to know the Balkans—Bucharest, Jassy, Vienna, and Hanover etc. His cousin married

---

[1] From 'The Night-Piece: to Julia'.
[2] A. M. Syrett. Killed with First R.W.F. in April 1917. S.S.

1916

Ionescu the Roumanian statesman. So I talked myself silly, and said everything rash I could; what a funny life it is!

December 27

Medical Board gave me another month's home service. Went to Repertory Theatre to meet Dent and lunch with Bridges-Adams, the manager;[1] But Dent missed his train from Manchester, or something, so I went back to the Adelphi and lunched with Bobbie Hanmer, just back from a bombing-course; he's gone to Clapham Bombing School this evening, leaving a noble-looking pipe in my hut—and a scrawl—'With love: just off to bloody Clapham. R.H.H.' Very characteristic.

Another sharp frost and thick fog this morning. Reading Curzon's *Monasteries in the Lavant*[2] which Meiklejohn[3] sent me at Christmas. More amusing than *Eothen*,[4] but Doughty's *Arabia Deserta* spoils one for every other book of that sort. About a dozen officers in the waiting-room this morning, all looking conscious of their ailments, real and imaginary, probably all got tight or something last night, in order to look their worst: apparently I did too, but the two drowsy old Colonels hardly glanced at me; blue papers are what they rely on.

Those four months away from the Army blotted out the slight sense of discipline I had managed to acquire, much against my will. I want to go off and play golf and be independent and alone, all the time. My absurd decoration is the only thing that gives me any sense of responsibility at all. And the thought of death is horrible, where last year it was a noble and inevitable dream. And nothing left but to watch the last flare-up, and try to dodge through to the end, 'the victory that is more terrible than defeat' —exhaustion, and blind men with medals, and everyone trying to clear up their lives, like children whose little make-believes have been smashed and ruined in the night.

Mr Britling says: 'Everywhere cunning, everywhere

[1] William Bridges-Adams (1889–1965), theatrical producer, designer and historian. Director at Stratford-upon-Avon 1919–34.

[2] *Visits to Monasteries in the Levant* by Robert Curzon (1849).

[3] Roderick Sinclair Meiklejohn (1876–1962), senior Treasury official. Knighted 1931.

[4] *Eothen, or Traces of Travel brought home from the East* (1844) by A. W. Kinglake (1809–91).

small feuds and hatreds, distrusts, dishonesties, timidities, feebleness of purpose, dwarfish imaginations, swarm over the great and simple issues . . . It is a war now like any other of the mobbing, many-aimed cataclysms that have shattered empires and devastated the world; it is a war without point, a war that has lost its soul, it has become mere incoherent fighting and destruction, a demonstration in vast and tragic forms of the stupidity and ineffectiveness of our species.'[1]

Remembering places by sounds is best. Litherland sounds are sirens from factories, and fog-horns out on the Mersey mouth; bugles, generally rather flat and badly blown. The hooters and fog-horns combine sometimes and make huge unhappy dissonances; once or twice I heard a rich ultra-modern chord, Stravinsky-ish. Then there are little noises, like servants' feet bustling up and down the hut-passages, and the more deliberate tread of sedate officers coming and going from meals and parades and anteroom vacuities. And the wind moans and soughs and hurooshes and rain spatters and hail drums over the hut-roofs. And all these noises and sounds and camp-clatterings make a picture of the grey, foggy, smoke-drifted factories and villas and roads that one sees from the Mess; all the disconsolate vignettes of the country round here, meagre trees, drab fields, and flatness dotted and heaped with sheds and munition-making gear. And the canal, and the few farms, that look scared of the encroaching suburbs—sooty-looking farms with no touch of bucolic cheeriness about them; dishevelled parcels of land, whose chief features are manure-heaps and pigsties. On the P.T. field this afternoon, frost gone out of the ground left everything liquid squash. A grey, darkening sky, and warm west wind: haze settling down with dusk. Clumsy recruits and (*sic*) 'trained-men', doing bayonet-exercises. '*On* garrrd! Long-point at the stomach' etc. Red-and-black-striped-jersey instructors with well-poised bodies and wasp-waists, moving easily among the bunchy, awkward privates—pathetic crowd of willy-nilly patriots and (?) heroes! Johnny Basham the boxer, still wearing the bruises of his big fight two nights ago, grim brute, bullying a squad. 'At the throat: point!' and so on, till they all march away in the twilight,

---

[1] *Mr Britling Sees it Through* by H. G. Wells (1916), Bk II, Chap. 4.

back to the dreary huts; and a funeral-cortège trots merrily down the road from the cemetery, showing faint lamps, leaving its burden safe among the glimmering monuments. Hooot! goes a factory siren. And I turn away in a drizzle of rain.

> O sleepless heart and sombre soul unsleeping,
>> That were athirst for sleep and no more life
>> And no more love, for peace and no more strife!
> Now the dim gods of death have in their keeping
>> Spirit and body and all the springs of song.
>
> (Swinburne, 'Ave atque Vale')

December 30

Cheshire: Tiverton Smithy. A fine, warm sort of day, breezy with clouds about. Found at Huxley and ran nicely for about a mile, then turned left-handed and hunted him very slowly back to Clotton cover and lost him. Took a goodish fall over some post-and-rails with a big ditch on the far side. All grass, but a lot of wire. Very little to jump—typical Cheshire fences. Drew Stapleton and Waverton blank. Found at Crow's Nest at 2.30, but he was twice headed on the road and ran a short circle out by the railway and back past the cover, and after that they never had the line. A very disappointing hunt; scent very moderate all day. Went back to Beeston Station and on to Spittal with Brocklebank,[1] and had a cheery evening at his home. Back to the huts at 12.

December 31

Played golf at Formby and got rather wet. Robert [Graves] (with niblick) played the fool and rather annoyed my serious golfing temperament.

[1] R. Brocklebank. Killed with First R.W.F. in May 1917. S.S.

1917

I have beheld the agonies of war
Through many a weary season; seen enough
To make me hold that scarcely any goal
Is worth the reaching by so red a road.
                    Hardy, *The Dynasts*, III, 5, v

1917

January 4

Coming out of the dreary hour-and-a-half of Mess and utter boredom, there was a cold north wind blowing, and a bright, high moon, and enormous clouds moving toward Liverpool, dark clouds with broad white-shining edges and crowns, piled half-way up the sky—one making a huge canopy for the lights and shuttered smoky glare and muffled din of the munition-works.

Out at Knowsley all day, in the wind and scudding showers and cold hastening sunshine, we did a silly attack on a brown ferny hill with a statue on the top.

A Copenhagen paper (December 2) says, 'The sons of Europe are being crucified in the barbed wire enclosures because the misguided masses are shouting for it. They do not know what they do, and the statesmen wash their hands. They dare not deliver them from their martyr's death.' Is this true?

1917

January 6

Cheshire: Peckforton Gap. Found in the Gardens at Chol-
mondeley but lost him as soon as he went away. Found at Bar
Mere about 12.50 (a brace) and went away toward Bickley and
back past the cover and toward Norbury Common and right-
handed ring to Marbury, where he got in a big earth. About
fifty minutes: they ran nicely at times. Had another slow hunt
round the same country and lost him. Got back to Tilston
about 5. Best day I've had with the Cheshire, but nothing won-
derful. Very little wire about.

ENEMIES

He stood alone in some queer sunless place
Where the dead soldiers go: perhaps he longed
For what he'd lost with life; but his quiet face
Gazed out untroubled; and suddenly there thronged
Round him the hulking Germans that I shot
When my mad anger for his death was hot.

He stared at them unmoved and grave; and then
They told him that I'd killed them for his sake;
Those patient, stupid, sullen ghosts of men;
And still there was no answer he could make.
At last he turned and smiled; and all was well,
Because his face could lead them out of hell. [1]

January 8

The most Mondayish of Monday mornings—rain and howl-
ing wind. Twenty officers going to France to-morrow, including
Brocklebank and Barter V.C. [2]

There were three Company Commanders going over the
parapet for a peculiarly nasty attack. Two of them made the
usual sort of remarks to their officers. They were shortly after-
wards killed. The third Company Commander said very little to

---

[1] Published, slightly revised, in *The Old Huntsman*. Further revised for *Collected
Poems*.
[2] Company Sergeant-Major Barter had won the Victoria Cross at Festubert in
May 1915.

his officers—until the zero-time was due in a few minutes. For
he was very much afraid. But before they started for their objec-
tive he spoke to them and said with a most determined air:
'Remember that I shall not recommend any of you until I have
got something myself.' He was not killed, nor even wounded.
But he has got the Military Cross for bragging to the Brigadier.

> When I am in a blaze of lights,
> With tawdry music and cigars
> And women sipping cheap delights,
> And officers at cocktail bars;
> Sometimes I think of garden-nights,
> And elm trees nodding at the stars.
>
> I dream of a small firelit room,
> With yellow candles burning straight,
> And glowing pictures in the gloom,
> And some kind book that holds me late.
> Of things like these I love to think,
> Where I can never be alone,
> Till someone says 'Another drink?'
> And turns my living heart to stone.[1]

January 10
  A typical Wednesday night (Guest night; the only guest being
Captain Moody on leave from the Second Battalion, with two
years' trench service and M.C. and bar). A little nonentity with
a pudding face and black hair, but a stout soldier and worthy of
his laurels. I left them singing any old drivel to the strains of the
tin-kettle piano, and the rain pattering on the roof. Why should
a little silver rosette on an M.C. ribbon make one want to go
back to hell? If I had a crimson ribbon [i.e. a V.C.] I should be
no better soldier, no worse. It is blood and brains that tell; blood
in the mud, and brains smashed up by bullets. Where's all the
poetry gone then? But my book will be in print next month.
Robert was very excited and portwineish. Shouting catches
louder than any of them. And yet he's hundreds of aeons in front
of most of them, and a magical name for young poets in 1980, if
only he survives this carnage.

[1] Published, slightly revised, in *The Old Huntsman*.

January 12

I sent Ottoline Morrell a book of poems[1] the other day, and this morning comes her reply, full of superlatives. Does she really admire my things as much as all that?

January 15

Down on Seaforth sands this morning everything was drab and white and lead-grey. Snow on the sand and grey-brown fog at sea and a lowering snow-sky. And snow quietly filling up the wrinkles in the hard sand. It has stopped in the afternoon, but freezes now. Searchlight reflected made a bar of light on the canal to-night.

On Saturday (January 13) the Cheshire were at Calverley Hall, near Tarporley; after a rather frosty morning, they found at Calverley New Gorse and ran quite nicely by Paradise and Hills Gorse, and over the railway at Wardle Bank, and along on the right of it—by the canal to point 147, where they appeared to be beat. Short made a cast up toward Cholmondeston Hall, but did no good, and cast right-handed on to Poole Hall, where a fresh fox got up in one of the covers and they were hunting him for two hours. He ran two rings left-handed and back to Poole and then away again and on to Acton where he got in at ten past four. Quite good fun but a bad fox. He got in a wet drain, very hard luck for the bitches. I rode back to Catebrook with them—only one other stayed to the end. Stayed the night at Wistaston Hall and danced at Alvaston. Came home yesterday afternoon.

A few hours in the pre-war surroundings—'Loderism' and so on. Pleasant enough; but what a decayed society, hanging blindly on to the shreds of its traditions. The wet, watery-green meadows and straggling bare hedges and grey winding lanes; the cry of hounds, and thud of hoofs, and people galloping bravely along all around me; and the ride home with hounds in the chilly dusk—those are *real* things. But comfort and respectable squiredom and the futile chatter of women, and their man-hunting glances, and the pomposity of port-wine-drinking buffers—what's all that but emptiness? These people don't reason. They echo one another and their dead relations, and what they read in

[1] The privately printed *Morning-Glory* (1916).

papers and dull books. And they only *see* what they want to see—
which is very little beyond the tips of their red noses. Debrett is
on every table; and heaven a sexless peerage, with a suitable
array of dependents and equipages where God is [*page torn
out*].

Another bright spark is [*name obliterated*], who has just re-
turned from three weeks' sick leave with his mistress, a widow
at Waterloo, quite near. He has been suffering from gonorrhoea
(he called it an injury caused by riding). He has been here nearly
eighteen months since he was sent home from the First Bat-
talion. What earthly use are all these people? They don't
instruct anyone; they simply eat and drink. I think nearly half
the officers in our Army are conscripted humbugs who are paid
to propagate inefficiency. They aren't even willing to be killed;
I can at least say *that* for myself, for I've tried often. Twelve
months ago to-day my poem appeared in *The Times*: 'To
Victory',[1] and it's not arrived yet—not the sort of victory I
meant. And since then I've been lucky. Things might have gone
just a little differently, and all those decent poems I've done
since then might never have been written. Now I've got my
book fixed up, and there's nothing to do but wait for something
else to happen to set my emotions going in a blue and crimson
flare-up—mostly blue—with a touch of yellow (for liver). Now
I've really got a grip of the idea of life and describing it, I hope I
shan't get myself killed in 1917. There's such a lot to say. Love
and beauty and death and bitterness and anger.

> England has many heroes; they are known
> To all who read of German armies beat.
> One chap got drunk and took a trench alone,
> And grinned to cheering mobs in every street.
> Though England's proud of him—her stuffed V.C.—
> No medal was attached to his D.T.
> Think of the D.C.M's and D.S.O's
> And breasts that swell with Military Crosses;
> They are the pomps of War; and no one knows
> Nor cares to count the bungling and the losses.
> But I would rather shoot one General Dolt
> Than fifty harmless Germans; and I've seen

[1] See p. 32.

1917

Ten thousand soldiers, tabbed with blue and green,
Who, if they heard one shell, would crouch and bolt.
But when the War is done they'll shout and sing,
And fetch bright medals from their German King.

January 17
A draft of a hundred and fifty 'proceeded' to France to-night.
Most of them half-tight, except those who had been in the
guard-room to stop them bolting (again), and the Parson's
speech went off, to the usual asides and witticisms. He ended:
'And God go with you. I shall go as far as the station with you.'[1]
Then the C.O. stuttered a few inept and ungracious remarks.
'You are going out to the Big Push which will end the war' etc
(groans). And away they marched to beat of drums—a pathetic
scene of humbug and cant. How much more impressive if they
went in silence, with no foolishness of 'God Speed'—like
Hardy's 'men who march away . . . To hazards whence no tears
can win us'.[2]

January 18
Gulls were flapping and calling; the tide was low; the sea
level; ships—one full-rigged—and steamers and a liner slipped
along, grey ghosts across the water, and the houses ashore were
grey ghosts too—only *they* did not move. So I stood on the sand-
flats between the two with a quiet cloudy hazy sky overhead and
a little frosty wind blowing the smoke from the north. Then the
sun began to come out, as I stood on the huge, green-stained
sewer-pipes, and the mud-flats were beaten-silver with level
water creeping in as level as a sheet, and across the Mersey
mouth the sea was shining pale coppery-gold. Then the sun
went in again, and the arena of sand and sea was drab. And some
soldiers flapped and wagged their signal-flags—tiny figures
hundreds of yards away along the shore; crusted with melt-
ing ice.

[1] This has since been attributed to the Commanding Officer. J. C. Dunn gives him
(through hearsay) the story (p. 345 of *The War the Infantry Knew*). S.S.
[2] The fifth line of 'Men who March Away' as printed in *The Times* of 9 September
1914 and in *Satires of Circumstance* (1914). In *Moments of Vision* (1917) and
subsequently it became 'Leaving all that here can win us'.

1917

This afternoon I sent Robert's new poems to the Chiswick Press.[1] Only nine of them—but the best work he has done, or will do for some time, I am afraid.

A Captain from the Second Battalion, on leave, was here last night. He said the soldiers in France regard the end of the war in the summer as certain. It will be a successful Push and victory, or else—failure and a patched-up peace!

January 20

Robert left for France to-day with nine other officers. This little pamphlet of verse he is getting out will keep his mind occupied and take away a little of the blankness of going out for the third time. We have had more than six weeks here together. Lucky to get that in these uncertain times. I wonder if he will *really* get killed this time. One never expects anything else, so perhaps the green of summer will bring relief. I don't think it will. I don't, I don't. It was a raw drizzling day—suitable for the event.

Cheerful Bobbie Hanmer is in the hut with me now. His conversation consists mainly in winding his watch and brushing his hair. But he is a dear, though not *quite* so adorable as he was in October 1915, when his radiance first broke in on me. And I fell in love with his kind eyes and ingenuous looks. But he would be a good person to die for, and suffer with, and I hope I'll get the chance.

No hunting to-morrow as it has been freezing all the week. And Robert's gone.

April will come again, and sunrays be shafting among the hazels and beeches, and birds be flitting low and startled, and shallow brooks be juggling with the glitter of noon. Slowly the big white clouds will sail across to Lebanon and its blue-green slopes. And all the music of the earth and of men's hearts must be destroyed, because man desires only the things that he had put behind him—killing, and the pride of women with child by a warrior. O their gluttonous eyes: I think they love war, for all their lamenting over the sons and lovers.

When I go out again I will be mad as ever. And the others will laugh at my secret frenzy. But the loveliness of earth will

[1] *Goliath and David*, of which two hundred copies were privately printed.

be a torment and a sweet tumult in my heart. And I shall be
longing for the humility of green fields and quiet woods. I shall
be longing for lonely hills and skies flushed with morning glory.
And nights that were one rich chord that echoes and murmurs
from a thousand strings, and fades not, until the stars go out and
the birds begin their merry jargon in thicket and garden.

January 21

A funny mixture—reading *The Brook Kerith*[1] and talking to
simple, white-souled Bobbie about 'religion and the war' in a
rambling sort of monologue. (I don't remember B. saying any-
thing at all!) But it all came back to me—the anxious unsettled
ideas of last spring and summer—desire of death—emotion at
facing danger unafraid—repugnance at the commonplace gross-
ness of the majority and their incessant chatter about 'Blighty'
and 'cushy wounds'—their little souls wanting nothing nobler
than to creep safely home to—what? But Bobbie at least under-
stands the feeling of self-sacrifice—immolation to some vague
aspiration—whether our cause be a just one or not. Yet I never
could find anyone who really got any value out of the Christian
theology—out there. It was all 'Carry on' and 'Get there some-
how'. They did not 'walk the secret way with anger in their
brain'[2] or see 'Love, a great Angel stand Gazing far beyond
Time', as Abercrombie says so finely.[3]

From *The Brook Kerith*

> Very soon, he said, the hills will be folded in a dim blue
> veil, and sleep will perchance blot out the misery that has
> brooded in me all this livelong day, he muttered. May I
> never see another, but close my eyes for ever on the broad
> ruthless light. Of what avail to witness another day? All
> days are alike to me.
> It seemed to Joseph that he was of a sort dead already,

---

[1] By George Moore. First published on 23 August 1916.
[2] From S.S.'s poem 'A Mystic as Soldier', written in November 1916:
    I walk the secret way
    With anger in my brain.
[3] Presumably Lascelles Abercrombie (1881–1938), but I have failed to trace this
    line.

for he could detach himself from himself, and consider himself as indifferently as he might a blade of grass. My life, he said, is like these bare hills, and the one thing left for me to desire is death.

(p. 104)

He recalled with singular distinctness and pleasure the fine broad brow curving upwards—a noble arch, he said to himself—the eyes distant as stars and the underlying sadness in his voice oftentimes soft and low, but with a cry in it; and he remembered how their eyes met, and it seemed to Joseph that he read in the shepherd's eyes a look of recognition and amity.

(p. 97)

January 22
'Old Man' Greaves came back to-day, fat, belted and burly, after five months sick-leave since he got wounded at Bazentin last July. Fat red cheeks and shining pince-nez, just the same. And the laugh that used to be so much inspired by whisky in those dirty dug-outs on the Somme.
Lieutenant X is a nasty, cheap thing. A cheap-gilt Jew. Why are such Jews born, when the soul of Jesus was so beautiful? *He* saw the flowers and the stars; but they see only greasy banknotes and the dung in the highway where they hawk their tawdry wares. 'In Whitechapel was heard a voice' . . .

He began to speak to Joseph of God, his speech moving on with a gentle motion like that of clouds wreathing and unwreathing, finding new shapes for every period, and always beautiful shapes. He often stopped speaking and his eyes became fixed, as if he saw beyond the things we all see.
(*The Brook Kerith*, p. 122)

I am no suicide, I am condemned to die. Do not make the struggle too hard for me! I may not live. My body has taken possession of my soul, therefore I must let it escape and go to God.
(*Gösta Berling*)[1]

[1] *Gösta Berlings Saga* (1891), a novel by the Swedish author Selma Lagerlöf (1858–1940).

1917

January 23

[A few bars of Elgar's Violin Concerto] *pp nobilmente* etc
made me glorious with dreams to-night. Elgar always moves me
deeply, because his is the melody of an average Englishman (and
I suppose I am more or less the same).

And Ravel painted a Spanish garden nocturne for me; and
there was the Irish Derry tune too. The Ravel was exquisitely
delicate and brilliant. In all the noblest passages and the noblest
strains of horns and violins I shut my eyes, seeing on the dark-
ness a shape always the same—in spite of myself—the suffering
mortal figure on a cross, but the face is my own. And again there
are hosts of shadowy forms with uplifted arms—souls of men,
agonised and aspiring, hungry for what they seek as God in
vastness.

THE ELGAR VIOLIN CONCERTO

I have seen Christ, when music wove
Exulting vision; storms of prayer
Deep-voiced within me marched and strove.
The sorrows of the world were there.

A God for beauty shamed and wronged?
A sign where faith and ruin meet,
In glooms of vanquished glory thronged
By spirits blinded with defeat?

His head forever bowed with pain,
In all my dreams he looms above
The violin that speaks in vain—
The crowned humility of love.

O music undeterred by death,
And darkness closing on your flame,
Christ whispers in your dying breath,
And haunts you with his tragic name.[1]

A bitter attack on Oliver Lodge's[2] spook book in the *Daily*

[1] Published, slightly revised, in *Siegfried's Journey*.
[2] Physicist and leading spiritualist (1851–1940). His book *Raymond* (1916)
described his spirit-communications with his dead son.

[124]

Mail. Stuff like *Raymond* repels me utterly. Having discovered the fatuity of it in my own case, and watched that pathetic, foolish clinging to the dead which goes on among so many women who (like my own mother) have nothing else to distract their minds from war and wretchedness. It is the *worst* confession of weakness—a ridiculous hiding of one's head in a stuffy cupboard, when there is the whole visible earth outside the windows. If I am killed, no doubt my [*page torn out*].

Shrivelled by icy blasts, I went an hour's footpath-walk among starved, colourless fields and cowering, straggly thorn-hedges; skirting chimney-pots and the factories whose thin smoke-streamers flew with the sunless, bitter north wind. Once I watched a scattering of gulls that followed the newly-turned furrows; their harsh wrangle mingling with the faint creak and rattle of the plough, as they swung and settled like enormous grey snow-flakes. While the team halted at the hedge, and the man was turning, with a grumble at the wretchedness of the afternoon, they all sat still like some cloaked, attentive congregation, yet their bills were busy at the soil: then the big steady horses moved forward again, with a confusion of dull-silvery wings flickering in the wake of the toilers, as the queer procession began another journey across the stubble.

The rain has ceased. Broken clouds drift slowly from the west, glorious with fringes of evening colour. On a hillside I am alone with my happiness, hearing everywhere the faint drip and rustle of summer green: there is a stirring in the grass; each flower has a message to give me. All sounds are small and distinct, as though they expressed the liquid clarity of the air. The country is now properly arrayed in a sort of rich calm, shining and yet subdued and gracious.

The roofs and stacks of the farm among its trees below the hill, the farm-house chimney with its wisp of smoke, a bird winging out across the valley-orchards, and the sound of a train going steadily on, miles away—all are as I would have them, as I would keep them remembered. I am back in childhood; home with my kind dreams; soon I shall hear my brother's voice along the garden, where moths will be fluttering like flowers that are free from their hot parades in sunshine, free to go where they will among the dimness of quiet alleys. O brother, tell me what you have seen to-day, what have you done?

He will not answer, for he is dead. And I am far from the garden, far from the summer that is past. I am alone in this bitter winter of unending war.

I don't think purely descriptive verse should be rhymed, but should sometimes give a feeling of rhyme-endings (a sort of 'singing-touch' effect).

Shall I ever be alone, until I am dead? Having settled down in the hope of a couple of hours' quiet to try and get this poem worked out, I do three lines and am fairly under way; in comes old Greaves and squats down for nearly an hour talking about the war (and advising me not to go back to it!). Then a few minutes' peace, and I get started again with poetry. But Bobbie must needs return from Liverpool laden with apples and magazines and pipe-cleaners etc and I could almost cry, or else shout and break something. Even Bobbie is not welcome when I am trying to write verse. Somehow or other I got the thing finished anyhow. But my serenity suffered, and probably the poem did too.

SERENITY

The storm was done; low wreathing drifts of cloud
Drove outward from the sunset, fringed with flame
And splendid as the wind whereon they came.

I listened; and there fell faint rhythmic tunes
Of drip and rustle along the oak-thronged hill;
With stir of rain-washed grass, and tinkling rill.

A lonely kestrel winged across the vale,
High over fields and orchards; and these words
Came with the evening voices of the birds.

January 24–25

The twilight had vanished and the stars were coming out, and Joseph said to himself: there will be no moon, only a soft starlight, and he stood gazing at the desert showing through a great tide of blue shadow, the shape of the hills emerging, like the hulls of great ships afloat in a shadowy sea.

(*The Brook Kerith*, p. 238)

May we start to-night? Jesus asked, and Joseph said: if a
man be minded to leave, it is better that he should leave
at once.

(p. 287)

January 27

There were two silver-haired men in khaki uniforms sitting
at a table; they peered at blue and white sheets of paper, the one
with waxed moustaches half-turned as the door opened for the
twentieth time that morning, and a young man came into the
dreary office. 'Feel fit to go out?' 'Yes, quite well, thank you.'
The pen began to move on a blue sheet: 'Has been passed fit for
General Ser . . .' 'Don't shake the table!' (The young officer was
tapping his fingers nervously.) The other colonel looked mildly
up over his pince-nez. All the shaking in the world wouldn't stop
that War. Waxed-moustache had signed another death-warrant.
Mine. As I went out into the grey street and the bitter east wind
I felt as if a load had been lifted from my sullen heart. I'd got
another chance given me to die a decent death. And a damned
uncomfortable one, probably. But I can't leave at once; it will be
three or four weeks before I go away.

Got the first lot of proof-sheets of my book this morning. 'The
Old Huntsman' looks first-class in print.

EPITAPH

If I should ever be in England's thought
    After I die,
Say, 'There were many things he might have bought,
    And did not buy.

Unhonoured by his fellows, he grew old,
    And trod the path to hell,
But there were many things he might have sold,
    And did not sell.'

(T. W. H. Crosland)

January 28

I have lived and dreamed so immune, since August, that
without knowing it I had forgotten the significance of 'going out

again', although the thought of it has passed in my head a thousand times, but only as a shadow, not the real storming tumult of fiends and angels.

Now the wings of death are over me once more. And while my body cries out that they are a savage threat (cowering as a bird under the hawk's shadow in the sun) something within me lifts adoring hands, something is filled with noble passion and desire for that benison and promise of freedom. And all the greatness that was mine last year shall be mine again; and what that happiness means, who shall say, or foretell the end and the sequel?

January 29

Went to a concert of chamber music in a restaurant with glaring electric light and people sitting at tables. There was a curious old man next to me—very blind, dirty, with a flowing beard and a lop-sided wig and the most tattered raiment. But he knew all about music and modern composers and performers, and had a pleasant, refined voice. 'The first thing was melodious; the second trivial, and the third music with the right stuff in it' was his accurate summary of the concert, which consisted of Fauré's Quartet, Delius's Violin and Piano Sonata (new), and César Franck's Quintet—all very well played by Arthur Catterall[1] and his men (the pianist R. J. Forbes).

January 30

Weather still dreary and harsh, looks like snow, very severe frost since January 22. Procter in here very elated as he'd been passed for General Service again. Having been wounded at the first Battle of Ypres in November 1914, at Gallipoli in November 1915, and gassed at Plug Street Wood in October 1916, one would think he's had enough of General Service!

This time last year we'd just got up to Morlancourt for the first time. And *two* years ago I left Canterbury with my broken arm and got home for two months of writing nature-poems. And three years ago I was having my hunting stopped by a week's frost, and wondering if life would ever be anything but utterly futile!

[1] Violinist (1883–1943). Leader of the Hallé Orchestra.

And now I'm sitting by a stove in a stuffy hut and reading a silly book by Arnold Bennett. And it don't matter to him whether I like his book or not, or whether I'm dead by breakfast-time.

February 1

Heard from Robert to-day. He has reached the Second Battalion and is in trenches at Frise—on the Somme.

February 2

Weather rather warmer, and glimpses of the sun this morning. I was walking on the sands, alone with gulls (and the *Mauretania* in Gladstone Dock). Then an hour after lunch taking evidence about some ridiculous 'bulged rifles', then an hour till 5.30 handing silver coins to the men, to the value of £75 odd. And now reading Charles Lister's letters[1] in the hut and feeling deadly tired and depressed. I suppose I'll worry along somehow in France. How, I don't quite know.

Wilfrid Gibson's new poems[2] arrived to-day. He seems laying himself out to be a sort of Crabbe (modernised on Masefield lines). Some of it is very good, but diffuse; the rhymed endings don't tell at all—might as well be blank-verse, or prose. And surely 'Ten thousand, seven hundred and eleven' (printed in figures) is a pretty poor line!

February 5

Went to concert at Crane Hall—a most tawdry-looking place. Josef Holbrooke (that third-rate composer and second-rate pianist) played some very bad things of his own, absolute trash. They also did his Diabolique Quintet, which was very little better. But Glazounov Quartet, Op. 26, was fine. Came out into the dark streets, with a tram moaning like a huge sorrowful bass-viol. The tall buildings and narrow streets behind the Exchange loomed magical in mist and moonlight, towers and

---

[1] The Hon. Charles Lister, only son of the fourth Lord Ribblesdale, had died of wounds at Gallipoli in August 1915, aged twenty-seven. His *Letters and Recollections, with a Memoir by his Father* were published in January 1917.
[2] *Livelihood* (1917).

chimneys vast and strange-looking. Up by the camp, black-and-white scheme of hedges and frozen snow—and the hell-workshop hissing and throbbing at making T.N.T.

Off on leave for a week to-morrow.

Viscount Morley says of Lloyd George: 'In Veracity an Ananias; in Friendship a Brutus; for the rest of his character refer to Marconi.'[1]

Jangling bell calling people back—Marlborough, early morning in dormitory, white horse hill—back to fiddles tuning up and yammer of concert-audience, via Sorley. Then Beethoven's Fifth Symphony begins and I go out from the gallery—miles away across the open air with the music following me, following the music.

Man with black beard—sallow—a little like Cockerell[2]—Cowen[3] taps sharply—people cough and stop talking. Finish with jolly tune and Hardy rustics dancing round Shepherd's Hey—and down the hill in a tram.

February 7 (Weirleigh)

At home again—for the last time before I go back to the unmitigated hell of 'the spring offensive'.

A bright fire burning, Topper licking his paws in an armchair, two candles alight, the friendly books all round me on their shelves, and blue moonlight filtering through the white curtains from the dazzling white snow and clear stars outside, while the wind makes a little crooning in the chimneys, and the hall clock strikes ten. And poor old Mother quite cheerful. I am afraid she don't realise that I am for France this month. And I was playing Morris dances and old English airs on the piano, so gay and full of green fields.

February 11

Breakfast with Eddie Marsh[4] at Gray's Inn. Lunch at the

---

[1] See *The Marconi Scandal* by Frances Donaldson (1962).
[2] Sydney Cockerell (1867–1962). Director of the Fitzwilliam Museum, Cambridge 1908–37. Knighted 1934.
[3] Sir Frederic Cowen, composer and conductor (1852–1935). Knighted 1911.
[4] Edward Marsh (1872–1953), civil servant, translator, patron of poets and painters. Knighted 1937. See *The Weald of Youth.*

Reform with Meiklejohn and Robbie Ross. Tea at Gower Street with 'Brett'[1] to inspect her vast portrait of Ottoline Morrell. Dinner at Gosse's.[2]

At 1.45 a.m. bed. S.S: 'To cheer you I will tell you, as a good end to the day, that the Poet Laureate's house was burnt to the ground last Friday. I wonder what caused the conflagration!' Robbie Ross: 'Dry rot, I expect.' (*Exeunt.*)

> Let me enjoy the earth no less
> Because the all-enacting Might
> That fashioned forth its loveliness
> Had other aims than my delight . . .
>
> From manuscripts of moving song
> Inspired by scenes and dreams unknown
> I'll pour out raptures that belong
> To others, as they were my own.
>
> And some day hence, toward Paradise
> And all its blest—if such should be—
> I will lift glad, afar-off eyes,
> Though it contain no place for me.
>
> (Thomas Hardy)[3]

Books taken to France
  Shakespeare's Tragedies
  Hardy's *Dynasts*
  Hardy's (Golden Treasury) Poems
  Conrad, *Nostromo* and *A Set of Six*
  Lamb's Essays and Letters (selection)
  Chaucer, *Canterbury Tales*

15 February
  Left Waterloo 12 noon. Irish Hussar in carriage. Sunshine at Southampton. Skite by Haig in daily papers: 'we shall demolish the enemy' etc.

[1] The Hon. Dorothy Brett (1883–1977), daughter of the second Viscount Esher. Painter, friend and disciple of D. H. Lawrence.
[2] Edmund Gosse, critic and man of letters (1849–1928). Knighted 1925. S.S. first met him in 1910. See *The Weald of Youth*.
[3] From 'Let Me Enjoy' in *Time's Laughingstocks* (1909).

Left London feeling nervous and rattled; but the worried feeling wears off once aboard the *Archangel*. People seem to become happy in a bovine way as soon as they are relieved of all responsibility for the future. Soldiers going to the War are beasts of burden, probably condemned to death. They are not their own masters in any way except in their unconquerable souls.

Yet, when they have left their relatives and friends blinking and swallowing sobs on Waterloo platform, after a brief period of malaise (while watching the Blighty landscape flitting past) they recover. When the train has left Woking and the Necropolis in the rear they begin to 'buck themselves up'. After all, becoming a military serf or trench galley-slave is a very easy way out of the difficulties of life. No more perplexities there. A grateful Patria transports them inexpensively away from their troubles—nay, rewards them for their acquiescence with actual money and medals. But nevertheless they are like cabbages going to Covent Garden, or beasts driven to market. Hence their happiness. They have no worries, because they have no future; they are only alive through an oversight—of the enemy. They are not 'going out' to *do* things, but to have things *done* to them.

LIFE-BELTS (SOUTHAMPTON TO HAVRE)

The Boat begins to throb; the Docks slide past;
And soldiers stop their chattering, mute and grave;
Doomed to the Push, they think 'We're off at last!'
Then, like the wash and welter of a wave,
Comfortless War breaks into each blind brain,
Swamping the hopes they've hugged to carry abroad;
And half-recovering, they must grope again
For some girl-face, or guess what pay they'll hoard
To start a home with, while they're out in France.
For, after all, each lad has got his chance
Of seeing the end. Like life-belts in a wreck,
They clutch at gentle plans—pathetic schemes
For peace next year. Meanwhile I pace the deck
And curse the Fate that lours above their dreams.

February 15

February 22 (No. 25 Stationary Hospital, Rouen)[1]

My fifth night in this squalid little 'compound'. Four of my fellow-patients play cards all day; their talk is all the dullest obscenity. The other two are good enough, one a rather charming little Scot in the gunners.

There are miles of pine-woods on one side of the camp; I went a walk among the quiet stems yesterday. The silence and the clean air did me good. It seemed easier to think clearly, a sore need now. My brain is so pitifully confused by the war and my own single part in it. All those people I have left in England have talked me nearly to death. The people I have seen out here so far have made me feel that there is no hope for the race of men. All that is wise and tender in them is hidden by the obsession of war. They strut and shout and guzzle and try to forget their distress in dreary gabble about England (and the War!). It is all dull and hopeless and ugly and small.

And while I lie awake staring at the darkness of the tent my own terrors get hold of me and I long only for life and comfort, and the weeks before me seem horrible and agonizing. I haven't the physical health to face the hardship and nerve-strain. Nothing seems to matter but a speedy release from the hell that awaits me.

Yet I should loathe the very idea of returning to England without having been scarred and tortured once more. I suppose all this 'emotional experience' (futile phrase) is of value. But it leads nowhere now (but to madness). There is little tenderness left in me: only bitter resentment and a morbid desire to measure the whole ignominy which men are brought to by these fearful times of 'sanguinary imbecility' (as Conrad calls it).[2]

For the soldier is no longer a noble figure; he is merely a writhing insect among this ghastly folly of destruction. His kingly reason is fooled and debauched by the dire pangs that his body must endure. 'Life, life' he cries—and then 'food—and warmth, and sleep'. He does not cry for wisdom. The best that a brave and thoughtful creature can hope for now is to become a sort of ignoble Hamlet, driven from pillar to post by his own

[1] On 16 February S.S. reached the Infantry Base Depot at Rouen, and two days later was taken to hospital with German measles. He rejoined the I.B.D. on 27 February.
[2] From 'Gaspar Ruiz' in *A Set of Six*.

remorse for men and their dirty devices. He watches curiously to see how long patient humanity will suffer.

'And still the War goes on; he don't know why.'[1] I *want* to find someone who has *some* faith in the war and its purposes. But they see nothing but their own tiny destinies.

The 'joke' I have heard a hundred times repeated here in five days has been: 'I will arise and will go to my Father and will say unto Him; "Father, *Stand-at*—ease!"' So much for God. He is a cruel buffoon, who skulks somewhere at the Base with tipsy priests to serve him, and lead the chorus of *Hymns Ancient and Modern*.

> 'O God our hope in ages past!'
> 'Rock of ages, cleft for me.'
> 'Lead, Kindly Light'—O the stupid cynicism of it!

I can see God among the pine-trees where birds are flitting and chirping. And spring will rush across the country in April with tidings of beauty. But spring in this cursed *'year of victory'* will be but a green flag waving a signal for devilish slaughter to begin. The agony of armies will be on every breeze; their blood will stain the flowers. The foulness of battle will cut off all kindliness from the hearts of men.

Such things come from a distempered brain: an infantry officer only sees the stupidest side of the War.

> 'There's no amendment to be got out of mankind except by terror and violence.' You can imagine the effect of such a phrase . . . upon a person like myself, whose whole scheme of life had been based upon a suave and delicate discrimination of social and artistic values.
>
> (Conrad)[2]

February 23

The stillness of the pine-trees is queer. They stand like blue-green walls fifty or sixty feet high with the white sky beyond and above. They seem to be keeping quite still, waiting for the war to end. This afternoon, off the road by the training-ground, I found an alley leading downhill to a big shuttered red house that overlooks the valley and the distant wall of hills. It was so

[1] The last line of S.S.'s poem 'In the Pink'. See p. 39.
[2] From 'The Informer' in *A Set of Six*.

quiet along the paths with green moss growing under the pine-stems. And chiffchaffs and tits chattering; and some Frenchmen chopping timber in a brown copse down below. It might almost have been England (though I don't know what difference that would make). I could hear a dog barking in the stable-yard, a cow lowing, and hens clucking. These homely things come strangely when one is up to the neck in camps and suchlike. And it is good to think of spring being near, and daylight at 6 o'clock soon. Blackbirds scolding among bushes in gardens, and red sunsets fading low down, and the smell of late March, and daffodils shining in the dusk and the orchard grass.

February 24

'To-night returning from my twilight walk,'[1] among the glooming pines with the young thin moon and a few stars over-head, suddenly I felt an intense craving for simplicity, or even for stupidity. Just to be a good boy (like Bobbie Hanmer) and to have done with this itch to pull everything to shreds. For there is something very alluring in that Sunday-evening peace-fulness of heart, where a church-bell rings, and the landscape twinkles with cottage-lights.

Bobbie Hanmer can kneel down every night and say his simple prayers to nothing, and fall asleep content to die or lose an arm or a leg for king and country. For him all England's wars are holy. His smooth head is no more perplexed with problems than a robin in a hedgerow. He cocks his bright eye at you like a bird, bless him. To-night I felt that I should like to be the same: and all my unhappiness and discontent and hatred of war and contempt for the mean ways of men and women and myself seemed so easy to put away and forget: my morbid heresies seemed like a lot of evil books that one might push into a dark shelf to gather dust. And even the ranks of solemn, brooding pines took on a sort of tenderness, and there was homeliness in the lights of the camp; and I couldn't hear a bugle anywhere.

I think this craving for something homely is a feeling that overcomes all others out here; even my pseudo-cynical heart is beginning to be filled by it. I am not so angry with the world as I was a week ago. Soon I shall be utterly domestic, asking no

[1] Meredith, 'A Ballad of Past Meridian'.

more than a fireside and a book by Trollope, and the parson in to supper.

St Ouen. Much the best of three churches I saw. Lofty effects of dull silver stone and rich coloured glass. At one end above organ a very good rose-window, a sort of cheery futurist effect of terra-cotta red, powder-blue, and arsenic-green. At the other end some delicate colour and design. Someone chanting. Sound of motor-horns and traffic outside: horn-like effect of a religious nose-blower inside the sacred edifice.

'The necessary supply of heroes must be maintained at all costs.' (Sir Edward Carson[1] at Dublin.)

The hotel lift came sliding down from nowhere and stopped with a dull bump: a very stout Colonel in a green-and-gold cap came heavily out.

Young officers—furtively glancing round—obviously feeling themselves 'abroad'—people talking French. The lift slips upward again; murmur of voices and clatter of feet on the wooden floor. Officers, conscious of their leather gaiters, straddling in, pulling down tunics.

27 February

Reinforcements at Rouen

He sat and watched the officers who came through the swing-doors of the hotel in twos and threes. He leaned back in his wicker chair and puffed his pipe, enjoying the sensation of luxurious comfort after his hot bath. Soon he would be munching a good lunch: then he'd smoke a cigar and drive up the hill to the cheerless Base Camp in a taxi-cab. He thought of his bath, the first he'd had for more than a week. At any rate *his* body was strong and healthy; *he* wouldn't be 'fading away' to the Venereal Hospital like so many of the 'reinforcements', unlucky victims of a 'last night in town' before 'going out'.

He stared across the crowded hall at the Colonels and Majors and Captains—Assistant Provost Marshals, Military Liaison Officers, Base Commandants, and others with less distinctive occupations, who were smoking and sipping whiskies and cock-

---

[1] Irish barrister and politician (1854–1935). From 1917 First Lord of the Admiralty and a member of the War Cabinet.

tails in their easy-going way—fortunate creatures who could write home 'from the Front' (more or less) and yet could face the future as a certainty of so many years and meals (unless apoplexy intervened). He wondered if they were really as stupid as they appeared to be. Three subalterns sat at the next table; they were for the real war anyhow; trench-coats were hung across their chairs, trench-boots impeded their thick legs: their dissatisfied, clumsy faces wore the look of the man who has something nasty in front of him. 'Up the line' they'll go to-morrow or the day after, in a crawling, stuffy train, with all their 'trench' gear, hoping vaguely that 'down the line' will mean a Red Cross train for them, and the certain prospect of 'good old Blighty'.

Meanwhile this discerning young officer watched the crowd and tried to fit things together. He had loathed the business of 'coming out again', had talked wildly to his pacifist friends about the cruel imbecility of the war, and the uselessness of going on with it. He came out with his angry heart, resolved to hate the whole show, and write his hatred down in words of burning criticism and satire. Now he is losing all that; he has been drawn back into the Machine; he has no more need to worry. 'Nothing matters now.' He must trust to fate: the responsibility of life has been taken from him. He must just go on until something happens to him. And through his dull acquiescence in it all, he is conscious of the same spirit that brought him serenely through it last year; the feeling of sacrifice.

He doesn't know for what he is making the sacrifice; he has no passion for England, except as a place of pleasant landscapes and comfortable towns. He despises the English point of view and British complacency. Some day perhaps he will be able to explain this feeling of unreasoning acquiescence. For the moment he is glad enough to accept it and go on his pilgrimage resolved to get all he can out of ugliness and destruction and death, and the intolerable dull-wittedness of his fellow-officers. He gets up and walks across to the dining-room. In a few minutes he is plying a good knife and fork and sipping Chambertin—an average young Englishman with a more than average appetite.

1917

In the Cathedral (purple passage)

He pushed into the Cathedral, leaving the bustling square, while the gusty March evening began to close, under a colourless sky. A few lights were burning, low down among the grey columns that soared and branched to the dim roof. At intervals there was some chanting of monotonous antiphonies along the nave, where the altar was lit as though by some warm yellow moonshine.

The place was full of dark, shifting figures; their footfalls echoed in the dusk. Sometimes a chair scrooped when a soldier got up to go out. Candles burned in clusters of clear golden flowers, at the shrines where the devout were kneeling and whispering, and gazing apparently rapt in ludicrous idols and pictures of their patrons. He had wandered into this astonishing Roman Catholic temple to stare at the coloured windows. And now, in the gathering gloom, glory faded slowly from those gateways of heaven, those jewelled frescoes of tracery and brightness. There were smouldering flames in the great rose above the organ—hell-fires stoked for heretics. Elsewhere the blazoned petals faded to ivory and silver and brown, till most became mere patches and blurs of remembered colour. But there was one that became lovelier in its eclipse, spreading delicate wing-feathers from a central ember of red. Gazing upward, he seemed to find it swaying like silver blossom in moonlight. The delicate structure of branching stonework became a living tree, a miraculous garden full of rustling angels.

In the house of God he had found, not God, but beauty. The half-lit arches and the noble columns were transfigured in his eyes to a mystery that was motionless, and yet quivering with some inward transparency. He was going away from all this, going away to the naked horror of the War, that he already knew so well.

A priest was standing in the pulpit, gesticulating like a marionette, until from reiteration his fervent attitudes became ridiculous. The priest spoke clear, but in a foreign tongue; he was urging the Lenten significance of '*Jésu*' in a self-conscious oration, brandishing his arms and tilting his pale square face from side to side. His adjectives were innumerable. Then he suddenly stopped, and the chanting began once more.

The officer turned to go; a little child was staring up at him, and he smiled at the awed innocent face. The child could not understand the sermon any more than it could understand the War; seeing only a man standing high up and alone, clenching his hands and shouting; seeing only the tall figures of things called soldiers, kindly things that went away. Somehow that child made him feel alive again; but the people worshipping in the great cathedral seemed no more real than the prophets and martyrs standing up in the windows that were merged now in the walls and the outer darkness. So he went out to the streets and the crowds moving between lamp-lit shops. 'What's the good of it all?' he thought. Then he bumped into a stout Staff Major who was hastening to his dinner. The Major glared and gobbled like a turkey.

So he too bethought him of his evening meal. And the War went on, pitiless, threatening to continue for ever.

Lunch on Sunday in Rouen

He poured out another glass of the delicate-flavoured, honey-coloured wine. Over a meditative sip he glanced across the room, whose white walls made a background for the red and blue 'tabs' and coronation-medals of the Staff Officers. Grey-haired colonels with fierce eyebrows lingered over a chicken casserole with the tenderness of a lover. Everyone seemed to be munching. The waiters made a clatter with steaming white and brown dishes; and there was a continual murmur of male military voices. After lunch these soldiers would return to their offices, to make lists of young men who are going up the line, or to read lists of young men who have been killed and wounded. But they will have lunched well; so that their nerves may be equal to the strain.

A Brigadier-General came and sat down a few feet away. He had the puffy, petulant face of a man with a liver who spends most of the year sitting in London clubs. He began guzzling hors d'oeuvres as though his life depended on the solidity of his meal.

The cynical subaltern who was staring at him from the next table felt an almost irrepressible desire to walk across and pour a plate of soup down his neck. 'O you bloody Brigadier! you bloody Brigadier! you are a professional soldier; I am not. Why

can't you go and show the Germans how to fight instead of
guzzling at the Base? You have never been within thirty miles
of a front-line trench, and yet you call yourself a general. And
you will be alive, over-eating yourself in a military club, when I
am dead in a shell-hole up on the Somme. *You* will guzzle your-
self to the grave and gas about the Great War, long after I am
dead with all my promise unfulfilled.

'O damn all these bald-headed incompetent belly-fillers!' he
thought. And he glanced at a Gunner colonel with a D.S.O. who
was cutting himself a big slice of cheese, hoping that he at least
might be a brave man. But all the really brave men were dead,
or else maimed or 'up the line'.

These people at Rouen were no use except to swear at
orderly-room clerks and promote the prosperity of French
restaurants. 'Damn them all!' he thought, and longed for the
morning when one of them would send him up in a crawling
train to join his Battalion.

BASE DETAILS

If I were fierce, and bald, and short of breath,
   I'd live with scarlet Majors at the Base,
And speed glum heroes up the line to death.
   You'd see me with my puffy petulant face,
Guzzling and gulping in the best hotel,
   Reading the Roll of Honour. 'Poor young chap,'
I'd say—'I used to know his father well;
Yes, we've lost heavily in this last scrap.'
And when the war is done and youth stone dead,
I'd toddle safely home and die—in bed.

March 4[1]

March 4

Half-an-hour in the glorious Église de St Ouen, with soft
notes of the organ and chanting voices, and burning blossoms of
colour in the high windows; one was a narrow arch of green and
silver, with touches of topaz and pale orange—most delicate and
saintly. Below was the huddle of black-cloaked and bonneted

[1] Published in the *Cambridge Magazine*, 28 April 1917, then in *Counter-Attack*.

women and grey-headed men, with a few soldiers, French and English, and children.

Then a train hurried me up the hill to Bois Guillaume—about five kilometres out of the city, and by 4.30 I was alone in some woods with a chilly wind soughing in the branches of beech and oak, and a grey sky overhead, and a carpet of dry beech-leaves underfoot. And one thrush singing a long way off, singing as if he did not yet quite believe in the end of winter.

The delicate, aspiring grey pillars of St Ouen are noble, and the rich colours there do not change, except when darkness falls outside. There will be such beauty in these woods at the end of April as no mediaeval builder could imitate. But they had the idea in their heads, when they lifted up that miracle of stone and crystal, and crowned it with deep-toned bells, calling down the peace of God to comfort the good citizens of Rouen.

IN THE CHURCH OF ST OUEN

Time makes me a soldier; but I know
That had I lived six hundred years ago,
I might have tried to build within my heart
A church like this, where I could dwell apart,
With chanting peace; my spirit longs for prayer,
And, lost to God, I seek him everywhere.
Here, while the windows burn and bloom like flowers,
And sunlight falls and fades with tranquil hours,
I could be half a saint, for like a rose
In heart-shaped stone the glory of Heaven glows.
But where I stand, desiring yet to stay,
Hearing rich music at the close of day,
The Spring Offensive (Easter is its date)
Calls me. And that's the music I await.

March 4[1]

This will never do. I remember old Greaves in the trenches saying he would like to be a cathedral organist after the war—the music was a minor canon of his scheme. All he wanted was a sedentary life with lots to eat and a little vague emotion such as

---

[1] First published in Dame Felicitas Corrigan's *Siegfried Sassoon: Poet's Pilgrimage* (1973).

might as well be caused by a couple of liqueurs after a good dinner. Now to be a saint one must suffer. And I am more qualified for the job after six months in the front line than after sixty years in a cathedral cloister. *Religious feeling* is a snare set by one's emotional weakness. *Religion* is a very stern master, who promises nothing and demands *all*.

The distant rumble of guns can be heard from the line, as the wind blows from that direction. There is a sort of unreasoning, inhuman gaiety in the air which is beyond description. The English are supposed to be mad in their way of treating the War as a joke, but I think it is only their inherent stupidity and unwillingness to face things. I sometimes feel that everyone (even the Base-Colonels) will suddenly go stark mad and begin shooting one another instead of the Germans. The whole business is so monstrously implacable to all human tenderness. We creep about like swarms of insects. And all the while there is the spectacle of Youth being murdered.

March 6

It was raining to-night. I went out about 10, leaving the bridge-playing officers in their smoky hut—oh such a dreary lot of people! The pine-trees stood up dark and peaceful, looming against the pale sky where the moon was hid by clouds. The rain (that Sorley loved) was dripping quietly down, and there was the endless murmur of the wood like surf miles away. And the guns still rumbling at their damned bombardment. There's a line of beeches by the path to the camp. They are silent, they've no night-music like the pines. They are waiting to sing their April lyric of young leaves. Waiting to dress themselves in their glory of green and luminous yellow. Trees are friendly things.

And I am very lucky to be able to find happiness so quickly. A few hundred yards and I am alone with the trees and the rain. So all is well. It is my evening prayer. And the war is of no importance as long as there are some trees left standing upright, with a clean wind to shake their branches. Beside these things, how grotesque and dull and licentious human nature appears. That mysterious life of growing things doesn't seem to have any significance for it. A few slang phrases, war-shop, a woman, a plate of food, a glass of beer and a smoke, is that really all? I can't believe it.

March 11

Left Rouen about 4 o'clock in sunlight. Got to Corbie at midnight, and was turned out there. Slept at Field Ambulance and went out to Rest Camp at Chipilly next day, to join Second R.W.F.

Slept on the floor with a blanket at Corbie—very wretchedly —with some grumbling officers, two or three of them out again after being wounded last year: one, in the King's Royal Rifles, had been hit in both lungs. My two R.W.F. companions are both cadet-officers, quite dull and suitably impressed by the occasion. Everything seems conspiring to lower my spirits (our kits were lost and plundered on the way up, and we didn't recover them for over a week).

RETURN

I have come home unnoticed; they are still;
No greetings pass between us; but they lie
Hearing the boom of guns along the hill,
Watching the flashes lick the glowering sky.

A wind of whispers comes from sightless faces;
'Have patience, and your bones shall share our bed.'
Their voices haunt dark ways and ruined places,
Where once they spoke in deeds; who now are dead.

They wondered why I went; at last returning,
They guide my labouring feet through desolate mud.
And, choked with death, yet in their eyes discerning
My living strength; they are quickened in my blood.

March 11[1]

---

[1] Written in the train at night. An example of entirely artificial emotionalism. The dead are underground all right, but they don't care whether I come back or not. This is the sort of poetry I'm always trying to avoid writing. (Note, March 29.) S.S.

March 21

Eight days passed in this place, without event except changes of weather, which has been warm and sunny at times, but now blows very cold, and has rained hard since Monday night. This afternoon I'm off to Amiens for a night, going with Orme (late of C. Company, First R.W.F.). A good dinner, a bath and a bed are something to be thankful for after this dirty place. The journey thither is seventeen miles of bumping in an Army Service Corps lorry.

News of 'fall' of Péronne and other places seems to 'fall' rather flat. My brain is steadily getting more sluggish as my body grows healthier with air and exercise. Life is reduced to a series of efforts to keep clean, warm, well-nourished and dry.

March 22

5 o'clock outside the Gare du Nord at Amiens—a day of cold winds and snow-showers and sunshine. Sitting in a hospital ambulance waiting for it to make up its mind to start for Corbie, whence we must catch a lorry to take us as near the camp as possible. I suppose one might just as well be sitting here as in a dug-out or in that beastly camp. Had a good dinner last night and a bath and a clean bed to sleep in; and to-day lunch with old Perrineau, the old First R.W.F. interpreter. He was as delightful as ever. Vague news comes of the German retreat.

March 25

After five weeks in France (and two with Second R.W.F.) I have not yet been within five miles of a German gun. Instead of getting nearer, the war has actually receded, and I don't think there are any Germans (except the shivering prisoners one sees working half-heartedly on the roads) within ten or even fifteen miles of this place.

Yesterday afternoon I got on to a lorry and went bumping along the Corbie road for three or four miles, with a bitter-cold north wind blowing dust, and glaring sunshine on the rolling brown, ploughed country. Then I walked down the hill to Heilly on the Ancre, where we camped for four days early in July last year, and marched away to the line again on a hot dusty afternoon. The water still sings its deep tune by the bridge, and the narrow stream goes twinkling away past the bend, and past the garden where I used to walk when I came over from Morlancourt to the Field Cashier. About 5 o'clock I started off up the hill again with the sun setting low and red and the valley hazy and quiet, the wind blowing shrewd, and a plough-team working on the ridge.

I could imagine myself walking home to some friendly English village, until the aerodromes loomed in the dusk, and I came to the main road with lines of lorries, and a brazier glowing red where the sentry stands at the cross-roads. And so down the hill to this abominable camp, and a foul dinner in the smoky hut and early to bed, too fed-up to read. And summer begins to-night— which means an hour less in bed, and absolutely nothing else.

March 26

> Give me the passion to re-build
> Bright peaks of vision stormed in vain;
> That, though in fight my flesh be killed,
> The noise of ruin may be stilled,
> And beauty shine beyond my pain.

March 27

Yesterday afternoon I rode on a lorry to Corbie; walked six kilometres to Pont Noyelles; then got a lift to Amiens on an Army Service Corps motor (Ford), standing up on a sort of platform behind, amid showers of mud. The weather still very windy with heavy showers blowing across the sky. Reached Amiens about 5.30.

After dinner (alone, thank heaven) walked round the cathedral for half-an-hour in the rain. The city is pitch-dark by 9 o'clock. Rose late to-day, and after a bath and quiet lunch, returned to the place whence I came, per lorry and feet. These little outings break the monotony: very lucky to get them. The officers one sees about in Amiens don't appear quite so repulsive as the Rouen lot.

We expect to be at Camp 13 till the end of this week; then

probably go to St Pol, 'before proceeding to the battle'—whatever that may mean. I felt last night (after a bottle of decent wine) that I would gladly die to guard Amiens Cathedral from destruction, but one can't feel like that in the light of day.

Anyhow, I would rather be in a battle than at Camp 13. It would be interesting, though uncomfortable; and there would always be the possibility of release, to Blighty, or Elysian fields. In these days I drug myself with dreams. I have seen the *Spectator* for March 17, in which Heinemann advertises my book as 'ready shortly'. Being about ten days behind the civilised world of London, I suppose I'm published by now![1]

March 30 (Hotel Belfort, Amiens)

Alone at last after a typical 'war evening'. After yet another 'lorry-journey' in rain and westerly wind, I got to this town again for a 'final jolly'. On 30 March 1914 I was looking forward with acute anxiety to the Atherstone point-to-point meeting (to be held next day). All my world was centred in the desire to steer old Cockbird first past the post in some silly, jolly race over hedge and ditch.

And I did it. And the world went on just the same! 30 March 1916 I was in the trenches at Fricourt-Mametz, hating the Germans for killing my friend, and wondering if they'd kill me. *But they didn't!* And to-night I've been guzzling at the Godbert restaurant with a captain of the Dublin Fusiliers, and a captain of the Cameronians, and three other Welsh Fusiliers; and the bill was 230 francs; and we drank Veuve Clicquot; and the others have gone into the dark city to look for harlots; and I'm alone in my room; looking out of a balconied window at the town, with few lights, and the moon and silver drifts of cloud going eastward; and the railway station looming romantic as old Baghdad. And next week we march away 'to hazards whence no tears can win us'.[2]

Dream Pictures

I wish I could write a book of 'Consolations for Homesick Soldiers in the Field'. There must be many whose dreams need

[1] *The Old Huntsman* was not published until 8 May.
[2] See note p. 120.

stimulating, when the letters from home grow monotonous (always the same two or three handwritings when they are sorting their mail so eagerly). They need someone to refresh the familiar scenes and happenings which they remember and long for. Someone to make them exclaim 'Damn it, how that takes one back to the dear old times!'

When there's 'nothing doing', and they are fed up with reading newspapers full of 'war restrictions' and no sacrifices must be spared, and they are having a smoke and watching the sun go down behind some straggling poplar-trees on the hill above the disconsolate rest-camp, while they listen to the muffled thudding of an artillery-strafe miles away in the line; in such moments they are starving for a healthy dose of domestic sentimental recollection.

I would turn them loose in some dream-gallery of Royal Academy pictures of the late-nineteenth century. I would show them bland summer landscapes, willows and meadowsweet reflected in calm waters, lifelike cows coming home to the byre with a golden sunset behind them; I would take them to gateways in garden-walls that they might gaze along dewy lawns with lovers murmuring by the moss-grown sundial; I would lead them 'twixt hawthorn hedgerows, and over field-path stiles, to old-world orchards where the lush grass is strewn with red-cheeked apples, and even the wasps have lost their stings. From the grey church-tower comes a chiming of bells, and the village smoke ascends like incense of immemorial tranquillity. And at the rose-grown porch of some discreet little house a girl in a print-dress is waiting, waiting for the returning footsteps along the twilight lane, while the last blackbird warbles from the may-tree. And then I would leave Mrs Florence Barclay[1] to take up the thread of the tale, drowning them in intolerable sweetness.

April 1 (Palm Sunday)

Last day in Camp 13. To-morrow we move to Corbie, twelve kilometres away.

---

[1] Immensely popular author (1862–1920) of *The Rosary* (1909) and other romantic novels.

April 2

Very cold morning. Left Camp at 9.15. As we went up the hill to the Bray–Corbie road the smoke of the incinerators gave the impression that we had fired the camp on leaving it. Reached Corbie at 12.30.

April 3

Left Corbie 9 a.m. First halt on the hill toward Pont Noyelles.[1] Second between P.N. and Allonville (crucifix and apple-trees). Third just beyond Allonville (muddy road and château-wall). Fourth Croissy (on hill between two copses—cemetery and waving yew-trees). Arrived Villers-Bocage 2 p.m. Brilliant sunshine and real April clouds. Snow in night—a little lying on the hills. Marched twenty-one kilometres.

Woman in our billet says that troops have been coming through (going toward Doullens and Arras) for fifteen days, never staying more than one night. The movements of our (33rd) Division are nebulous. Left four officers at Corbie; they go to St Pol to be held in reserve. Kirkby,[2] Soames, Casson, and Evans are with B. Company, also self. Soames is an Etonian, was a sergeant in Fifth Dragoon Guards early in the war, went through the Mons retreat, and the fighting till May 1915, then came to Second R.W.F. as Second Lieutenant. Left after one tour of trenches and became a Flight Commander; now returns here as Second Lieutenant again. Seems to have had some sort of a row with the Royal Flying Corps people. He is, I imagine, just like any other member of the Soames family. Casson was at Winchester and Christ Church, Oxford (twenty-three years old). Comes from Wales and is rather a young snob, but amusing in a mild, gossiping way, and fairly well-informed.

Kirkby is short, red and round, thirty-three and good-humoured (except early in the morning) with a slight weakness for standing on his dignity as a senior captain. A Welsh landowner (owns part of Harlech Golf Course, which is to his credit). Evans is a Caradoc Evans type of Welshman, very noisy and garrulous and licks his thumb when dealing cards; an awful hooligan, rather ape-like in countenance; has been out about

---

[1] Landscapes toward Amiens like a background by Charles Sims [1873–1928]. S.S.
[2] The Captain Leake of *Memoirs of an Infantry Officer*.

three months, and is fairly efficient. If one says anything to him
he invariably answers 'Pardon?' Our billet is adorned with
mouldy stuffed birds, with spread wings; a jay, a small hawk
over the fireplace, and a seagull slowly revolving in draughts,
hung from a string in the ceiling. Also two squirrels and a stork.

Feeling much better since we started moving, except for usual
cold in head and throat. Same old 'point-to-point' feeling about
going into the show—the 'happy warrior' stunt cropping up as
usual. Letters from Robert Graves and Julian Dadd yesterday
which cheered me no end. R.G. at Harlech—lucky devil. J.D.,
still voiceless, at Stamford Hill.

The Second R.W.F. are gradually taking me to their bosom.
It will be best for me to stay here now and try to become a hero.
The First, without Cotterill, Hawes, Adams and Anscombe,
would be rather empty.

No sign of my book yet. I do want to see it before I get killed
(if death is the dose which April means me to swallow).

First Battalion are up at Croisilles; having a rough passage, I
am afraid.

FOOT INSPECTION

The twilight barn was chinked with gleams; I saw
Soldiers with naked feet stretched on the straw,
Stiff-limbed from the long muddy march we'd done,
And ruddy-faced with April wind and sun.
With pity and stabbing tenderness I see
Those stupid, trustful eyes stare up at me.
Yet, while I stoop to Morgan's blistered toes
And ask about his boots, he never knows
How glad I'd be to die, if dying could set him free
From battles. Shyly grinning at my joke,
He pulls his grimy socks on; lights a smoke,
And thinks 'Our officer's a decent bloke'.

April 3

April 4

A dull morning; we marched eight miles to Beauval in wet
snow—falling all the way—along the main Amiens–Doullens

road. Spent the night in a cheery little brick-floored cottage in the main street.

April 5

Warm, sunny morning. Battalion left Beauval at 4 p.m. and marched to Lucheux (the other side of Doullens) about seven miles. Got there about 8. Billeted in huts. Rather steep wooded hills all round, quite nice. Dined in moonlight, sitting round a brazier with plates on our knees. A wonderfully calm night.

April 6 (Good Friday)

Woke with sunshine streaming through the door, and broad Scots being shouted in the next huts by some Scottish Rifles. We remain here to-day. Weather turned very wet about mid-day.

So we slowly crawl along the roads to our destination; rumours floating in to meet us, from 'up the line'. I don't think battle-nightmares haunt many of us. There isn't time for thinking. We are 'for it'—that's enough for most of us. The wind is gone round to the east and we can hear the huge firing up at Arras.

I saw a signpost last evening with Arras 32 kilometres. I suppose that's about the nearest point where hell begins. Going down the hill into Doullens in sunshine was pleasant. And the town looked clean and cheerful. And I was walking with nice old Major Poore, and talking about cricket and hunting.

And everywhere spring is not quite ready to break out in a sudden glory of flowers and leaves. The big woods round here are brown and sombre; in a fortnight they'll be flashing and quivering, bowers of beech-trees, cages full of sunbeams, swaying alleys of Paradise.

Last night I went and stood in the moonlight, watching the stems and leafless branches against the sky, and dreaming of summer dawns, till the startled birds rustled overhead, and something went plunging blindly through the undergrowth—it might have been Pan, or a roebuck, or a mule escaped from the Transport lines. This morning romance had fled. Soldiers were practising on bugles and bagpipes at the wood's edge.

1917

April 7   7 p.m.

We are now at Saulty, a village just off the Doullens–Arras
road (about twelve miles from Arras). Marched fifteen kilo-
metres to-day, reaching Saulty at 2.30. A sunny day with cold
east wind. I am sitting on a tree-stump, in the peaceful park of a
big white château which one sees among the trees. The sun is
looking over the tree-tops now, and birds singing a way off, and
a few little deer grazing; nothing to remind me of the battle,
except the enormous thudding of guns from eastward. The
brown of the trees and undergrowth grows purple, and the
birds sing, thrushes and blackbirds, while a few rooks flap over-
head. The bombardment must be terrific. Three Army Corps are
reported to be attacking between Arras and Lens. We move to
our final concentration area to-morrow (Easter Sunday!)—
about four miles from here.

I don't suppose anyone would believe me if I said I was abso-
lutely happy and contented. Of course this is written after a good
meal of coffee and eggs. But the fact remains that if I had the
choice between England to-morrow and the battle, I would
choose the battle without hesitation. Why on earth is one such a
fool as to be pleased at the prospect? I can't understand it. Last
year I thought it was because I had never been through it before.
But my feeling of quiet elation and absolute confidence now is
something even stronger than last summer's passionate longing
for death and glory.

> I keep such music in my brain
> No din this side of death can quell.[1]

(I never wrote truer words than those.)

This battle may be nothing at all, or it may give me a fine
chance. I only hope we are in the forefront of it. Sitting in sup-
port and getting shelled is no fun at all. I may even be left out,
awful anticlimax for the hero!

The men seem very cheery and have done the forty-odd miles
well. These occasions when soldiers are on the verge of hell
always seem to show them at their very best. Of course the
officers are very prone to a sentimental *ave atque vale* frame of

---

[1] The first lines of S.S.'s poem 'Secret Music', written in December 1916 and
published in *The Old Huntsman*.

mind. For the men it is a chance of blighty, and 'anything for a change'.

Aeroplanes are humming in the clear sky, and the sun is a glint of crimson beyond the strip of woodland. And still that infernal banging continues away on the horizon.

Holmes has applied for me to go to the First Battalion, but I suppose I'll stay here now.

April 8 (Easter Sunday)

Left Saulty 9 a.m., reached Basseux 11.30 (about eleven kilometres south-west of Arras). Until recently this place was only a mile or two from the line, but doesn't appear to have been shelled. We are living in a dismantled château which must have been quite nice before the war. I am sitting with my feet out of the window of an attic under the roof, looking down on the courtyard where some officers are playing cricket with a stump and a wooden ball, and a brazier for wicket. Glorious sunshine, and pigeons flying about over the red and grey roofs. A little grey church with a pointed tower a hundred yards down the street. Three balloons visible, and the usual confused noise of guns from Arras.

April 9

Attack began 5.30 a.m. Still at Basseux. Weather windy and cold, with snow-showers and fine intervals. The usual pre-operation-orders, restlessness and forced gaiety. Everyone talking very loud about successes reported from the line—'our objective gained', '5000 prisoners', and so on. I try to be serene through it all—and get into a corner and read *Far from the Madding Crowd* in a desultory way.

The cold weather does its best to take the heart out of one—and I've got my usual sore throat and no clean handkerchiefs or socks. A bloody life. Mail to-day—mine including little India-paper edition of Keats bound in green vellum.[1]

April 11

Battalion left Basseux at 5 p.m. and marched about eight miles

[1] A present from Lady Ottoline Morrell.

in heavy snowstorm—we are relieving the 30th Division (21st Brigade) to the right of Héninel which was taken today.[1] Writing this in a very small dug-out by a sunken road near Mercatel where we bivouac. Self, Casson, a trench-mortar sergeant-major, two B. Company servants and two others huddled round a brazier (for which thank God). We are about six kilometres from the line. It is now 2 a.m. and April 12. Must make an effort to sleep. Passed through villages absolutely levelled with the ground. Ficheux was one of the worst. 'Fish-hooks!' the men called it.

April 12   10 p.m.

Moved to St Martin-Cojeul, a demolished village about four kilometres north-west of Croisilles, three kilometres south-east of Wancourt where the Germans counter-attacked to-day. We take over an old German third-line trench from the 17th Manchesters. Arrived about 3 o'clock in wet weather after a fine morning. The snow has gone and left bad mud. The British line is about a mile in front of us. A dead English soldier lying by the road as we came to the village, his head hideously battered. I visited the underground Dressing Station this evening, and got my hands seen to. Several wounded in there—one groaning with broken leg. A few five-nines dropped in the village, which is the usual heap of bricks. Absolute desolation—and the very strong line of German wire which they left. They have cut down even the pollard willows by the river.

Writing this in a tiny dug-out, but luckily it has a stove. Just room for Kirkby and self to sit. He is asleep. Rations getting very short. Only one meal to-day, and that scrappy to a degree. Casson and I finished our last orange to-night but feeling fairly fresh (just the usual trench-mouth). A fair amount of gun-rumbling going on all round. Héninel believed taken by 56th Division, but doubtful if they hold it. Up to the neck in war this time, anyhow. Quite impossible to sleep as it is bitter-cold and nowhere to lie down.

[1] And I heard afterwards that the Southdown had the hunt of the season that afternoon from Plashett! S.S.

April 13

Remained in same trench. Weather fine. 62nd Division
[Brigade] attacked in front this morning—from a hill about
three quarters of a mile away. Objective was a village called
Fontaine-les-Croisilles—and the wood, Fontaine Wood. Attack
failed owing to left flank being unsupported. Casson and I walked
up the hill after tea. A good many dead lying in front of our
trench. Our troops are a little way down the far slope: on the
left they are still in the Hindenburg Line, above the village and
River Sensée. Our Brigade attacks the same place to-morrow at
5.30. We are in reserve. We are astride the Hindenburg Line on
the hill. Went and looked at it. One of our tanks stuck in the
mud getting over the trench—very wide.

April 14

At 9 p.m. we started off to relieve the 13th Northumberland
Fusiliers in Hindenburg support (Second R.W.F. being in sup-
port to the First Cameronians). It was only an hour's walk, but
our Northumberland Fusilier guides lost themselves and we
didn't arrive and complete the relief until 4 a.m. Luckily it was
fine. I went to bed at 5 a.m., after patrolling our 900-yard front
alone!—in a corridor of the underground communication-trench
of the Hindenburg Line—a wonderful place. Got up at 9.30 after
a miserable hour's sleep—cold as hell—and started off at 10.45
with a fatigue-party to carry up trench-mortar bombs from
dump between St Martin-Cojeul and Croisilles. Got back very
wet and tired about 4.30. Rained all day—trenches like glue.

Was immediately told I'd got to take command of a hundred
bombers (the Battalion is only 270 strong!) to act as reserve for
the First Cameronians in to-morrow's attack. The Cameronians
are to bomb down the two Hindenburg Lines, which they tried
to do on Saturday and had rather a bad time. We may not be
wanted. If we are it will be bloody work I know. I haven't slept
for more than an hour at a time since Tuesday night, but I am
feeling pretty fit and cheery. I have seen the most ghastly sights
since we came up here. The dead bodies lying about the trenches
and in the open are beyond description—especially after the rain.
(A lot of the Germans killed by our bombardment last week are
awful.) Our shelling of the line—and subsequent bombing etc—

has left a number of mangled Germans—they will haunt me till I die. And everywhere one sees the British Tommy in various states of dismemberment—most of them are shot through the head—so not so fearful as the shell-twisted Germans. Written at 9.30 sitting in the Hindenburg underground tunnel on Sunday night, fully expecting to get killed on Monday morning.

April 16

At 3 a.m. the attack began on Fontaine-les-Croisilles. I sat in the First Cameronians H.Q. down in the tunnel until nearly 6, when I was told to despatch twenty-five bombers to help their B. Company in the Hindenburg front line. I took them up myself and got there just as they had been badly driven back after taking several hundred yards of the trench. They seemed to have run out of bombs, failing to block the trench etc, and were in a state of wind-up. However the sun was shining, and the trench was not so difficult to deal with as I had expected.

My party (from A. Company) were in a very jaded condition owing to the perfectly bloody time they've been having lately, but they pulled themselves together fine and we soon had the Bosches checked and pushed them back nearly four hundred yards. When we'd been there about twenty-five minutes I got a sniper's bullet through the shoulder and was no good for about a quarter of an hour. Luckily it didn't bleed much. Afterwards the rest of our men came up and the Cameronians were recalled, leaving me to deal with the show with about seventy men and a fair amount of bombs, but no Lewis-guns.

I was just preparing to start bombing up the trench again when a message came from Colonel Chaplin [of the Cameronians] saying we must not advance any more owing to the people on each side having failed to advance, and ordering me to come away, as he was sending someone up to take over. I left the trench about 9.45. Got wound seen to at our Aid Post in the tunnel, walked to Hénin—and was told to walk on to Boyelles. Got there very beat, having foot-slogged about four kilometres through mud. Was put on a motor-bus and jolted for an hour and a half to Warlencourt (20th Casualty Clearing Station) and told to expect to go to England. Written about 7.30 p.m., with rain pelting on the roof and wind very cold. I hate to think of the poor old Battalion being relieved on such a night after the ghastly discomforts of the last six days. The only blessing is that our losses have been very slight. Only about a dozen of my party to-day—most of them slight. No one killed. My wound is hurting like hell, the tetanus injection has made me very chilly and queer, and I am half-dead for lack of sleep, sitting in a chair in my same old clothes—puttees and all—and not having been offered even a wash. Never mind—'For I've sped through. O Life! O Sun!'[1]

April 17

After a blessed eight hours' sleep (more than I'd had since last Wednesday) I waited till 3 o'clock reading *Far from the Madding Crowd*, when we got on board a Red Cross train of serpentine length. Five hundred men and thirty-two officers on board. Warlencourt is eighteen kilometres from Arras—quite near Saulty, where we stayed on April 7. We passed through Doullens about 6 p.m. and Abbeville at 8.30 and reached Camières at midnight.

An officer called Kerr is with me—one of the First Cameronians. He was hit in the bombing show about an hour before I got up there on Monday morning, so I've got some sidelights on what really happened.

At present I am still feeling warlike, and quite prepared to go back to the line in a few weeks. My wound is fairly comfortable, and will be healed in a fortnight, they say. I know it would be best for me *not* to go back to England, where I should probably be landed for at least three months, and return to the line in July or August, with all the hell and wrench of coming back and settling down to be gone through again. I think I've established a very strong position in the Second Battalion in the five weeks I was with them. My luck never deserts me; it seems inevitable for me to be cast for the part of 'leading hero!'

Things to remember

The dull red rainy dawn on Sunday April 15, when we had relieved the 13th Northumberland Fusiliers—our Company of eighty men taking over a frontage of nine hundred yards.

[1] The last words of Robert Graves's poem 'Escape'.

During the relief—stumbling along the trench in the dusk, dead men and living lying against the sides of the trench—one never knew which were dead and which living. Dead and living were very nearly one, for death was in all our hearts. Kirkby shaking dead German by the shoulder to ask him the way.
On April 14 the 19th Brigade attacked at 5.30 a.m. I looked across at the hill where a round red sun was coming up. The hill was deeply shadowed and grey-blue, and all the country was full of shell-flashes and drifting smoke. A battle picture.
Scene in the Hénin Dressing Station. The two bad cases—abdomen (hopeless) and ankle. The pitiful parson. My walk with Mansfield.
Sergeant Baldwin (A. Company) his impassive demeanour—like a well-trained footman. 'My officer's been hit.' He bound up my wound.

April 18

A quiet day in bed in the tent of D. Ward. A pouring wet, raw day outside. Ten officers in the tent, including a charming little R.F.C. boy called D. T. Leyshon (late of the Second Welsh). Been in France since January *1915* and is now only eighteen and a half! A gunner major opposite me has been gassed. He is only about twenty-six, and carries on the usual discussions common among such gatherings of officers who don't know one another's failings. 'Seniority'—'Decorations'—'Wound-stripes' etc. These discussions are always an airing of personal grievances. The man who has received a decoration never complains of the unfairness of the system. The man who *has* got one listens, and knows damn well how much it is worth to him. The conscientious professional soldier is the dullest man on earth.

April 19

Expecting to be 'evacuated' to England any time.[1]
On 20 April *1916* I left the trenches in front of Mametz and went for those four divine, sunlit weeks at the Fourth Army School, half-way between Amiens and Abbeville. This year I am

[1] Next day, 20 April, he was moved to the Fourth London Hospital at Denmark Hill.

being set free from even more hellish places, and before me lies
a vision of green fields sloping to a vale full of white orchards—
mazes of cherry-blossom where tiny rills tell their little tales,
while the 'shy thrush at mid-May flutes from wet orchards
flushed with the triumphing dawn'. And beyond it all a deep
blue landscape chequered.

Groping along the tunnel in the gloom
He winked his tiny torch with whitening glare,
And bumped his helmet, sniffing the hateful air.
Tins, boxes, bottles, shapes too vague to know,
And once, the foul, hunched mattress from a bed;
And he exploring, fifty feet below
The rosy dusk of battle overhead.
He tripped and clutched the walls; saw someone lie
Humped and asleep, half-covered with a rug;
He stooped and gave the sleeper's arm a tug.
'I'm looking for Headquarters'. No reply.
'Wake up, you sod!' (For days *he'd* had no sleep.)
'I want a guide along this cursed place.'
He aimed a kick at the unanswering heap;
And flashed a beam across that livid face
Horribly glaring up, whose eyes still wore
The agony that died ten days before,
Whose bloody fingers clutched a hideous wound.
Gasping, he staggered onward till he found
Dawn's ghost that filtered down a shafted stair,
To clammy creatures groping underground,
Hearing the boom of shells with muffled sound.
Then with the sweat of horror in his hair,
He climbed with darkness to the twilight air.[1]

April 22

TO THE WARMONGERS

I'm back again from hell
With loathsome thoughts to sell;
Secrets of death to tell;
And horrors from the abyss.

[1] First draft of 'The Rear-Guard', published in *Counter-Attack*.

Young faces bleared with blood,
Sucked down into the mud,
You shall hear things like this,
Till the tormented slain
Crawl round and once again,
With limbs that twist awry
Moan out their brutish pain,
As the fighters pass them by.

For you our battles shine
With triumph half-divine;
And the glory of the dead
Kindles in each proud eye.
But a curse is on my head,
That shall not be unsaid,
And the wounds in my heart are red,
For I have watched them die.

I remember seeing a heap of earth thrown up by a big shell-explosion; two mud-stained hands were sticking out of the wet ashen chalky soil, like the roots of a shrub turned upside down. They might have been imploring aid; they might have been groping and struggling for life and release: but the dead man was hidden; he was buried; his hideous corpse was screened from the shame of those who lay near him, their agony crying to heaven.

April 23 (*In the Ward*)

Morning sunshine slants through the many tall windows of the ward with its grey-green walls and forty white beds. Daffodils and primroses, red lilies and tulips make spots of colour; there are three large red-draped lamps hung from the ceiling down the centre. Officers lie humped in beds smoking and reading morning papers; others drift about in dressing-gowns and slippers, going to and from the washing-room where they scrape the bristles from their contented faces. The raucous gramophone keeps grinding out popular airs. 'Somewhere a Voice is Calling' and the other sentimental songs are reserved for the lamplit glow of evening, when men's hearts turn to the consolations of emotion. In the morning it is ragtime—'Everybody's doing it' and 'At the Fox-Trot Ball'. Everyone is rather quiet. No one has the energy or the desire to begin talking war-shop till noon. Then one catches scraps of talk from round the fire-places.

'barrage lifted at the first objective'
'shelled us with heavy stuff'
'couldn't raise enough decent N.C.O.s'
'our first wave got held up by machine-guns'
'bombed them out of a sap'—etc etc.

There are no serious cases in this ward; only flesh-wounds and sick. No tragedies of gapped bodies and heavily bandaged faces; no groans at night, and nurses catching their breath while the surgeon deals with some ghastly gaping hole. These are the lucky ones, whom a few days of peace have washed clean of the squalor and misery and strain of ten days ago. They are lifting their faces to the sunlight: the nightmares have slunk away to haunt the sombre hearts of the maimed and shattered.

WOUNDED

Waking, I seem to float upon a mere
Of swaying silence; windless gleams the way
Where I may drift from darkness into day.
Through gracious healing languors I can hear
Rumours of strife I need no longer share;
Slowly through fallen eyelids growing aware
Of colour, warmth of light, and songs unseen
From leaves along some shore, when breezes bear
Peace through a forest murmurous with green.
I lift my hands only to touch the flowers,
Rose and narcissus, ranged beside my bed;
Morn comes with mercy of the clean fresh hours,
And lays cool hands on my untroubled head.
And the sombre evening dyes my glowing dreams
With tranquil glory clov'n by fiery streams.

April 24

In the Ward (ii)

They are playing cards at the table opposite my bed; the blinds are drawn and the electric lights on, and a huge fire glows on walls and ceiling. I can see the faces of the card-players; the lean flying-man in his usual grey dressing-gown, his narrow whimsical face (can't get him described at all) below the turban-like bandages bound on his small round head, coming down low over his narrow forehead. He has rather a sour grin, and the look of a man interested in machines; one can imagine him in a white dust-coat at the door of a big garage in some Midland town. This is the young man who was 'brought down' by the Germans behind Arras, and spent three days in a dug-out with Bavarians and Russians until they retired and our men came along and found him.

Next him lolls a burly, swarthy, wide-faced Canadian: the lights make his face look even more gross than usual—heavy loose mouth, low beetling forehead, sneering negroid eyes, deeply shadowed, loose fleshy cheeks, sallow and unhealthy. He wears a dark jacket and a dark muffler, which heighten the criminal effect of his appearance. And where he leaned on his elbows last night, this morning I can see a bowl of daffodils and narcissus with a ray of sunshine dazzling their little faces.

In the ward they talk of little else but war:
'counter-attacked from the redoubt'
'permanent rank of captain'
'didn't draw any allowances for six weeks'
'failed to get through their own wire' and so on.

Very sore is my need of escape from these things—even a week or two might put me right. My brain is screwed up like a tight wire. All day I have to talk to people about the war, and answer the questions of friends, getting excited and over-strained and saying things I never meant to. And when the lights are out, and the ward is half shadow and half glowing firelight, and the white beds are quiet with drowsy figures, huddled out-stretched, then the horrors come creeping across the floor: the floor is littered with parcels of dead flesh and bones, faces glaring at the ceiling, faces turned to the floor, hands clutching neck or belly; a livid grinning face with bristly moustache peers at me over the edge of my bed, the hands clutching my sheets. Yet I found no bloodstains there this morning. These corpses are silent; they do not moan and bleat in the war-zone manner approved by the War Office. They are like dummy figures made to deceive snipers: one feels that there is no stuffing inside them.

That is always the impression given by the genuine article; here of course there is no stench; the hospital authorities probably made that a stipulation when they admitted these intruders. I don't think they mean any harm to me. They are not here to scare me; they look at me reproachfully, because I am so lucky, with my safe wound, and the warm kindly immunity of the hospital is what they longed for when they shivered and waited for the attack to begin, or the brutal bombardment to cease. One boy, an English private in full battle order, crawls to me painfully on hands and knees, and lies gasping at the foot of my bed; he is fumbling in his tunic for a letter; just as he reaches forward to give it me his head lolls sideways and he collapses on the floor; there is a hole in his jaw, and the blood spreads across his white face like ink spilt on blotting-paper. I wish I could sleep.

April 26
My sixth day in this hospital. Roderick came this afternoon. And afterwards Robbie and Edmund Gosse who was in delightful good humour.

April 29
A lovely morning after a sleepless night. The trees outside have become misty with green since last night. I am just emerging from the usual beautiful dream about 'not going back'—'war over in the autumn'—'getting a job in England' etc. These ideas always emanate from one's friends in England, and one's own feeble state of mind when ill, and fed up, and amazed at being back in comfort and safety.

Things must take their course; and I know I shall be sent out again to go through it all over again with added refinements of torture. I am no good anywhere else: all I can do is to go there and set an example. Thank heaven I've got something to live up to. But surely they'll manage to kill me next time! Something in me keeps driving me on: I must go on till I am killed. Is it cussedness (because so many people want me to survive the war)—or is it the old spirit of martyrdom—'ripe men of martyrdom', as Crashaw says?[1]

[1] Richard Crashaw (1613?–49), 'A Hymn to the Name and Honour of the Admirable Saint Teresa'.

May 1

My first time out of hospital: lunched with Roderick at the Reform. A warm day, lit with quiet sunshine, a little hazy.

May 2

Lunch with Robbie Ross and Roderick at Reform. Talked to Wells and Arnold Bennett—the latter very affable. Also Harold Williams, a correspondent from Petrograd (and Lance-Corporal in New Zealand forces).[1] Sat in Hyde Park 3.30–4.30 in warm sun—very pleasant. Book published to-morrow. (Delayed till May 8th.)

May 9

Lunched with Bennett and J. C. Squire.[2] S. upheld Bridges strongly. Bennett's mannerisms very marked. A trick of pausing in the middle of a remark and finishing it quickly.

e.g. Shall . . . we . . . ⎫ ⎫
   (Slow drawl ⎬ pause ⎬ go upstairs?
   Largo) ⎭ ⎭ (Allegro)

Habit of pursing up mouth—very middle-class. Air of finality.

Squire—vegetarian—sad-looking type of poetical person with hair rather long brushed tidily over right eyebrow. Slouching gait, hands in pockets. Distinct charm in face when lit up. Looks more like an actor. Seemed amused by some of my remarks (pacifist cussedness about the conduct and effect of the war).

May 13   3.30 a.m. (in a white bedroom at Chapelwood Manor)[3]

This notebook began not many miles from Arras in the bloody month of April, when guns began to bellow. And now my disciplined wanderings have sent me to a very pleasant country house, where perfect good taste prevails, and nobody sleeps in the clothes he wore last week and this.

[1] This remarkable man (1878–1928) had lived in Russia since before the 1905 Revolution and had a Russian wife. He spoke thirty-five languages, including dialects from remote parts of Russia. Foreign Editor of *The Times* from 1922.

[2] John Collings Squire (1884–1958), poet, parodist and critic. Founder and editor of the *London Mercury*. Knighted 1933.

[3] The home of Lord and Lady Brassey at Nutley in Sussex, to which S.S. had been moved on 12 May. Thomas, first Earl Brassey (1836–1918), held many government and other posts. He married in 1890, as his second wife, Sybil de Vere, daughter of the seventh Earl of Essex.

It is a grey-timbered and many-gabled house, built twelve years ago. Dark yew-hedges and formal gardens are round it. And its windows look across Sussex toward Lewes and Beachy Head—all woods and sloping meadows and hedges in their young green, and growing wheat, with clumps of daffodils in the field beyond the gardens.

Sleepless, I am waiting for the dawn and the first English birds I have heard sing out their maytime madrigals since 1915. The gables of the house begin to show distinct against a clear, starry sky. Cocks are crowing; an owl hooting away in the woods; and the busy clock ticks on the mantelpiece. I feel as if I were soon to get up and dress for a cub-hunt—swallow my cocoa and boiled eggs, and then hear the horses' feet trampling the gravel outside.

All this is a long way from Arras and the battles. I am back in the years before battles were invented or Rolls of Honour thought about at all. As I lie on my bed with a yellow-shaded electric lamp shining (on my pink pyjamas) I can see the sky through the open, uncurtained window. The sky is a wonderful deep-blue colour, as I see it. When I turn out the light the window is a patch of greyish white on the darkness, with tree-tops standing up, very shadowy and still. It is the quietest of mornings; not a breath of wind.

I hear a cuckoo—a long way off. Then a blackbird goes scolding along the garden trees. Soon the chorus will begin. Put out the light.

May 15

Marvell's poems are the best vintage for these days of tranquillity. In the morning I wake to hear a gardener whetting his scythe beyond the yew-hedges. And I know that a tree of silver blossom shakes in the morning sunshine above his head, and a blackbird sings to all the world, crying that life is fresh and sweet and jolly.

> Ye glow-worms, whose officious flame
> To wandering mowers shows the way,
> That in the night have lost their aim,
> And after foolish fires do stray.[1]

[1] Andrew Marvell, 'The Mower to the Glow-worms'.

And in the afternoon I breathe the country air blown up from weald and wood—the smell of earth after rain, the kindest smell that ever came to make me glad.

All the morning I sit under oaks and beeches in the glory of young leaves, a book on my knee—John Morley on some eighteenth-century Frenchman, the kind of book where one can read a page or two and then turn to the morning sky and the garden and the distant line of downs as infinitely preferable, like listening to a bird singing outside the church during a dry sermon, as one watches the shadows of leaves and wings against the coloured windows.

Old Lord Brassey has gone to London to a dinner in the House of Lords where General Smuts is being entertained. Brassey is an interesting figure to study; serene old age going down hill too fast to keep its tranquillity: he has not far to go with his dragging feet and body bent double with rheumatics. Sometimes he is querulous, and almost childish. And at times he is the oracular proconsul, with snatches of urbane oratory, as he sits huddled at table, his chin on his chest and his red-rimmed eyes almost closed. His face, once gravely impressive, has become puffy and loose. Death presses him hard; he is losing his grip on life, in spite of his indomitable resistance. A pattern Englishman, no doubt, very wise in the ways of his generation, a useful servant of the State, but a strange figure to Youth in Revolt, and Youth torn by sacrifice. His wisdom has had its day, and his life has been blandly arranged, full of honest work and genial prosperity and interest.

But the way of martyrdom and doubt is the best. They see the flaming heavens opened, and angels and fiends at war. Theirs is the fiery path, storm-cloven with light.

A Conversation

He told her how he'd been trying to make up his mind. It was all quite simple; a tale re-told in many hearts. Twice he had been to the war, and twice had come home wounded; and now his friends had half-persuaded him to take a 'safe job'.

She listened to him, with her grey hair and tired white face, kind, aristocratic and emotionless, leaning a little forward over a piece of embroidery. She represented the patrician distinctions that he had fought for—the climbing woods and green fields that soldiers learn to love when death is over them. She was a Great Lady. And he was only a poet; but he knew that life was taking shape in his heart, and reputation a thing of small value compared with his hidden passion for utterance and truth and beauty. For a while he thought that she understood.

He spoke without reserve of his longing for life and the task that lay before him, setting against it his mystical joy in the idea of sacrifice and the disregard of death. 'But death is nothing', she said, putting away her high-bred reserve like a rich cloak; 'Life, after all, is only the beginning. And those who are killed in the war—they help us from "up there", *they are all helping us to win.*'

For a moment he was struck dumb: he had forgotten that he spoke to an alien intelligence, that would not suffer the rebellious creed that was his. She was a good woman as well as a Great Lady. But her mind dwelt in another kingdom from his. He was the starry wind on the hills, and the beast writhing in the mire, the strange traveller who had come to her gates and had been suffered to sit by the fire and rest his tired limbs. What was this 'other world' that she spoke of? It was a dream he had forgotten years ago—the simplicity of his childish prayers, the torment of his mocking youth that denied the God of priests, and triumphed in the God of skies and waters.

She spoke again, kind yet unrelenting, from the dais of her noble rank. 'It isn't as if you were an only child, with a big place to inherit. No; I can't see any excuse for your keeping out of danger.' And again, half-compassionate, yet still tinged with the prejudice of caste, 'But of course you can only decide a thing like that for yourself.' And he knew she was right. He was heir to a dukedom that would never exist in the Peerage that moulded her judgements. Had he been the only son of an accredited Lord Parnassus, she would have said, in her clear firm voice: 'The name must be preserved; it would never do for the place to go to that impossible creature in Canada.'

But she would pray for him with all the strength of her generous perfect-mannered soul. And when he had died of his wounds she would say: 'He was such a good boy, I am sure he is happier "up there". And he did so splendidly.'

And he would rot in his shallow grave, with all his plays and

poems blown away on the smoke of some senseless battle—
because his name was not worth preserving, and his 'place' was
only a little book of the songs he had made, bidding farewell to
earth as he stood on the verge of his promised kingdom. For he
was not even the younger son of an obscure barony; he was only
a poet who used to read the Bible for the glory of the language.
But death forgives many things; and he *had* died for England,
after all.

May 16
For a while I am shaking off the furies that pursued me. I am
an Orestes freed from the tyranny of doom. The War is a vague
trouble that one reads about in the morning paper. The com-
muniqués are almost insignificant. I no longer visualise the
torment and wretchedness there.

The world is just a leafy labyrinth with clouds floating above
the silence of vivid green woods and clean meadows bright with
cowslips and purple orchis. My thoughts have the voices of the
tiny brook that runs along the woodland, slipping and twisting
over mossy stones, and bubbling out into a rushy field to gurgle
merrily in its narrow bubbling channel.

I am a country wanderer once more—climbing gates and
staring through tangled hedges at the mossy boughs of apple-
trees laden with blossom, while the sun comes out after a passing
shower. I roam the narrow lanes, light-hearted as a lambkin,
emotionless as a wise gander. I desire nothing more than to stop
and discuss the weather with an old gaffer mending the gaps in
a hedgerow. I could almost praise the Apostles Creed to the
village parson if I chanced to meet him in the road, or saw him
leaning over his garden gate as I passed. And the sunsets are
yellow and serene—never dyed with crimson or hung with
banners of war.

From Letters and Reviews about my Book[1]

Your recent pieces are solid, vigorous and full of substance.
Edmund Gosse

[1] *The Old Huntsman*, published on 8 May.

The book is full of good and simple and personal things, and gives me the real excitement of poetry.

John Drinkwater

If this is not a great poet, true as well as new, then I have wasted a lifetime on trying to find what is, and what is not, the sovereign stuff.

E. B. Osborn

I appreciate thoroughly 'When I'm among a Blaze of Lights' and 'Blighters', and much like the grim humour of 'The Tombstone-Maker' and 'They', the pathos of 'The Hero', and the reticent poignancy of 'The Working-Party'.

Thomas Hardy

The book has much pleased me. The general spirit, choice of subject, energy, and 'don't care-a-damness', and youthfulness, give me deep satisfaction. I say naught of the versification as I know nearly nothing of the mystery thereof.

Arnold Bennett

'The Old Huntsman' is 'stunning' throughout, and so are lots of the others, especially in the first half of the volume.

Hamo Thornycroft

What Mr Sassoon has felt to be the most sordid and horrible experiences in the world he makes us feel to be so in a measure which no other poet of the war has achieved. As these jaunty matter-of-fact statements succeed each other, such loathing, such hatred accumulates behind them that we say to ourselves 'Yes, this is going on; and we are sitting here watching it', with a new shock of surprise, with an uneasy desire to leave our place in the audience, which is a tribute to Mr Sassoon's power as a realist. *It is realism of the right, of the poetic kind.*

The Times Literary Supplement
Second review (by Virginia Woolf)

I saw the Poet Laureate . . . and he had seen your poems in

a shop. He could not cut the leaves, but he read where he could. He is a rare and grudging praiser, and therefore I was much gratified at his warm commendation of several of your pieces. He said you had 'got more of the real stuff in you than almost any other of your generation'.

(Letter from Edmund Gosse)

> For these I fight,
> For mine own self, that thus in giving self
> Prodigally, as a mere breath in the air,
> I may possess myself, and spend me so
> Mingling with earth, and dreams, and God: and
> In them the master of all these in me,
> Perfected thus.

(Frederic Manning)[1]

Second R.W.F. Ten killed, fifteen wounded in six weeks. The casualties occurred mainly on April 23 and in another show five weeks later. First Battalion casualties at Bullecourt April–May 18—*350*.

May 18

Lord Brassey returned from town to-day. He discoursed during coffee and port-time about the War, while we four young soldiers sat round the table putting in a respectful word now and again.

I was next to him and had plentiful opportunities of noting the wreckage of his fine face—the head and brow are still there, and the firm nose, but the mouth is loosened and the lower lip pendulous and unhealthy-looking, like his hands. I think he is always on the verge of a 'stroke'. He talks in carefully pompous phrases as though he were Chairman of a Meeting—with the usual repetitions: 'I declare to you, my dear fellow (voice sinking to a mumble), I declare to you (louder), have you—can you say you have—any consciousness (pause) of *Sierra Leone*?' He is strong on the uselessness of a lot of our small colonies—says we (in the language of Lord Morley) might just as well give them to Germany. *Anything* to end the war (bless him). Lays stress

[1] From 'αυταρκεια' published in Manning's *Eidola* (1917).

on the uselessness of trying to 'redeem Belgium'—wouldn't
they be just as happy under the German Empire? and so on.
Probably he's quite right. He ended by saying 'I'm only an old
dotard,' and we tried to laugh naturally, as if it were a good
joke, instead of a tragedy, to see a fine man the victim of Time,
his body worn-out, his spirit undaunted.

But I won his heart with my piano-playing afterwards—and
probably made him sad as well as happy (possibly sleepy!). He
seems unable to lift his chin from his chest. We young men are
strangers in the land of his mind. He will go out into the night,
and the world will be ours.

'I declare to you, my dear fellow, that it is my *profound* convic-
tion that the present ecclesiastical administrative functions are
entirely, yes, *entirely* and undisputably inefficacious. O what
worlds of dreary self-sustainment are hidden by the *gaiters* of
our episcopal dignitaries!'

'I declare to you, my dear fellow, that it is my profound con-
viction that the preponderance of mankind is entirely, O yes,
most grievously, impervious to the deliberations of that obtuse
but well-meaning body of men, the Ecclesiastical Commis-
sioners!'

He is a very old man: his sententious periods quavering
between the querulous and the urbane. But his face is often lit
up by the human tenderness that the wise years have taught
him. He is a good man.

And he has never heard of Rupert Brooke! How refreshing.
And Lady Brassey has never heard of Hardy's *Dynasts*. But they
both admire Tagore!

May 20

When I woke early this morning to hear the bird-voices, so
rich and shrill in the grey misty dawn, piping hoarse and sweet
from the quiet fragrance of the wet garden and from the green
dripping woods far off—lying in my clean white bed, drowsy and
contented, I suddenly remembered 'At zero the infantry will
attack'—Operation Orders! Men were attacking while I lay in
bed and listened to the heavenly choruses of birds. Men were
blundering about in a looming twilight of hell lit by livid flashes
of guns and hideous with the malignant invective of machine-

gun fire. Men were dying, fifty yards from their trench—failing
to reach the objective—held up.

And to-night the rain is hushing the darkness, steady, whisper-
ing rain—the voice of peace among summer foliage. And men
are cursing the downpour that drenches and chills them, while
the guns roar out their challenge.

May 21

Lady Brassey and I discuss religion. Agree that C. of E. 'is a
bit *passé*'. But some formula is necessary until 'people have
learned to do without a Church'. 'Our Lord never told us to go
to church.'

But I cannot believe that such faith is beyond question if it
cannot join issue with wholesome disbelief. Grim, wise fatalism
like Hardy's has never touched her; she would not allow it to
disturb her serene optimism. Hardy is merely 'an unpleasant
writer', as my own mother would say. Lady B. dabbles in
Christian Science. She is fond of the word mystical (so meaning-
less). 'Mock-turtle Religions.'

She is very kind; and judicial about things. Apropos of the
idea of my taking a job in England till 'my nerves' are all right,
she doesn't want me 'dangling about and writing poetry'. She is
undoubtedly right, but I still think I'd better go back to the First
Battalion as soon as possible, unless I can make some protest
against the War.

Song (To an old Tune)

THE HAWTHORN-TREE

Not much to me is yonder lane
Where I go every day;
But when there's been a shower of rain,
And hedge-birds whistle gay,
I know my lad that's out in France,
With fearsome things to see,
Would give his eyes for just one glance
At our white hawthorn-tree.
Not much to me is yonder lane

Where he so longs to tread;
But when there's been a shower of rain
I think I'll never weep again
Until I've heard he's dead.

May 25[1]

DEATH IN THE GARDEN

I never thought to see him; but he came
When the first strangeness of the dawn was grey.
He stood before me, a remembered name,
A twilight face, poor lonely ghost astray.
Flowers glimmered in the garden where I stood
And yet no more than darkness was the green.
Then the wind stirred; and dawn came up the wood;
And he was gone away: or had I seen
That figure in my brain? for he was dead;
I knew that he was killed when I awoke.
At zero-hour they shot him through the head
Far off in France, before the morning broke.

May 25

A WAR WIDOW

'Life is *so* wonderful, so vast!—and yet
'We waste it in this senseless war', she said,
Staring at me with goggling eye-balls set
Like large star-sapphires in her empty head.

I watched the pearls that dangled from her ears,
Wondering how much was left for *her* to buy
From Time but chattering, comfortable years,
And lust that dwindles to a jewelled sigh.

May 26

A QUIET WALK

He'd walked three miles along the sunken lane,
A warm breeze blowing through the hawthorn-drifts
Of silver in the hedgerows; sunlit clouds
Moving aloft in level, slow processions.

[1] Published in the *Spectator*, 27 October 1917, then in *Counter-Attack*.

And he'd seen nobody for over an hour,
But grazing sheep and birds among the gorse.

He all-but passed the thing; half-checked his stride,
And looked—old, ugly horrors crowding back.

A man was humped face downward in the grass,
With clutching hands, full-skirted grey-green coat,
And something stiff and wrong about the legs.
He gripped his loathing quick . . . some hideous wound . . .
And then the stench . . . A stubbly-bearded tramp
Coughed and rolled over and asked him for the time.

June 1

IN AN UNDERGROUND DRESSING-STATION

They set him quietly down: I think he tried
To grin . . . moaned . . . moved his head from side to side.

He gripped the stretcher; stiffened; glared, and screamed,
'Oh put my leg down, doctor, do!' (He'd got
A bullet in his ankle; and he'd been shot
Horribly through the guts.) The surgeon seemed
So kind and gentle, saying, above that crying,
'You *must* keep still.' But he was dying . . . dying.

June 2[1]

[S.S. left Chapelwood Manor on 4 June, and spent his time
until 12 July in his London club and at Weirleigh.]

June 15

I am making this statement as an act of wilful defiance of
military authority, because I believe that the War is being
deliberately prolonged by those who have the power to end
it. I am a soldier, convinced that I am acting on behalf of
soldiers. I believe that this War, upon which I entered as a
war of defence and liberation, has now become a war of
aggression and conquest. I believe that the purposes for
which I and my fellow-soldiers entered upon this War

---

[1] First draft of a poem, begun in April, published in the *Cambridge Magazine*,
9 June 1917, and in *War Poems* (1919).

should have been so clearly stated as to have made it impossible for them to be changed without our knowledge, and that, had this been done, the objects which actuated us would now be attainable by negotiation.

I have seen and endured the sufferings of the troops, and I can no longer be a party to prolonging those sufferings for ends which I believe to be evil and unjust.

I am not protesting against the military conduct of the War, but against the political errors and insincerities for which the fighting men are being sacrificed.

On behalf of those who are suffering now, I make this protest against the deception which is being practised on them. Also I believe that it may help to destroy the callous complacence with which the majority of those at home regard the continuance of agonies which they do not share, and which they have not sufficient imagination to realise.[1]

Copies of Statement sent to:

Thomas Hardy O.M.	H. W. Massingham[5]
Lord Brassey G.C.B.	Lord Henry Bentinck M.P.[6]
J. F. Hope M.P.[2]	Horace Hutchinson[7]
H. B. Lees-Smith M.P.	J. A. Spender[8]
C. K. Ogden[3]	Harold Cox[9]
Arnold Bennett	Eddie Marsh
Edward Carpenter[4]	H. G. Wells[10]

[1] This is the statement which S.S. sent to his Commanding Officer on 6 July. It was read out in the House of Commons on 30 July by Mr H. B. Lees-Smith, Liberal M.P. for Northampton, and printed in *The Times* next day.

[2] James Fitzalan Hope (1870–1949), Conservative Member for Sheffield Central and a Junior Lord of the Treasury. Later Deputy Speaker of the House of Commons. Created Baron Rankeillour in 1932.

[3] (1889–1957) Editor of the pacifist *Cambridge Magazine*, where many of S.S.'s war poems were published. Inventor of Basic English.

[4] (1844–1929) Writer and teacher. S.S. had written to him about homosexuality in 1912.

[5] Liberal journalist (1860–1924). Editor of the *Nation* 1907–23. The Markington of *Memoirs of an Infantry Officer*.

[6] (1863–1931) Brother of Lady Ottoline Morrell. A great hunting man.

[7] Pen-name of Horatio Gordon Hutchinson (1859–1932), twice amateur golf champion, author of many books on golf, cricket and a variety of other subjects.

[8] (1862–1942) Editor of the Liberal *Westminster Gazette*.

[9] (1859–1936) Liberal journalist and M.P. Brother-in-law of Hamo Thornycroft.

[10] This is not a complete list, since copies were certainly sent to Robbie Ross, Bertrand Russell (see note, p. 178) and Robert Graves.

June 19

I wish I could believe that Ancient War History justifies the indefinite prolongation of this war. The Jingos define it as 'an enormous quarrel between incompatible spirits and destinies, in which one or the other must succumb'. But the men who write these manifestos do not truly know what useless suffering the war inflicts.

And the ancient wars on which they base their arguments did not involve such huge sacrifices as the next two or three years will demand of Europe, if this war is to be carried on to a knock-out result. Our peace-terms remain the same, 'the destruction of Kaiserism and Prussianism'. I don't know what aims this destruction represents.

I only know, and declare from the depths of my agony, that these empty words (so often on the lips of the Jingos) mean the destruction of Youth. They mean the whole torment of waste and despair which people refuse to acknowledge or to face; from month to month they dupe themselves with hopes that 'the war will end this year'.

And the Army is dumb. The Army goes on with its bitter tasks. The ruling classes do all the talking. And their words convince no one but the crowds *who are their dupes.*

The soldiers who return home seem to be stunned by the things they have endured. They are willingly entrapped by the silent conspiracy against them. They have come back to life from the door of death, and the world is good to enjoy. They vaguely know that it is 'bad form' to hurt people's feelings by telling the truth about the war. Poor heroes! If only they would speak out; and throw their medals in the faces of their masters; and ask their women why it thrills them to know that they, the dauntless warriors, have shed the blood of Germans. Do not the women gloat secretly over the wounds of their lovers? Is there anything inwardly noble in savage sex instincts?

The rulers of England have always relied on the ignorance and patient credulity of the crowd. If the crowd could see into those cynical hearts it would lynch its dictators. For it is to the inherent weakness of human nature, and not to its promiscuous nobility, that these great men make their incessant appeals.

The soldiers are fooled by the popular assumption that they are all heroes. They have a part to play, a mask to wear. They are allowed to assume a pride of superiority to the mere civilian. Are there no heroes among the civilians, men and women alike?

Of the elderly male population I can hardly trust myself to speak. Their frame of mind is, in the majority of cases, intolerable. They glory in senseless invective against the enemy. They glory in the mock-heroism of their young men. They glory in the mechanical phrases of the Northcliffe Press. They regard the progress of the war like a game of chess, cackling about 'attrition', and 'wastage of man-power', and 'civilisation at stake'. In every class of society there are old men like ghouls, insatiable in their desire for slaughter, impenetrable in their ignorance.

> Soldiers conceal their hatred of the war.
> Civilians conceal their liking for it.

'How vastly the spiritual gain of those who are left behind outweighs the agony and loss of those who fight and die . . . the everlasting glory and exaltation of war.' (From a review in *The Times Literary Supplement*)

This is the sort of thing I am in revolt against. But I belong to 'a war-wearied and bewildered minority which regards "victory" and "defeat" as rhetorical terms with little precise meaning'.

June 21

A long statement of the war-aims etc by Belloc in *Land and Water* leaves me quite unconvinced. He argues from the point of view of British rectitude: and it is *that* which I am questioning. Worst of all, he argues on the assumption that 'the next few months' will bring a military decision; he has done this since 1915, so one cannot put much faith in him.

I am revolting against the war being continued indefinitely; I believe that Carson, Milner,[1] Lloyd George and Northcliffe *intend* the war to continue at least two more years. To carry out the scheme of 'crushing Kaiserism and Prussianism' by means of brute force, the war *must* go on two more years.

If they stated our terms definitely, once and for all, and those terms were the ones we went into the war to enforce, the German people would realise that they had been enforced; and

[1] Alfred, first Viscount Milner (1854–1925), proconsul. Member of the War Cabinet. Secretary of State for War 1918–19.

would insist on the war being stopped. (But the one thing which our side ignores is the true psychology of the Germans.) We are aggravating their obstinacy and will to resist by our own intolerant arrogance.

It is obvious that nothing could be worse than the present conditions under which humanity is suffering and dying. How will the wastage and misery of the next two years be repaired? Will Englishmen be any happier because they have added more colonies to their Empire? The agony of France! The agony of Austria-Hungary and Germany! Are not those equal before God?

July 4
Adjutant Third R.W.F. wires me 'Join at Litherland immediately'. (I have now overstayed my leave a week.) This is the first step.

Copy of letter to the C.O. of the Third R.W.F.   Sent off July 6
I am writing you this private letter with the greatest possible regret. I must inform you that it is my intention to refuse to perform any further military duties. I am doing this as a protest against the policy of the Government in prolonging the War by failing to state their conditions of peace.

I have written a statement of my reasons, of which I enclose a copy. This statement is being circulated. I would have spared you this unpleasantness had it been possible.

My only desire is to make things as easy as possible for you in dealing with my case. I will come to Litherland immediately I hear from you, if that is your wish.

I am fully aware of what I am letting myself in for.

[From this point there is no surviving diary until December, but from *Memoirs of an Infantry Officer*, *Sherston's Progress* and *Siegfried's Journey* the outline of the missing months can be sketched out. On 12 July S.S. reported at Litherland and stayed in Liverpool. After refusing one medical board he was persuaded by Robert Graves to attend another on 20 July, at which he was ordered to report to Craiglockhart War Hospital for shell-shocked officers at Slateford, near Edinburgh. He arrived there on 23 July and stayed till, after a month's sick-leave, he was boarded fit for General Service on 26 November.

At Craiglockhart he wrote a number of his finest war poems, and among his fellow-inmates was the young poet Wilfred Owen, whom S.S. encouraged and introduced to Robbie Ross and others.

A selection of letters will add some details of the following months.]

Bobbie Hanmer to S.S.

Tuesday   1 *War Hospital, Block C 11, Reading*
My dear old Sassons, What is this damned nonsense I hear from Robert Graves that you have refused to do any more soldiering? For Heaven's sake man don't be such a fool. Don't disgrace yourself and think of us before you do anything so mad. How do you propose to get out of the Army for the first thing? You are under age and will only have to join the ranks unless you become a Conscientious Objector, which pray Heaven you never will.

Let me have a line soon.   Yours ever   Robert H. Hanmer

Lady Ottoline Morrell to S.S.

Garsington
I saw Bertie [Russell][1] in London yesterday and he showed me your statement which I thought extraordinarily good. It really couldn't have been better, I thought. Very condensed and said all that's necessary. It is *tremendously fine* of you doing it. You will have a hard time of it, and people are sure to say all sorts of foolish things. They always do—but nothing of that sort can really tarnish or dim the value and splendour of such a True Act. Nor rob it of its fruition. Such deeds always bear splendid fruits however much people may carp. It is beastly being a woman and sitting still, irritating. Sometimes I feel I must go out and do something outrageous.

[1] Bertrand Russell (1872–1970), philosopher, mathematician, pacifist. The Thornton Tyrrell of *Memoirs of an Infantry Officer*. Massingham had introduced S.S. to him, and Russell had helped and encouraged S.S. with his protest, as well as introducing him to Lees-Smith.

Robbie Ross to S.S.

8 July 1917   *Hotel Albion, Brighton*
Dearest Siegfried, I am quite appalled at what you have done. I can only hope that the C.O. at Litherland will absolutely ignore your letter. I am terrified lest you should be put under arrest. Let me know at once if anything happens.

Ever your devoted   Robbie

Eddie Marsh to S.S.

10 July 1917   *5 Raymond Buildings, Gray's Inn*
My dear Siegfried, Thank you very much for telling me what you've done. Of course I'm sorry about it, as you expect. As a non-combatant, I should have no sort of right to blame you, even if I wanted to. But I do think you are intellectually wrong—on the facts. We agree that our motives for going to war were not aggressive or acquisitive to start with, and I cannot myself see that they have changed. And it does seem strange to me that you should come to the conclusion that they have, at the very moment when the detached Americans have at last decided that they must come in to safeguard the future of liberty and democracy—and when the demoralised Russian Army seem—after having been bitten with your view—to have seen that they must go on fighting for the sake of their freedom.

I cannot myself see any future for decent civilisation if the end of the war is to leave the Prussian autocracy in any position of credit and trust.

But now dear boy you have thrown your die, and it's too late to argue these points. One thing I do beg of you. Don't be more of a martyr than you can help! You have made your protest, and everyone who knows that you aren't the sort of fellow to do it for a stunt must profoundly admire your courage in doing it. But for God's sake stop there. I don't in the least know what 'They' are likely to say or do—but if you find you have a choice between acceptance and further revolt, accept. And don't proselytise. Nothing that you can do will really affect the situation; we *have* to win the war (you must see that) and it's best that we should do it without more waste and friction than are necessary.   Yours   Eddie

1917

Edward Carpenter to S.S.

10 July 1917 *Millthorpe, Holmesfield, near Sheffield*
Well done, good and faithful! Let me know if I can be of any use
in the matter. I shall be in London in ten days or so, and could
see you if feasible. Edward Carpenter

Arnold Bennett to S.S.

20 July 1917 *Comarques, Thorpe-le-Soken*
My dear S.S. It is a pity you didn't get my previous letter, as it
was rather a judicious document. As you now sort of invite my
notions I will tell you that I think you are very misguided and
that your position cannot be argumentatively defended. Your
conclusions may be right. I think they are wrong, but they may
be right. That is not the point. The point is that you are not in
a position to judge the situation. For you are not going to tell
me that you have studied it in all its main bearings and branches.
In my opinion a citizen is not justified in acting in such a way
as will, so far as he is concerned, fundamentally thwart the
desires of the majority as expressed by the accepted channels,
unless he has with reasonable fullness acquainted himself with
the facts of the case. If you were acting from an objection to all
war, your position would be comprehensible and justifiable. But
you are acting from an opinion that this particular war has
reached a particular stage and that civilians have reached a
particular degree of inhumanity. The overwhelming majority of
your fellow citizens are against you. You may say that your
action affects only yourself. Not so. It affects the whole State.
You did not bind yourself as an officer on the understanding that
you should be free from obligations whenever you happened to
conclude that the war ought to be over. You are arrogating to
yourself a right to which you are not entitled. A most important
principle is involved—unless you declare for anarchy. You have
asked for this plain speaking, and dash it! you have got it! And
do not imagine that we chaps over age have not realised to a
considerable extent what you soldiers have been through and
are going through, and do not appreciate it. But we say that
only the accident of age put you into it, and kept us out of it. For
various reasons, further, we are better able to judge the war as

a whole than you are. There is no sort of callousness in this. I read your poem in the last *Cambridge Magazine* and much liked it.[1] I rely on you not to resent this epistle. Your suspicion is correct. The Army will ultimately lay it down that you are 'daft'. You aren't of course, but that's how it will end. What is the matter with you is spiritual pride.   Yours ever   A.B.

S.S. to Robert Graves

Sunday night [15 July 1917]   *Exchange Hotel, Liverpool*
Dearest Robert, No doubt you are worrying about me. I came here on Friday, and walked into the Orderly Room feeling like nothing on earth, but probably looking fairly self-possessed. Found 'Floods' there (the C.O. away on holiday).

Of course F. was prepared for the emergency (and Tony Pryce had also been told). F. was nicer than anything you could imagine, and made me feel an utter brute. But he has a kind heart. They have consulted the General, who is consulting God —or someone like that. Meanwhile I am staying at the Exchange, having sworn not to run away to the Caucasus.[2]

No doubt I shall in time persuade them to be nasty about it. I don't think they realise that my performances will soon be very well known. I hate the whole thing more than ever—and more than ever I know that I'm right, and shall never repent of it.

Things look better in Germany, but Lloyd George will probably say it is 'a plot'. These politicians seem incapable of behaving like human beings. *Don't answer this.*   S.S.

Robbie Ross to Edmund Gosse

19 July 1917   *40 Half Moon Street, W.1.*
Dear Gosse, Your letter reached me at Brighton this morning just as I was leaving. The case of Siegfried is very distressing. Before telling you about it I had hoped that some fortunate resolution would have supervened, but alas I have no news good or bad. This is what happened.

Some three weeks ago, Siegfried, who was in fair spirits (but

[1] 'To Any Dead Officer', *Cambridge Magazine*, 14 July 1917.
[2] See p. 98.

in a very abnormal state I thought), was told that if he applied to a certain colonel at Cambridge he would get a berth there, connected with the officers training corps. This was the kind of thing he had wanted, but I observed that he delayed writing, for some reason I did not suspect. At last at my instance he wrote from here and I posted the letter.[1]

He returned to his mother's house at Weirleigh. After writing a few ordinary letters, in one of which he stated that he had *not* heard from Cambridge, he posted a short note containing a copy of a statement that he had forwarded to his Commanding Officer at Liverpool, the headquarters of the Welch Fusiliers. This statement briefly set forth that he would no longer obey orders, would not go back to the front in any eventuality, that he disapproved of the war and the conduct of the war, etc etc. Unhappily he has circulated copies to various people, including Robert Graves.

Graves wrote an excellent letter to the C.O. at Liverpool and received a most kind sympathetic letter in reply, saying that Siegfried would be ordered a Medical Board and the best would be done to treat the whole thing as a medical case. Siegfried consented to go to Liverpool and passed through London last Thursday, slept at my rooms and *said* he was going to Liverpool. I was away at the time. He is hurt with me because I am unsympathetic and to be precise that I did not give my blessing to his insane action. I came on Tuesday and met Graves by appointment but he had no news. He (Graves) went to Liverpool on Wednesday (yesterday) and is to let me know how things are going. Meanwhile all Siegfried's letters have been returned from Liverpool here! His mother's letters come here. I fear lest Siegfried is under arrest, but in a way that is the best that could happen. I have promise of powerful help if necessary at the War Office. At present it is premature to do anything. When I have news you shall have it.   Yours   Robbie Ross

---

[1] S.S. did go to Cambridge and was accepted as an instructor in the Cadet Battalion there.

1917

S.S. to Robbie Ross

26 July [1917] 　　　　　　　　　　*'Dottyville'*
　　　　　　　　　　　Craiglockhart War Hospital
　　　　　　　　　　　　Slateford, Midlothian

My dear Robbie, There are 160 Officers here, most of them half-dotty. No doubt I'll be able to get some splendid details for future use.

Rivers, the chap who looks after me, is very nice. I am very glad to have the chance of talking to such a fine man.[1]

Do you know anyone amusing in Edinburgh who I can go and see?

It was very jolly seeing Robert Graves up here. We had great fun on his birthday, and ate enormously. R. has done some very good poems which he repeated to me. He was supposed to *escort* me up here, but missed the train and arrived four hours after I did!

Hope you aren't worried about my social position.

　　　　　　　　　　　　　　　Yours ever 　　　S.S.

S.S. to Lady Ottoline Morrell

30 July 　　　　　　　　　　　　　　　　*Craiglockhart*

My dear Ottoline, I am quite all right and having a very decent time. Letters aren't interfered with. It's simply an opportunity for marking time and reading steadily.

The Pentland hills are glorious. I leap on their ridges like a young ram.

My fellow-patients are 160 more or less dotty officers. A great many of them are degenerate-looking. A few are genuine cases of shell-shock etc. One committed suicide three weeks ago. The bad ones are sent to another place.

My doctor is a sensible man who doesn't say anything silly. His name is Rivers, a notable Cambridge psychologist. But his arguments don't make any impression on me. He doesn't *pretend* that my nerves are wrong, but regards my attitude as

---

[1] Dr W. H. R. Rivers F.R.S. (1864–1922), psychologist and anthropologist, Fellow of St John's College, Cambridge, was now a temporary captain in the Royal Army Medical Corps. For his beneficent treatment of S.S. see *Sherston's Progress* and *Siegfried's Journey*. S.S. appears briefly as Patient B in Rivers's posthumously published *Conflict and Dream* (1923).

abnormal. I don't know how long he will go on trying to persuade me to modify my views. Yours ever S.S.

I have got lots of books, and go in to Edinburgh whenever I like.

S.S. to Lady Ottoline Morrell

19 August   *Central Station Hotel*
                                              Glasgow

I am never sniffy or snubby with my friends—as you ought to know by now! I thought you understood that when I don't feel like writing letters I don't write them.

Barbusse's French is beyond me, but the translation[1] is good enough to show the truth and greatness of his book, so you needn't be so superior about it!

I have been working at new poems lately, and a few of them are shaping themselves all right.

A man has motored me over to this large city and I have lunched ponderously.

Your delightful tiny Keats has been my companion lately, but most of my days have been spent in slogging golf-balls on the hills above Edinburgh. I admire the 'views' prodigiously: they are bonny. A month ago seems like a bad dream. 'And still the war goes on, *he* don't know why'.[2]   S.S.

S.S. to Lady Ottoline Morrell

5 September 1917   *Craiglockhart*

My dear Ottoline, I am glad you have forgiven me! I would have written, but have been knocked flat once again by the best sporting friend I ever had getting killed on August 14—in France. He was indeed my greatest friend before the war—a Winchester boy named Gordon Harbord, whom I met in 1908 and saw constantly afterwards. When the *un*intellectual people go it is much the worst—one feels they've so much to lose.

I had been busy writing a cub-hunting poem for him during the days between August 15 and the time I heard of it.

---

[1] *Under Fire* (1917), English version of *Le Feu* (1916), the war-novel of Henri Barbusse (1873–1935).
[2] The last line of S.S.'s poem 'In the Pink' (see p. 39).

Things go on the same here.
I wonder if Massingham would care to use the sonnet in *The
Hydra*[1]—show it to him when you see him.

A WOODEN CROSS (TO S.G.H.)
August 14, 1917

My friends are dying young; while I remain,
Doomed to outlive these tragedies of pain
And half-forget how once I said farewell
To those who fought and suffered till they fell—
To you, the dearest of them, and the last
Of all whose gladness linked me with the past.
And in this hour I wonder, seeing you go,
What further jest war keeps, having laid you low.

Men grey with years get wisdom from the strange
Procession of new faces, and the change
That keeps them eager. I am young, and yet
I've scores of banished eyes I can't forget;
The dead were my companions and my peers,
And I have lost them in a storm of tears.

I cannot call you back; I cannot say
One word to speed you on your hidden way.
Only I hoard the hours we spent together
Ranging brown Sussex woods in wintry weather,
Till, blotting out to-day, I half-believe
That I shall find you home again on leave,
As I last saw you, riding down the lane,
And lost in lowering dusk and drizzling rain,
Contented with the hunt we'd had, and then
Sad lest we'd never ride a hunt again.

You didn't mean to die; it wasn't fair
That you should go when we'd so much to share.
Good nags were all your need, and not a grave,
Or people testifying that you were brave.

[1] The Craiglockhart magazine, in which S.S.'s sonnet 'Dreamers' had appeared
on 1 September.

The world's too full of heroes, mostly dead,
Mocked by rich wreaths and tributes nobly said,
And it's no gain to you, nor mends our loss,
To know you've earned a glorious wooden cross;
Nor, while the parson preaches from his perch,
To read your name gold-lettered in the church.

Come back, come back; you didn't want to die;
And all this war's a sham, a stinking lie;
And the glory that our fathers laud so well
A crowd of corpses freed from pangs of hell.

Craiglockhart, August 24

S.S. to Robbie Ross

17 September [*1917*]   *Craiglockhart*
My dear Robbie, Robert sent me his proofs. His new poems
are delightful, and the whole book is a wonderful expression of
him. I hope you are feeling refreshed by your country visits.

I have got about 300 lines of verse for you to inspect, but am
too lazy to copy it out. I have done some good ones since
Roderick was here. The lot I showed him were mostly failures
which I have since destroyed.

I was rejoicing in my luck in getting a room to myself—my
late companion having gone—but after two days a man of forty-
five with iron-grey hair, an eyeglass and an aquiline nose has
floated in.

You were right about poor Julian Dadd. I hear from Robert
that J.D. has brain-fever or something bad.

Is Wells's new book amusing?

I am reading *South Wind*.[1] It is fairly funny, but rather re-
minds me of Dent (when not at his best). I play golf every day,
and say 'Ha ha,' among the captains.[2] But in the dusk of day I
whet my trusty Waterman and slay them all with songs!

Yours ever   S.S.

---

[1] By Norman Douglas, published in June 1917.
[2] 'He saith among the trumpets Ha, ha; and he smells the battle afar off, the
thunder of the captains, and the shouting' (Job 39: 25).

1917

S. S. to Robbie Ross

25 September 1917   *Craiglockhart*
My dear Robbie, Many thanks for the photos, which are excellent. Philpot has undoubtedly made a good job of it.[1]

A man called Aylmer Strong called here today with an invitation from Lady Margaret Sackville,[2] who lives six miles away, to go and see her. Do you know her? Her verse is fairly rotten, isn't it? Strong confessed that he, too, is a poet![3]

I will send you some new things shortly. Ogden (the *Cambridge Magazine* man) is getting them in proof for me to look at. I am full of poetry, but rather hampered by the constant presence of an iron-haired Theosophist in my room all the time. But perhaps my verse will be better for being bottled up a bit longer. I hope it won't lose its bubbles, like old champagne.

I hear an R.W.F. friend of mine has had one arm amputated, and will probably lose the other.[4] As he was very keen on playing the piano this seems a little hard on him, but no doubt he will be all the better in the end. At least the Theosophist thinks so.   Love from   Siegfried
Did you see my poem in the *Cambridge Magazine* for September 22? (The one about the Editor who'd been to the front.)[5]

S. S. to Robbie Ross

3 October 1917   *Craiglockhart*
My dear Robbie, I hope the air-raids haven't annoyed you? I am sending you some *Cambridge Magazine* cameos. Let me know if you think they are worth publishing in that noble organ. I see Ogden has queried my most uncontrolled line—sheer temper! One might put in something about 'went out to dine'—or 'I wished such fatherhood were mine'.[6]

---

[1] Glyn Philpot's portrait of S.S., painted in June 1917, which was reproduced as frontispiece to *Siegfried's Journey*. It is now in the Fitzwilliam Museum, Cambridge.

[2] (1881–1963) Daughter of the third Earl De La Warr. Published much verse and prose.

[3] For an account of the effect of his verse on S.S. and Wilfred Owen, see *Siegfried's Journey*, pp. 64–5.

[4] Ralph Greaves, the Ralph Wilmot of *Memoirs of an Infantry Officer*.

[5] 'Editorial Impressions', reprinted in *Counter-Attack*.

[6] The last line of 'The Fathers', which finally appeared as 'Those impotent old friends of mine'.

I have great difficulty in doing any work as I am constantly disturbed by nurses etc and the man who sleeps in my room—an awful bore. It is pretty sickening when I feel like writing something and have to dry up and *try* to be polite (you can imagine with how much success!). However, Rivers returns on Friday and may be able to get me a room to myself (or get me away from these imbeciles). Lady Margaret Sackville has sent me her war poems and asked me to lunch! A rival to Lady Ottoline; and quite ten years younger! Get *Nothing of Importance* by Bernard Adams (Methuen).[1] He was in the First R.W.F. with me for eight months (and mentions me once under the name of Scott). The book is by no means bad and he was a nice creature.

Love from S.S.

I sent Massingham a *very good* sonnet, but he hasn't replied. It is called 'Glory of Women'—and gives them beans.[2]

S.S. to Robert Graves

4 October [*1917*]   *Craiglockhart*
My dear Robert, Thanks for photograph. It is like you, except the forehead, which looks too flat and receding. I believe you washed your face before being taken! Hope you didn't catch cold. You might write to me when you aren't too busy. I am reading Bill Adams's book.[3] If you and I had re-written and added to it it would have been a classic; as it is it is just Bill Adams—and a very good book—expressing his quiet kindliness to perfection. He saw a lot through those spectacles of his.

The *Nation* quoted my 'syphilitic' poem[4] in an article on 'Venus and Mars' last Saturday.

I am on the way to doing a good, long poem in blank verse— sort of reminiscent of the wars, with stress on the heroism of Private Morgan-Hughes-Davies-Evans-Parry. But I can't get a room alone, and 8–11 p.m. is my brainy time, so I am rather hung up at present. Rivers returns on Friday, I hope. He has been rather ill.

[1] A record of service at the front in the First R.W.F. in 1915–16, by J. B. P. Adams (see p. 104). He died of wounds aged twenty-seven. S.S. gave his annotated copy of the book to Wilfred Owen.
[2] Published in the *Cambridge Magazine*, 8 December 1917, then in *Counter-Attack*.
[3] See previous letter. Bill was Bernard Adams's nickname.
[4] 'They', published in the *Cambridge Magazine*, 20 January 1917, then in *The Old Huntsman*.

I have been playing golf every day with a chattering R.A.M.C.
man who is a very fine player—partly to try and become im-
mensely healthy, but mainly to escape from the truly awful
atmosphere of this place of wash-outs and shattered heroes.
Result: go to bed every night tired and irritable, and write
querulous peace-poems.   Love from S.S.

S.S. to Robbie Ross

7 October 1917   *Craiglockhart*
Dearest Robbie, I am much relieved that the new poems have
passed safely through your judgment—always unfailing.
'Walking' puppies is a very well-known and quite technical
hunting expression and will be all right, and your suggestion
for the last two lines of 'The Fathers' shall be adopted forthwith.
I see Ogden has put two of the poems in this week. They look
pretty decent, I think.[1] I will send you copies of all new stuff
when I have the energy to copy them out. I have two longer ones
which aren't too bad. Rivers is back, and I hope he will get me a
room to myself, as I can't do anything with a prosy Theosophist
there all the time—he maddens me with his stilted talk. When I
told him our casualties (by official reports) were 102,000 for
September, he remarked 'Yes, Sassoon; it is the Celestial
Surgeon at work on humanity.' But he may provide material
for a poem some day!
I received the enclosed from Bedford Street.[2] It's some beastly
Harmsworth stunt, isn't it?
They acted *The Silver Box*[3] here last night—very badly, no
doubt. I didn't see it, but I hear a dotty padré who is here was
most upset and said 'Such a play is pernicious, and calculated to
set class against class.' Aren't people wonderful?
I suppose Robert's book won't be out for a few weeks.
Vernede's poems are wretched stuff, aren't they?[4] Have you seen

[1] 'Does it Matter?' and 'How to Die' in the *Cambridge Magazine* of 5 October.
[2] i.e. the office of William Heinemann Ltd.
[3] By John Galsworthy.
[4] Robert Ernest Vernede (1875–1917). British poet and novelist of French
   extraction. Although over-age he enlisted as a private in September 1914, was
   commissioned in the Rifle Brigade, served through the Battle of the Somme and
   died of wounds on 9 April 1917. His *War Poems and Other Poems* were published
   posthumously in 1917, with an introductory note by Edmund Gosse.

Horatio's article on his G.H.Q. visit, in *John Bull*?[1] It is the most astounding thing. Sir D. Haig was obviously pulling his leg all the time.   Yours ever   Siegfried

S.S. to Lady Ottoline Morrell

Wednesday [*17 October 1917*]   *Craiglockhart*
My dear Ottoline, Your letter reached me just as I was moving my belongings into the 'garret' which I have at length secured and am now free from theosophy and conversation, though somewhat chilly. As they say, the war situation looks more hopeless than ever, and the bolstering speeches only make it seem worse. I am afraid I cannot do anything 'outrageous'. They would only say I had a relapse and put me in a padded room. I am at present faced with the prospect of remaining here for an indefinite period, and you can imagine how that affects me. Apparently nothing that I can do will make them take me seriously (and of course it is the obvious course for them to adopt). I have told Rivers that I will not withdraw anything that I have said or written, and that my views are the same, but that I will go back to France if the War Office will give me a guarantee that they really will send me there. I haven't the least idea what they will do. But I hope you and others will try to understand what I mean by it.

After all I made my protest on behalf of my fellow-fighters, and (if it is a question of being treated as an imbecile for the rest of the war) the fittest thing for me to do is to go back and share their ills. By passing me for General Service (which Rivers says is 'the only thing they can do') they admit that I never had any shell-shock, as it is quite out of the question for a man who has been three months in a nerve-hospital to be sent back at once if he really had anything wrong. If the War Office refuse to promise to send me back I shall let the people here pass me for General Service and then do a bolt to London—and see what

---

[1] Horatio Bottomley (1860–1933), journalist, Member of Parliament, litigant in person, patriot, orator, and swindler on a gigantic scale. In 1906 he founded *John Bull*, an immensely popular weekly scandal-sheet which encouraged recruiting in the war. Having coaxed several million pounds out of willing admirers, and by his courtroom advocacy repulsed several charges of dishonesty, he was finally convicted of fraudulent conversion in 1922 and sentenced to seven years penal servitude.

course they adopt. Oh I wish I could talk to you about it. It's so hard to say what one means. I have written to Lees-Smith telling him what is happening. You *must* see how futile it would be for me to let them keep me here in these intolerable surroundings.

Surely my poems in the *Cambridge Magazine* are enough to show that I've not altered my views!

Let me know what you think, and if you are angry with me— say so.   Yours ever   S.S.
This poem will show you what I feel like. And it is the truth.

DEATH'S BROTHERHOOD

When I'm asleep, dreaming and drowsed and warm,
They come, the homeless ones, the noiseless dead.
While the dim charging breakers of the storm
Rumble and drone and bellow overhead,
Out of the gloom they gather about my bed.
They whisper to my heart; their thoughts are mine.

'Why are you here with all your watches ended?
'From Ypres to Frise we sought you in the Line.'
In bitter safety I awake, unfriended;
And while the dawn begins with slashing rain
I think of the Battalion in the mud.
'When are you going back to them again?
'Are they not still your brothers through our blood?'[1]

S.S. to Robert Graves

19 October [*1917*]   *Craiglockhart*
Dearest Robert, I am so glad you like Owen's poem. I will tell him to send you on any decent stuff he does. His work is very unequal, and you can help him a great deal.

Seeing you again has made me more restless than ever. My position here is nearly unbearable, and the feeling of isolation makes me feel rotten. I had a long letter from Cotterill to-day. They had just got back to rest from Polygon Wood and he says

[1] First published in the *English Review*, January 1918, then, retitled 'Sick Leave', in *Counter-Attack*.

the conditions and general situation are more bloody than any-
thing he has yet seen. Three miles of morasses, shell-holes and
dead men and horses through which to get the rations up. I
should like the people who write leading articles for the *Morning
Post* (about victory) to read his letter.

I have told Rivers that I will go back to France if they will
send me (making it quite clear that my views are exactly the
same as in July—only more so).

They will have to give me a written guarantee that I shall be
sent back at once. I don't quite understand how it is that Rivers
can do nothing but pass me for General Service as he says, be-
cause I am in the same condition as I was three months ago, and
if I am fit for General Service now, I was fit then.

He says I've got a very strong 'anti-war' complex, whatever
that means. I should like the opinion of a first-class 'alienist' or
whatever they call the blokes who decide if people are dotty.
However we shall see what they say. Personally I would rather
be anywhere than here.

It's too b....y to think of poor old Joe [Cotterill] lying out
all night in shell-holes and being shelled (several of the ration-
party were killed) but, as he says, 'the Battalion got their
rations'. What a man he is.

O Robert, what ever will happen to end the war? It's all very
well for you to talk about 'good form' and acting like a 'gentle-
man'. To me that's a very estimable form of suicidal stupidity
and credulity. You admit that the people who sacrifice the troops
are callous b.....rs, and the same thing is happening in all
countries (except some of Russia). If you had real courage you
wouldn't acquiesce as you do.   Yours ever   Sassons

S.S. to Lady Ottoline Morrell

28 October 1917   *Craiglockhart*
My dear Ottoline, The trouble is that if I continue my protesting
attitude openly after being passed for General Service they will
call it a 'recrudescence' or relapse and keep me shut up here or
elsewhere. They will *never* court-martial me. The only chance
would be—after being passed fit—to get an outside opinion
from a man like Mercier.[1] I don't quite know how they'd act if

[1] Charles Arthur Mercier (1852–1919), physician for mental diseases.

he said I was normal. At present the War Office has been informed that the only conditions under which I will undertake soldiering again are *with my old Battalion in France*, which makes it fairly clear. I mean to get a written guarantee from them before I do anything definite, as I know their ways too well. I am glad you like 'Death's Brotherhood'. It is the best that is in me, however badly I may have expressed it. I think the one this week—'Fight to a Finish'—is fairly effective in its way.

I am going to try and make Heinemann publish my recent stuff in a small book of about forty pages next spring. If he won't do it I'll get them printed for private circulation. I think 'The Rear-Guard' and another very terrible one will appear in the *English Review* in December or January.

It isn't worth while your coming all the way to Edinburgh in this awful weather. Wait a bit—I may be getting away soon. If you came I would ask Lady De La Warr to put you up. She would be pleased, I know. But they will be away for at least a fortnight after Monday.

I am not depressed—only strung up for supreme efforts—whether they'll be out in that charnel-place or not is in the hands of chance. Only I want to be active *somehow* because I know I can do it. Strength is something to be glad for—and one needs it to be able to face the bare idea of going back to hell. Yours S.S. Have you seen Gosse's remarks in the *Edinburgh*!!![1]

S.S. to Lady Ottoline Morrell

[Postmark 29 October 1917]   *[Craiglockhart]*
My dear Ottoline, It would be jolly to see you; but it seems a terrible long way for you to come, especially if you are rather broke, as I gather you and Philip generally are! However, if you decide to come, let me know what time you arrive.[2]

I can't see any way out of it except in France. Nothing definite has been heard from the War Office. They are very fed up with me here, as I was supposed to attend a Board last Tuesday, and didn't go.

[1] Gosse's essay 'Some Soldier Poets' appeared in the October 1917 issue of the *Edinburgh Review* and was reprinted in his *Some Diversions of a Man of Letters* (1919). In it he discussed and praised the poems of, *inter alios*, Graves and S.S.
[2] Lady Ottoline nobly undertook the long journey and stayed several days in Edinburgh.

Rivers thinks my 'Fight to a Finish' poem in the *Cambridge Magazine* very dangerous!

Love to Julian.[1]   Yours ever   S.S.

Italy! Things get worse and worse. 1920 now, I suppose (and peace and plenty).

FIGHT TO A FINISH

The boys came back. Bands played and flags were flying,
   And Yellow-Pressmen thronged the sunlit street
To cheer the soldiers who'd refrained from dying,
   And hear the music of returning feet.
'Of all the thrills and ardours War has brought,
This moment is the finest.' (So they thought.)

Snapping their bayonets on to charge the mob,
   Grim Fusiliers broke ranks with glint of steel,
At last the boys had found a cushy job.

   I heard the Yellow-Pressmen grunt and squeal;
And with my trusty bombers turned and went
To clear those Junkers out of Parliament.[2]

S.S. to Lady Ottoline Morrell

21 November   *Craiglockhart*

My dear Ottoline, I was afraid you would dislike the portrait.[3] It *is* a little popular. No doubt it will help to sell my posthumous works when used as a frontispiece!

And I feel pretty posthumous tonight. Reading about 'The New British Triumph' in the evening paper. Those things always bring black despair. I can visualise the horror too clearly, and the result is *not* triumphant. O God the yellings of politicians seem to get worse and worse.

But the poets will get the upper hand of them—some day (when bound in half-calf, suitable for wedding presents). I went

[1] Lady Ottoline's daughter.
[2] First published in the *Cambridge Magazine*, 27 October 1917, then in *Counter-Attack*.
[3] See note p. 187.

to town for two days last week, and saw an intermediary (about going back) but the result hasn't come through yet. Rivers has gone to town to his new hospital job, but will do his best for me, I know.

I will write a suitable letter to Lees-Smith as soon as I am passed fit—if ever. The First Battalion are for Italy soon, but I don't expect I'll get back to them again.

I met R. Nichols in town; and liked him.[1] (Probably because he behaved so charmingly to me.) R. Ross gave us dinner, and we went on to see some people called Colefax,[2] and I found it was a small at-home and that I was expected to read poems! Pretty thick, I thought; they might have given me *some* warning. However I slung a few ugly things at them—'The Bishop tells us',[3] and so on. Nichols read in a curious chanting manner which made me feel uncomfortable. But his things are very fine, when one reads them in the right mood. He is *the* poet for people emotionally wallowing in the blues.

I shall be here till November 28th. Perhaps longer. Litherland has moved to somewhere in Ireland, so I may have to go there for a bit.

Robert Graves writes that he is 'very happy'—and still at Rhyl. I don't seem to remember 'feeling very happy' since before I was wounded. Sometimes I feel as if I were very nearly used up. Funny how one recovers. I don't think R.G. feels things as deeply as some—certainly not as much as Nichols—with all his egotism.

This isn't much of a letter, but it's a relief to write to someone who understands things, and doesn't raise pitying eyebrows.

Yours S.S.

S.S. to Robert Graves

21 November [1917]   *Craiglockhart*
Dear Robert, *Please* forget about that d....d money. Surely you know me well enough. And some day a first edition of *Over the Brazier* (with the author's compliments) will be worth all that.

---

[1] Robert Nichols, poet (1893–1944).
[2] Arthur and Sibyl Colefax. He was a barrister and Unionist M.P., later knighted; she became a relentless society hostess. He died in 1936, she in 1950.
[3] 'They', see note on p. 188.

Your new photograph (profile) is awfully nice. I was wondering whether Litherland had gone to Dunsinane. Does that mean that I shall have to trek over to Ireland if passed General Service next week? Why can't I come to your shop—and then you can give me unlimited leave? I wish you'd try and find out something, as I may be leaving here next Wednesday. I hear the First Battalion are preparing to visit 'Nero's native city'. Joe writes me asking for an Italian dictionary! I wish to God I were with them—the prospect of being messed about and finally sent out to the 19th Battalion haunts me badly.

Robbie is always cursing me for using 'blood' and 'mud'—but the enclosed poem isn't too bad. Anyhow it is *true*. ('When I'm asleep'.)[1] You talk cheerily of our being established as poets and going far together. It is all very jolly, but I can't see beyond the war, and I don't care if I'm dead or alive—except to look after the two Roberts, and they can do quite well without me.

S.S.

Little Owen went to see Robbie in town and made a very good impression. You'd better make him the third in your triangle. I am sure he will be a very good poet some day, and he is a very loveable creature.

S.S. to Robert Graves

7 December [1917]   *Sussex*

Dear Robert, I am having some leave and return to Litherland next Tuesday. I was passed General Service at Craiglockhart on November 26. The Board asked if I had changed my views on the war, and I said I hadn't, which seemed to cause surprise. However Rivers obtained, previously, an assurance from a high quarter that no obstacles would be put in the way of my going back to the sausage machine.

I am not sure if I shall go up to this Poetry Show on Wednesday.[2] It will be an awful bore, and means going up for the day from Liverpool. Bob Nichols came to Weirleigh for two nights and was charming. He is quite different when in town among a lot of people. I forgot the war to-day for fifty minutes when the

[1] 'Death's Brotherhood', see p. 191.
[2] A charity poetry reading at the Colefaxes'. The readers included Aldous Huxley, the three Sitwells, Robert Nichols, T. S. Eliot, and Irene Rutherford McLeod (who read poems by S.S.).

hounds were running and I was taking the fences on a jolly old grey horse.

But the safety curtain is always down and I can't even dream about anything beyond this cursed inferno. The air-raid on Thursday gave me an awful fright (I was at Half Moon Street). I don't think I'll be any good when I get to the war.

Yours S. S.

December 19

Left Edinburgh on November 26, after being passed for General Service. Came to Liverpool, and found the Third Battalion had gone to Limerick. Kit Owen and Attwater still here, and about three hundred details. About thirty officers.

Went on leave November 29. Friday, Saturday and Sunday at Weirleigh. Bob Nichols came for Saturday and Sunday. Monday December 3 went to Lewes and hunted with Southdown at Offham. Poor day: very sharp frost. Stayed at Middleham. To town on Wednesday. Air-raid early on Thursday morning. Wednesday evening went to *Dear Brutus*[1] with Robbie Ross and Heinemann.[2] Thursday back to Middleham. Hunted Friday. Good hunt from Trueleigh Osiers—forty-five minutes. Back to the Stone Staples and to Toddington. Rode Stamp's old grey. Saturday lunched at Hove; to London after. Awful conversations in Pullman carriage by Jew profiteers. Breakfast at 5 Raymond Buildings Sunday—with Eddie Marsh and Bob Nichols. Received copy of *Georgian Poetry 1916–17* and showed E.M. my new poems. To Nuneaton after lunch. Evening at Portland House. Rode to Witherley on Monday; weather frosty. Got on Chamberlayn's black horse and rode on to Upton. Scent poor all day, but good fun, and lots of Atherstone hedges to jump. Back to Witherley.

Came to Litherland on December 11. Since then have eaten, slept, played a few rounds of golf at Formby, walked on the shore by the Mersey mouth, and am feeling healthy beyond measure. I intend to lead a life of light-hearted stupidity. I have done all I can to protest against the war and the way it is prolonged. At least I will try and be peaceful-minded for a few

[1] By J. M. Barrie.
[2] William Heinemann (1863–1920), S.S.'s publisher.

months—after the strain and unhappiness of the last seven months. It is the only way by which I can hope to face the horrors of the front without breaking down completely. I must try to think as little as possible. And write happy poems. (Can I?)

Christmas Day (Litherland)

Alone in the hut, after a day of golf at Formby, in fine, cold weather; dine to-night with Colonel Jones Williams and family at Crosby.

Last Friday went to Rhyl to see Robert Graves, and received his apologies for his engagement to Miss Nicholson. On Sunday went to Manchester and spent the day at Lawrence Haward's;[1] Dent was staying there. Went to tea with some Germans (Eckhards) and met Lowes Dickinson.[2] Trains late; and got back here at midnight, cold and tired.

Eddie Marsh writes that A. J. Balfour is much interested in my new poems; and Maurice Baring says they are 'too terrible to be published'. *Georgian Poetry* already in its third thousand. Expect to leave here soon.

[1] Author, translator and bibliographer (1878–1957). Curator of Manchester Corporation Art Galleries (1914–45).
[2] Goldsworthy Lowes Dickinson, philosophical writer and essayist (1862–1932).

1918

1918

January 7 (New Barracks, Limerick)

Left Liverpool 10.30 Sunday night and arrived Limerick this morning. Weather cold and snow on ground. Came across with Attwater and Hickman (the Quartermaster).

About 120 officers here. Four who were in France with First R.W.F. in 1915–16, C. D. Morgan, Freeman (both wounded for second time up at Ypres in October), Dobell and Garnons-Williams. Also J. V. Higginson who went out with me in November 1915. Very glad to get away from Litherland. Had been there since December 11 and done nothing but play golf and eat expensive dinners at the Adelphi.

Bells tolling from Limerick Cathedral; much nicer than sirens from Bryant & May's factory.

A MOMENT OF WAKING

I awoke; evilly tired, and startled from sleep;
Came home to seeing and thinking; shuddered; and shook
An ugly dream from my shoulders: death, with a look
Of malice, retreated and vanished. I cowered, a horrible heap,

1918

And knew that my body must die; that my spirit must wait
The utmost blinding of pain, and doom's perilous drop,
To learn at last the procedure and ruling of fate.
. . . I awoke; clutching at life; afraid lest my heart should stop.

January 8

JOURNEY'S END (TO W.M.M.)[1]

Saved by unnumbered miracles of chance,
You'll stand, with war's unholiness behind,
Its years, like gutted villages in France,
Done with; its shell-bursts drifting out of mind.
Then will you look upon your time to be,
Like a man staring over a foreign town,
Who hears strange bells, and knows himself set free;
And quietly to the twinkling lights goes gladly down,
To find new faces in the streets, and win
Companionship from life's warm firelit inn.

January 8[2]

IN BARRACKS

The barrack-square, washed clean with rain,
Shines wet and wintry-grey and cold.
Young Fusiliers, strong-legged and bold,
March and wheel and march again.
The sun looks over the barrack gate,
Warm and white with glaring shine,
To watch the soldiers of the Line
That life has hired to fight with fate.

Fall out; the long parades are done.
Up comes the dark; down goes the sun.
The square is walled with windowed light.
Sleep well, you lusty Fusiliers;
Shut your brave eyes on sense and sight,
And banish from your dreamless ears
The bugle's dying notes that say,
'Another night; another day.'

January 9[3]

[1] Perhaps Second Lieutenant W. M. Morgan of the R.W.F.
[2] Published, slightly abbreviated, in *Siegfried's Journey*. It was the beginning of a sonnet which S.S. never finished.
[3] Published in *Counter-Attack*.

January 12

Peace of mind; freedom from all care; the jollity of health and good companions. What more can one ask for? But it is a drugged peace, that *will* not think, dares not think. I am home again in the ranks of youth—the company of death. The barrack-clock strikes eleven on a frosty night, 'Another night; another day'.

January 19

And another week has fled. Frost and snow till Wednesday. Now it's warm and rainy. I walked out to Adare this afternoon. At the end of the journey I suddenly came upon the wide, shallow, washing, hastening, grey river; the ivy-clad stones of a castle-ruin planted on the banks, amid trees. Very romantic scene, on a grey evening. Then a hurried tea at the Dunraven Arms; rushed to catch a train which crawled back to Limerick. Strange peace of mind now. The last two weeks have been a complete rest for mind, while body stood about for hours on parade, watching the boys drill and do P.T., or lecturing lance-corporals in barrack-room of an afternoon. Their young eyes always meeting mine—frank and happy.

Robert Graves is married on Tuesday. Sent me his new poem 'The God Poetry' yesterday. Very fine. Hunt Monday, and go to Cork for Anti-Gas Instruction till the end of the week. Hunt Saturday with Jerry Rohan's hounds.

Reading Colvin's *Keats*, Hardy's new poems, and dipping into Barbusse now and then (all this apart from my military text-books which I study again!!).

How many miles to Craiglockhart? Hell seems nearer.

THE DREAM

Moonlight and dew-drenched blossom, and the scent
Of summer gardens; these can bring you all
Those dreams that in the starlit silence fall:
Sweet songs are full of odours.
                    While I went
Last night in drizzling dusk along a lane,
I passed a squalid farm; from byre and midden
Came the rank smell that brought me once again
A dream of war that in the past was hidden.

Up a disconsolate, straggling village street
I saw the tired troops trudge: I heard their feet.
The cheery Q.M.S. was there to meet
And guide our Company in . . .
                              I watched them stumble
Into some crazy hovel, too beat to grumble;
Saw them file inward, slipping from their backs
Rifles, equipment, packs.
On filthy straw they sit in the gloom, each face
Bowed to patched, sodden boots they must unlace,
While the wind chills their sweat through chinks and cracks.

I'm looking at their blistered feet: young Jones
Stares up at me, mud-splashed and white and jaded;
Out of his eyes the morning light has faded.
Old soldiers with three winters in their bones
Puff their damp Woodbines, whistle, stretch their toes:
They can still grin at me; for each of 'em knows
That I'm as tired as they are . . .
                              Can they guess
The secret burden that is always mine?
Pride in their courage; pity for their distress;
And burning bitterness
That I must take them to the accursèd Line.

I cannot hear their voices; but I see
Dim candles in the barn: they gulp their tea:
And soon they'll sleep like logs. Ten miles away
The battle winks and thuds in blundering strife.
And I must lead them nearer, day by day,
To the foul beast of war that bludgeons life.

January 17[1]

DEAD MUSICIANS

From you, Beethoven, Bach, Mozart,
The substance of my dreams took fire.
You built cathedrals in my heart,
And lit my pinnacled desire.

[1] Published in *Counter-Attack*.

You were the ardour and the bright
Procession of my thoughts toward prayer.
You were the wrath of storm, the light
On distant citadels aflare.

Great names, I cannot find you now
In these loud years of youth that strives
Through doom toward peace: upon my brow
I wear a wreath of banished lives.
You have no part with lads who fought
And laughed and suffered at my side.
Your fugues and symphonies have brought
No memory of my friends who died.

For when my brain is on their track,
In slangy speech I call them back.
With fox-trot tunes their ghosts I charm.
'Another little drink won't do us any harm.'
  I think of ragtime; a bit of ragtime;
  And see their faces crowding round
  To the sound
  Of the syncopated beat.
  They've got such jolly things to tell;
  Home from Hell
  With a Blighty wound so neat . . .

And so the song breaks off; and I'm alone.
They're dead . . . For God's sake smash that
                              gramophone!
                              January 19[1]

January 21
    This morning I hear that my name has come through on a list
of officers going to Egypt.

    Points in favour of going:
New country—conditions not so trying (probably Palestine)
—less chance of being killed.

[1] Published in *Counter-Attack.*

Points against going:
I want to go back to one of the regular battalions. The other place is only a side-show, and I'd be with an inferior battalion. Am known with the others, and know more people.
Can't make up my mind.[1]

January 22
Went to Cork for Anti-Gas Course. Very boring: hearing lectures on tedious details which I learned two years ago, and a year ago.

Sitting in the Country Club, I talked to an old parson, red-faced and patrician-nosed, about hunting etc. Becher by name, and was parson at Castle Townshend, where Miss Somerville[2] lives. His son is in the First Cameronians, and was in that H.Q. dug-out with me on April 16 last year, before I went up to the bombing show when I was wounded.

January 26
Motored with two Irishmen to a place eighteen miles from Cork—Roore's Bridge—to meet of the Muskerry Hounds. A grey, windy day, south-west wind. Rode a chestnut of J. Rohan's —good performer. A poor day's hunting, but very enjoyable. Fine country—along the River Lee—a wide, rain-swollen stream, flowing down long glens and reaches. The whole landscape grey-green and sad and lonely. Ireland is indeed a haunted, ancient sort of land. It goes deep into one's heart.

January 27
Returned to Limerick.

[1] Private Frank Richards D.C.M. in his book *Old Soldiers Never Die* (1933) recorded that Major Kearsley of the Second Battalion R.W.F. received a message: 'AM ORDERED TO EGYPT CAN YOU DO SOMETHING TO GET ME BACK TO FRANCE SASSOON.'
[2] Edith Œnone Somerville (1858–1949), joint author with 'Martin Ross' (1862–1915) of *Some Experiences of an Irish R.M.* (1899) and other stories set in Ireland.

January 28
  Limerick Hounds at Fedamore. Found at once in Lower Feda-
more Gorse; ran nicely to Kilpeacan, on toward Friarstown, and
back to Old Fedamore—and to ground close to where we found.
A good hunt of an hour and fifteen minutes—the first half-hour
very good. Found two at Rockbarton and dug one out (both bad
foxes). Rode Sheeby's bay mare—a lovely ride. Strong south-
west wind, and rain later in day. Home 5.30. Best hunt I've had
since the war. Took one fall—my own fault.

January 30 (Limerick. Kilfinny Cross)
  Drove thirteen miles in taxi to meet. A fine, breezy morning,
with drifts of sunshine. Rode Sheeby's little white-faced bay
horse (rather lame all day, and slow, but clever jumper). Drew
Kilfinny, Croome Gorse, and two other small places blank.
Found at 2 o'clock at Durrach and ran down wind to Croome
Gorse, through there and over the river at Caherass, straight
through the demesne, and on toward Killonehan; turned left-
handed (slow hunting) and crossed river beyond Fanningstown.
Long check there, but he was viewed going into Adare Deer
Park, and they picked him up after forty minutes, and killed him
in Adare village, in the Police Station! To Fanningstown it was
forty minutes, and a six-mile point. Obviously he took a strange
line, as he didn't try any of the earths in Adare. Very amusing
day and got to know some jolly people.

TOGETHER

Splashing along the boggy woods all day
And over brambled hedge and holding clay,
I shall not think of him;
But when the watery fields grow brown and dim
And hounds have lost their fox and horses tire,
I know that he'll be with me on my way
Home through the darkness to the evening fire.

He's jumped each stile along the glistening lanes;
His hand will be upon the mud-soaked reins;

Hearing the saddle creak,
He'll wonder if the frost will come next week.
I shall forget him in the morning light,
And while we gallop on he will not speak;
But at the stable-door he'll say good-night.

January 30[1]

MEMORY

When I was young my heart and head were light,
And I was gay and feckless as a colt
Out in the fields, with morning in the may,
Wind on the grass, wings in the orchard bloom.
  O thrilling sweet, my joy, when life was free
  And all the paths led on from hawthorn-time
  Across the carolling meadows into June.

My heart is heavy-laden now; I sit
Burning my dreams away beside the fire:
For death has made me wise and bitter and strong;
And I am rich in all that I have lost.
  O starshine on the fields of long-ago,
  Bring me the darkness and the nightingale;
  Dim wealds of vanished summer, peace of home,
  And silence; and the faces of my friends.

February 1[2]

IDYLL

In the grey summer garden I shall find you
With day break and the morning hills behind you.
There will be rain-wet roses; stir of wings;
And down the wood a thrush that wakes and sings.
Not from the past you'll come, but from that deep
Where beauty murmurs to the soul asleep:
And I shall know the sense of life re-born
From dreams into the mystery of morn

---

[1] Published in *Counter-Attack*.
[2] First published in *To-Day*, March 1918, then in the privately printed *Picture Show* (1919).

Where gloom and brightness meet. And standing there
Till that calm song is done, at last we'll share
The league-spread, quiring symphonies that are
Joy in the world, and peace, and dawn's one star.

February 1[1]

February 1 (Limerick. Maine)

Went to the meet (to ride Harnett's chestnut mare), but
weather very wet and stormy, and hounds went home from the
meet, as the draw was on some bad hill-country. Lunched at
Glenwilliam with Tom Atkinson. (Twenty-three miles for
nothing.) Very sad.

February 4 (Limerick. Four Elms)

Hacked to meet—four miles from Limerick. Fine sunny
morning. Rode Sheeby's big bay mare (quite a good ride).
Found in Cahervally, but he was headed twice, and finally went
away, and ran very twisting (a vixen). Slow hunting for about
forty minutes, ran toward Limerick, and killed at a farm. Scent
poor, but they hunted nicely. Mostly wall-jumping. Chopped a
mangy one in Friarstown, and drew the bog and Fedamore Old
Gorse blank. Home 5.15. A poorish day, but very jolly. Tea
with Mrs Marshall, the finest lady-rider I've ever seen. Happy
days.

REMORSE

Lost in the swamp and welter of the pit,
He flounders off the duck-boards; only he knows
Each flash and spouting crash; each instant lit
When gloom reveals the streaming rain. He goes
Heavily, blindly on. And, while he blunders,
'Could anything be worse than this?' he wonders.
Remembering how he saw those Germans run
Screaming for mercy among the stumps of trees;
Green-faced, they dodged and darted: there was one
Livid with terror, clutching at his knees;

---

[1] Published in the *New Statesman*, 29 June 1918, then in *Picture Show*.

Our chaps were sticking them like pigs. 'Oh hell!'
He thought—'There's things in war one dare not tell
Poor father sitting safe at home, who reads
Of dying heroes and their deathless deeds.'

February 4[1]

February 6 (Limerick. Ballingrane)

A wet day, south-west wind. Found in some gorse a mile from Nantinan (after drawing N. blank). And ran nicely back a half-circle to Nantinan, where he tried the earths, and went back to where we found, and ran us out of scent. A nice twenty minutes. Drew Castle Hewson and two other small places blank. Rode the Master's second horse as my hireling never turned up. A glorious ride—very sad that we did so little. Nigel Baring drove me back to Adare where I changed and dined. Home 9.50.

February 7

Orders to embark Southampton next Monday.

Books to take to Egypt

Oxford Book of English Verse	Barbusse, *Le Feu*
Keats	Pater, *Renaissance*
Wordsworth	Trollope, *Barchester Towers*
Shakespeare's Sonnets	Surtees, *Mr Sponge's Sporting*
Hardy, *Moments of Vision*	*Tour*
Crabbe, *The Borough*	*Tracy Romford's*
Browning, *The Ring and the*	*Hounds*
Book	Bunyan, *Holy War*
A Shropshire Lad	Plato, *Republic*
Meredith, Poems	Tolstoy, *War and Peace*
Oxford Dictionary	(3 vols)
Hardy, *The Woodlanders*	Scott, *The Antiquary*

February 8 (County Limerick. Ballingarry)

A fine, sunshiny day. Rode same mare as last Monday. Stayed with hounds till 2.30. They found several foxes on the rough hills above Ballingarry, and we scrambled about over walls and

[1] Published in *Counter-Attack*.

rough places. Scent was poor. The country all round looked beautiful—shining with water and grey villages, and white cottages, and the green fields, and soft, hazy, transparent hills on the horizon—sometimes deep blue, sometimes silver-grey. Good-bye to Dorothea Conyers[1] and Nigel Baring Esq and Mike Sheeby and hard-riding Mrs Marshall and all the jolly Limerick field. Into the Ford-taxi and back to Balinacurra for a hasty lunch of salmon and woodcock and champagne, with 'the Mister' and Mrs Macdonnel. Then to the station, and the 4.25 to Dublin. Billy Morgan, Jim Ormrod and Kit Owen saw me off (and of course the old 'Mister'). Reached London 7 a.m. February 9 and stayed the night at 40 Half Moon Street. Lunched with Robbie and Eddie Marsh and quiet dinner with R. and saw Rivers after. Heard Beethoven's Fifth Symphony, Lalo's Concerto (by Sammons),[2] César Franck's Symphonic Variations (Miss Hess)[3] and a new Schmitt[4] Tone Poem, at Queen's Hall in the afternoon. Sunday at Melbury Road, after seeing Heinemann and Lousada.[5] To Shannon's[6] after tea. Mother brave as usual. Left Waterloo Monday 12 noon. Robbie and Roderick saw me off. Left Southampton 7 and reached Cherbourg 2 a.m. Stayed one night in rest-camp three miles out.

February 13

A mild, grey morning, with thrushes and other birds singing like spring's first prelude. I am a little way off the rest-camp, sitting on a bundle of brushwood under a hedge. The country round, with its woods of pine, oak and beech, and its thorn and hazel hedges, might be anywhere in the home counties—Surrey for preference. I came on deck on the *Antrim* yesterday morning at 6.30, and found we were in Cherbourg harbour. It was just dawn—everything dark and strange—with lights burning round the harbour and on shore. Slowly the dark water grew steel-grey, and the clouded sky whitened, and the hills and houses

[1] Irish author and sportswoman (1873–1949).
[2] Albert Sammons, violinist (1886–1957).
[3] Myra Hess, pianist (1890–1956). Created Dame 1941.
[4] Florent Schmitt, French composer and pianist (1870–1958).
[5] J. G. Lousada, S.S.'s friend and solicitor.
[6] Probably the American-born portrait-painter J. J. Shannon (1862–1923), who lived in Holland Park Road.

emerged from obscurity. All the while the ship hissed and
steamed and the wind hummed in the rigging. By 8 it was sun-
shine and we were alongside the quay.

The rest-camp is close to a large château (used as Red Cross
place). Handsome park etc. A jay (magpie) is scolding among
the beeches a little way off, and the wind (south-west) bustles
among the bare twigs of trees. I have just recaptured that
rather pleasant feeling of isolation from all worldly business,
which comes when one is 'at the war'. Nothing much to worry or
distract one except the ordinary irritations and boredom of 'be-
ing messed about' by the Army. To-day we start our 1446 miles
by train to Taranto. It takes over a week. My companions are
S. W. Harper, M. Robinson[1] and H. G. Howell-Jones, all decent
chaps—Harper of course charming. It was he who went to
Edinburgh with Robert Graves, as my supposed 'escort', last
July.

Dinner last night—Hotel des Etoiles, rather bad—Corton
Burgundy. Hot bath this morning in shower-place. Fifty-six
young officers on our boat going to Indian Army straight from
Sandhurst (mostly children). I am reading *Barchester Towers*,
The Woodlanders and Pater's *Renaissance* in the train. (Camp-
commandant, Major Flux's speech—'anythink else you may
wish to partake of—etc').

Later. Have just picked a primrose. How touching!

February 14 (On the train. Notes)
6.30 p.m. after reading Pater's 'Leonardo'. Train stops. Black
smoke drifting. Got out for a minute. Trees against pale sky—
clouds higher, with three stars. The others playing cards by
candlelight. Scraps of talk—'Twist—Stick etc' 'Any more for
any more' (men drawing rations). Jock officer going back to
Seventh Division. Halt at Bourges—French and English soldiers
on platform. American camps on the way. Black men in khaki at
Cherbourg. Brown landscapes.

The beginning of a new adventure. I am already half way into
my campaigning dream-life. Funny mixture of reality and crude
circumstance with inner 'flame-like' spiritual experience. But
this time I know myself, and am quite free to study the others—

[1] The Marshall of *Sherston's Progress*.

equipped to interpret this strangest of all my adventures—ready
to create brilliant pictures of sunlight and shadow. In the 'awful
brevity' of human life I seek truth.

February 15
Awoke in the railway carriage to find a bright, frosty morning
—and the train in a station. We started about 9 and crawled to
St Germain (fifteen kilometres from Lyons) arriving there at
12.30. The morning journey was through fine country—fir-clad
hills and pleasant little valleys threaded by brooks and shallow
rivers.
Notes (oxen pulling a tree: boy standing among trees looking
down at the train). Yesterday was through level, brown, buff,
sand-coloured places. To-day dark-green firs are the colour-
note, and the sun shines gloriously on all, and warms my face as
I crane from the window to see the unfolding prospects.
We stay at a rest-camp near the station—bath and lunch—in
the afternoon go marketing. The blue Saone River flowing nobly
along. We leave again to-night. Singing in Mess-place. Jock.
Bad show. Service[1] poem etc.

February 17   1.30 p.m.
Train crawling toward the Italian frontier. Bright sun and
cold wind. Hard frost last two nights. Feeling ill with touch of
fever and chill on insides. Left St Germain 2 a.m. yesterday—
bitterly cold in the train. Went through Avignon, and through
Cannes, Nice, etc along by the sea in late afternoon. A gaudy,
parched-looking, tourist region—richly-scented flowers thrown
to the troops, and general atmosphere of Cook's tour. Throngs
of black soldiers in red fez and blue uniforms seen at street-ends
in the brassy sunshine. Beyond Nice the sea looked less 'popular'
—softly crashing on the brimming shore in the dusk, and so I
heard it at times during the night—half-sleeping on the seat
with drowsy M. Robinson. Daylight, red and frosty, found us
beyond Genoa (after much rumbling and clanking through short
tunnels in the dark).

[1] Robert W. Service (1874–1958), 'the Canadian Kipling'.

1918

February 18

Through Novi and Vochera, where we halt for lunch 12–1. Glaring sunlight and cold wind—dried-up land. All afternoon we crawl through vinelands, with the low, blue, delicate-edged hills on the right—a few miles away, till the sun goes down and leaves an amethyst glow on that horizon, and at 7.30 we reach Bologna.

Reading *Lewis Seymour and Some Women*[1] all day—an easy-flowing, unpleasant-flavoured book—great relief to turn to Pater's Botticelli essay, and then to Hardy's *Woodlanders*. Nasty old man, George Moore.

Jolly companionship of the journey, in spite of the animal squalor and so on. Harper rather hipped and fussy—bad campaigner, I fear. Howell-Jones sensible and philosophical. M. Robinson has my heart with his dear impetuous ways, kind and willing and cheery.

February 19

After a night-journey of freezing gloom, the train stopping occasionally in cavernous stations, we reached Faenza about 2.30 a.m. and slept in the train. Turned out at 8 to a sunlit morning and soon found ourselves washing and drinking coffee in a hotel, moderately comfortable. Clean, narrow tall streets, a market-place full of gossip and babble of cloaked, unshaven, middle-aged men, with a sprinkling of soldiers in grey with yellow collars. We stay here twelve hours. The fountain in the *place* was festooned with ice, like melted lead.

February 20

Left Faenza 9 a.m. and began the journey along the Adriatic shore. A cold morning, snow lying thin and half-melting, grey sky. On our right the low, drab hills, streaked with white, on the left the flat, lavender sea, flecked and broken with foam, and the pink slate-coloured horizon. Breakfast at Castellammarie. Reached Foggia about 11 p.m. Still very cold.

[1] By George Moore, first published in 1917.

1918

February 21

Awoke to find the train going through a region of olive-orchards, hoar and ancient, bent and twisted, with rough stone walls, and Primavera spreading her arms in a dazzle of almond-blossom, sunlit and joyous, with the Adriatic, in delicate glimpses of level blue, a mile or two away beyond the bleached-grey boles and branches. Quite an idyll.

About noon we come to Brindisi; and I take a shower-bath and dry myself in the sun and the bracing breeze, in a garden close to the railway, where 'ablution-sheds' etc are put up among fig-trees, vine-pergola, and almond-blossom, with a group of umbrella-pines at one end overshadowing an old stone seat for summer afternoons. Lunch in Brindisi city gate. Sailors. Picturesque. Spanish effects.

About 3—on again—the final stage to Taranto—across a flat, cultivated plain, fringed and dotted with the tufts and cloudy haze of bloom, rose and white, and the wind-swayed dull silver of tossing olive-trees, all in the glare of spring sunshine, with green of cactuses and early wheat. Bare fig-trees; silver; the most naked trees ever seen. Further on we came to a stony region with dry rocky hillsides—always the olive-trees.

Grottaglie at sunset A city crowning a hill: ivory-white houses, flat-roofed, climbing one above another, a dim brown castle with tower and sheer wall, the whole rising from a cloudy tangle of rosy fruit-orchards in blossom. Dim with dusk, the city shines in the last glow of a clear sunset; it faces the west and seems lit from within, smouldering and transparent with its own luminous beauty, magical, enchanted; to the left a long sweeping line of dim trees, a narrow border fringing an expanse of open country. A city of fiery opal, moonstone, amethyst, set in silver and turquoise. Oriental, not Italian—perhaps more Spanish than either —a dream-city girdled with orchards (and probably a damned smelly place for all that).

Reached Taranto about 9 in moonlight.

February 22

In a tent at rest-camp, Taranto 6 p.m. after a day of glaring sunshine and shrewd wind. Walked along the harbour after lunch. Blue water, and rusty, parched hills away on the other side. Towns like heaps of white stones, far away. One on a hill. Glad of my good field-glasses. Sat on a rock and listened to the slapping gurgle of the brimming water—clear as glass, while the others swung their sticks and straddled along the path, looking queerly out of place without a pier and bathing-machines.

This journey will always come back vividly when I hear or think of an utterly absurd song which everyone sings, hums, whistles and shouts always. 'Good-bye-ee—don't cry-ee; wipe the tear, baby dear, from your eye-ee,' etc.

Slept in the train again last night, and had my watch stolen—very irritating. All sorts of officers here, many going home for three weeks' leave. Very few intelligent, sensitive faces. (The doctors, of course, stand out from the others, with their kind, wise faces.)

The usual riff-raff, always playing poker in the Mess. Staff-officers, Colonels, Majors, Australians, Flying-men—all sorts—their eyes meet one's face and then slide down to one's left breast to look for medal-ribbons. But it would need a Joseph Conrad to picture the scene in the Mess here.

After dinner I came out to the chilly moonlight and the moonlight-coloured bell-tents with tracery of shadows falling on them from the poor old olive-trees that are left high and dry among this upstart camp, like wise old men among a flashy, jostling crowd coming from a race-meeting.

Someone was strumming the piano in the large concert marquee behind our tent-lines, so I lifted a flap and peered into the fantastic dimness—the few lights in there made a zany-show of leaping shadows and swaying whiteness. On the stage (looked at from behind) a little group rehearsing—Jews (of the Battalion here awaiting embarkation). A big man was doing a bit of gag before stepping back two paces to start his song. 'Give 'em a bit of Fred Emney' shouts someone, then a little man jumps into the light, and does some posturing, chin out, with his curved Hebrew beak coming down to the thin-lipped mouth. Another little Jew whispered to me (I was inside the tent by then) 'That's Sid Whelan—the other's his brother Albert'— evidently expected me to be thrilled. Probably well-known London comedians.

1918

February 24

Midway of the longest journey of my life. Aboard the liner
Kashgar in Taranto gulf. The evening sun hangs low upon the
sea. Across my cabin steals a patch of dusty glare. I hear feet
pacing on the deck above, and slamming doors in cabins down
below: the swish of the sea, the droning of the gusty breeze.
Soon the wind will fall; the twilight will be fair; and the hurry-
ing waves will lull the reflected stars. And the moon will hang
the shore with magical veils.

February 26   7 a.m.

Feeling much better this morning. Boat got under way
yesterday at 4.30 p.m. and has since been ploughing along the
smooth Mediterranean—a very well-mannered voyage. When
going on deck for boat-drill, officers sing 'Nearer my God to
Thee'.

Sat reading Conrad's *Chance* in the dark saloon after dinner
(shaded lights). Moonlight outside.

Can't say I've discovered any 'sensations' on this journey. The
sea is rather like an Academy picture, and the officer conversa-
tions dull beyond description. (I am too deep in my self; must
try to soften a bit, but have felt so damned ill since coming on
board.) When I look round at them, I feel no sympathy for
them; they seem so self-satisfied, with their card-playing, and
singing *Chu-Chin-Chow*[1] etc—while outside the saloon-door one
passes from the smell of cheap cigarettes to 'clear, starry nights,
oppressing our spirit, crushing our pride, by the brilliant evi-
dence of the awful loneliness, of the hopeless obscure insig-
nificance of our globe lost in the splendid revelation of a glitter-
ing, soulless universe' (Conrad).[2] The sea was darker than the
sky.

Last night the level plain of the bay was steel-blue, glimmer-
ing in deepening twilight. Low and sheer on the horizon stood
the coast; the Apennines, steel-blue as the water, appeared like
a soft rain-cloud on the sea, a ragged, receding line of hills,
spreading to dim capes and shoals jutting into a hazy brightness

[1] A musical play by Oscar Asche and Frederic Norton, which ran at His Majesty's
Theatre from 1916 to 1921.
[2] *Chance*, Pt One, Chap. 2.

[217]

of sunset. Above and beyond these blue ridges the west was saffron-hued, deepening to an edge of cloth-of-gold, rose-flushed and slowly fading. This was the last I saw of the land and of Italy. On the other side of the ship it was already night, with a full moon dancing on the waves.

N.B. Don't be too bloody serious.

February 27

Weather fine. Brain refuses to work. Feeling rather seedy still.

Read Hardy's 'Waiting Supper' and Wells's *Research Magnificent* (ship's library).

February 28

Arrived Alexandria 4 p.m. after exactly three days' voyage. A clear, soft-coloured afternoon, blue sea, creamy, brick-red terra-cotta and grey city, wharves and docks and so on, with smoke drifting and sunshine (no glare) and thickets of masts and funnels. Everything breezy, cheerful, and busy. English officers watch it for a while, nonchalantly, then go below for tea. I also, no more thrilled than the rest of 'em.

Backgrounds: exploring the picturesque. It doesn't satisfy at all. My 'travel sketches', 'landscape poems' and so on—no use. Merely exercises. *Must* concentrate on the tragic, emotional, human episodes in the drama. Shall I find them out here? Little Welsh officers in a warm-climate side-show. An urbane existence. Like this dock, with its glassy dark water, and warm night —stars, and gold moon, and the dark ships—the quiet lights— sounds of soldiers singing—safe in port once more. No tragedy. Nothing heroic. I *must* have the heroic. So good-bye to amiable efforts at nature-poems. If I write I'll write tense and bitter and proud and pitiful.

March 2

Left Alexandria 10.30 last night; arrived Base Camp, Kantara, 10 this morning.

No. 1 Base Depot Glare of sunshine. Splitting headache. Lying

in tent—valise spread on sand. Sounds: thrumming of piano not
quite out of earshot—in Officers' Mess. Lorries rumbling along
road fifty yards away. Troops marching and whistling. Bagpipes
a long way off. Egyptian labourers go past, singing monotonous
chorus (it seems to go up into the light somehow).
Officers' Mess analysis Drinks: drinks: writing some letters.
Only one mail the last three weeks, stale *Bystanders* etc. Piano
thrumming Amy Woodforde-Finden[1] and 'Somewhere a voice
is calling'.

A wounded officer (53rd Division) in the latrines. 'They bung
you back quick enough nowadays. Can hardly walk.'

This morning: Suez Canal from train. Garden at Ismailia—a
spot of blossom among green. Then sandy wastes. Huts: tents:
sand. Cool breeze. At the station. Waiting at bridge. Two large
ships go by. Cool anterooms. Birds in the roof. Slim, grey
chirpers. Onions for lunch. Two Irish officers in train who knew
Ledwidge and Dunsany.[2] Ledwidge 'could imitate birds, and
call them to him'. A tiny glimpse of 'real life' in this arid waste
of officer mentality. I feel damned ill. Coughing all the time.

March 4
Posted to 25th R.W.F. to-day. Moved across to Yeomanry
Base Camp. Another day of arid sunshine and utter blankness.
This place is the absolute visible expression of time wasted at
the war. The sand and the huts and the tents and the faces, all
are meaningless. Just a crowd of people killing time. Time
wasted in waste places. I wish I could see some meaning in it all.
But it is soul-less. And it seems an intolerable burden—to
everyone, as to me.

People go 'up the line' almost gladly—for it means there's
some purpose in life. People who remain here scheme to 'get
leave'. And, having got it, go aimlessly off to Cairo, Port Said,
or Ismailia, to spend their money on eating and drinking and
being bored, and looking for lust.

[1] Writer of popular songs, particularly settings of the *Indian Love Lyrics* of
Laurence Hope. Died 1919.
[2] Francis Ledwidge, an Irish peasant-poet, was killed in Flanders on 31 July 1917
while serving as a lance-corporal in the Fifth Royal Inniskillin Fusiliers. He was
twenty-six. He had been much helped and encouraged by the Irish writer Lord
Dunsany (1878–1957).

1918

One hears a certain amount of war-shop being talked. But it hasn't the haggard intensity of Flanders war-shop. This is only an antechamber to the real hell of France with its shelling and mud and agony. The whole place, with its glaring sunshine, has the empty clearness of a moving picture. Movements of men and munitions against a background of soul-less drought. The scene is drawn with unlovely distinctness; every living soul in this great caravanserai is here against his will. And, when the war ends, the whole place will vanish, and the sand will blot out the footprints of the men who came here.

Along the main road that runs through the camp parties of Turkish prisoners march, straggling and hopeless, slaves of war, guarded by a few British soldiers with fixed bayonets. These prisoners are killing time. One of them was shot last week, for striking an officer. A moment of anger, then probably fear, and swift death. He has escaped.

March 8
Went to Port Said for day; with M. Robinson. Bought a few books and some pipe-cleaners, a penny each. Tolstoy, *War and Peace*, Scott, *Antiquary* (Everyman) and pocket edition of Meredith's poems. (Funny books to buy at Port Said of all places in the world.)

Sunset waves foaming white, and breeze blowing.

March 9
On District Court Martial in the morning. President pompous and incompetent. A major in the 19th Rifle Brigade. Going 'up the line' to-morrow. (Walk this evening. Remount train. Grey faces.) Drunk officer. Nurses in Mess. Concert.

March 10
Left Kantara 7.15 p.m. and travelled up to Gaza; thirteen officers in a cattle-truck. Got to Gaza 7 a.m.

March 11
Reached Railhead (Ludd) at 2.30 p.m. Olive-trees, almond-

orchards, reddish soil. Fine hills on the right all the way—not unlike Scotch hills.

Last night we went through level sandy places. Country began to be green about daybreak. Tents among crops and trees all the way up from Gaza. Weather warm and pleasant, with clouds. One glimpse of sea after leaving Gaza. Thousands of camels in one camp. A few Old Testament pictures, people and villages.

March 12

Reading Scott's *Antiquary*. Slept in tent at bad rest-camp a mile from the station. Self and M. going there after curious meal in canteen-tent. 'Abdul' and the omelettes. Mountain Battery Major (who'd ridden down from Bethlehem).

Beauty of stars and clouds; soft candle-glow of bell-tents among olive-trees. Birds: four large black-headed tits among cactuses. A sort of small rook (made same noise as rook). Distant hills: very white and stony and dry-looking. Rain in the night, and between 7 and 8. Sunshine and larks singing. Soft, warm air; like English summertime.

Between 6 and 7 a rumble of gun-noise miles away, for ten minutes. Officers grumbling, 'bad organisation' etc. Loading camels. Nothing grim about this front so far. France was grim, even at Rouen.

Started at 9.30. Twelve officers and baggage in a lorry. Reached Division H.Q. at 4.30 at Ramallah, eight miles north-west of Jerusalem. The road climbed and sank and twisted among the stony hills. At the first halt (Latrun), at the foot of the hills, a running stream; ruined garden; wind in trees; birds' strange notes; and frogs croaking; wildflowers.

These hills are wild and desolate, strewn with rocks and stones —like thousands of sheep. Tractors going up with six-inch howitzers. Ambulances coming down. Leaving Ludd, a long line of grey donkeys with troops' blankets.

About 2.30 we entered Jerusalem. Not a very holy-looking place. Then into another stony region of hills; very desolate.

At Ramallah I saw Sergeant Stone of the Sussex Yeomanry. He was in the Lewes troop with me in August 1914. Ramallah is on a hill-top. Taken by us two months ago. A line of cypress-trees by Divisional H.Q.—a large house. Weather cold, grey, and rainy. Yellow, flaring sunset; hills faint-purple. Strange medley of soldiers and inhabitants in the dusky, narrow village-street. A silent landscape all round—the hills getting dark; some hoary in the twilight—sad, lonesome glens and ravines. No sound of artillery.

March 13

A very wet morning. Our tent became very wet and wretched. We remain here till to-morrow. About 11 I went out walking. The weather improved about 12. Sat in a tent talking to a private (Middlesex Regiment) for nearly an hour, while it rained. He had been twelve years in America with a circus, training trick-horses, he said. Gave me a gloomy account of 'the line' here. 'Very bad country for troops; great hardships, and not much to eat.'

When I got away from the village the sun shone; and with the increasing light and warmth the landscape revealed itself to me slowly; and what had seemed a cruel, desolate, unhappy region, was now full of a shy and lovely austerity. Along the terraces of the hillsides where vines and fig-trees grow, and the young wheat is green among the reddish, stony slopes, there are innumerable wildflowers; the red anemone lords it over the rest; and the bashful pink cyclamen; and a small purple flower makes carpets of colour below the fig-trees; but in the crannies of rocks older than Jerusalem are rock-plants; everywhere are shy blossoms of tiny delicate plants. I wandered back to Ramallah by a glen with a cheerful stream, small but companionable; birds came down there to drink: birds whose colours were grey and brown and any colour which the rocks are. Later in the afternoon four Arabs came driving two asses and some small black-and-white cattle up the glen. I sat as still as a stone to watch them pass on the other side of the brook. But the cattle turned and looked at me, and their owners, two men, a woman and a youth, shouted greetings. I waved back and shouted 'Cheeroh!' The bells of the cattle sounded pleasantly.

The scene made me think of Doughty's *Arabia Deserta*. But this valley will be lovely in May, with fig-trees in leaf, and tall green wheat. I escaped from the war completely for four hours.

I felt like one of the rocks; or perhaps like a budding prophet.

Back in the village the business of war goes on; motors, lorries, camel-columns, limbers, are going and coming, laden and empty. The roads are liquid mud; *c'est la guerre*—in an Old Testament environment.

March 14

Left Ramallah at 8.30. A fine morning. Walked up to 74th Divisional Supply Dump, about six miles. Then on to Battalion, another three, all through the usual wild hills and rocks, where the Division have been attacking since last Saturday. (They have advanced about six miles since then.) Reached 25th R.W.F. about 4.15. They are bivouacked on a hillside among the rocky terraces. A ragtime show, evidently. I am in command of C. Company. R. Harrison is the only other Company officer. They have had two killed and three wounded in the recent attacks, and are now resting. Picturesque warfare—apparently one needs to be able to climb like a goat.

March 15

Out from 9 till 4 with the Company working at road-mending. Got very wet. Silly speech by the Brigadier before we started. He addressed the Battalion, praising them for their recent exploits in chasing 'Johnny Turk' over the hills and far away and admitted that 'all he cared about was getting a Division' (over our dead bodies?).

March 15–16

Very heavy rain; Battalion stayed in camp. This evening I walked up the hill for a couple of hours. Down below in the glen (or wadi) the brown water galloped along among the rocks with a rustling sound. Brown birds flitted and whistled among the rocks. The wind shook the dingy olive-trees. Clouds were over all the sky, with a yellow gleam in the west above the gloom of hills.

In the village on the hill-top no one was to be seen except two soldiers, 'looking after the place,' they said. Eight of them live up there. The inhabitants were all in their warren-like houses, crouching over damp wood-fires. Lonely hills; the freedom of them makes me glad. Occasionally one hears the bang and reverberation of a gun, or shell bursting in some neighbouring valley. And there are camps on many a distant slope. But one hardly sees them—the tents might be rocks. A little smoke goes up in places.

Now I sit with my one candle; men's voices sing and chatter in the tents below. Some are singing hymns (it is Sunday evening).

This place is not soul-less, not soul-deadening, like France (in the war-zone). Two officers (B. Company) in the tent, Barker, a 'commercial' gent from Welshpool—'quite a character' and very garrulous and amusing, with a broken nose and a slight stammer (aged thirty-five). Charlesworth, an Oxford (Magdalen) man, aged twenty-four—pleasant; reads Kipling, Shakespeare, and novels—a sentimentalist—not strong.

I should be very contented with life if it would stop raining. I have a strong feeling of escape. I have slipped away 'from fields where glory does not stay'.[1] Here I can start afresh. And if death happens to meet me on these hills—the ragged old Syrian rascal —who cares? I'll go along with him to the Prophet's Paradise, or any dusty old tomb where he's got my number up. But it'll be a wooden cross in France after all, I fear.

March 23
Moved three miles down the Nablus (Shechem) road to fresh camp. Hot day. Camp on terraces among fig-trees. Thousands of small purple irises in flower. In tent with F. R. Charlesworth. Concert at night. Huge white clouds blowing across moonlit hills.

March 24
Weather thundery with heavy showers. Walked up hill in morning. Strong breeze up there. Landscape grey with drifts of sunshine.

Woke feeling ill, with strong 'Blighty hunger'. First attack I've had. This place is much finer really, but the longing for

[1] A. E. Housman, 'To an Athlete Dying Young'.

English countryside recurs. Feeling of mental heaviness prob-
ably due to incessant heavy cold I've had for over a month.
Can't think vividly yet. And no one seems to say anything
illuminating. Church parade this morning. Singing National
Anthem standing at the salute. O God, O Montreal![1]

March 26

The Medical Officer (Captain Bigger), late of Emmanuel
College, Cambridge. Lean, grimy and brown—goes out grub-
bing roots on the hills—knows every bird a hundred yards off—
rather like a bird himself—different species to the other officers
anyhow. The sort of man who used to cruise about on rivers and
canals and remote streams, looking at the by-ways of English
counties and studying wild life. Eyes like brown pools in a Scotch
burn—scrubby moustache—foul pipe—voice somehow suggests
brown water flowing. Knows tenderness for dumb and piping
creatures. O, the coarse stupidity of some of the others. Minds
like the front page of the *Daily Mirror*. Cairo; cocktails; war-
shop; etc. Suffocating boredom of the forced intimacy of living
with them. They see nothing clearly. Minds clogged with
mental deadness.

Wet day yesterday. Brown water pouring down the wadis.
Saw kestrel, shrike, Critchman's bunting, lesser whitethroat,
woodlark, Syrian jays, partridges, tits, blackcap, redstarts,
wheatears, goldfinch.

March 28

A quiet warm late-afternoon. Frogs croaking in the wet
ground up the wadi, east of camp. Small thorn-trees make clumps
of young green up the terraces. There is a water-spring at the
top of the wadi, and small rills of water sing their way down
among the stones and over the slabs of rock. Wheatears, pipits,
whitethroats, flit and chirp among the bushes, perch on rocks,
or are busy in the olive-branches. On the way home a gazelle got
up and fled away up hill among the boulders. It stood quite still
on a terrace five hundred yards away, turning its head to watch
us. Then trotted quietly away over the ridge. A free creature.

[1] From 'A Psalm of Montreal' by Samuel Butler (1835–1902).

Evening; warm dusk; the hills looming dark and solemn all around; here and there a single dim tree on the skyline; the moon came up hazy and clouded with quiet pearl-grey drifts. A warm wind blows across the darkling heights. The camp below is a shrouded litter of tiny lights scattered on the dusk. Sounds of voices and rattling wheels come far-off and clear. Small sounds of life in the vast silence of the night and the hills under dim stars.

Once there begins a sudden yelping, high-pitched and long-drawn, like people being tortured. Jackals; eerie and wild; suddenly breaking off in silence.

I look down on the dusky olive-trees below. The terraces wind and climb, a labyrinth of endless quiet and mystery—wild gardens among the rocks. The huge slabs, headstones, shafts and crags glimmer silver and ancient in the clouded moonlight. They seem like tombs of giants or titans, ruinous, tilted and heaved-sideways. Some rise like gigantic well-heads; some are cleft and piled to form narrow caves. Ghosts might inhabit there, but they are older than man. They are as he first found them. Ramparts of rock tufted with flowers and tangled with clematis and honeysuckle and briar. Unutterable peace and sense of freedom . . . But as a finish to this someone comes into the tent with more ghastly news of the French battle.[1]

March 30
Says Wordsworth:

> I hear the echoes through the mountains throng,
> The winds come to me from the fields of sleep.[2]

IN PALESTINE

On the thyme-scented hills
In the morning and freshness of day
I heard the voices of rills
Quietly going their way.

[1] The German break-through south of Arras.
[2] From Ode, 'Intimations of Immortality from recollections of early childhood'.

Warm from the west was the breeze;
There were wandering bees in the clover;
Grey were the olive-trees;
And a flight of finches went over.

On the rock-strewn hills I heard
The anger of guns that shook
Echoes along the glen.
In my heart was the song of a bird,
And the sorrowless tale of the brook,
And scorn for the deeds of men.

March 30

March 31 (Easter Sunday)

On the hills all afternoon with the Doctor. Clouds came down
and blotted the landscape and we squatted in a vineyard and
smoked our pipes by the blaze of a fire of dry olive-branches. In
the cloudy weather after rain the clearness of the hills and glens
shifted from shadow to gleams of watery light, and the skylines
were clean-cut and delicate-edged. The hills looked green and
the wet rocks were not so visible as usual—there was a look of
Ireland about it.

And when we got home to camp I found a mail and a letter
from Dorothea Conyers, the good soul, full of Limerick hunting,
and hounds flying over the big green banks and grey walls.

And the news from remote France grows more ominous every
day, though no one else seems to worry much.

I read *War and Peace* of an evening; a grand and consoling
book—a huge vista of life and suffering humankind which makes
the present troubles easier to endure, and the loneliness of death
a little thing.

Our padré rather drunk to-night after all the Communion
wine he'd blessed and been obliged to 'finish up'. Consolations
of religion!

April 3   9 a.m.

Alone in a terraced garden on a hill, with the morning sun
warm on my face and big white clouds moving slowly along the

blue. Bees and flies make a pleasant droning around the silver rocks, butterflies wander and settle on the thick white clover, where a few late scarlet anemones make spots of lordly colour in the lush green grass. An old mine is half-hidden by the spring growth of grass and weeds. A tiny flycatcher perches six feet away on a bush; and a redstart preens himself a little further away. Further off a whitethroat[1] is singing delightfully in a bright-green thorn-bush—a small delicate fantasia played on an Arcadian pipe. From the far hillside across the valley I hear the notes of a cuckoo. Down the hill some gunners are busy around the sixty-pounder guns, turning some sort of wheel with a rattling sound. I can see their tiny arms working like piston-rods. Then the warbler begins again with a low, liquid phrase; and a pair of buntings flutter down to sit on a crab-apple tree a few feet away from the ledge of rock where I sit.

Then someone blows a whistle down by the battery; a motorbike goes along the rough road; machine-gun-fire rattles and echoes to crashes away over the hills—probably only practicefiring.

It is a heavenly morning, and a heavenly place; and the war is quite subsidiary to the landscape—not a sprawling monster, as in France. As the shadows of huge clouds on the ancient hills—spreading from slope to glen, and moving on—so do our battles pass, leaving no trace of the evil that has been.

Files of camels move along the road below, and limbers and waggons crushing the stones with a rattling noise—eight mules to each waggon. The fig-trees have a few young leaves sprouting. Clematis is over. Wild roses soon, on great jolly bushes.

April 4 (Transferred from C. Company to A. Company)

A hot cloudless day. Saw a large flock of griffon vultures; and a flock of black storks (?)—about forty—moving steadily northward, with effect of airplanes.

Everyone has quite decided that we shall go to France. Probably untrue. (Funny to think that I tried to get to France in January.)

The hills are more lovely each day, with all the plants and bushes bursting into flower and leaf.

[1] Orphean Warbler (not whitethroat). S.S.

1918

We move down to Ludd on Sunday. I don't want to leave these hills. Perhaps we shall return. I wonder if I can stand another dose of France.[1]

April 5

After dinner last night the Colonel started a 'selling sweep' on 'where we go to'. Palestine £20, France £15, etc. Total in pool was over £94. Subalterns wishing to please the Colonel (who acted as a most efficient and lifelike auctioneer) bid for tickets which were obviously absurd—'Home' fetched £14 and Italy about the same. The money will go to Major R. (the second in command) who is very rich. A thoroughly puerile and ill-bred show altogether. I gave £10 for 'Submarined' in sheer exasperation at the snobbery of it all (after refusing to take a ticket or make a bid until the proceedings were more than half over).

At the back of it all one felt that they all feared the nightmare of the Western Front and would have paid anything to avoid going there. It was a sort of raffish effort to turn the thing into a joke; for everyone knows we *are* going to France. All maps handed in to-day, and hot-weather kit cancelled.

The Colonel is odiously vulgar and snobbish; a very bad type of British nobleman. (And known to be both 'windy' and incompetent.) He would look exactly right in a grey top-hat yelling the odds in Tattersall's ring at race-meetings.

April 7   6.45 a.m.

A quiet, warm morning, with the clouds low on the hill-tops and the sun shining through. Blue smoke goes up from the incinerators of our camp and the 24th Welsh, on the other side of the Nablus road. Everyone busy clearing up our camp among the fig-trees which are slowly becoming a mist of green. To-day we begin our forty-five-mile march down to railhead (Ludd). It is also the first day of our journey to France, or wherever it is we are going.

These diaries of mine are full of notes written in that hour of departure when the men are loading limbers and putting on their packs and everyone is in a fuss, except, perhaps, the present writer, who invariably slopes off to some quiet place beyond the

[1] Yes; the men make me able to stand it. May 16. S.S.

camp or village; there he hears the sounds of preparation, high shouts, and rattlings, and murmur and grumble of voices, clatter of tins, and sounds of feet. 'Come on; fall in, headquarters!' someone shouts.

Birds whistle and pipe small in the still morning air, flitting among the clematis and broom, perching on fig-boughs or small bright-green thorn-trees. The hillside seems more like a garden than ever before—a garden just outside the life of men. In an hour I shall be trudging along behind the column with a lot of heavy-laden mules—trudging away from Arcadia. (cf. a morning early in December 1915 when we were starting from a village near Lillers.)

April 8   7 p.m.

In my bivouac on a hill-top near Suffa—after two days' marching (nine or ten miles each day). This morning we started from a point near Ramallah, well over 3000 feet up. The early morning sky was clear, and down toward the sea and over the lower hills northward were low grey banks of clouds, like snow-mountains. Up at 5.15 and away by 7.40. Reached here 1.30. Passed General Allenby[1] on the way. Weather perfect. Hot sun, and a breeze from the sea. Pink and white rock-roses along the wadis. From this hill I can see a city of tiny lights below and on the opposite hill, where the Brigade are camped. Stars overhead, and sound of men's voices singing and chattering; they seem contented with their lot.

Away in the darkness jackals howl, and some night-bird calls. My bivouac is pitched in a tangle of large golden-yellow daisies. A mule brays among the murmur of men's voices. We are nearly in the plains again; a mile away from the grey, stony hills, crowned with villages and towers.

Horrid smell of dead camels along the road this morning. Saw a fine Syrian Pied Woodpecker this evening. Grey with scarlet head and tail. Reading Hardy's *Woodlanders*. Like going into a cool parlour with green reflections on wall and ceiling after the heat and sweat of marching.

[1] (1861–1936). Under his command the Egyptian Expeditionary Force had captured Jerusalem (undamaged) from the Turks in December 1917. In October 1918 he captured Damascus, Tripoli and Aleppo with the last great cavalry campaign in history.

1918

April 9   10.45 a.m.

We marched away at 6.45 this morning. A clear still dawn; very hot by 8 o'clock. Reached Latrun by 10. They are now settling down on a bare hot slope. Treeless, green and brown, low, rolling country, growing vines and corn. The dusty main road with its crawling, droning lorries, and files of pack-animals. The sea, hazy and far away, on the edge of the land-scape, shown by a line of sandhills.

After seeing to the Company, I have escaped to the shadow of a thin belt of small fir-trees. Tents and camps and horse-lines are only a hundred yards away, but the place is green and cool, filled with the drowsy hum of insects, and the noontide chirp of a few sparrows and crested larks. Out in the vineyard, or vine-field, brimstone-yellow with weeds, some (Arabs?) are hoeing busily, making it more pleasant than ever to be in the shade. Came through dull country to-day. Two ancient Arabs sit under a tree ten yards away. After a while a fresh breeze comes blow-ing from the sea, and sways the trees to a sound of breaking waves. Then a flight of blackcaps and whitethroats begin their busy flittings among the boughs.

And, best of all, a nightingale[1] sits on a twig quite near, and gives me a charming fantasia on the flute.

To-morrow we start at 5.30 and go twelve miles to Ludd, to entrain for the Base.

Out after tea, and found a charming garden by a clear, quick-running stream with willows and tall rushes; the garden be-longed to the French monastery here; oranges and lemons, bananas, and 'ascadinias' growing. 'Ascadinias', as the Arab gardener called them, seemed to be small apple-like fruit with large seeds in them. Came back through a tangle of huge golden daisies—knee-deep and solid gold, as if Midas had been walking there among the almond-trees and cactus-hedges.

April 10

Up at 3.30: started at 5.30. Reached camping-ground at Ludd about noon. Came thirteen miles. Clear dawn with crested larks singing, and large morning star and shaving moon above dim blue hills; firefly lights of camps below us. Marched through

[1] It was a bulbul! S.S.

[231]

green country and low hills in the cool morning, till Ramileh, a white town with olives and fruit-trees all round, and full of British. Weather very hot after 7.30, and roads awful dusty; marching between cactus-hedges, with motors passing. Clouds of dust and glaring pale-blue sky. One thought of cool green woodlands and chuckling water-brooks.

On the March

Left; left; left, right, left. 110 paces to the minute. The monotonous rhythm of the marching troops goes on in his brain. His eyes blink at the glaring sky; the column move heavily on in front; dust hangs over them; dust and the pale blue, quivering sky. As they go up a hill their round steel helmets sway from side to side with the lurch of their heavy-laden shoulders. Vans and lorries drone and blunder and grind along the road; the cactus-hedges are caked with dust. The column passes some Turk prisoners, in dingy dark uniform and red fez, guarded by Highlanders. 'Make the fuckers work, Jock' someone shouts. He sees and hears these things through the sweat-soaked weariness that weighs him down; his shoulders a dull ache; his feet burning hot and clumsy with fatigue; his eyes tormented by the white glare of the dusty road. Men before and behind him—no escape. 'Fall out on the right of the road.' He collapses in the dry ditch.

Lord X's story at lunch of how some friend of his turned a machine-gun on to Turkish prisoners in a camp he was in charge of, and killed 280 (they had been causing trouble, but it seemed an atrocious affair; the story was received with appreciative sycophantic laughter from the company commanders).

SHADOWS

In the gold of morning we march; our swaying shadows are long;
We are risen from sleep to the grey-green world and our limbs move free.
Day is delight and adventure, and all save speech is a song;
Our thoughts are travelling birds going southward across the sea.

1918

We march in the swelter of noon; our straggling shadows
    are squat;
They creep at our feet like toads,
Our feet that are blistered and hot:
The light-winged hours are forgot;
We are bruised by the ache of our loads.

Sunset burns from behind; we would march no more;
    but we must:
And our shadows deride us like dervishes dancing along in
    the dust.

April 10

April 11
    Left camp at 1 p.m. with first party; awful hot; scent of
orange-bloom. Left Ludd station about 5 p.m. Reached Kantara
9.15 next morning. Travelled in covered trucks.

Birds seen in Judaea since March 15

Black-throated Wheatear	Linnet	Kestrel
Arabian Wheatear	Blue Thrush	Raven
Black-eared Wheatear	White Wagtail	Little Owl
Great Tit	Syrian Jay	Meadow Pipit
Redstart	Syrian Partridge	Water Pipit
Robin	Graceful Warbler	Bee-eater
Masked (Nubian) Shrike	Ruppell's Warbler	Chiff-chaff
Woodchat Shrike	Bonelli's Warbler	Cuckoo
Crested Lark	Sardinian Warbler	Swift
Woodlark	Orphean Warbler	Swallow
Cretzschmar's Bunting	Blackcap	Egyptian Swallow
Nightingale	Whitethroat	
Goldfinch	Lesser Whitethroat	Griffon Vulture
Greenfinch	Long-legged Buzzard	Black Stork
Egyptian Kite	House Sparrow	Peregrine Falcon

Hooded Crow ⎫
Wryneck   ⎬ *April 9*
Bulbul   ⎭

White Stork   ⎫
Syrian Pied Woodpecker ⎬ *April 8*
Hoopoe   ⎭

[233]

April 11 etc

Flamingos	Redshank
Ring Plover	Sandpiper
Kentish Plover	Egyptian Nightjar
Stint	

April 12

Kantara again! When I left here on March 10 I thought I'd seen the last of it for a long time—beastly place. Horribly tired yesterday; not much improved by the sixteen hours of jolting and excruciating noise of the cattle-truck. It was warm, and I had my valise, though.

It is positive agony to leave these Palestine hills in all their beauty and glory. Here I sit in a flapping tent, close to the main road. The wind is strong, and sand blows everywhere. Nearest tree God knows how far off.

Escaped from 1 to 4 o'clock, to a salt-lake about a mile behind the camp in the salt-marshes, where nothing grows. It was quite lonely except for an aeroplane overhead and a flock of flamingos some way off. The tents and huts of Kantara were a sand-coloured blur on the edge of the hot quivering afternoon. The water came merrily in wavelets blown by the hot wind. So I had a bathe in the shallow salt water with deep mud below; and the sun and wind were pleasant enough as I ran up and down; happy, because there wasn't a soul within a mile of me, though it was a dreary sort of place when one came to think about it. Miles of flat sand and nothing green; and the dried mud glistening with salt. Only the water was light blue-green, and the flamingos had left a few feathers at the water's edge, before they flapped away with the light shining through their rosy wings.

Battalion arrives to-morrow morning.

April 15

Another day gone and wasted. Up at 5.30. On parade 6.30 to 10.15. Endless small, stupid details to be worried through. And at the end of the day, exhaustion and exasperation, and utter inability to think clearly, or to marshal any kind of thought. Two men going on leave to Cairo tomorrow—their happy, excited faces, when they came to my tent for their pay—the only human thing in all the past fourteen hours.

April 17

Concert Party

Night of stars; half-moon overhead; two men with grey soft hats; three women in short silk skirts; jangling ragtime piano, a few footlights shining upwards, just reaching the faces of these puppets—these players; and over all the serene canopy of night in Egypt. They sing their songs, perform their skilful antics from the tent; and all around—a mass of men—dim, moonlit hour. I see their faces that are no more than a mere rufous brown—sometimes glowing with the ember of a cigarette— keeping the spark of life alight. These men, sitting—standing —tier beyond tier—row beyond row—excluded from life—the show is what they long for—LIFE with its song and dance—life with its brief gaiety. I see dim faces of soldiers, chins and cheeks leaning on their hands. I know their hearts and the longing in them. I know the tears half-risen in their eyes—their thoughts of home—the past—Blighty.

Suddenly I recognise that this is indeed the true spectacle of war—that these puppets are the fantastic delight of life played to an audience of ghosts and shadows—crowding in like moths to a lamp—to see and hear what they must lose—have lost. In front there are half-lit ruddy faces and glittering eyes, and behind they grow more dusky and indistinct—ghosts, souls of the dead —the doomed—till on the edge high above the rest one sees silhouetted forms motionless, intent—those who were killed three years ago—and beyond them, across the glimmering levels of sand, legions of others come stealing in—till the crowd is limitless; all the dead have come to hear the concert party in this half-lit oasis of Time.

It is too much; I cannot bear it; I must get up and go away. For I too am a ghost, one of the doomed.

Join in the chorus, boys—'It's a long, long trail'—'I hear you calling me'—'Sweet lovers love the spring'—'Dixieland'.

April 19

A week at Kantara. Company training each day 6.30–10, and in afternoon. Sand . . . sunlight. Haven't been half a mile from camp since I got here, except to take a party down to get their clothes and blankets boiled last Sunday night—when we waited two and a half hours for the boilers to be disengaged, and then —from 9 to 10—a hundred stark-naked men standing about while most of their worldly possessions stewed in a boiler.

This afternoon A. Company got beat by C. Company in the football tournament. C. had my sympathies—my old Company —with young Roberts running about with nothing on but a pair of tight shorts—a sort of Apollo—and Jim Linthwaite (the First Battalian chap) looking his best in any attire, and playing an energetic game. I think he knew I was watching him all the time.[1]

The Lena Ashwell Concert on Wednesday was very impressive. But that will go into a poem, if I can get it written.[2] The scene moved me far more than anything I've seen since I left England. But I'd had a tumbler full of stout and champagne at dinner. Nevertheless I believe that I saw below the surface, being by nature a seer and dreamer of dreams.

CONCERT PARTY

(EGYPTIAN BASE CAMP)

They are gathering round . . .
Out of the twilight; over the grey-blue sand,
Shoals of low-jargoning men drift inward to the sound—
The jangle and throb of a piano . . . tum-ti-tum . . .
Drawn by a lamp, they come
Out of the glimmering lines of their tents, over the
    shuffling sand.

O sing us the songs, the songs of our own land,
You warbling ladies in white.

[1] He was drunk when we disembarked at Marseilles, and is now awaiting a Field-General Court Martial. May 14. S.S. The Stonethwaite of *Sherston's Progress.*
[2] Lena Ashwell, actress and impresario (1872–1957) organized concerts in all theatres of war from 1914 to 1920.

1918

Dimness conceals the hunger in our faces,
This wall of faces risen out of the night,
These eyes that keep their memories of the places
So long beyond their sight.

Jaded and gay, the ladies sing; and the chap in brown
Tilts his grey hat; jaunty and lean and pale,
He rattles the keys . . . some actor-bloke from town . . .
God send you home; and then *A long, long trail*;
I hear you calling me; and *Dixieland* . . .
Sing slowly . . . now the chorus . . . one by one
We hear them, drink them; till the concert's done.
Silent, I watch the shadowy mass of soldiers stand.
Silent, they drift away, over the glimmering sand.[1]

The little doctor, W. K. Bigger, goes away to join the 10th
Division, who are staying in Palestine. I shall miss him and his
bird-lore much; also his cheery, whimsical companionship.

FLAMINGOES (Imitation of T. Hardy)

From camp I went; across the sand
To a wide, salt, blue mere
That lipped the crusted, drear
Expanse of desert-land.
And I said, 'The place is dead:
'No light of dawn can bless
'Such barren emptiness.'

I plodded slow, with vacant gaze
That pictured in my brain
Green fields and quiet rain
Hushing the woodside ways.
And still the place was dead:
No arch leaned overhead
Of leafy-glinting maze.

Then flocked flamingoes, wheeling by,
Crowded the air with white,
Warm-flushed in rosy light
That *flowered* across the sky;

---

[1] First published in the *New Statesman*, 17 August 1918, then in *Picture Show*.

Until they sank once more
To the bleached, songless shore.
Thus beauty comes and brings
New life to desolate things;
And far aloft men hear the rustle of her wings.

April 22

April 23 (Kantara)

As I lie in my little bivouac a few yards from the dusty white road, I watch the dim shapes of men passing along in the blue dusk of clouded moonlight. I listen to scraps of their talk as they pass, many of them full of drink and thick-voiced. Others flit past in silence; from the men's tents behind come confused shouts and laughter; from the road the noise of tramping boots. The pallor of the sand makes the sky look blue. A few stars appear, framed in the triangle of my bivouac door, with field-glasses and haversack slung against the pole. Sometimes a horse goes by, or a rumbling lorry. So I puff a pipe and watch the world, ruminating on all things that lie within the narrow chamber of my philosophy, lit by the single lantern-candle of my faith—in people like Tolstoy and Hardy. *War and Peace* and *The Woodlanders* have been my guides of late. And Marty South[1] is as great as anything in English.

When I compare my agony of last year with the present, I am glad to find a wider view of things. I am slowly getting outside it all. Getting nearer the secret places of the heart also, and recognising its piteous limitations. I recognise the futility of war more than ever, and, dimly, I see the human weakness that makes it possible. For I spend all my days with people who, with a very few exceptions, are too indolent-minded to think for themselves. Sometimes I feel as if this slow and steady growth of comprehension will be too much to bear. But, if I am not mad, I shall one day be great. And if I am killed this year, I shall be free. Selfishness longs for escape, and dreads the burden that is so infinitely harder to carry than three years, two years, one year ago. The simplicity that I see in some of the men is the one candle in my darkness. The one flower in all this arid sunshine. Half-baked aspirations and reasonings are no good. *I will not go mad*.

[1] Heroine of *The Woodlanders*.

1918

April 26

Saw Charles Wiggin last night. To-day he is gone up to
Jerusalem, and on to his regiment which is going to Jordan on
some small show. I found him in a bell-tent after dinner, with
four of his Eton friends—two of the Barclays, Toby Buxton
(looking like a tailor's advertisement of a staff-officer) and
another. They talked about the Yankees' army, and 'our big
offensive *next year*'! Dear old Charles shares most of my own
views on the subject. We talked old hunting days and were very
pleased with life and old brandy supplied by his hosts; who were
all majors except the Colonel (Norfolk Yeomanry). Eton
manner was somewhere in the offing, but not too noticeable.
Charles is just the same nice creature as he was four years ago.
Wonder if I'll ever see him again. We leave here on Sunday for
Alexandria and Marseilles, and the rest of it.

April 27

As I said before, we leave to-morrow night for Alex (where
I hope to see E. M. Forster, who wrote *The Celestial Omnibus*
and other good books).

If there were anything to be gained by analysing one's feel-
ings, what curious stuff would be distilled from the yeomen who
are leaving this country. Many of them have gone through over
two years of campaigning, which would have satisfied most of
our professional soldiers before 1914, as a life-experience of
war. Yet these men, who ask only to go home to their farms,
towns, parks, manors, flats, mansions, cottages, granges, etc are
doomed to suffer far worse things than any they've yet known.

Fortunately the fact that the Western Front is over two
thousand miles nearer Leicester Square seems to console them.
Nor can they realise what they are going to, not having seen it
with their own eyes. Torpedoes are nothing! And my own bloody
self: here I am after nearly four years of this business, faced with
the same old haggard aspect of soldier-life—a very small chance
of complete escape unblemished—a big chance of being killed
outright—ditto of being intolerably injured—a certainty of
mental agony and physical discomfort—prolonged and exas-
perating—a possibility of going mad or breaking down badly:
in fact, the whole landscape of the near future bristling with

unimaginable perils and horrors, and overshadowed by the gloom of death.

It is an amazing thing that men can go on their way in apparent serenity. Only an occasional stabbing moment of realisation, seen in the sudden, half-concealed disquiet of a haunted look, a bitter, uneasy laugh—and the skeleton pops back into the cupboard.

Tolstoy's battle-pictures help me a lot. They make me remember my own experiences—the ugly anticipations of wounds and failure, then the excitement and devil-may-care ardours before going into action, the mental gesturing and limelight postures of 'facing death', playing the hero before one's men, the angry joy of being 'up against it' and 'carrying on' to the end. Then the disillusion and nerve-shattered exhaustion— broken in mind and body—the shock of seeing one's comrades killed and maimed. And, worst of all, the futile longing for home and comfort, the rat-in-a-trap feeling that escape will never come. Well, well.

April 28

Reading through these notes of the past two months, I find, as usual, that they represent my self, my thoughts at odd moments, against a background of change and varying camps and landscapes. There are lists of birds and flowers, snatches of emotion and experience. But the people I meet and mix with are scarcely mentioned. Why should I write a description of Lord X. the coarse sporting nobleman, who is so entirely occupied with the material aspect of things? Of Major R. the quiet, efficient soldier, a true Briton and 'white man', whose only fault is his British reticence, and stereotyped manner? Of the little adjutant, who is 'rather an outsider', tactless, stupid, and diligent—a nonentity. Of the four captains: B. densely stupid, grossly selfish, narrow-minded, fussy, important, a half-baked product of Eton and Sandhurst, addicted to country pursuits, and (from all accounts) by no means a hero. E. a suburban snob, who used to 'go to the city' and thinks of nothing but his own comfort, luxury, and social advancement; easy-going but not an attractive personality, with his red, florid face, and ingratiating manner: a glutton. F. a product of Winchester and New College, Oxon, who cultivates an artificial loquacity, never saying what he means, fond of getting a rise out of some butt; very snobbish; very intolerant and narrow; with a hard, light-blue eye and regular features; apparently conceited; fussy and excitable; the type that is precocious and popular at school and college, and then ceases to develop in any way. I get on well with S., a well-informed barrister, posing as an amusing cynic—pleasant-mannered, with a taste for sport. But, like the rest of them a snob, for all his assumption of being 'a judge of human nature'. He of course is infinitely superior in mind to the others.

And in all four of these captains one realises that the human element probably appears in their 'home life'—all that they are exiled from; they hate soldiering, and resent being herded up with people of inferior social status. They like their men, in a patronising way, but it doesn't strike one as a very genuine or deep emotion.

None of the remaining thirty officers seems in any way remarkable. The usual gambling and drinking element—but not a large one. Perhaps there's a Bernard Adams or a Robert Graves among them; if so, he's very well camouflaged! The usual splendid qualities will appear when we get fighting; *that* is always a certainty, anyhow.

May 1   S. S. *Malwa* (10,833 tons) P. & O. (3300 troops on board). Six other boats in convoy.

Conversations

'I myself believe . . . I think, myself . . . my own opinion is . . .' Scraps of conversations come clearly up from the saloon below the gallery where I am reading. The speaker continues to enunciate *his* opinions, in a rather too well-bred voice. The War—always the war—and the politics of the world—and a few other matters of importance—are being discussed, quite informally, by a small group of staff-officers. After a while they drift away; their leisurely talk is superseded by the jingle of knives, forks and spoons; the stewards are preparing the long tables for our next meal. A dissipated-looking subaltern is jingling the piano—fragments of flashy, stale ragtime which makes such a strong appeal to the majority of our officers.

May 4

Still trying to get at the psychology of the average officer on
board. One can only pick up vague hints and clues from their
talk and general behaviour. I am beginning to suspect that their
mental deadness is an effective protection for them against the
impending disasters. They refuse to *face* facts. And their mental
atrophy makes it easy. Cards and drinks and routine and healthy
bodies and trashy novels carry them through. They know they
are 'for it', and hope for luck and a Blighty wound or a cushy job.
It is every man for himself. Their attitude appals me. Is it a
proof of the human folly which will accept war as an inevitable
and useful part of the world's workings?

I watch the *men* lying about on the decks in the sunlight, star-
ing at the glittering, glorious blue sea and the huge boats
ploughing along in line—six of us, and nine or ten destroyers.
They lie in indolent attitudes, and their minds are just as stoical
as the 'average young officer's' I suppose. I like to see them lean-
ing against each other with their arms round one another—it is
pathetic and beautiful and human (but that is only a sexual
emotion in me—to like them in those attitudes). Anyhow they
are simple and childlike.

Day by day I watch and try to learn something from all this.
But I am confused by it all, and still intolerant and superficial. It
is all like a pilgrimage—leading me deathward. It seems an
irresistible procession of events—toward completion and fulfil-
ment. Everything seems to fit in. I am working up to another
climax—steadily. The nearer I get to the war the more I desire
to share its terrors again—that I may learn yet more the mean-
ing of it—and the effect. But I can't believe that I'm going there
to kill people—or to help in the destruction of human life. It is
inconceivable. But I am throwing off my haunting fears and
apprehensions. *No limelight, please!*

The liner, ominously cleaving the level water with a per-
turbed throbbing vibration, is bearing us, day and night, away
from the unheeding mystery and warmth of Egypt. Leaving
nothing behind us, we are bound for the heavily-rumoured
grimness and horror of the battles in France. Some of us have
already been there, and have escaped through wounds or sick-
ness. But even these are aware that something worse awaits
them. Each day brings the ordeal closer—a perceptible leap

toward the abyss of torment; 'by next month . . . next week,' we murmur to ourselves—until, at last, we shall know that 'to-morrow' the storm will break above our heads, and we shall be one with the swarming barrier of tortured creatures who cower and march under swooping shells and vulture-airmen, 'trapping the Hun!'

The liner goes steadily on under a night of stars. It is bearing a few Generals, with their staff-officers, toward the achievement of further strategic efforts, renewed decorations and promotions. Unfortunately the champagne on board is not very good, and the food is only moderate, but many cocktails drown much dis-content and discomfort. The smoking-room is filled with a jabbering crowd of officers. The boat is overcrowded. The troops are herded on the lower decks in stifling, dim-lit mess-rooms, piled and hung with a litter of equipment. There are three bat-talions on board. Like the staff, they are 'for it', doomed to share the perils and hardships of the Western Front and its battles. They do not discuss world-politics, nor drink cocktails; they have no facilities for such efforts. Their time is short; they read *John Bull* and drink ginger-beer. They have no smart uniforms, no bottles of hair-oil, no secret information to make their con-versations important and intriguing. Neither their photographs, nor those of their female relations, have ever appeared in the *Tatler*. They are a part of the huge dun-coloured mass of victims that passes across the shambles of war into the gloom of death where all ranks revert to private. But in their vast patience, in the simplicity of their anger and their mirth, they are as one soul. They are the tradition of human suffering, stripped of all its foolish decorations and ignoble strugglings for individual success and social advancement.

'Tarry no longer; toward thine heritage
Haste on thy way, and be of right good cheer.
Go each day onward on thy pilgrimage;
Think how short time thou hast abided here.
Thy place is built above the starres clear,
None earthly palace wrought in so stately wise.
Come on, my friend, my brother most entire!
For thee I offered my blood in sacrifice.'
(*John Lydgate*) [1370?–1447]

In the circular gallery above the dining-saloon a few electric lamps are glowing with an orange and subdued light that reveals the vulgar oak-panelling and carved balustrades, the bilious-green curtains neatly looped with tassels, and the tawdry gilt and painted ceiling, blue and gold and red, with its hideous patterns, and the crude clumsy decorations of dancing women in the two lunette wall-spaces under the skylight (an atrocity of blue and green coloured glass with P. & O. crests, etc, but now invisible). Electric fans hum and revolve, hurling faint whizzing shadows on the dim buff-hued walls, like ghostly wings, flickering and insubstantial.

The ship throbs and quivers, straining onward as if conscious of her own danger, which keeps every light shrouded from the menacing gloom outside, and makes the buzzing air close and stifling. In the saloon below some officers are playing cards; others are busy with a small roulette-wheel. I look down on their oiled heads, bending over the green tables. I listen to the clink of coins, and the empty jargon of their ejaculations and comments on the play. The dusky stewards continually bring them drinks. These are the things that drug their alarm and exasperation; for, like the ship, they are straining toward safety, environed by the night that menaces their piteous frailty.

Outside, on the decks, one finds the haunted darkness and the sea. One stumbles over the sleeping soldiers, wrapped in their blankets. The sea is darker than the sky, but the escort of destoyers is dimly seen, long shadows, scarcely more than a blur on the water. Nothing is heard but the throbbing of the engines. The sentries loom in doorways, standing upright and silent above the recumbent sleepers, like men watching over a litter of dead bodies.

Lights and drinking card-players and wireless operators and navigators within; chart-rooms, and kitchens and engine-rooms; all that is life, struggling to keep above water. And outside the mystery and unpitying hugeness of death and sleep, the terror that walks by night, and the impossibility of escape.

This is rather portentous stuff. I have obviously been re-reading *Lord Jim*; and the mixture of *War and Peace* and *Howards End* contributes to the mental hotch-potch.

1918

May 7

A quiet morning with rain-clouds and sunshine. We came into Marseilles Harbour about 8.30 a.m.

The Divisional General was playing bridge last night in the 'music-room' (gallery above the dining-saloon). By his special request 'I hear you calling me', 'Because' and 'The Rosary' were sung. 'They may be hackneyed,' he said, 'but I love them!' He was quite moved by the music. A kindly, stupid sort of man, with all the qualities needed by a Major-General.

Reading Arnold Bennett's *These Twain*, and a Charles II romance by Father Benson—quite pleasant stuff.[1]

May 8

Rest-camp just outside Marseilles. We marched away from the docks in drizzling rain at 3.15 yesterday afternoon and got here about 6.45. Very pleasant streets lined with plane-trees— bright green—soldiers childishly pleased at seeing a European city and people (many of them having been in Egypt since October 1915).

People seem delighted and refreshed at being able to read yesterday's *Daily Mail*. But it doesn't cheer me to read that 'we advanced our line a little nearer Morlancourt—a position of great tactical importance'. Two years ago we were living there, when not in the line, which was five miles in front of it.

Blood-curdling stories are being circulated about our trip in the Mediterranean. From these accounts (straight from the Captain's cabin) one gathers that we passed through shoals of submarines; cheerful people also say that if we'd been torpedoed no one would have been saved. It is a fact that there were 3300 troops on board (not counting the crew) and the boat and raft 'accommodation' was for about 1000.[2] But we like to make much of our incredible escapes when the danger is past.

I dined last night in Marseilles with Lord X. and two others. Champagne was Pommery 1900, and '58 Brandy, both very fine, as my tongue tells me this morning, for no ill effects are felt. We went on to a music hall and X. went into ecstacies over an

---

[1] *Oddsfish!* (1914) by Monsignor Robert Hugh Benson (1871–1914), younger brother of A. C. and E. F. Benson.

[2] The transport behind us struck a mine outside Alexandria and most of them drowned (Warwickshire Yeomanry included). S.S.

acrobat-strong-man, who was certainly very good. X. watched him from our box, with a real appreciation of the muscular demonstration, just as he would watch a fine horse or boxer. He certainly has a fine zest for material things. Perhaps he's not such a fool as I thought at first. We came back in a 'special' train, crowded with officers, many of them drunk and jabbering about their exploits (with harlots).

Went to the Zoo with Stable after lunch. A blackbird sat in one of the aviaries, like a priest among a lot of bright-plumaged little birds; he sat and sang his heart out, quite indifferent to the others, throwing his head back and opening his yellow bill wide. It was pathetic to see and hear him.

Marseilles is a very pleasant-looking place, with its climbing streets and green trees and the grey stony hills that guard it.

May 9

To-day is warm—a proper May-day, with glory in the air. Lots of letters came for me, including a cheque from Heinemann for the first 1000 copies of my book; and news that Bunny Tattersall has been given a D.S.O. and had his leg taken off at the thigh. From what I've seen of him, he seemed the sort that needs sport and activity to keep him from going wrong. *Now* he will probably end with D.T. like his father. 'Does it matter, losing your legs?'[1]

I must never forget Rivers. He is the only man who can save me if I break down again. If I am able to keep going it will be through him. So I get to the end of another notebook, and five months have gone by since I left Craiglockhart. The next note-book begins when we march away from camp this afternoon to entrain for some place in Picardy or Pas de Calais.

And all my future is 'to-morrow', or at the most two or three weeks of training for battle. Beyond that the fire-proof curtain comes down (as it did in the music hall last night). And it is covered with placards advertising my new volume of remarkable and arresting poems. I cannot believe that the curtain will go up this year and disclose the painted scene of Peace and Plenty. But I am quite prepared to leave my seat in the stalls and go away

---

[1] The first line of S.S.'s poem 'Does it Matter?', first published in the *Cambridge Magazine*, 6 October 1917, then in *Counter-Attack*.

with Mr Mors, in case he calls for me at the theatre. But all this is silliness—the facts are what we want in our notebooks, and events. So here's to the *next* five months, and the harvest.

Gossip

'Fitz'—'handsomest man in the army fifteen years ago! A perfect Adonis!' says the Colonel. I saw Fitz—on the boat—a tall Brigadier with huge eyebrows, an eyeglass, and a lust-ridden debauched expression on his commonplace features. I also caught a glimpse of him in Marseilles, talking to a very obvious tart.

X's story of Lord Kitchener in South African war. He imported fifteen well-known harlots from London to Pretoria and some other town. They were paid to give away officers who gave them military information. When will someone write the true life of Lord Kitchener, Britain's syphilitic hero?

May 10   11 p.m.

The other three—Morgan, Phillips and Jowett[1]—are asleep in various ungainly attitudes. J. looks as if he were dead. The train has rumbled along all day through the Rhone valley—the country green and lovely with early summer and a blue-and-white day. Now it goes on in the dark, emitting eldritch shrieks which echo along the glens. Nightingales have been singing from every bush and thicket all day; and I hear one now, while the train stops—warbling in the darkness, to an orchestral accompaniment of croaking frogs; I hear the muttering voices of some officers in the next compartment.

Yesterday afternoon we marched for three hours to the station, through Marseilles between lines of staring French people *en fête*, and down to the dock, where we got on the train. Officers went for a meal aboard our late home, the P. & O. liner *Malwa* (who was in dry dock a few hundred yards away).

B. (the fourth platoon officer of my company) came on parade yesterday afternoon very drunk, and was removed. He is a bad hat; was formerly a lance-corporal in this battalion. Will probably be court-martialled. Am reading *Kipps*.[2]

[1] The Howitt of *Sherston's Progress*.
[2] By H. G. Wells (1905).

1918

May 13

Yesterday morning we reached Noyelles-sur-Mer, and marched to Domvast, a village thirteen kilos from Abbeville. We marched about eleven miles and got here at 6.30 p.m. Into billets—farmyard smells etc—all just like two years ago. Weather fine with a breeze behind us all the way. Country looking very beautiful—while 'the May month flaps its glad green leaves like wings'.[1]

Domvast is a straggling village lying low among orchards and trees, with the Forest of Crécy a mile away westward. I went there this morning in the rain. Wind in the beech-wood; endless avenues of branching green. All very comforting.

I feel rather ghost-like coming back to the familiar country and happenings. Buying eggs and butter from 'Madame'. The servants in the kitchen stammering Blighty French to the girls. The men in barns, still rather pleased at the strange conditions. All the queer Arcadian business of settling down in a village unspoiled by continuous billeting and (still) thirty or forty miles away from the war.

Five weeks ago we were marching away from Ramallah, and Jerusalem!

May 14

Sitting in the Company Mess on a fine, breezy afternoon copying out a lecture on consolidation of captured trenches (for T. B. Bardwell to spout to the Company). I sit at the window watching soldiers go up and down the lane; now and then a lorry passes or an officer on a horse, or a peasant with grey horse. On the opposite side of the road is a jolly hawthorn-hedge, and an orchard with two brown cows eating lush grass. A bell begins tolling from the church down the road.

This morning we took the Company up to the Forest and did a little training under the beech-trees. 'It's like being at home again, sir,' one of the sergeants said to me.

It was nice to watch the groups of men under the green arches, although they were doing 'gas drill' and bayonet-fighting—loathsome exercises. Nice, too, to walk home behind the column, a breezy mile or two, with the men chattering gaily,

[1] Hardy, 'Afterwards' in *Moments of Vision* (1917).

to

and the cloud-shadows floating across the peaceful, spacious landscape.

A blackcap was singing in the hornbeam-bushes outside the forest, and a crow sat watching me a little way off, among the young wheat. Then a column of infantry appeared along the Abbeville road, slogging along in their tin-hats, with a few officers on horses, six hundred yards away—a miniature of war. Beside that road, or where it runs along the ridge, the battle of Crécy was fought 572 years ago.

May 15

Another golden day, fine and warm. In the afternoon Colonel Campbell delivered his famous lecture on 'the spirit of the bayonet' to the 24th and 25th R.W.F. He stood on a farm-waggon in a bright-green field. He certainly has an amazing power of stimulating the 'spirit' of the troops; it is a stunt, of course, and has little permanent effect on men of moderate courage. His lecture is much the same as when I heard it at Fourth Army School two years ago: and only disgusted me this time. It was the spirit of Militarism incarnate. A fine piece of bluff to keep up the fighting morale of the army. 'Every Bosche you fellows kill is a point scored to our side; every Bosche you kill brings victory one minute nearer and shortens the war by one minute' etc, etc. His coarse jokes of the butcher variety were finely judged and went down well. But he made an error in constantly referring to the Colonial troops and their exploits with the bayonet.

Last night I went about 10.30 in the warm dusk along twilight lanes, past glimmering farms with a few yellow-lit windows, and the glooming trees towering overhead. Nightingales were singing. Beyond the village, below the eastward slopes, I could see the dark masses of the copses on the hill; a nightingale was singing very beautifully, and the stars were showing among a few thin clouds. But the sky winked and glowed with swift flashes of the distant bombardments at Amiens and Albert, and there was a faint rumbling, low and menacing. And still the nightingales sang on while I strolled back to billet. O world God made![1]

[1] The last words of S.S.'s poem 'At Carnoy' (see p. 87).

May 17

Started off at 10 a.m.[1] with 180 men, and went *eight miles* to Brigade Baths. Beautiful day, but much too far. Baths very inadequate (at Nouvions) but the men sat around under trees among lush grass and daisies, and seemed happy enough. Crécy Forest looked superb as we skirted the beech-glades on our way home.

May 18

Extracts from censored letters.

(i) 'Well, lad, this is a top-hole country, some difference to Palestine. It gives a chap a new inside to see some fields and hedges again. Just like old Blighty . . . There is great talk of *leave* just now. In fact a party goes to-morrow. 'T.X.' (Time-expired) men first: I'm a *duration* man: what hopes! Never mind, Cheer-oh!'

(ii) 'Well dear I dont sea any sighn of my leave but if we dont get it soon it will be a grate disapointment to us all for we all expected to get one when we came to England.'

(iii) 'Our Coy. have been for a bath to-day and had a clean shirt given us, and socks. We had to march eight miles each way so we had a good walk for it didn't we. *Everywhere we go here seems such a long way.* My feet are absolutely minus of all the top skin and I've got them wrapped up like an old woman.'

(iv) 'I hope to go (on leave) soon. I've not been since Xmas 1915. You are fed up, are you. I don't wonder. I've gone past that.' (To a soldier.)

(v) 'The weather has been lovely since ive been here; we are nowhere near the line yet, ive been going to the Doctor these last few days, *sore feet*, so all I do now is going round these farms bying eggs for myself, so you can see I'm not doing so bad.'

And this is the war. 'Everywhere we go here seems such a long way' . . . 'hope to get leave soon' . . . 'our officers are fairly putting us through it' . . . 'expect we'll be going to the line soon' . . .

Then I go down the lane and watch them sitting about in the sun outside their 'same old barn', gobbling their stew out of

---

[1] *Route-march* equipment ordered by Brigade, but I got this cancelled. S.S.

canteen-lids, scribbling their letters, lying asleep in the long grass under the apple-trees, chattering and smoking, while blankets are spread out everywhere to dry, old shirts and socks hung on currant-bushes after being washed; the two Company cooks probably busy with the 'cooker', and the orderly sergeant making a list of something on a packing-case (the Quartermaster's stores are in our yard).

Some of them look up as I pick my way among the litter of men and equipment. I think they begin to realise, for I've never before worked harder for men's 'comfort and efficiency' than I have in this Company.

May 19

B., our 'drunk' officer, has got off with a severe reprimand from Corps Commander. He is lucky. Apparently quite unashamed; swaggers about, noisy and vulgar as ever. Reads out a letter of one of his platoon, which he's censoring (the man is breaking with some girl who's been unfaithful to him). 'Pretty 'ot, that!' says B. with a loud guffaw. Must try and make the best of him, I suppose, but he's a bad officer, quite irresponsible and not trustworthy.

I read in the *Nation* about Secret Treaties, and the Lloyd George-Maurice affair,[1] but it doesn't make much impression on me. Life is circumscribed by the effort of campaigning, and I can see no further than the moment when I have got this Company back from its first 'show' on the Western Front. All my efforts centred on that, and I have, for the time, escaped from my own individuality (as much as possible). This is a very blessed state to arrive at. War has its compensations—for the happy warrior type of officer.

Written as I lay on my bed after lunch; mice trickling about among the kit lying on the dusty floor of this ramshackle room with its musty old cupboards: the mice live in them among old

---

[1] After the successful German offensive in March 1918 Major-General Sir Frederick Maurice, Director of Military Operations at the War Office, published a letter accusing the Prime Minister, Mr Lloyd George, of misleading the country by falsifying the numbers of British troops in France, and all the evidence suggests that Maurice was right. The subsequent debate in the House of Commons rocked the Coalition Government and caused a split in the Liberal Party which led to its decline.

black dresses and other rubbish. Handsome Jowett asleep on the floor, with his smooth, sensual face and large limbs (as usual, he looks as if dead). He is a shy, simple, rather uncouth boy. Stiffy Phillips, our other nineteen-year-old officer, is small and self-possessed. Both are very good lads, but inclined to indolence.

The fourth officer, Harry Morgan, is aged thirty-nine—clean-shaven, saturnine, and full of jests. Has 'knocked about the world' in East Africa and Cardiff. Result; ruined digestion and considerable amount of good sense. But addicted to orgies of wine and women when he gets a chance. A knowing old bird. Not sure how much he can be trusted.

After tea I leave them—all four—scribbling down a lot of notes on training etc which Bardwell[1] dictates to them. (He has just come from a Company Commanders' conference at Battalion H.Q. and is primed with all 'the latest wind'.)

It is 5.30 and the sun blazes from a clear sky; in the orchard where I sit the trees begin to lengthen their shadows on the green and gold and white floor of grass, buttercups, and daisies. Aeroplanes drone overhead, but the late afternoon is full of mystical peace and beauty. I walk in my garden. No one can take this loveliness from my heart. I am sure St Francis would have liked a Dunhill pipe.

MILITARISTIC CURIOSITIES

(General Routine Order 2901)

'It has been ruled by the Army Council that the act of voluntarily supplying blood for transfusion to a comrade, although exemplifying self-sacrifice and devotion, does not fall within the qualification "Acts of gallantry or distinguished conduct" in paragraph 1919 (xiv) of King's Regulations.'

(Blood must be *spilt*, *not* transfused. S.S.)

(G.R.O. 3055) Exhumations

It is notified for information that no Exhumations will be permitted in the area occupied by the British Army in the

[1] I read of T. B. Bardwell's death in *The Times* in March 1928. S.S.

Field except for purely sanitary reasons, and then only with special permission from G.H.Q.

May 20

This afternoon we marched over to Cauchy, two miles away, through the hot sunshine, green wheat and barley and clover, with occasional whiffs of hawthorn along the narrow lanes skirting Domvast and Cauchy; two red may-trees over a wall, and the silver hawthorn appearing everywhere.

The 231 Brigade (or a part of it) formed a hollow square on a green hillside above the red-roofed village, snug among its trees. The Brigadier stalked on to the scene, and the Divisional General followed, receiving the salute of flashing bayonets, a small forest of them. The General (who is so fond of 'The Rosary' and 'Because') is a shortish, thick-set, well-nourished, red-faced and kindly man. He told us, speaking loud and distinct, though rather fast, that he had never been more honoured and proud and pleased etc than to-day, when he had come (like a dear, middle-aged turkey-cock) to do honour to one of the most gallant men he had ever known. He felt sure we were all equally proud and honoured. (D. Company came along using awful language, owing to their having been turned out for this show before they'd finished their mid-day meal.) He read out and descanted on the exploits which had won Harold Whitfield[1] (10th King's Shropshire Light Infantry) the V.C. Nothing was finer in the whole history of the British Army (the rest of the Brigade, of course, say that Whitfield's deeds were much exaggerated, but the K.S.L.I. are pleased and proud). Whitfield had captured a machine-gun-post single-handed, shot and bayoneted the whole team (they were Turks—probably harmless conscripts—but *possibly* Bosches or Austrians). He had killed immense numbers of the enemy, and redeemed the situation on his battalion front. The General then called for 'Corporal Whitfield', and a clumsily-built, squat figure in a round steel helmet ran out of the front rank of his Company, stopped, and saluted. He did not look a heroic figure. The General then pinned something on his breast (after dropping the pin, which a Brigade Major quickly recovered from the long grass). In a

[1] The Whiteway of *Sherston's Progress*.

loud voice the General wished Whitfield a long and happy life to wear it, and wrung him by the hand; and the little Corporal turned and was escaping to the shelter of the bayonet-forest; but was recalled, to stand out there beside the General, who called for the General Salute 'to do honour to Whitfield'. 'Present-Arms!' Everyone saluted the stumpy little soldier, including the Generals. Three cheers were then given for Whitfield. And he escaped.

It was an absurd show; not dignified in any way; not impressive because one suspected that a lot of the men realised that it was only a 'stunt' (like Campbell's lecture) to raise the morale of the troops. The man who 'voluntarily supplies blood for transfusion to a comrade' does not—technically—perform an act of gallantry. But one who, in a spirit of animal excitement and over-strain, kills a certain number of Turks is acclaimed by his comrades, and made a fool of by the Mayor and Corporation when he goes on leave, shakes hands with George V and sees his face on the front pages of the gutter-press illustrated papers. The whole thing is childish—not manly—although the man and the deed are intrinsically fine things. The Army is kept going by 'stunts' like these. General Maurice is the man who should stand out to be honoured and acclaimed by his comrades.

May 21

Another cloudless day. Lectured Company fifteen minutes on 'Morale and Offensive Spirit' in morning. Forty-minute talk to senior N.C.O.s after tea; under apple-trees; very jolly and successful effort. This Company is the best I've struck, in spite of having a dead-stale Company Commander who is suffering from nervous sexual repression, having been away from his young wife for twenty-seven months, and worried about his financial affairs at home. After lunch we did a two hours' march (full order) into the Forest. Very nice among the green of the beeches, with sunshine filtering through. Prolonged wearing of gas-masks on parade rather trying.

Shattering din and sky-high organ-drone of planes going on now (10.30 p.m.) on a moonlit night with hawthorn-scents and glimmerings and nightingale songs. (The Bosche are overhead, dropping bombs on neighbouring villages. They have been

hammering Abbeville heavily the last few nights.) We move to
St Pol on Thursday. Nothing matters now but the welfare of the
Company I am with. Working hard and sleeping badly. Never
mind.

May 22

Another cloudless day. Quiet day's training. Began to read
Duhamel's *Vie des Martyrs*[1] yesterday. I expect *he* felt he was in
a groove while he wrote it, patiently studying the little world of
his hospital. But as I began to read I suddenly saw the narrow-
ness of the life a soldier leads on active service. The better the
soldier, the narrower is his groove. Duhamel is quite equal to
Barbusse.

I am getting to understand soldiers and their ideas; intelligent
instruction of them teaches me that. But I find them very difficult
to describe. And in these days of hawthorn and young leaves they
seem a part of the passing of the year. Autumn will bring many
of them to oblivion and decay. 'Their lives are like the leaves . . .
O martyred youth and manhood overthrown, The burden of
your wrongs is on my head.'[2]

> It was written that you should suffer without purpose
> and without hope. But I will not let all your sufferings be
> lost in the abyss.
>
> (Duhamel)[3]

Tomorrow morning we leave Domvast. Breakfast 3.45; move
off 5. March sixteen miles to station (Rue).

Somewhere between Arras and St Pol will be our training
area. In April 1917 I was marching up from Doullens toward
Arras in the cold weather and sleet-showers. 80% of those
officers were killed last year, and a large proportion of the men.

> What became of you, precious lives, poor wonderful
> souls, for whom I fought so many obscure great battles, and
> who went off again in the realm of adventure?
>
> (Duhamel)[4]

[1] Published in 1917. The novelist Georges Duhamel (1884–1966) was an army
surgeon during the war and this book is a moving account of the terribly wounded
soldiers in his hospital. S.S. was reading the English translation, *The New Book
of Martyrs* (1918).
[2] From S.S.'s poem 'Autumn', published in *Counter-Attack*.
[3] *Op. cit.*, p. 32.   [4] *Op. cit.*, p. 53.

There are ancient graveyards which the centuries filled
slowly, and where woman sleeps beside man, and the child
beside the grandfather. But this burial-ground owes nothing
to old age or sickness. It is the burial-ground of young,
strong men. We may read their names on the hundreds of
little crosses which repeat daily in speechless unison: 'There
must be something more precious than life, more necessary
than life . . . since we are here'.

(Duhamel) [1]

May 24

Magnicourt. 'Yesterday' began at 2.30 a.m. and ended at
11 p.m. when our Company were safely settled down in their
billets after twenty miles' marching and five hours in the train
(covered trucks). We left Domvast at 5 a.m. A warm still
morning with a quiet sunrise glinting behind us beyond the trees
and the village.

We crossed the Abbeville-St Omer road and went through
Crécy Forest for about eight miles. There had been some rain
in the night and the air smelt of damp leaves and dust. Glim-
mering aisles of green. Entrained at Rue, 1 o'clock and reached
St Pol about 6.30. Marched five miles to billets. Strong breeze;
much colder. It has rained all day to-day. Billets good. The
whole Company in one huge, lofty barn, with nice clean straw.

Have got a room up a lane, with churchyard view, and clock
ticking peacefully on a shelf. We are about twenty kilometres
behind the Arras-Albert sector, and ten kilometres from
Lucheux, where I passed with the Second Battalion toward
Arras in April 1917. *But we have just received orders to march
again to-morrow!*
Note on my servant (I put this in in case I was killed, for Law's
benefit).

I have been saved from innumerable small worries and ex-
asperations in the last ten weeks by my servant, 355642 Private
John Law. [2] He is the perfect servant. Nothing could be better
than the way he does things, quiet and untiring. I can imagine
him figuring as an ideal 'patient' in one of Duhamel's hospital

[1] *Op. cit.*, p. 87.
[2] The Bond of *Sherston's Progress*.

interiors. Of him it might have been written: 'He waged his own war with the divine patience of a man who had waged the great world war, and who knows that victory will not come right away.'[1] He is simple, humble, brave, patient and loving: he is reticent, yet humorous. How many of us can claim to possess these things, and ask no reward but a smile?

> To make up one's mind to die is to take a certain resolution, in the hope of becoming quieter, calmer, and less unhappy. The man who makes up his mind to die severs a good many ties, and indeed actually dies to some extent.
>
> (Duhamel)[2]

I glance over my right shoulder at my little row of books, red and green and blue; they stand waiting for my hand, offering their accumulated riches. I think of the years that *may* be in store for me, and of all the pages I *may* turn. Then I look out at the falling rain and the grey evening beyond the churchyard wall, and I wonder if there is anything awaiting me that will be truer or more human than my feeling of satisfaction yesterday. What was the thing I did to win that satisfaction? There were five of my men on the train who had come too late for their tea. They had stared disconsolate at an empty 'dixie', tired out by the long march and herded into a dirty van to travel toward hell. But I was able to get some tea for them. Alone I did it. Without my help they would have had none. And I was proud of myself. It is these little things, done for nameless soldiers, that make the war bearable. So I sit and wonder if I'm really a good chap, or only rather a humbug.

Little ginger-haired Cowan, our shy Company clerk, who works so hard, goes home for a month's leave to-morrow. Funny to think that some of us may be dead when he returns to his documents and 'returns'.

May 25 (Habarcq, twelve kilometres from Arras)

We left Magnicourt at 9 a.m. A warm day, beastly march of ten miles; very slow owing to congestion. Arrived about 2. Bardwell and I in the Château; a barrack of a place. Village very

[1] *Op. cit.*, p. 38.
[2] *Op. cit.*, p. 145.

much overdone with troops. B. goes on leave to-morrow, so I
shall be in command of the Company for the next five weeks.

This place is only five miles from Basseux, where we stayed
for three days in April 1917 before going up to the Arras battle.
A girl watching us pass through a village to-day cried out '*Ne pas
des anciens!*' Youth going to the sacrifice.

One of our platoons is billeted close to a burial-ground. They
refer to it as 'the rest-camp'. 'No reveille and route marches
there,' said one chap, a long, tired-looking man with a walrus-
moustache. Getting nearer the line is working me up to a
climax. Same old feeling of confidence and freedom from worry.

May 26

Feeling very tired to-night. The guns are making a noise
eight miles away. But I will read Lamb's letters, and then go to
sleep. I am alone in this large room now (B. gone to England
to-day). Small things have conspired to exasperate me to-day.
My windows look out on tree-tops, and a huge cedar. (I am on
the third storey.) Am no use to-night.

May 28

After two days' hard work with the Company too tired to read
or think. Devilish noise last night when the next village was
being bombed, and anti-aircraft and Lewis-guns firing. They are
over again tonight.

> Believe thou, O my soul,
> Life is a vision, shadowy of Truth;
> And vice, and anguish, and the wormy grave,
> Shapes of a dream.
>
> (Coleridge)[1]

May 29

Inspection by Divisional General. He made a very pleasant
impression. A. Company turned out devilish smart. Letter from
Robert Graves (from another world, talking of 'leave' and all

[1] From 'Religious Musings'.

that is life). Damn leave; I don't want it. And I don't want to be wounded and wangle a job at home. I want the next six weeks, and success; do I want death? I don't know yet; but the war is outside of life; and I'm in it. 'Those we loved were merely happy shadows.'[1]

May 30
Another cloudless day. Working hard all day with the Company. After tea the Brigadier made a speech to his officers—a rambling discourse which lasted an hour and a quarter. He is a stupid, fire-eating professional soldier—brave, no doubt (but that word means nothing now). He said things that matter! and prepared us for the fall of Paris! But I am still happy and healthy, and proud of my Company.

June 2 (Three weeks ago we reached Abbeville district)
The weather continues cloudless. On Friday the Company were out nearly eleven hours; marched to the range, eight miles each way (near Magnicourt). Yesterday we paraded at 6 a.m. and marched seven miles to take part in Brigade field-day. (The men have not had a half-holiday, except Sundays, for a fortnight. This afternoon they are not free till 4 o'clock.) But they are in wonderful form in spite of sore feet. Only three have gone on leave since we arrived in France (all 'time expired' men). *One* goes next week! But the rest are *hoping*. I have got a fine grip on them now.

After breakfast to-day I sat under the apple-blossom behind our Mess and read a Homeric Ode to Hermes. It was a great relief after a week of unremitting toil over small details. But it was only half-an-hour. What a life. I feel stronger and more confident than ever before. We are now on GHQ Reserve and liable to move at twenty-four hours' notice.

The papers are full of this foul 'Billing Case'. Makes one glad to be away from 'normal conditions'.[2] And the Germans are on

---

[1] Duhamel, *op. cit.*, p. 3.
[2] In early June 1918 Noel Pemberton Billing (1880–1948), eccentric Independent M.P. for East Herts, was sued for criminal libel by the dancer Maud Allan, on account of his review, in his own paper *The Vigilante*, of her performance in Oscar Wilde's *Salome*. Billing, who conducted his own defence, maintained that there existed a Black Book containing the names of 47,000 leading Britishers,

the Marne and claim 4500 more prisoners. The world is stark
staring mad, and I don't regret the prospect of leaving it, as
long as my friends go with me.

This morning I was shaving at 8.30 (got up at 4.30 yesterday,
and 5.15 the day before). Below my window a voluntary service
was taking place, and I heard about twenty male voices strike up
with 'How sweet the name of Jeeesus sounds'. It seemed funny,
somehow. Later on the smug Padre was preaching about 'the
spiritual experiences of the righteous'. Righteous! what a
Church of England word it is!

After bolting a hasty lunch at 12.45, I must spend one-and-a-
quarter hours at a 'Commanding Officers' Conference' and listen
to a lecture on Trench Warfare, and discuss yesterday's Field
Day. No peace for poets. But I have my large airy upper chamber
in the Château, where I am alone, and can retire and *be alone* for
an hour. Through the window one sees the upper parts of large
trees which crowd round the front of the Château; a huge cedar,
two fine ashes, a very fine walnut, with a background of chest-
nuts and others. All very magnificent and towering with foliaged
limbs. Birds chirp; the guns rumble twelve miles away. And my
servant has picked some syringa and wild roses which are in a
bowl by my bed.

A jolly young lance-corporal (headquarters signaller) came in
to cut my hair this morning, and chattered away about the
Germans and the war and so on. He likes France, but doesn't
think the war can be ended by fighting. Very sensible. So he
clatters down the stairs (echoing boards) whistling 'Dixieland';
and it's a bright summer morning, the first Sunday in June.

After tea an exciting mail came in—Walter de la Mare's new
book of poems.[1] I went out and read some of them under a
hawthorn-hedge, sitting in the long grass, with a charming
glimpse of the backs of barns and men sitting in the sun, and the
graveyard—but no mouldering headstones with 'a time-worn
cupid's head'.[2] All the graves are men killed in the war—most of
them French; but there are flowers—white pinks and pansies—

whose sexual perversions rendered them liable to blackmail by the Germans.
Mr Justice Darling lost control of the court, in which disorder reigned and
Lord Alfred Douglas was removed by force. Billing won the case.

[1] *Motley and other Poems* (1918).

[2] An echo of 'one rain-worn cherub's head' in De la Mare's poem 'The Stranger',
published in *The Listeners* (1912).

and long grass and sunshine. Then I watched the Company play football and get beaten.

But the most exciting thing in the mail-bag was Bob Nichols's long letter, and four new poems—very fine. I wish to God he were with me now. I hate to think of him alone and sex-ridden—the daemon of poesy leading him from gloom to gloom. Could he but share my present happiness! Could I but breathe into his haunted mind something of the golden-skinned serenity of my own St Martin's Summer of happy warrior youth! He says in his letter, 'You have the act-of-being-a-soldier to help you. I wish I was a soldier again.'[1] Pathetic cry for help, and hope, and pride.

June 4

Out with the Company from 7.15 till 4.15. Did a Battalion attack, and after lunch a gas-lecture and we were bombarded with smoke and gas etc. I was feeling jumpy and nerve-ridden and exasperated all day. It would be a relief to shed tears now. But I smoke on my bed, and the Divisional brass band is tootling on the grass in front of the Château. I will read de la Mare and try to buck up. It is the result of working so hard and being worried with trivial details from morning till night. After all, I am nothing but what the Brigadier calls 'a potential killer of Germans (Huns)'. O God, why must I do it? *I'm not.* I am only here *to look after* some men.

Dreams

Last night I dreamed that I was leading my Company into battle. I was afraid they wouldn't follow me (in my dream I'd forgotten that I should be trying to control them *from behind*). And everything went wrong; and I lost them; and I knew they were on in front somewhere; and it all got mixed up with 'getting left' in a hunt and I'd lost hounds. I'd gone to sleep tired out and unhappy and exasperated by soldiering and never being alone and free. But I awoke in the grey of the June morning with the bird-songs coming through veils of twilight and drowsiness. And I was still unhappy; even that beauty failed to touch my heart. 'When earth is no more mine though night goes out, And stretching forth these arms I cannot be Lord of winged

[1] Nichols had been invalided out of the army after some three weeks at the front.

sunrise and dim Arcady.'[1] Have I got to that yet? I wrote that
sonnet ten years ago.

June 5   9.30 p.m.

Yesterday was the first bad day I've had for three weeks at
least; and I finished the day with nerves racked and life hideous.
But this morning I got up, with great difficulty, at 6.30, and
started off with the men at 7.45 for a Brigade field-day. A hot
day and not too strenuous. We only went a mile from here and
finished two miles from home. Did an attack from 10.30 till 2.30.
I became a 'casualty' as soon as they got fairly started on their
2000-yard assault. And I lay among the rustling barley and
listened to the larks and soaked in the sunshine; the rumour of
death was very far away—a low rumble of guns. So I am in good
spirits again to-night, and the furies have sailed away into the
blue air.

When I rode into the transport lines this afternoon I saw Jim
Linthwaite toiling at cleaning a limber, under the supervision of
a military policeman. (He has still ten days to do of his twenty-
eight Field Punishment No 2 for getting drunk at Marseilles.)
But I gave him a cheery word and a grin, and he smiled at me,
standing there in his grimy slacks and blue jersey. I wonder if he
thought it a strange thing to do? I hadn't spoken to him since I
talked to him like a father when he was awaiting his court-
martial. Something drew me to him when I saw him first.
'Linthwaite, a nice name' I thought, when they told me he was a
First Battalion man. Then I saw him, digging away at road-
mending, and he'd got a rotten pair of boots, which were an
excuse for conversation, and I've loved him ever since (it is
just as well he's not in my present Company). And when he got
into trouble I longed to be kind to him. And I talked to him
about 'making a fresh start, and not doing anything silly again',
while he stood in front of me with his white face, and eyes full
of tears. I suppose I'd have done the same for any man in the
Company who had a good character. But there was a great deal
of sex floating about in this particular effort. No doubt he dreams
about 'saving my life'. I wish I could save his.

[1] From 'Before Day', published in S.S's privately printed *Sonnets* (1909), then
in *The Old Huntsman*.

1918

REWARD

Months and weeks and days go past,
And my soldiers fall at last.
Months and weeks and days
Their ways must be my ways.
And evermore
Love guards the door.

From their eyes the gift I gain
Of grace that can subdue my pain.
From their eyes I hoard
My reward.
O brothers in my striving, it were best
That I should share your rest.

Habarcq, June 5

June 7

Golden weather. Starting this morning with C.O. and Ellis for three days in the line with the Canadians. Our days here are numbered. From all accounts people spend half their time wearing gas-masks (in spite of this the casualties are very heavy; a great many of them get gassed on purpose). Discipline among the conscripts is reported as very bad, and the Commander-in-Chief can't get many men from England. I am taking Lamb's letters in my pocket. I can't think of a better book for the trenches. No doubt I shall 'gather big impressions'!

June 8

Another fine day. Yesterday I rode to Avesnes-le-Comte, and was conveyed thence in a lorry to Basseux[1] (where the Second Canadian Division H.Q. are) and then on to Agny. Lunched at Brigade H.Q. and came up to Battalion H.Q. Reached B. Company

---

[1] Basseux was the last billet I was in with the Second R.W.F. Left there on 11 April 1917 and marched up to near Mercatel—a few hundred yards from where I sit writing. Less than three miles from here died little Orme, and Conning, and L. Ormrod was mortally wounded, and all those others went west, in April and May last year. And I come blundering into it all again, guffawing with Canadians. S.S.

H.Q. in the front line about 7.30. (Like Mr Bottomley in the trenches, I feel!)

The 24th Victoria Rifles are many of them French Canadians (from Quebec). I stay with Captain Duclos, who has been wounded twice, and in France twenty-one months, and if he gets one more 'blighty' he'll stay there. Jake! In spite of his name, he speaks no French. Seems a fine chap.

Expect I'll see a good deal of the Neuville-Vitasse-Mercatel sectors, so I'll let them wait to be described.

There was a fair amount of shelling last evening, considerable patrolling activity by our side, much sending up of flares by the Bosche; in fact, things are much the same as two years ago, except that we didn't sniff then for whiffs of mustard-gas. I don't think I'm any worse than I was at Fricourt and Mametz. I would have enjoyed doing a patrol last night.

These trenches are narrow and not sandbagged; they will be very bad when it rains. At present they are dry as dust. Very few rats. Company H.Q. in a steel hut which would stop a whizz-bang.

Duclos was very friendly last night, and we sat and jawed about old battles and cursed names and the Billing Case, and the Fifth Army rout, and people with cushy jobs at home, and all the usual dug-out talk. And I went to sleep at stand-to (2.30) and woke up with the usual dug-out mouth. I have come back into the past, but none of my old friends are here. (Old Greaves is with the Second Battalion; Stansfield back in Canada; Julian Dadd insane?; Orme dead; and the First Battalion away in Italy.) But I have got A. Company to look after. And Stiffy Phillips and Jowett are as good as the old crowd. ('Everything *jake*'?)

The landscape here is of the deadly-conventional Armageddon type—low green-grey ridges fringed with the usual decorations of a few isolated trees, half-smashed, with a broken wall or two, straggling trench-grey silhouettes that once were villages. Then there are open spaces broken only by ruined wire-tangles, old trenches, and the dismal remains of an occasional rest-camp of huts. The June grass waves, poppies flame, shrapnel bursts with black puffs, an aeroplane drones, larks sing; someone comes along the trench, clinking a petrol-tin. And this is about all one sees, as one stumps along the communication-trenches, dry and crumbling, with a dead mole lying about here and there.

Inside our H.Q. I watched another conventional trench-warfare interior. The Captain snores on his bed. I sit at a table with a large yellow candle burning.[1] At the other end of the Nissen Hut (curved steel) daylight comes unnaturally in at the door—evening sunshine—the servants are cooking (fire made of sandbag soaked in candle-grease). The H.Q. runner, a boy of nineteen, leans against the doorpost, steel-hat tilted over his eyes (long eyelashes showing against the daylight). The signaller sits at a table with his back to me, making a gnat-like obbligato on his instrument. Outside one hears dull bumpings of guns, and the leisurely trickle of shells sailing overhead. Now and then tap, tap of machine-gun-fire.

It is all exactly the same as two years ago. But this is one of the very few quiet places on the British front.

Went out about 10 this evening and dropped in for a damnable half-hour. Bosche sending over a lot of stuff, including aerial torpedoes. Half-a-dozen men hit in the left Company: only one man in this Company. Supports heavily shelled also. Everything quiet again now. Didn't feel as frightened as I expected to, but the noise was hideous. No gas. Came back to H.Q. and read Lamb's letters now.

June 9

The Bosche came over on our left last night, a small raid against the next battalion. Only a few got into our trenches. This battalion had two killed and eight wounded.

I left the front line at 3 p.m. to-day, and after various delays got back to Habarcq at 11 p.m. So here I am in my quiet room again, with the trees rustling outside, and a very distinct series of war-pictures in my head. Coming into it, for a short time, and then straight out and clear away, leaves one with a very solid impression (like Mr Bottomley's). The business-like futility of it is amazing. Those Canadians were fine fighters, decent chaps, bloodthirsty brutes. They were holding their trenches very well; patrols, raids, and complete absence of 'wind up'.

[1] On the table, spread-out and covered with grease, is a sheet of the *Sussex Express*. God knows why! So I look down and read 'Whist-Drive at Heathfield', 'Weak Milk from Hellingly, Hastings prosecution', 'Lewes Tribunal', and such-like items. S.S.

June 10

A dull, rainy morning. Among my letters I find the South-down Hunt balance sheet. (The late) Capt. G. S. Harbord gave £10. The hunt accounts always make me homesick . . . I am made a temporary Captain. What drivel it all is!

A good letter from E. M. Forster.

An article on Scott in the *Literary Supplement* adds to my war-misery this morning. I think of the Pentlands, and the charm of Scotch landscapes. Peace. Then I switch on to Canadians and Lewis-guns again.

Demeanour (in the trenches)

Captain D. of the –th Canadians has got the right manner, whether it be studied imitation or spontaneous gallantry. He knows just how to walk along a trench when there's a 'trench-mortar strafe' on, and the half-darkness is full of booms and flashes. He never hurries; quietly, with a wise, half-humorous expression masking his solid determination and mastery of the situation, he moves from sentry to sentry; now getting up on the fire-step to lean over beside a flinching youngster who stares fearfully into the drifting smoke that hides the wire where the Bosche may be lying ready to rush forward; now he cracks a joke with some old 'tough'. 'Everything Jake here?' he says, as he passes from one to another—always making for the place where he expects trouble—or where the din is loudest. He leaves a feeling of security in his wake. Men finger their bayonets and pull themselves together. The end of his cigarette glows in the dusk—a little planet of unquenchable devotion. Captain D. is a soldier-type. But his own company always thinks there never was such an officer. And someday he'll light his last 'gasper' and something will knock him flat; and he'll make way for Captain E. 'There never was such an officer as Captain E.' they'll say, a few months later.

June 12

Yesterday we did an Attack with Tanks. I was sitting on the back of a tank, joy-riding across the wheat and rye-grass in afternoon sunshine; suddenly I remembered my tank poem.[1]

[1] 'Blighters', published in *The Old Huntsman*.

Busy again all to-day. Another fine day. The weather is miraculous. Like the sunlit opening scene of a melodrama—Chorus of haymakers. Act II Thunder and Lightning. Heavy firing in the wings. Act III Limelight; dying speeches; 'Kiss me, Hardy.' Act IV Memorial tablet erected in parish church.

After lunch to-day I glanced at *The Times*—killed in action Lt. C. N. Dobell, R.W.F. Little Colin who was with me at Mametz Wood. And I took him out hunting with the Limerick Hounds last February, his first real day's hunting. 'It can't be true; it can't be true,' I thought. But it's there in print.

Fool-poems in the *Spectator* about 'our unforgotten dead'. 'We must live more nobly, remembering those who fell,' etc. Will *that* comfort *Colin*, or his girl? *He* wanted life; fox-hunting, and marriage; and peace-soldiering. Now he's lost it all; aged twenty-one.

COLIN

One by one they've passed across the scene;
One by one; the lads I've known and met;
Laughing, swearing, shivering in the wet.
On their graves the grass is green;
Lads whose words and eyes I can't forget.

Colin's dead to-day; he's gone away;
Cheery little Colin, keen to hunt;
Firm and cool and quiet in a stunt.
   Is there any more to say?
Colin's name's been printed in *The Times*,
'Killed in Action'. *He* can't read my rhymes.

June 12

June 14

I have seen a lot of soldiers at the war, but I have never seen a more well-behaved crowd than my present Company. They are living now in good billets, in a fairly good village. They are well fed. Their mental attitude is far less abject than is the case with the 1917–18 conscripts. But when their day's work is ended they have about four hours left with nothing to do, nowhere to go. Not so much as a cinema or a YMCA hut.

Perhaps they watch a football match till 6.30. There is only one ground, used by the Canadians as well.

So they go to the *estaminets*. I calculate that at least 10,000 francs are spent in *estaminets* in this village by our battalion alone every week, probably £500 a week is the figure. And 50% of the battalion goes to bed drunk every night. Why do they do it? Because they all know that they will be in hell within a month; most of them have been away from home for nearly two and a half years. (Ten men go on leave each week from this battalion of eight hundred men.) They are having what is called a good time. Drink and death.

The noise of the bombardments—miles away—as I lie awake at night sounds like heavy furniture being moved in a room overhead. Every night I come back to my large empty room, where I sleep alone; and from 8.30 till 10.30 I read and write and do my day's thinking. Sometimes I am too tired to think at all. I read the *Nation*, or the *Literary Supplement*; Lytton Strachey's book;[1] Duhamel; *Trivia*;[2] a Tolstoy; Lamb's letters.

(All day I have been worrying about Lewis-guns and small Company details; usually I've been out and about from 8 a.m. till 5. Is this self-pity?)

While I'm reading, someone drops in for a talk, and I must put down my book and listen to someone else's grievances against the War (or Battalion arrangements). And outside the wind hushes the huge leafy trees. Usually I awake early and hear the chorus of birds through the half-dissolved veils of sleep. But those songs have ceased to thrill me as of old.

At dinner in our Company Mess I was arguing with Phillips, who has strong convictions of his own infallibility (like many nineteen-year-old officers). But it was only about some detail of Lewis-gun training. Also he had said that I had 'got a downer' on some N.C.O., which I stoutly denied. We got quite hot over it. Then the discussion dissolved into jolly merriment and fled from our minds for ever. After all, we'd had a good feed and some red wine; to-morrow was to be Saturday, an easy day's work; and Phillips and Jowett had come in to the meal flushed and happy after a platoon football match. And we are all so amazingly healthy.

[1] *Eminent Victorians* (1918).
[2] By Logan Pearsall Smith (1918).

'Damn it, I'm fed up with all this training!' I exclaimed in a loud voice, pushing back my chair on the brick floor and getting on to my feet. 'I want to go up to the Line and *fight!*' said I, with a reckless air. 'Same here' agreed handsome boy Jowett in his soft voice. J. always agrees with me. He is brave and gentle, and rather shy. Stiffy Phillips is thick-set and short and confident, and inclined to contradict his elders. He too is brave and tender-hearted and clean-souled.

I went out into a cool, grey, breezy evening. Miles away the guns growled and rumbled. 'Come on, then; come on, you mug!' they muttered. I shivered, and walked quickly up to the Château —to the quiet room where I spend my evenings with one candle, scribbling notes on the monstrous cruelty of war and the horrors of the front line. 'I want to go and fight!' Thus had I boasted in a moment of folly, catching my mood from the lads who look to me as their leader.

How should they know the shallowness of those words? The dark and secret pools of my mind are hidden from their under-standing. They see me in the sunshine, when I must acquiesce in the evil that is war, building my pride of its bravery and brief jollity. But in the darkness of the night my soul goes down into the valleys of death, and my feet move among the graves of dead youth.

Stiffy, grey-eyed and sensible and shrewd; Jowett, dark-eyed and lover-like and wistful; how long have you to live, you, in the perfection of youth, your pride of living, your ignorance of life's narrowing road? O let my pity be poured out upon you; let my love be spent to make your time more happy. And if you must die, and I be left alone, let me be strong to endure the injustice that dooms you to banishment from all that is your desire.

'I want to go and fight!' That was an hour ago; and they are still in the mood of flushed confidence and ardour. And I with my one candle in the gloom; and the wisdom of my books; and the knowledge that my years have given me. 'Whom the gods love'. Bless their little hearts; and bring them safety.

June 15

This afternoon I was lying on my bed reading a letter from young H., quite an ordinary Midland youth, who is left in

Egypt. He had no nerve for fighting, but his affection touched me. At the end of his long letter he says 'You may think me a queer sort of being, but I am really awfully bucked at having met someone who had a little sympathy for me, the only particle I ever had the whole twelve months of my perfectly wretched existence with the 25th Battalion.' So a certain mood was stirred in me. And I began reading *Sea-Drift*, with an emotion I'd not felt for many months—the *passion* of poetry. And then the brass band struck up outside the Château (our Saturday afternoon treat). So starved am I for music that even those inane tootlings didn't jar on my enjoyment of the poem. A strange substitution for the storms of lovely sound that Delius made to those words:

> O throat! O throbbing heart!
> And I singing uselessly, uselessly all the night.
> O past! O happy life! O songs of joy!

More than three years ago I listened to that music of Delius. And now a brass military band playing 'I feel so lonely' etc. And the same tumult and conflict and thrilling pain in my heart.

> The messenger there aroused, the fire, the sweet hell within,
> The unknown want, the destiny of me.[1]

Result of Reading Whitman

To O.C. A. Coy. Ref. Return of Books and Pamphlets at present in possession of Companies. This should have been passed on by you at 6 p.m. last night instead of which it was not passed until 11.45 this morning. As this entails additional work in the office please ensure that this does not occur again.

Adjutant, 25th R.W.F.

I am beginning to realise the difficulties of combining the functions of soldier and poet.[2]

When I was out here as a platoon-commander I spent half my time in day-dreams. I avoided responsibilities. But since I've been with this battalion responsibility has been pushed on to me, and I've taken soldiering very seriously. A conscientious and

[1] Both these extracts are from Walt Whitman's 'Out of the Cradle Endlessly Rocking' in his collection *Sea-Drift*, which was set to music by Frederick Delius.
[2] Soldier and pacifist. S.S.

efficient company-commander has rather a harassing time, especially during prolonged periods of training. For several weeks I hardly thought of anything but the Company. Now that their training is coming to an end I've been easing off a bit; have allowed myself to enjoy books. The result is that I immediately lose my grip on soldiering, and begin to find everything intolerable except my interest in the humanity of the men. One cannot be a good soldier and a good poet at the same time. Soldiering depends on a multitude of small details; one must not miss any of the details. Poetry depends on wayward moods and sudden emotions. Life will be easier and simpler when we get into the line again. There one alternates between intense concentration on the business in hand and extreme exhaustion. Everything up there is 'soul-deadening'; there is no time for emotion, no place for beauty. Only grimness and cruelty and remorse. And the well-known 'gaiety' which is a defence against these. (The 'gaiety' of men in a scuttled ship.)

I wish you to understand that I have never been more healthy, physically, than I am to-day. But under all that mask of animal satisfaction the mind rebels and struggles to dominate the situation as it should do. For all these details of soldiering are not exercises for the mind; they are mechanical and utterly stupid, and (to me) unnatural.

I don't write this for self-advertisement, or in self-pity; nor am I a pompous prig. I am merely recording what thousands of sensitive gifted people are enduring in the name of 'patriotism'. And O how I long for music. *That* is what I need *most of all*.

June 16

'What's the weight of *your* pig?' asked a witty Colonial. Coming up a communication-trench, he squeezed himself against the chalky side of the trench to make room for two men who were coming down; they were carrying a dead body slung on a pole. This is how the Canadians take their corpses away from the front-line. They tie the hands together at the wrists; feet ditto. Then sling the body on a pole. What splendid common-sense! And how jolly the War is! But I wish they'd put a sandbag over the face.

1918

What the Bishop said

<table>
<tr><td>(Deputy-Chaplain</td><td>(or the Spiritual Equivalent of</td></tr>
<tr><td>General)</td><td>Campbell's Bayonet Fighting Lecture)</td></tr>
</table>

The Bishop is an old friend of our Divisional General: knew him in the Soudan in fact. The Bishop is a well-nourished, Anglican Gramophone. He would have made an admirable Butler, had he been called to that profession. To-day he gave us one of his well-worn Records: Patriotism, Insular Imperialism, Hun-Hatred, all with a strong flavour of *Morning Post*, and the Bishop of London somewhere in the offing. After a preliminary pre-oration, beginning 'I am very proud, and very pleased, to have the privilege etc of welcoming you to the Western Front, on behalf of my Branch of the Service . . .' He told us that every heart had thrilled with pride when the news came that we had taken Jerusalem. The armies in France had been most enthusiastic.

He went on with his manly address, and gave us a few facts about the war, suitable for the troops. As follows:

(i) The Germans have got the initiative and are hammering us very hard (due to the Russian Revolution).

(ii) The troops are more enthusiastic about winning the war than they were last year. They feel they'd rather die than see their own land treated like Belgium.

(iii) Thank God, we hold the seas!

(iv) It is religion that keeps their morale so high.

(v) The Americans are coming across in large numbers.

(vi) A distinguished General told him last week that the Germans are getting weaker every week. *Time is on our side!*

(vii) He compared us to the Early Christians, who were burnt alive and thrown to the lions. (How nice!)

(viii) Referred to J. Christ as 'not the effete figure in stained glass windows, but the *Warrior Son of God* who moves among the troops and urges them to yet further efforts of sacrifice (and slaughter?)

(ix) Concluded by reciting two verses of the American hymn 'God goes marching on', with lifted hand. (Strong smell of Parish Room.)

And the troops rather liked it.

I figure the Bishop with one hand on the knob of God's drawing-room door; 'What name, sir?' Or talking to an old friend of the family as he relieves him of his overcoat and umbrella in the Celestial Entrance Hall. 'Yes, m'lord, all the family are in the best of health. Mr Jesus has been a little worried by this terrible war, like most of us. Likewise the Holy Ghost, the Comforter . . . Yes, m'lord, the Almighty is in the library, and has enquired for you several times lately.' And so, with deliberate, confidential mien, he leads the way up the soft-carpeted stairs.

I STOOD WITH THE DEAD

I stood with the Dead, so forsaken and still:
When dawn was grey I stood with the Dead.
And my slow heart said, 'You must kill, you must kill:
'Soldier, soldier, morning is red'.

On the shapes of the slain in their crumpled disgrace
I stared for a while through the thin cold rain . . .
'O lad that I loved, there is rain on your face,
And your eyes are blurred and sick like the plain.'

I stood with the Dead . . . They were dead; they were dead;
My heart and my head beat a march of dismay:
And gusts of the wind came dulled by the guns.
'Fall in!' I shouted: 'Fall in for your pay!'

Habarcq, June 18[1]

Left Habarcq June 20 and went to St Hilaire, near Lillers. Went to the line a fortnight later. Wounded July 13.[2]

July 15 (In hospital at the Base)
It all gets blurred: time drifts between me and last week. I am amputated from the Battalion. When I was hit it seemed an un-speakable thing to leave my men in the lurch, to go away into

[1] Published in the *Nation*, 13 July 1918, then in *Picture Show*.
[2] Returning from a patrol in no-man's-land, S.S. was shot in the head by one of his own sergeants, who mistook him for an advancing German. See *Sherston's Progress*.

safety. 'I won't say good-bye; I'm coming back,' I said to the little Company Sergeant-Major. Then I turned and climbed out of the big shell-hole where my Company H.Q. hid itself. Down the path among wheat and oats and beans, over the bullet-swept willow-bordered road, and so I came to the red-roofed farm that is Battalion H.Q.—a mile and a half from the front-line. Five o'clock on a summer morning. I passed the little cluster of crosses, and blundered in to the Aid-Post to get my head seen to. Long farewells to C.O. and adjutant and other H.Q. officers— sleepy men, getting 'situation reports' from the front line. 'You'll see me back in three weeks,' I shouted, and turned the corner of the lane with a last confident gesture of defiant determination, undefeated by a mere bullet-graze on the head. And so from one Dressing Station to another on motor ambulances, steadily leaving the battle-zone. Then a night at the big Casualty Clearing Station. 'We're sending you down to the Base to-day.' And yesterday I was trying to persuade an R.A.M.C. Colonel to keep me up at the Main Dressing Station till my wound was healed. Still I persistently hang on to my obsession that I'll not go to Blighty . . . 'I won't, I won't.' Write letters to people at home, saying I'm wounded, and staying in France till I can go up the line again. But an angry, tortured feeling has come over me. 'I'll stay in France just to spite those blighters who yell about "our alien enemies" in Trafalgar Square.' But, after all, what do *they* care about me? And I'd be dead now, if I'd moved my head an inch to the right before that bullet whizzed down. Then I remember my (J. Law) servant's kindly, loving face, and see him putting my kit on to the ambulance. I smile at him, 'Back soon'. He promised to walk over to the C.C.S. next day and see me there, bringing letters and the latest news from the line. But I'd gone when he got there. Not my fault. They sent me straight on to the place near St Omer where I slept. If I'd made a scene and refused to go on, everyone would have thought me mad, especially with a head-wound. Who ever heard of anyone refusing to go down the line with an honourable wound?

Now I'm at Boulogne, trying to be hearty and well. 'How are you feeling?' says the doctor. 'Quite well, thank you; it's only a graze on the scalp.' But I daren't look him in the face. And I can't swallow my food. Nurses and sisters are sympathetic.

They've heard I'm a poet and a bit of a celebrity in my way. Young, too, and picturesque-looking. So they make a fuss over me, till I hardly dare to behave like a healthy man.

Still the memory, growing dimmer now, of 'the Company' in the Line, haunts me and wrings my heart. I hear them saying, 'When's the Captain coming back? Oh, he's a proper lad, he is!' It seemed that across the Channel I had nothing to go back to, as long as the war went on. My world had shrunk to a Company H.Q. All the people in England who mattered were inaccessible owing to their own war activities. I wanted to be back with good old de Sola[1] and Stiffy and Jowett and the men in my Company. There at least I had been something real, and I had lived myself into a feeling of responsibility for them—inefficient and excitable though I was when in close contact with Germans. All that was decent in me disliked leaving them to endure what I was escaping from. And somehow the idea of death had beckoned to me—ghastly though it had been when I believed that I had been killed.

But I think to myself, 'Perhaps half of 'em 'll be in Blighty by the time I go back, even if I stay in France to get well'. And again, I think, 'How many officers are there in the Battalion who would refuse to go to Blighty if it were made easy for them?' I swear to God there's not one. Why should I be the only one? They'd only think me a fool, if they believed it to be true that I'd really done it. And then in my heart I know that it is the only way I can keep my soul clean, and vindicate my pride in the men who love and trust me. It is the supreme thing that is asked of me. And already I am shying at it. 'We'll be sending you across to England in a few days,' murmurs the nurse who is washing my blood-clotted hair. And my heart stops beating for a moment. She says it so naturally, as if it were the only possible thing that could happen.

I am weakening in my proud, angry resolve; all my tenderness is fading into selfish longing for safety. I close my eyes, and all I can see is the door into the garden at home, and Mother coming in with a basket of roses. And my terrier . . . and the piano . . .

---

[1] Vivian de Sola Pinto (1895–1969) had been S.S.'s second-in-command in France. He was a poet, critic, and eventually a Professor of English Literature. The Velmore of *Sherston's Progress*.

In a final effort to banish those longings, I try to see in the gloom the far-off vision of the Line, with flares going up and the crash and whine of bursting shells scattered along the level dusk. Men flitting across the gloom, low voices challenging, 'Halt, who are you?' Someone gasping by, carrying a bag of rations. 'Jesus—ain't we there yet?'—he stumbles into a shell-hole and disappears, crouching from the hiss of bullets going high overhead. I see the sentries in the forward posts, staring patiently into the night, sombre shapes against the flickering sky. O yes, I see it all, from A to Z—*my* Company holding its four hundred yards of the Line. And I remember how they shelled us with five-nines the night before I was hit. Not many shells, but very close.

I listen to the chatter of the other wounded officers in my room, talking about people being blown to bits. I remember the chap at the C.C.S. with his jaw blown off by a bomb ('a fine looking chap, he was,' they said). He lay there on the bed with one hand groping about on the bandages that covered his whole head and face, gurgling every time he breathed. His tongue was tied forward to stop him swallowing it. The war had gagged him—smashed him. (Me it had spared.) People looked at him and tried to forget what they'd seen. 'Not expected to live . . .' Surely he would be better dead. All this I remembered, while the desirable things of life, like living phantoms, stole quietly into my brain; looked at me wistfully, and crept away again . . . beckoning . . . pointing . . . 'To England in a few days . . .' and I know it's wrong . . . I know that I shall go there, because it is made so easy . . .

Looking Forward to Something

He was longing for the day when they'd take the bandages off his face. He wondered whether his nurse was pretty: she had a nice, soft voice. And she seemed so sorry for him. He hoped his face wouldn't be badly disfigured.

The Doctor said to the Sister, 'I'm afraid to tell him. He hasn't the slightest idea how bad his face is. And he thinks he'll be able to see.'

The Sister was half-crying. For the soldier's face had been marred beyond recognition. He had practically no face left. And his eyes were absolutely destroyed.

Next note-book lost. (While walking on the Cheviot Hills with Prewett[1] when at Lennel.)[2]

July 18 Arrived Lancaster Gate.

S.S. to V. de S. Pinto

August 4   *American Red Cross Hospital No 22*
for Officers
98–99 Lancaster Gate W.2.

My dear Pinto, My conscience has at last awakened and told me to write you a letter. My only excuse is that I've written as few as possible by order of the doctor. Letters from the Battalion are rather agonizing—they just give one a heart-pain, that's all. My servant Law puts the most poignant simple things in (apparently quite unconsciously). You know what I feel about Blighty. The callous vulgarity of the majority here is beyond anything. I have been in this place since July 18, and haven't yet 'put my uniform on' to dazzle the V.A.D.s. Have had a dose of fever or something which left me rather futile and I see practically no one, nor do I want to. One can't have a 'good time' without peace of mind, and I got more of that commodity with A. Company than anywhere else. I lie and sweat in bed at night and wonder what you're all up to, my dears. I wish to God I could lend you some of the empty luscious comfort that is heaped around me. How poor old Bardy[3] would revel in it!

I beg you not to worry about what reviewers say of your book. It is finished, as far as *you* are concerned. Your job is to begin writing from a fresh point of view, saying the things which are true and vivid and life-giving. You can do it, and you have humour to save you from pitfalls of pomposity. I will send you a few books when I can get out and find something amusing.

You will see Solomon Eagle's[4] remarks about *Counter-Attack* in the *New Statesman*, I expect. Very warm. The *Clarion* and the

---

[1] Frank Prewett (1893–1962), Canadian poet and farmer. Nicknamed Toronto.
[2] The home, near Coldstream in Berwickshire, of Major Walter and Lady Clementine Waring, which had been turned into a convalescent home for officers.
[3] T. B. Bardwell.
[4] A pen-name of J. C. Squire.

Labour Leader have produced *columns* of eulogy!! And that queer old girl who brought forth the man-child Winston[1] comes in several times a week and pours melted butter over the poet Sass. What a mixture! *Eve*[2] has not yet spoken . . . There was an outburst of national vulgarity yesterday—Thanksgiving for the War or something. A 'Shrine' in the Park (gift of Waring & Gillow, 'erected at a cost of several hundred pounds')—one of our insults to the dead. The Marne Show is very cheering, though, from the strategic point of view, if that is worth anything. I'm off to the country soon for a month's further treatment!

God knows how long I'll be in England—months and months, I expect. I've tried hard to be well, but it was no use.

Best of luck, and love to all.   S.S.

I sent old Dodds some cigars.

Do look after Law, please, and keep him safe, if you can.

Jowett's show was first-rate. He is one of the best young officers I've ever seen.

I had forgotten all about your strafing me for patrolling!

CAN I FORGET? . . .

Can I forget the voice of one who cried
For me to save him, save him, as he died? . . .

Can I forget the face of one whose eyes
Could trust me in his utmost agonies? . . .

I will remember you; and from your wrongs
Shall rise the power and poignance of my songs:
And this shall comfort me until the end,
That I have been your captain and your friend.

August 10

August 17   Left Lancaster Gate.

Arrived Lennel August 20 after Craiglockhart (three days). Went to London September 30.

[1] Lady Randolph Churchill.
[2] A weekly paper for women.

1918

October 1

Lunched with Robbie Ross, Arnold Bennett and Maurice Baring,[1] at the Reform Club. Went to Russian Ballet with Robbie in the evening, and on to Gordon Square with Maynard Keynes,[2] Duncan Grant,[3] and Lytton Strachey. (Ballet was *Papillons*.)

October 2

Lunched with Robbie at Automobile Club; Massingham, Edith Sitwell and Clive Bell[4] were there also. Ottoline Morrell came to tea at Half Moon Street. Dined with Eddie Marsh and went to Ballet—*Prince Igor*. Stayed at Raymond Buildings.

October 3

Long interview with Winston Churchill at Metropole in the morning. Lunched with Billy Greaves at Waldorf*; and went to Ballet—*Carnaval*. Dined with Maynard Keynes at United Universities Club, and went to Ballet—*Cleopatra*. Met the Sitwells, Ottoline, Gertler,[5] Roger Fry,[6] Sheppard** etc and was taken behind to see Leonide Massine[7] and Lopokova—both charming. Awful headache, and back to Half Moon Street, where Charles Scott Moncrieff[8] appeared with a young actor called Noel Coward.

* took him to tea at Half Moon Street	** (Later Provost of King's, Cambridge.)

October 4

Saw Heinemann before lunch. Third impression of *Counter-Attack* ready (completing 3500 copies). Saw Rivers. Lunch with Ottoline and Desmond MacCarthy[9] in Soho (Eiffel Tower).

[1] Poet, novelist, diplomat and man of letters (1874–1946).
[2] Economist, Fellow of King's College, Cambridge, adviser to the Treasury, financier, writer, collector of books and pictures (1883–1946). Created Baron 1942.
[3] Painter (1885–1978).   [4] Art critic (1881–1964).
[5] Mark Gertler, painter (1891–1939).
[6] Art critic and painter (1866–1934).
[7] See S.S.'s poem 'To Leonide Massine', published in *Picture Show*.
[8] Translator of Proust (1868–1925).
[9] Literary critic and author (1877–1952). Knighted 1951.

1918

Dined at Carlton with Eddie, Toronto and Lady Clemmie, and went to *The Man from Toronto*. Was taken behind and talked to Iris Hoey. Stayed at Raymond Buildings and came back to Lennel on Saturday very exhausted. (Robbie died that day at about 7 p.m.)

October 7
Heard of Robbie's death (telegram from Burton[1]).

October 17
Board at Craiglockhart; left for four weeks' leave.

October 18–November 5 at Weirleigh.

November 5
At Raymond Buildings. Dined with Eddie Marsh and met Lawrence (the Hedjaz general—a little Oxford archaeologist).[2] Talked a lot about Doughty whom he knows. 'A viking' he called him. E.M. told stories of Henry James ('economy of *means*, and economy of effect,' H.J. at Gosses').

November 6
Saw Winston Churchill for a few minutes at the Ministry. Full of victory talk, and just off to a War Cabinet meeting. He looked well. One gets an inhuman impression from his talk—all words, like a leading article. Went to Dorchester; 12.30 from Waterloo. A clear, sunny day. Slept badly last night. Queer dream. A bit of Toronto in it.

E.M. has strong bias against Wilson.[3] (Lawrence is going across to see him soon: W. wants to give Mesopotamia to Portugal, so L. said.) One feels that England is going to increase in power enormously. They mean to skin Germany alive. 'A peace to end peace!'

[1] Nellie Burton, proprietress of 40 Half Moon Street, where she let rooms to single gentlemen.
[2] T. E. Lawrence (1888–1935).
[3] Thomas Woodrow Wilson (1854–1924). Democrat President of the U.S.A. 1913–1921.

November 7 (Max Gate)

Arrived 6.45 in darkness (having been delayed by being in wrong part of train at Bournemouth, and having to come on by a slow one). Cab rumbled up to door of small house among trees. Found small man in front of fire in candle-lit room, small wife with back turned doing something to a bookcase. Both seemed shy, and I felt very large and hearty. First impression of Thomas Hardy was that his voice is senile and slightly dis-cordant,[1] with a provincial accent, but that was only when he was nervous. Frail and rather gnome-like in the candle-shine and dim room, with his large round head, vast brow, beaky nose and pendulous grey moustache—impression not unlike the Max caricature,[2] but more bird-like—some sort of twilight bird. His voice improved, and was always pleasant and full-toned after-wards.

He knelt by the log-fire for a bit, still a little shy, but they both gained confidence after a while. Then there was a little scene of 'Which room is he in, dear?' etc. 'The West Room, my dear' (though of course they both knew, the dears!) and he lit me up the narrow staircase with a silver candlestick. I think he feared I should be a huge swell, and appear in a white waistcoat or something.

Both days were bright and frosty, and T.H. became more loveable all the time. A great and simple man. He thinks 'The Statue and the Bust' Browning's best. Said he 'feared (in 1914) more than anything else that English literature might be wiped out by the Germans'.

November 8

Left Max Gate about noon and went to Oxford. Toronto at Christ Church. We went out to Garsington.

November 9

A fine cold day. Started about 12 and bicycled over to Boar's Hill (by Abingdon) to see Masefield. He is a kindly, manly figure; deep rich voice and young-looking face, grey hair. Face

---

[1] Wrong word—I meant a sort of harshness or something like that. S.S.
[2] Probably 'Mr Thomas Hardy composing a lyric', published in Max Beerbohm's *Fifty Caricatures* (1913).

made on a small scale, but a lot of nobility and tenderness in it.
He took me to see the Poet Laureate, shaggy and self-conscious
and rather hectoring. He spoke intolerantly about 'those
Socialists', and I did not like him. Back to Garsington through
the dark streets of Oxford, leaving J.M. at hide-and-seek in the
twilight of his garden with his girl Judith and little boy, and a
Bridges girl. Francis Meynell[1] and his wife Hilda Saxe the
pianist came to Garsington at dinner-time; also Aldous Huxley,
who is a master at Eton. H.S. played two short Beethoven pieces,
two Brahms waltzes and a Moussorgsky, and F.M. talked a lot
of *Herald* Labour politics, and announced the Kaiser's abdica-
tion. Dear Toronto sat very quiet all the evening and listened.

The more I think of Hardy the greater his simplicity seems. It
is a deeply moving memory already. What a contrast to arrogant
old Bridges with his reactionary war-talk. The one a supreme
tragic artist, the other a splendid craftsman with a commonplace
mind.

November 11

I was walking in the water-meadows by the river below
Cuddesdon this morning—a quiet grey day. A jolly peal of bells
was ringing from the village church, and the villagers were
hanging little flags out of the windows of their thatched houses.
The war is ended. It is impossible to realise. Oxford had much
flag-waving also, and signs of demonstration.

I got to London about 6.30 and found masses of people in
streets and congested Tubes, all waving flags and making fools
of themselves—an outburst of mob patriotism. It was a wretched
wet night, and very mild. It is a loathsome ending to the loath-
some tragedy of the last four years.

S.S. remained on indefinite sick-leave until on 11 March 1919
the *London Gazette* announced: 'Lt (acting Captain) S. L.
SASSOON MC relinquishes his acting rank, is placed on the
retired list on account of ill-health caused by wounds 12 March
1919 and is granted the rank of Captain.'

[1] Son of Wilfrid and Alice Meynell. Book designer, publisher and poet (1891–
1975). Founder of the Nonesuch Press. Knighted 1946.

INDEX

Index

Index

Index

Index

Index